THE GREAT GATSBY

and Other Stories

The Great Gatsby
and Other Stories

F. SCOTT FITZGERALD

with a Foreword to *The Great Gatsby* by

NED HALLEY

The Great Gatsby was first published in 1925 and the short stories included in this volume were published between 1922 and 1939

This edition prepared and designed by Worth Press Ltd
for Monti Publishing & More, Canada

ISBN: 978 0 9878228 4 0

Cover and endpaper design by Bradbury & Williams, London
Typeset in Great Britain by Antony Gray
Printed and bound in China

10 9 8 7 6 5 4 3 2 1

Contents

Biography of the Author

Francis Scott Fitzgerald was born in 1896 in St Paul, Minnesota. His father manufactured cane furniture, but the business failed. He lost a subsequent job as a travelling salesman, but was rescued from financial disaster when his wife received a large legacy from her father, a wealthy wholesale grocer in St Paul.

The Fitzgeralds aspired to gentility. The given names of their only child (three sisters died in infancy) were those of an antecedent, Francis Scott Key (1780–1843), who had witnessed the Royal Navy's bombardment of Fort McHenry, Baltimore, during the British–American War of 1812–15. The sight of a lone American flag hoisted defiantly by the garrison inspired Key to write a poem, 'Defence of Fort McHenry', later taken as the lyric for 'The Star-Spangled Banner', the American national anthem.

In 1913 Scott enrolled at Princeton. An aspiring author and socialite, he neglected his studies in favour of drinking and writing for student magazines, then left without graduating in 1917 to join the army when America entered the First World War. He expected to be killed at the front, and hurriedly wrote a first novel. But he got no farther than a camp in Alabama, where he met Zelda Sayre, a Southern belle, and became engaged.

Discharged in 1919, he became an advertising copywriter in New York and revised his novel at the request of an interested publisher, Charles Scribner. When Zelda called off the engagement, doubting he could afford to keep her, he began to sell stories to magazines such as the *Saturday Evening Post.* His novel, *This Side of Paradise,* was then accepted by Scribner and was published in 1920 to a great fanfare. Scott and Zelda married a week later and took up a lavish lifestyle in New York, which inspired *The Beautiful and Damned,* the second novel, which appeared in 1922. In the same year they moved with their infant daughter, Scottie, to Great Neck, Long Island, adopted as the scene of his masterpiece, *The Great Gatsby*.

There followed years of travel, much of it in Europe, and extravagant living which diminished Fitzgerald's literary reputation as well as his funds, especially when Zelda descended into schizophrenia. Scott earned little from his novels, least of all from *Gatsby*, which was a commercial failure. He completed one further novel, *Tender is the Night*, and died in 1940.

THE GREAT GATSBY

Foreword

In the summer of 1922, the American century was well under way. Pride in the World War victory of 1918 (the US sent two million troops to Europe) and prosperity from a huge uplift in production, first of armaments, now of consumer goods, had ushered in a period of unprecedented affluence. In the Roaring Twenties, America was making whoopee.

F. Scott Fitzgerald, chronicler of this brassiest decade in American history – he christened it the Jazz Age – was perfectly placed to write the novel of the era. Princeton-educated, handsome and just twenty-six, by 1922 he was famous, though not quite rich, from the success of two novels and two collections of stories. He and his glamorous wife Zelda moved to Great Neck, New York, a smart beach community an easy commute from Manhattan on Long Island. The town, a magnet for the new millionaires and celebrities of the day, was to provide the thinly disguised setting for Fitzgerald's masterpiece, *The Great Gatsby.*

The location is key to the dramatic contrasts of this tale. Great Neck becomes a peninsula, jauntily called West Egg, projecting from the north shore into Long Island Sound. And across the bay, the author places another peninsula, which naturally he calls East Egg. It is at West Egg that Gatsby has his enormous beachfront home. Over the water, just visible at night from Gatsby's veranda, is the green light on the dock of the elegant East Egg home of Daisy and her husband Tom Buchanan. The Buchanans are archetypal East Egg inhabitants, scions of old American families, wealthy, idle and prone to the twin social disorders of snobbery and infidelity.

Fitzgerald takes the role of narrator Nick Carraway, a young, well-to-do Midwesterner restless after service in the war, who has moved to New York to seek his fortune in the bond market. Preferring not to live in the city, he has decided on a commuter life and rented 'a weather-beaten cardboard bungalow at eighty a month' that happens to stand next door to Gatsby's estate. He knows no one locally except Daisy, who is a distant cousin from back in the Midwest, and Tom, another Midwesterner whom he knew at Yale University. Carraway starts the narrative clock of the story by calling on the Buchanans.

The couple have a two-year-old daughter, and have formerly lived for a year in France. This strikes an autobiographical note. Fitzgerald and Zelda came to live here in what Carraway calls 'one of the strangest communities in North America' after the birth of their only child, a daughter they christened Scottie, soon after returning from a year in France. Daisy, along with other female characters in Fitzgerald's novels, is certainly inspired in part by Zelda, but also by another woman in the author's life, Ginevra King, his first love. She was a Chicago socialite who broke from Fitzgerald to marry a millionaire, the polo-playing William Mitchell, on whom Tom Buchanan is clearly modelled.

But after introducing us to these life-based characters in their all-too-real setting, Fitzgerald suddenly changes gear. The story that now unfolds is by far the most inventive of his four novels. The characters, particularly Gatsby himself, are sharply imagined, and the tragic narrative unwinds with a pace and tension that shows a master at work.

This might betray the circumstances in which the novel was written. Although Fitzgerald claimed he first had the idea of a novel of this kind when he was very young, it was not until 1923, after living for some months at Great Neck with Zelda and Scottie, that he began work on it. But the book was not completed *in situ*. The Fitzgeralds left Great Neck in May 1923 and moved to the South of France.

It was at this great distance from Long Island that *The Great Gatsby* was actually written. Fitzgerald later confessed he started work on the novel all over again while ensconced on the Riviera. By November of 1923, he had completed the first draft. He sent it to the New York publishers, Charles Scribner, telling his editor Maxwell Perkins he was convinced the book was a turning point in his literary life. It was 'a consciously artistic achievement' and 'not trashy imaginings as in my stories but the sustained imagination of a sincere and yet radiant world'.

Comparing *Gatsby* to Fitzgerald's two previous novels, *This Side of Paradise* (1920) and *The Beautiful and Damned* (1922), the author's self-assessment looks well understood. While both the earlier works display keen observation of manners and originality of style, only *Gatsby* demonstrates the crystallisation of character and classical unwinding of the mechanism of the romantic tragedy that are the keys to immortality.

Fitzgerald worked for a long time to make *Gatsby* ready for publication. In spite of his own certainties about the literary lionisation that awaited him, he co-operated closely with the publishers to produce the most marketable final version. The novel's tightness of narrative and unusual brevity – just under 49,000 words – probably owes much to the insistence by editor Perkins on cuts and improvements to the original manuscript.

Late in 1924 Maxwell Perkins wrote to Fitzgerald:

> I think you have every kind of right to be proud of this book. It is an extraordinary book, suggestive of all sorts of thoughts and moods. You adopted exactly the right method of telling it, that of employing a narrator who is more of a spectator than an actor: this puts the reader upon a point of observation on a higher level than that on which the characters stand and at a distance that gives perspective. In no other way could your irony have been so immensely effective, nor the reader have been enabled so strongly to feel at times the strangeness of human circumstance in a vast heedless universe.

Perkins was particularly taken with the device of the huge advertising billboard depicting the yard-high retinas of Dr Eckleburg that looms over the ash heaps and George Wilson's garage, midway between the lush lawns of the Eggs and the teeming streets of central New York City. 'Evidently some wild wag of an oculist set them there to fatten his practice in the borough of Queens, and then sank down himself into eternal blindness.'

In the eyes, Perkins told Fitzgerald, 'various readers will see different significances; but their presence gives a superb touch to the whole thing; great unblinking eyes, expressionless, looking down upon the human scene. It's magnificent!'

Scribners finally published *The Great Gatsby* in April 1925. But while Fitzgerald's friends, such as T. S. Eliot and Ernest Hemingway, were full of praise, sales were slow. The problem, soon evident, was that the novel was out of tune with the mood of the nation. America was, and remains, a nation in which progress and wealth are celebrated, unconditionally. Depicting the rich, even the new rich, as idle, adulterous, drunken (Prohibition outlawed alcohol in the US from 1920 to 1933), or even criminal, went against the grain. Critics in the popular press condemned Fitzgerald for his 'preoccupation with failure' and the 'really very unpleasant characters of this story'.

Fitzgerald might have coined the term Jazz Age for the 1920s, but he had less good to say about the period than other authors of the day. As a socialite who enjoyed the company of the rich and famous, he knew very well how they behaved and what their motives were. But he betrayed these truths at his peril. He had to write, not just as his artistic *raison d'être*, but in the urgent need to finance the extravagant, peripatetic lifestyle he and Zelda insisted upon. As a novelist, he was a commercial failure. He earned far more money from the short stories he at least pretended to despise – he could get as much for a couple of stories sold to the *Saturday Evening Post* as he did from the two modest print runs of *Gatsby* – and from the film treatments he produced towards the end of his life in Hollywood.

But Fitzgerald, despite his waywardness as a drinker, his notorious jealousy of his friends' successes, and the great sadness of Zelda's descent into schizophrenia, had the kind of self-knowledge that might just have given him the faith that it was all worth it. In the face of criticism of his realism about the American Dream he had this to say: 'An author ought to write for the youth of his own generation, the critics of the next, and the schoolmasters of ever afterward.'

He has been proven entirely correct. He completed only one further novel, *Tender is the Night*, published (again to muted acclaim) in 1934 and died, aged only forty-four, in 1940. Perhaps it was the reflectiveness felt by the American intelligentsia in the context of the new World War and then, in 1942, their own country's entry into it that stimulated the re-examination of Fitzgerald's role as the Cassandra of his age. The Wall Street Crash and ensuing Depression of the 1930s had done all too much to fortify Fitzgerald's hard-nosed views on America's movers and shakers. And the nobility of spirit often attributed in Fitzgerald's characters to soldierly honour (Gatsby's great redeeming feature is his war service) now began to be seen among the contrasts so carefully crafted into his stories.

During the Second World War, *The Great Gatsby* was among the novels distributed in pocket editions, with US Government approval, to American forces serving overseas. While sales of the book had totalled fewer than 25,000 to date, these editions amounted to 155,000 copies. Fitzgerald's reputation has been in recovery ever since and his masterpiece has been adapted to every kind of medium from radio and television to opera and computer games as well as cinema. Six major movies have been made so far, including the 1974 adaptation with Robert Redford as Gatsby and the 2012 production with Leonardo DiCaprio in the role.

The Great Gatsby is now unquestionably counted among the Great American Novels, and sometimes nominated as the greatest of the twentieth century. Agree or not, it will always say much about America. And America should be proud.

Principal Characters

Nick Carraway, the narrator, is a Midwestern newcomer to New York, aged about thirty, working as a bond dealer following service in the First World War. By chance, his rented bungalow at West Egg, Long Island, is next to Gatsby's estate.

Daisy Buchanan (née Fay) is Carraway's cousin and contemporary from the Midwest, now living with her husband Tom and infant daughter in a large mansion at East Egg.

Tom Buchanan is Daisy's husband, a millionaire sportsman and playboy. A contemporary of Carraway at Yale, he keeps a stable of polo ponies and a mistress for whom he rents an apartment in New York.

Jordan Baker is a New York socialite and golf champion. Her long-term friend Daisy believes Jordan should become attached to Carraway.

Jay Gatsby (born James Gatz) is from a poor farming family in North Dakota. As a young army officer stationed near her home, he met and fell in love with Daisy. In Europe during the war he lost touch with her, but after making a fortune he has bought an estate near the Buchanan mansion in hope of luring her away from her husband.

George B. Wilson keeps a garage on a grim industrial site on the route between the Eggs and New York City; he hopes to ease his money problems by selling on a car of Tom Buchanan's.

Myrtle Wilson is George's wife, and Tom's mistress. Tom openly flaunts their affair and treats her badly.

Chester and Lucille McKee are neighbours to Myrtle Wilson in New York. They live on the floor below the flat Tom Buchanan keeps for Myrtle.

Catherine is Myrtle's sister.

Meyer Wolfsheim is a shady New York businessman friend who claims long friendship with Gatsby.

Ewing Klipspringer is one of countless uninvited guests to be found at Gatsby's parties. A pianist, his presence is so persistent he is known as 'the boarder'.

Dan Cody is the rich yachtsman whose vessel was saved from destruction by the intervention of the seventeen-year-old James Gatz. In gratitude he gave the youth a job, and his first break in life.

Walter Chase is a friend of Tom Buchanan's who became involved in business with Gatsby, and wound up ruined and in jail as a result.

Michaelis is the young Greek café owner who is a compassionate neighbour to the Wilsons.

Henry C. Gatz is Jay Gatsby's father.

Then wear the golden hat, if that will move her;
If you can bounce high, bounce for her too,
Till she cry, 'Lover, gold-hatted, high-bouncing lover,
I must have you!'

THOMAS PARKE D'INVILLIERS

One

In my younger and more vulnerable years my father gave me some advice that I've been turning over in my mind ever since.

'Whenever you feel like criticising anyone,' he told me, 'just remember that all the people in this world haven't had the advantages that you've had.'

He didn't say any more, but we've always been unusually communicative in a reserved way, and I understood that he meant a great deal more than that. In consequence, I'm inclined to reserve all judgements, a habit that has opened up many curious natures to me and also made me the victim of not a few veteran bores. The abnormal mind is quick to detect and attach itself to this quality when it appears in a normal person, and so it came about that in college I was unjustly accused of being a politician, because I was privy to the secret griefs of wild, unknown men. Most of the confidences were three – frequently I have feigned sleep, preoccupation or a hostile levity when I realised by some unmistakable sign that an intimate revelation was quivering on the horizon; for the intimate revelations of young men, or at least the terms in which they express them, are usually plagiaristic and marred by obvious suppressions. Reserving judgements is a matter of infinite hope. I am still a little afraid of missing something if I forget that, as my father snobbishly suggested, and I snobbishly repeat, a sense of the fundamental decencies is parcelled out unequally at birth.

And, after boasting this way of my tolerance, I come to the admission that it has a limit. Conduct may be founded on the hard rock or the wet marshes, but after a certain point I don't care what it's founded on. When I came back from the East last autumn I felt that I wanted the world to be in uniform and at a sort of moral attention for ever; I wanted no more riotous excursions with privileged glimpses into the human heart. Only Gatsby, the man who gives his name to this book, was exempt from my reaction –

Gatsby, who represented everything for which I have an unaffected scorn. If personality is an unbroken series of successful gestures, then there was something gorgeous about him, some heightened sensitivity to the promises of life, as if he were related to one of those intricate machines that register earthquakes ten thousand miles away. This responsiveness had nothing to do with that flabby impressionability which is dignified under the name of the 'creative temperament' – it was an extraordinary gift for hope, a romantic readiness such as I have never found in any other person and which it is not likely I shall ever find again. No – Gatsby turned out all right at the end; it is what preyed on Gatsby, what foul dust floated in the wake of his dreams that temporarily closed out my interest in the abortive sorrows and short-winded elations of men.

My family have been prominent, well-to-do people in this Middle Western city for three generations. The Carraways are something of a clan, and we have a tradition that we're descended from the Dukes of Buccleuch, but the actual founder of my line was my grandfather's brother, who came here in fifty-one, sent a substitute to the Civil War, and started the wholesale hardware business that my father carries on today.

I never saw this great-uncle, but I'm supposed to look like him – with special reference to the rather hard-boiled painting that hangs in father's office. I graduated from New Haven in 1915, just a quarter of a century after my father, and a little later I participated in that delayed Teutonic migration known as the Great War. I enjoyed the counter raid so thoroughly that I came back restless. Instead of being the warm centre of the world, the Middle West now seemed like the ragged edge of the universe – so I decided to go East and learn the bond business. Everybody I knew was in the bond business, so I supposed it could support one more single man. All my aunts and uncles talked it over as if they were choosing a prep school for me, and finally said, 'Why – ye–es,' with very grave, hesitant faces. Father agreed to finance me for a year, and after various delays I came East, permanently, I thought, in the spring of 'twenty-two.

The practical thing was to find rooms in the city, but it was a warm season, and I had just left a country of wide lawns and friendly trees, so when a young man at the office suggested that we take a house together in a commuting town, it sounded like a great idea. He found the house, a weather-beaten cardboard bungalow at eighty a month, but at the last minute the firm ordered him to Washington, and I went out to the country alone. I had a dog – at least I had him for a few days until he ran away – and an old Dodge and a Finnish woman, who made my bed and cooked breakfast and muttered Finnish wisdom to herself over the electric stove.

It was lonely for a day or so until one morning some man, more recently arrived than I, stopped me on the road.

'How do you get to West Egg village?' he asked helplessly.

I told him. And as I walked on I was lonely no longer. I was a guide, a pathfinder, an original settler. He had casually conferred on me the freedom of the neighbourhood.

And so with the sunshine and the great bursts of leaves growing on the trees, just as things grow in fast movies, I had that familiar conviction that life was beginning over again with the summer.

There was so much to read, for one thing, and so much fine health to be pulled down out of the young breath-giving air. I bought a dozen volumes on banking and credit and investment securities, and they stood on my shelf in red and gold like new money from the mint, promising to unfold the shining secrets that only Midas and Morgan and Maecenas knew. And I had the high intention of reading many other books besides. I was rather literary in college – one year I wrote a series of very solemn and obvious editorials for the *Yale News* – and now I was going to bring back all such things into my life and become again that most limited of all specialists, the 'well-rounded man'. This isn't just an epigram – life is much more successfully looked at from a single window, after all.

It was a matter of chance that I should have rented a house in one of the strangest communities in North America. It was on that slender riotous island which extends itself due east of New York – and where there are, among other natural curiosities, two unusual formations of land. Twenty miles from the city a pair of enormous eggs, identical in contour and separated only by a courtesy bay, jut out into the most domesticated body of salt water in the Western hemisphere, the great wet barnyard of Long Island Sound. They are not perfect ovals – like the egg in the Columbus story, they are both crushed flat at the contact end – but their physical resemblance must be a source of perpetual wonder to the gulls that fly overhead. To the wingless a more interesting phenomenon is their dissimilarity in every particular except shape and size.

I lived at West Egg, the – well, the less fashionable of the two, though this is a most superficial tag to express the bizarre and not a little sinister contrast between them. My house was at the very tip of the egg, only fifty yards from the Sound, and squeezed between two huge places that rented for twelve or fifteen thousand a season. The one on my right was a colossal affair by any standard – it was a factual imitation of some Hôtel de Ville in Normandy, with a tower on one side, spanking new under a thin beard of raw ivy, and a marble swimming pool, and more than forty acres of lawn and garden. It was Gatsby's mansion. Or, rather, as I didn't know Mr Gatsby, it was a mansion, inhabited by a gentleman of that name. My own house was an eyesore, but it was a small eyesore, and it had been overlooked, so I had a view of the water, a partial view of my neighbour's lawn, and the consoling proximity of millionaires – all for eighty dollars a month.

Across the courtesy bay the white palaces of fashionable East Egg glittered along the water, and the history of the summer really begins on the evening I drove over there to have dinner with the Tom Buchanans. Daisy was my second cousin once removed, and I'd known Tom in college. And just after the war I spent two days with them in Chicago.

Her husband, among various physical accomplishments, had been one of the most powerful ends that ever played football at New Haven – a national figure in a way, one of those men who reach such an acute limited excellence at twenty-one that everything afterwards savours of anticlimax. His family were enormously wealthy – even in college his freedom with money was a matter for reproach – but now he'd left Chicago and come East in a fashion that rather took your breath away; for instance, he'd brought down a string of polo ponies from Lake Forest. It was hard to realise that a man in my own generation was wealthy enough to do that.

Why they came East I don't know. They had spent a year in France for no particular reason, and then drifted here and there unrestfully wherever people played polo and were rich together. This was a permanent move, said Daisy over the telephone, but I didn't believe it – I had no sight into Daisy's heart, but I felt that Tom would drift on for ever, seeking, a little wistfully, for the dramatic turbulence of some irrecoverable football game.

And so it happened that on a warm windy evening I drove over to East Egg to see two old friends whom I scarcely knew at all. Their house was even more elaborate than I expected, a cheerful red-and-white Georgian colonial mansion, overlooking the bay. The lawn started at the beach and ran towards the front door for a quarter of a mile, jumping over sundials and brick walks and burning gardens – finally when it reached the house drifting up the side in bright vines as though from the momentum of its run. The front was broken by a line of French windows, glowing now with reflected gold and wide open to the warm windy afternoon, and Tom Buchanan in riding clothes was standing with his legs apart on the front porch.

He had changed since his New Haven years. Now he was a sturdy straw-haired man of thirty with a rather hard mouth and a supercilious manner. Two shining arrogant eyes had established dominance over his face and gave him the appearance of always leaning aggressively forward. Not even the effeminate swank of his riding clothes could hide the enormous power of that body – he seemed to fill those glistening boots until he strained the top lacing, and you could see a great pack of muscle shifting when his shoulder moved under his thin coat. It was a body capable of enormous leverage – a cruel body.

His speaking voice, a gruff husky tenor, added to the impression of fractiousness he conveyed. There was a touch of paternal contempt in it, even towards people he liked – and there were men at New Haven who had hated his guts.

'Now, don't think my opinion on these matters is final,' he seemed to say, 'just because I'm stronger and more of a man than you are.' We were in the same senior society, and while we were never intimate I always had the impression that he approved of me and wanted me to like him with some harsh, defiant wistfulness of his own.

We talked for a few minutes on the sunny porch.

'I've got a nice place here,' he said, his eyes flashing about restlessly.

Turning me around by one arm, he moved a broad flat hand along the front vista, including in its sweep a sunken Italian garden, a half-acre of deep, pungent roses, and a snub-nosed motorboat that bumped the tide offshore.

'It belonged to Demaine, the oil man.' He turned me around again, politely and abruptly. 'We'll go inside.'

We walked through a high hallway into a bright rose-coloured space, fragilely bound into the house by French windows at either end. The windows were ajar and gleaming white against the fresh grass outside that seemed to grow a little way into the house. A breeze blew through the room, blew curtains in at one end and out the other like pale flags, twisting them up towards the frosted wedding-cake of the ceiling, and then rippled over the wine-coloured rug, making a shadow on it as wind does on the sea.

The only completely stationary object in the room was an enormous couch on which two young women were buoyed up as though upon an anchored balloon. They were both in white, and their dresses were rippling and fluttering as if they had just been blown back in after a short flight around the house. I must have stood for a few moments listening to the whip and snap of the curtains and the groan of a picture on the wall. Then there was a boom as Tom Buchanan shut the rear windows and the caught wind died out about the room, and the curtains and the rugs and the two young women ballooned slowly to the floor.

The younger of the two was a stranger to me. She was extended full length at her end of the divan, completely motionless, and with her chin raised a little, as if she were balancing something on it which was quite likely to fall. If she saw me out of the corner of her eyes she gave no hint of it – indeed, I was almost surprised into murmuring an apology for having disturbed her by coming in.

The other girl, Daisy, made an attempt to rise – she leaned slightly forward with a conscientious expression – then she laughed, an absurd charming little laugh, and I laughed too and came forward into the room.

'I'm p–paralysed with happiness.'

She laughed again, as if she had said something very witty, and held my hand for a moment, looking up into my face, promising that there was no one in the world she so much wanted to see. That was a way she had. She hinted in a murmur that the surname of the balancing girl was Baker. (I've heard it said that Daisy's murmur was only to make people lean towards her; an irrelevant criticism that made it no less charming.)

At any rate, Miss Baker's lips fluttered, she nodded at me almost imperceptibly, and then quickly tipped her head back again – the object she was balancing had obviously tottered a little and given her something of a fright. Again a sort of apology arose to my lips. Almost any exhibition of complete self-sufficiency draws a stunned tribute from me.

I looked back at my cousin, who began to ask me questions in her low, thrilling voice. It was the kind of voice that the ear follows up and down, as if each speech is an arrangement of notes that will never be played again. Her face was sad and lovely with bright things in it, bright eyes and a bright passionate mouth, but there was an excitement in her voice that men who had cared for her found difficult to forget; a singing compulsion, a whispered 'Listen', a promise that she had done gay, exciting things just a while since and that there were gay, exciting things hovering in the next hour.

I told her how I had stopped off in Chicago for a day on my way East, and how a dozen people had sent their love through me.

'Do they miss me?' she cried ecstatically.

'The whole town is desolate. All the cars have the left rear wheel painted black as a mourning wreath, and there's a persistent wail all night along the north shore.'

'How gorgeous! Let's go back, Tom. Tomorrow!' Then she added irrelevantly: 'You ought to see the baby.'

'I'd like to.'

'She's asleep. She's three years old. Haven't you ever seen her?'

'Never.'

'Well, you ought to see her. She's – '

Tom Buchanan, who had been hovering restlessly about the room, stopped and rested his hand on my shoulder.

'What you doing, Nick?'

'I'm a bond man.'

'Who with?'

I told him.

'Never heard of them,' he remarked decisively.

This annoyed me.

'You will,' I answered shortly. 'You will if you stay in the East.'

'Oh, I'll stay in the East, don't you worry,' he said, glancing at Daisy and then back at me, as if he were alert for something more. 'I'd be a God-damned fool to live anywhere else.'

At this point Miss Baker said: 'Absolutely!' with such suddenness that I started – it was the first word she had uttered since I came into the room. Evidently it surprised her as much as it did me, for she yawned and with a series of rapid, deft movements stood up into the room.

'I'm stiff,' she complained. 'I've been lying on that sofa for as long as I can remember.'

'Don't look at me,' Daisy retorted, 'I've been trying to get you to New York all afternoon.'

'No, thanks,' said Miss Baker to the four cocktails just in from the pantry, 'I'm absolutely in training.'

Her host looked at her incredulously.

'You are!' He took down his drink as if it were a drop in the bottom of a glass. 'How you ever get anything done is beyond me.'

I looked at Miss Baker, wondering what it was she 'got done'. I enjoyed looking at her. She was a slender, small-breasted girl, with an erect carriage, which she accentuated by throwing her body backwards at the shoulders like a young cadet. Her grey sun-strained eyes looked back at me with polite reciprocal curiosity out of a wan, charming, discontented face. It occurred to me now that I had seen her, or a picture of her, somewhere before.

'You live in West Egg,' she remarked contemptuously. 'I know somebody there.'

'I don't know a single – '

'You must know Gatsby.'

'Gatsby?' demanded Daisy. 'What Gatsby?'

Before I could reply that he was my neighbour, dinner was announced; wedging his tense arm imperatively under mine, Tom Buchanan compelled me from the room as though he were moving a checker to another square.

Slenderly, languidly, their hands set lightly on their hips, the two young women preceded us out on to a rosy-coloured porch, open towards the sunset, where four candles flickered on the table in the diminished wind.

'Why *candles*?' objected Daisy, frowning. She snapped them out with her fingers. 'In two weeks it'll be the longest day in the year.' She looked at us all radiantly. 'Do you always watch for the longest day of the year and then miss it? I always watch for the longest day in the year and then miss it.'

'We ought to plan something,' yawned Miss Baker, sitting down at the table as if she were getting into bed.

'All right,' said Daisy. 'What'll we plan?' She turned to me helplessly: 'What do people plan?'

Before I could answer her eyes fastened with an awed expression on her little finger.

'Look!' she complained; 'I hurt it.'

We all looked – the knuckle was black and blue.

'You did it, Tom,' she said accusingly. 'I know you didn't mean to, but you *did* do it. That's what I get for marrying a brute of a man, a great, big, hulking physical specimen of a – '

'I hate that word hulking,' objected Tom crossly, 'even in kidding.'

'Hulking,' insisted Daisy.

Sometimes she and Miss Baker talked at once, unobtrusively and with a bantering inconsequence that was never quite chatter, that was as cool as their white dresses and their impersonal eyes in the absence of all desire. They were here, and they accepted Tom and me, making only a polite pleasant effort to entertain or to be entertained. They knew that presently dinner would be over and a little later the evening, too, would be over and casually put away. It was sharply different from the West, where an evening was hurried from phase to phase towards its close, in a continually disappointed anticipation or else in sheer nervous dread of the moment itself.

'You make me feel uncivilised, Daisy,' I confessed on my second glass of corky but rather impressive claret. 'Can't you talk about crops or something?'

I meant nothing in particular by this remark, but it was taken up in an unexpected way.

'Civilisation's going to pieces,' broke out Tom violently. 'I've gotten to be a terrible pessimist about things. Have you read *The Rise of the Coloured Empires* by this man Goddard?'

'Why, no,' I answered, rather surprised by his tone.

'Well, it's a fine book, and everybody ought to read it. The idea is if we don't look out the white race will be – will be utterly submerged. It's all scientific stuff; it's been proved.'

'Tom's getting very profound,' said Daisy, with an expression of unthoughtful sadness. 'He reads deep books with long words in them. What was that word we – '

'Well, these books are all scientific,' insisted Tom, glancing at her impatiently. 'This fellow has worked out the whole thing. It's up to us, who are the dominant race, to watch out or these other races will have control of things.'

'We've got to beat them down,' whispered Daisy, winking ferociously towards the fervent sun.

'You ought to live in California – ' began Miss Baker, but Tom interrupted her by shifting heavily in his chair.

'This idea is that we're Nordics. I am, and you are, and you are, and – ' After an infinitesimal hesitation he included Daisy with a slight nod, and she winked at me again. ' – And we've produced all the things that go to make civilisation – oh, science and art, and all that. Do you see?'

There was something pathetic in his concentration, as if his complacency, more acute than of old, was not enough to him any more. When, almost immediately, the telephone rang inside and the butler left the porch, Daisy seized upon the momentary interruption and leaned towards me.

'I'll tell you a family secret,' she whispered enthusiastically. 'It's about the butler's nose. Do you want to hear about the butler's nose?'

'That's why I came over tonight.'

'Well, he wasn't always a butler; he used to be the silver polisher for some people in New York that had a silver service for two hundred people. He had to polish it from morning till night, until finally it began to affect his nose – '

'Things went from bad to worse,' suggested Miss Baker.

'Yes. Things went from bad to worse, until finally he had to give up his position.'

For a moment the last sunshine fell with romantic affection upon her glowing face; her voice compelled me forward breathlessly as I listened – then the glow faded, each light deserting her with lingering regret, like children leaving a pleasant street at dusk.

The butler came back and murmured something close to Tom's ear, whereupon Tom frowned, pushed back his chair, and without a word went inside. As if his absence quickened something within her, Daisy leaned forward again, her voice glowing and singing.

'I love to see you at my table, Nick. You remind me of a – of a rose, an absolute rose. Doesn't he?' She turned to Miss Baker for confirmation: 'An absolute rose?'

This was untrue. I am not even faintly like a rose. She was only extemporising, but a stirring warmth flowed from her, as if her heart was trying to come out to you concealed in one of those breathless, thrilling words. Then suddenly she threw her napkin on the table and excused herself and went into the house.

Miss Baker and I exchanged a short glance consciously devoid of meaning. I was about to speak when she sat up alertly and said 'Sh!' in a warning voice. A subdued, impassioned murmur was audible in the room beyond, and Miss Baker leaned forward unashamed, trying to hear. The murmur trembled on the verge of coherence, sank down, mounted excitedly, and then ceased altogether.

'This Mr Gatsby you spoke of is my neighbour – ' I began.

'Don't talk. I want to hear what happens.'

'Is something happening?' I enquired innocently.

'You mean to say you don't know?' said Miss Baker, honestly surprised. 'I thought everybody knew.'

'I don't.'

'Why – ' she said hesitantly, 'Tom's got some woman in New York.'

'Got some woman?' I repeated blankly.

Miss Baker nodded.

'She might have the decency not to telephone him at dinner time. Don't you think?'

Almost before I had grasped her meaning there was the flutter of a dress and the crunch of leather boots, and Tom and Daisy were back at the table.

'It couldn't be helped!' cried Daisy with tense gaiety.

She sat down, glanced searchingly at Miss Baker and then at me, and continued: 'I looked outdoors for a minute, and it's very romantic outdoors. There's a bird on the lawn that I think must be a nightingale come over on the Cunard or White Star Line. He's singing away – ' Her voice sang: 'It's romantic, isn't it, Tom?'

'Very romantic,' he said, and then miserably to me: 'If it's light enough after dinner, I want to take you down to the stables.'

The telephone rang inside, startlingly, and as Daisy shook her head decisively at Tom the subject of the stables, in fact all subjects, vanished into air. Among the broken fragments of the last five minutes at table I remember the candles being lit again, pointlessly, and I was conscious of wanting to look squarely at everyone, and yet to avoid all eyes. I couldn't guess what Daisy and Tom were thinking, but I doubt if even Miss Baker, who seemed to have mastered a certain hardy scepticism, was able utterly to put this fifth guest's shrill metallic urgency out of mind. To a certain temperament the situation might have seemed intriguing – my own instinct was to telephone immediately for the police.

The horses, needless to say, were not mentioned again. Tom and Miss Baker, with several feet of twilight between them, strolled back into the library, as if to a vigil beside a perfectly tangible body, while, trying to look pleasantly interested and a little deaf, I followed Daisy around a chain of connecting verandas to the porch in front. In its deep gloom we sat down side by side on a wicker settee.

Daisy took her face in her hands as if feeling its lovely shape, and her eyes moved gradually out into the velvet dusk. I saw that turbulent emotions possessed her, so I asked what I thought would be some sedative questions about her little girl.

'We don't know each other very well, Nick,' she said suddenly. 'Even if we are cousins. You didn't come to my wedding.'

'I wasn't back from the war.'

'That's true.' She hesitated. 'Well, I've had a very bad time, Nick, and I'm pretty cynical about everything.'

Evidently she had reason to be. I waited but she didn't say any more, and after a moment I returned rather feebly to the subject of her daughter.

'I suppose she talks, and – eats, and everything.'

'Oh, yes.' She looked at me absently. 'Listen, Nick; let me tell you what I said when she was born. Would you like to hear?'

'Very much.'

'It'll show you how I've gotten to feel about – things. Well, she was less than an hour old and Tom was God knows where. I woke up out of the ether with an utterly abandoned feeling, and asked the nurse right away if it was a boy or a girl. She told me it was a girl, and so I turned my head away and wept. "All right," I said, "I'm glad it's a girl. And I hope she'll be a fool – that's the best thing a girl can be in this world, a beautiful little fool."

'You see I think everything's terrible anyhow,' she went on in a convinced way. 'Everybody thinks so – the most advanced people. And I *know*. I've been everywhere and seen everything and done everything.' Her eyes flashed around her in a defiant way, rather like Tom's, and she laughed with thrilling scorn. 'Sophisticated – God, I'm sophisticated!'

The instant her voice broke off, ceasing to compel my attention, my belief, I felt the basic insincerity of what she had said. It made me uneasy, as though the whole evening had been a trick of some sort to exact a contributory emotion from me. I waited, and sure enough, in a moment she looked at me with an absolute smirk on her lovely face, as if she had asserted her membership in a rather distinguished secret society to which she and Tom belonged.

Inside, the crimson room bloomed with light. Tom and Miss Baker sat at either end of the long couch and she read aloud to him from the *Saturday Evening Post* – the words, murmurous and uninflected, running together in a soothing tune. The lamplight, bright on his boots and dull on the autumn-leaf yellow of her hair, glinted along the paper as she turned a page with a flutter of slender muscles in her arms.

When we came in she held us silent for a moment with a lifted hand.

'To be continued,' she said, tossing the magazine on the table, 'in our very next issue.'

Her body asserted itself with a restless movement of her knee, and she stood up.

'Ten o'clock,' she remarked, apparently finding the time on the ceiling. 'Time for this good girl to go to bed.'

'Jordan's going to play in the tournament tomorrow,' explained Daisy, 'over at Westchester.'

'Oh – you're *Jor*dan Baker.'

I knew now why her face was familiar – its pleasing contemptuous expression had looked out at me from many rotogravure pictures of the sporting life at Asheville and Hot Springs and Palm Beach. I had heard some story of her too, a critical, unpleasant story, but what it was I had forgotten long ago.

'Good-night,' she said softly. 'Wake me at eight, won't you?'

'If you'll get up.'

'I will. Good-night, Mr Carraway. See you anon.'

'Of course you will,' confirmed Daisy. 'In fact, I think I'll arrange a marriage. Come over often Nick, and I'll sort of – oh – fling you together. You know – lock you up accidentally in linen closets and push you out to sea in a boat, and all that sort of thing – '

'Good-night,' called Miss Baker from the stairs. 'I haven't heard a word.'

'She's a nice girl,' said Tom after a moment. 'They oughtn't to let her run around the country this way.'

'Who oughtn't to?' enquired Daisy coldly.

'Her family.'

'Her family is one aunt about a thousand years old. Besides, Nick's going to look after her, aren't you, Nick? She's going to spend lots of weekends out here this summer. I think the home influence will be very good for her.'

Daisy and Tom looked at each other for a moment in silence.

'Is she from New York?' I asked quickly.

'From Louisville. Our white girlhood was passed together there. Our beautiful white – '

'Did you give Nick a little heart-to-heart talk on the veranda?' demanded Tom suddenly.

'Did I?' She looked at me. 'I can't seem to remember, but I think we talked about the Nordic race. Yes, I'm sure we did. It sort of crept up on us and first thing you know – '

'Don't believe everything you hear, Nick,' he advised me.

I said lightly that I had heard nothing at all, and a few minutes later I got up to go home. They came to the door with me and stood side by side in a cheerful square of light. As I started my motor Daisy peremptorily called: 'Wait! I forgot to ask you something, and it's important. We heard you were engaged to a girl out West.'

'That's right,' corroborated Tom kindly. 'We heard that you were engaged.'

'It's a libel. I'm too poor.'

'But we heard it,' insisted Daisy, surprising me by opening up again in a flower-like way. 'We heard it from three people, so it must be true.'

Of course I knew what they were referring to, but I wasn't even vaguely engaged. The fact that gossip had published the banns was one of the reasons I had come East. You can't stop going with an old friend on account of rumours, and on the other hand I had no intention of being rumoured into marriage.

Their interest rather touched me and made them less remotely rich – nevertheless, I was confused and a little disgusted as I drove away. It seemed to me that the thing for Daisy to do was to rush out of the house, child in arms – but apparently there were no such intentions in her head. As for Tom, the fact that he 'had some woman in New York' was really less surprising than that he had been depressed by a book. Something was making him nibble at the edge of stale ideas as if his sturdy physical egotism no longer nourished his peremptory heart.

Already it was deep summer on roadhouse roofs and in front of wayside garages, where new red gas-pumps sat out in pools of light, and when I reached my estate at West Egg I ran the car under its shed and sat for a while on an abandoned grass roller in the yard. The wind had blown off, leaving a loud, bright night, with wings beating in the trees and a persistent organ sound as the full bellows of the earth blew the frogs full of life. The silhouette of a moving cat wavered across the moonlight, and turning my head to watch it, I saw that I was not alone – fifty feet away a figure had emerged from the shadow of my neighbour's mansion and was standing with his hands in his pockets regarding the silver pepper of the stars. Something in his leisurely movements and the secure position of his feet upon the lawn suggested that it was Mr Gatsby himself, come out to determine what share was his of our local heavens.

I decided to call to him. Miss Baker had mentioned him at dinner, and that would do for an introduction. But I didn't call to him, for he gave a sudden intimation that he was content to be alone – he stretched out his arms towards the dark water in a curious way, and, far as I was from him, I could have sworn he was trembling. Involuntarily I glanced seaward – and distinguished nothing except a single green light, minute and far away, that might have been the end of a dock. When I looked once more for Gatsby he had vanished, and I was alone again in the unquiet darkness.

Two

About halfway between West Egg and New York the motor road hastily joins the railroad and runs beside it for a quarter of a mile, so as to shrink away from a certain desolate area of land. This is a valley of ashes – a fantastic farm where ashes grow like wheat into ridges and hills and grotesque gardens; where ashes take the forms of houses and chimneys and rising smoke and, finally, with a transcendent effort, of ash-grey men who move dimly and already crumbling through the powdery air. Occasionally a line of grey cars crawls along an invisible track, gives out a ghastly creak, and comes to rest, and immediately the ash-grey men swarm up with leaden spades and stir up an impenetrable cloud, which screens their obscure operations from your sight.

But above the grey land and the spasms of bleak dust which drift endlessly over it, you perceive, after a moment, the eyes of Dr T. J. Eckleburg. The eyes of Dr T. J. Eckleburg are blue and gigantic – their retinas are one yard high. They look out of no face, but, instead, from a pair of enormous yellow spectacles which pass over a nonexistent nose. Evidently some wild wag of an oculist set them there to fatten his practice in the borough of Queens, and then sank down himself into eternal blindness, or forgot them and moved away. But his eyes, dimmed a little by many paintless days, under sun and rain, brood on over the solemn dumping ground.

The valley of ashes is bounded on one side by a small foul river, and, when the drawbridge is up to let barges through, the passengers on waiting trains can stare at the dismal scene for as long as half an hour. There is always a halt there of at least a minute, and it was because of this that I first met Tom Buchanan's mistress.

The fact that he had one was insisted upon wherever he was known. His acquaintances resented the fact that he turned up in popular cafés with her and, leaving her at a table, sauntered about, chatting with whomsoever he knew. Though I was curious to see her, I had no desire to meet her – but I did. I went up to New York with Tom on the train one afternoon, and when we stopped by the ash-heaps he jumped to his feet and, taking hold of my elbow, literally forced me from the car.

'We're getting off,' he insisted. 'I want you to meet my girl.'

I think he'd tanked up a good deal at luncheon, and his determination to have my company bordered on violence. The supercilious assumption was that on Sunday afternoon I had nothing better to do.

I followed him over a low whitewashed railroad fence, and we walked back a hundred yards along the road under Dr Eckleburg's persistent stare. The only building in sight was a small block of yellow brick sitting on the edge of the waste land, a sort of compact Main Street ministering to it, and contiguous to absolutely nothing. One of the three shops it contained was for rent and another was an all-night restaurant, approached by a trail of ashes; the third was a garage – *Repairs.* George B. Wilson. *Cars bought and sold.* – and I followed Tom inside.

The interior was unprosperous and bare; the only car visible was the dust-covered wreck of a Ford which crouched in a dim corner. It had occurred to me that this shadow of a garage must be a blind, and that sumptuous and romantic apartments were concealed overhead, when the proprietor himself appeared in the door of an office, wiping his hands on a piece of waste. He was a blond, spiritless man, anaemic, and faintly handsome. When he saw us a damp gleam of hope sprang into his light blue eyes.

'Hello, Wilson, old man,' said Tom, slapping him jovially on the shoulder. 'How's business?'

'I can't complain,' answered Wilson unconvincingly. 'When are you going to sell me that car?'

'Next week; I've got my man working on it now.'

'Works pretty slow, don't he?'

'No, he doesn't,' said Tom coldly. 'And if you feel that way about it, maybe I'd better sell it somewhere else after all.'

'I don't mean that,' explained Wilson quickly. 'I just meant – '

His voice faded off and Tom glanced impatiently around the garage. Then I heard footsteps on a stairs, and in a moment the thickish figure of a woman blocked out the light from the office door. She was in the middle thirties, and faintly stout, but she carried her flesh sensuously, as some women can. Her face, above a spotted dress of dark blue crêpe-de-chine, contained no facet or gleam of beauty, but there was an immediately perceptible vitality about her as if the nerves of her body were continually smouldering. She smiled slowly and, walking through her husband as if he were a ghost, shook hands with Tom, looking him flush in the eye. Then she wet her lips, and without turning around spoke to her husband in a soft, coarse, voice: 'Get some chairs, why don't you, so somebody can sit down.'

'Oh, sure,' agreed Wilson hurriedly, and went towards the little office, mingling immediately with the cement colour of the walls. A white ashen dust veiled his dark suit and his pale hair as it veiled everything in the vicinity – except his wife, who moved close to Tom.

'I want to see you,' said Tom intently. 'Get on the next train.'

'All right.'

'I'll meet you by the news-stand on the lower level.'

She nodded and moved away from him just as George Wilson emerged with two chairs from his office door.

We waited for her down the road and out of sight. It was a few days before the Fourth of July, and a grey, scrawny Italian child was setting torpedoes in a row along the railroad track.

'Terrible place, isn't it,' said Tom, exchanging a frown with Dr Eckleburg.

'Awful.'

'It does her good to get away.'

'Doesn't her husband object?'

'Wilson? He thinks she goes to see her sister in New York. He's so dumb he doesn't know he's alive.'

So Tom Buchanan and his girl and I went up together to New York – or not quite together, for Mrs Wilson sat discreetly in another car. Tom deferred that much to the sensibilities of those East Eggers who might be on the train.

She had changed her dress to a brown figured muslin, which

stretched tight over her rather wide hips as Tom helped her to the platform in New York. At the news-stand she bought a copy of *Town Tattle* and a moving-picture magazine, and in the station drugstore some cold cream and a small flask of perfume. Upstairs, in the solemn echoing drive, she let four taxicabs drive away before she selected a new one, lavender-coloured with grey upholstery, and in this we slid out from the mass of the station into the glowing sunshine. But immediately she turned sharply from the window and, leaning forward, tapped on the front glass.

'I want to get one of those dogs,' she said earnestly. 'I want to get one for the apartment. They're nice to have – a dog.'

We backed up to a grey old man who bore an absurd resemblance to John D. Rockefeller. In a basket swung from his neck cowered a dozen very recent puppies of an indeterminate breed.

'What kind are they?' asked Mrs Wilson eagerly, as he came to the taxi-window.

'All kinds. What kind do you want, lady?'

'I'd like to get one of those police dogs; I don't suppose you got that kind?'

The man peered doubtfully into the basket, plunged in his hand and drew one up, wriggling, by the back of the neck.

'That's no police dog,' said Tom.

'No, it's not exactly a pol*ice* dog,' said the man with disappointment in his voice. 'It's more of an Airedale.' He passed his hand over the brown wash-rag of a back. 'Look at that coat. Some coat. That's a dog that'll never bother you with catching cold.'

'I think it's cute,' said Mrs Wilson enthusiastically. 'How much is it?'

'That dog?' He looked at it admiringly. 'That dog will cost you ten dollars.'

The Airedale – undoubtedly there was an Airedale concerned in it somewhere, though its feet were startlingly white – changed hands and settled down into Mrs Wilson's lap, where she fondled the weatherproof coat with rapture.

'Is it a boy or a girl?' she asked delicately.

'That dog? That dog's a boy.'

'It's a bitch,' said Tom decisively. 'Here's your money. Go and buy ten more dogs with it.'

We drove over to Fifth Avenue, warm and soft, almost pastoral, on the summer Sunday afternoon. I wouldn't have been surprised to see a great flock of white sheep turn the corner.

'Hold on,' I said, 'I have to leave you here.'

'No you don't,' interposed Tom quickly. 'Myrtle'll be hurt if you don't come up to the apartment. Won't you, Myrtle?'

'Come on,' she urged. 'I'll telephone my sister Catherine. She's said to be very beautiful by people who ought to know.'

'Well, I'd like to, but – '

We went on, cutting back again over the Park towards the West Hundreds. At 158th Street the cab stopped at one slice in a long white cake of apartment-houses. Throwing a regal homecoming glance around the neighbourhood, Mrs Wilson gathered up her dog and her other purchases, and went haughtily in.

'I'm going to have the McKees come up,' she announced as we rose in the elevator. 'And, of course, I got to call up my sister, too.'

The apartment was on the top floor – a small living-room, a small dining-room, a small bedroom, and a bath. The living-room was crowded to the doors with a set of tapestried furniture entirely too large for it, so that to move about was to stumble continually over scenes of ladies swinging in the gardens of Versailles. The only picture was an over-enlarged photograph, apparently a hen sitting on a blurred rock. Looked at from a distance, however, the hen resolved itself into a bonnet, and the countenance of a stout old lady beamed down into the room. Several old copies of *Town Tattle* lay on the table, together with a copy of *Simon Called Peter*, and some of the small scandal magazines of Broadway. Mrs Wilson was first concerned with the dog. A reluctant elevator-boy went for a box full of straw and some milk to which he added on his own initiative a tin of large, hard dog-biscuits – one of which decomposed apathetically in the saucer of milk all afternoon. Meanwhile Tom brought out a bottle of whiskey from a locked bureau drawer.

I have been drunk just twice in my life, and the second time was that afternoon; so everything that happened has a dim, hazy cast over it, although until after eight o'clock the apartment was full of cheerful sun. Sitting on Tom's lap Mrs Wilson called up several people on the telephone; then there were no cigarettes, and I went out to buy some at the drugstore on the corner. When I came back they had both disappeared, so I sat down discreetly in the living-room and read a chapter of *Simon Called Peter* – either it was terrible stuff or the whiskey distorted things, because it didn't make any sense to me.

Just as Tom and Myrtle (after the first drink Mrs Wilson and I called each other by our first names) reappeared, company commenced to arrive at the apartment door.

The sister, Catherine, was a slender, worldly girl of about thirty, with a solid, sticky bob of red hair, and a complexion powdered milky white. Her eyebrows had been plucked and then drawn on again at a more rakish angle but the efforts of nature towards the restoration of the old alignment gave a blurred air to her face. When she moved about there was an incessant clicking as innumerable pottery bracelets jingled up and down upon her arms. She came in with such a proprietary haste and looked around so possessively at the furniture that I wondered if she lived here. But when I asked her she laughed immoderately, repeated my question aloud, and told me she lived with a girl friend at a hotel.

Mr McKee was a pale, feminine man from the flat below. He had just shaved, for there was a white spot of lather on his cheekbone, and he was most respectful in his greeting to everyone in the room. He informed me that he was in the 'artistic game', and I gathered later that he was a photographer and had made the dim enlargement of Mrs Wilson's mother which hovered like an ectoplasm on the wall. His wife was shrill, languid, handsome, and horrible. She told me with pride that her husband had photographed her a hundred and twenty-seven times since they had been married.

Mrs Wilson had changed her costume sometime before, and was now attired in an elaborate afternoon dress of cream-coloured chiffon, which gave out a continual rustle as she swept about the room. With the influence of the dress her personality had also undergone a change. The intense vitality that had been so remarkable in the garage was converted into impressive hauteur. Her laughter, her gestures, her assertions became more violently affected moment by moment, and as she expanded the room grew smaller around her, until she seemed to be revolving on a noisy, creaking pivot through the smoky air.

‘My dear,’ she told her sister in a high, mincing shout, ‘most of these fellas will cheat you every time. All they think of is money. I had a woman up here last week to look at my feet, and when she gave me the bill you’d of thought she’d had my appendicitis out.’

‘What was the name of the woman?’ asked Mrs McKee.

‘Mrs Eberhardt. She goes around looking at people’s feet in their own homes.’

‘I like your dress,’ remarked Mrs McKee, ‘I think it’s adorable.

Mrs Wilson rejected the compliment by raising her eyebrow in disdain.

‘It’s just a crazy old thing,’ she said. ‘I just slip it on sometimes when I don’t care what I look like.’

‘But it looks wonderful on you, if you know what I mean,’ pursued Mrs McKee. ‘If Chester could only get you in that pose I think he could make something of it.’

We all looked in silence at Mrs Wilson, who removed a strand of hair from over her eyes and looked back at us with a brilliant smile. Mr McKee regarded her intently with his head on one side, and then moved his hand back and forth slowly in front of his face.

‘I should change the light,’ he said after a moment. ‘I’d like to bring out the modelling of the features. And I’d try to get hold of all the back hair.’

‘I wouldn’t think of changing the light,’ cried Mrs McKee. ‘I think it’s – ’

Her husband said ‘*Sh!* and we all looked at the subject again, whereupon Tom Buchanan yawned audibly and got to his feet.

‘You McKees have something to drink,’ he said. ‘Get some more ice and mineral water, Myrtle, before everybody goes to sleep.’

‘I told that boy about the ice.’ Myrtle raised her eyebrows in despair at the shiftlessness of the lower orders. 'These people! You have to keep after them all the time.'

She looked at me and laughed pointlessly. Then she flounced over to the dog, kissed it with ecstasy, and swept into the kitchen, implying that a dozen chefs awaited her orders there.

'I've done some nice things out on Long Island,' asserted Mr McKee.

Tom looked at him blankly.

'Two of them we have framed downstairs.'

'Two what?' demanded Tom.

'Two studies. One of them I call "Montauk Point – The Gulls", and the other I call "Montauk Point – The Sea".'

The sister Catherine sat down beside me on the couch.

'Do you live down on Long Island, too?' she enquired.

'I live at West Egg.'

'Really? I was down there at a party about a month ago. At a man named Gatsby's. Do you know him?'

'I live next door to him.'

'Well, they say he's a nephew or a cousin of Kaiser Wilhelm's. That's where all his money comes from.'

'Really?'

She nodded.

'I'm scared of him. I'd hate to have him get anything on me.'

This absorbing information about my neighbour was interrupted by Mrs McKee's pointing suddenly at Catherine: 'Chester, I think you could do something with *her*,' she broke out, but Mr McKee only nodded in a bored way, and turned his attention to Tom.

'I'd like to do more work on Long Island, if I could get the entry. All I ask is that they should give me a start.'

'Ask Myrtle,' said Tom, breaking into a short shout of laughter as Mrs Wilson entered with a tray. 'She'll give you a letter of introduction, won't you, Myrtle?'

'Do what?' she asked, startled.

'You'll give McKee a letter of introduction to your husband, so he can do some studies of him.' His lips moved silently for a moment as he invented. ' "George B. Wilson at the Gasoline Pump", or something like that.'

Catherine leaned close to me and whispered in my ear: 'Neither of them can stand the person they're married to.'

'Can't they?'

'Can't *stand* them.' She looked at Myrtle and then at Tom. 'What I say is, why go on living with them if they can't stand them? If I was them I'd get a divorce and get married to each other right away.'

'Doesn't she like Wilson either?'

The answer to this was unexpected. It came from Myrtle, who had overheard the question, and it was violent and obscene.

'You see,' cried Catherine triumphantly. She lowered her voice again. 'It's really his wife that's keeping them apart. She's a Catholic, and they don't believe in divorce.'

Daisy was not a Catholic, and I was a little shocked at the elaborateness of the lie.

'When they do get married,' continued Catherine, 'they're going West to live for a while until it blows over.'

'It'd be more discreet to go to Europe.'

'Oh, do you like Europe?' she exclaimed surprisingly. 'I just got back from Monte Carlo.'

'Really.'

'Just last year. I went over there with another girl.'

'Stay long?'

'No, we just went to Monte Carlo and back. We went by way of Marseilles. We had over twelve hundred dollars when we started, but we got gypped out of it all in two days in the private rooms. We had an awful time getting back, I can tell you. God, how I hated that town!'

The late afternoon sky bloomed in the window for a moment like the blue honey of the Mediterranean – then the shrill voice of Mrs McKee called me back into the room.

'I almost made a mistake, too,' she declared vigorously. 'I almost married a little kike who'd been after me for years. I knew he was below me. Everybody kept saying to me: "Lucille, that man's way below you!" But if I hadn't met Chester, he'd of got me sure.'

'Yes, but listen,' said Myrtle Wilson, nodding her head up and down, 'at least you didn't marry him.'

'I know I didn't.'

'Well, I married him,' said Myrtle, ambiguously. 'And that's the difference between your case and mine.'

'Why did you, Myrtle?' demanded Catherine. 'Nobody forced you to.'

Myrtle considered.

'I married him because I thought he was a gentleman,' she said finally. 'I thought he knew something about breeding, but he wasn't fit to lick my shoe.'

'You were crazy about him for a while,' said Catherine.

'Crazy about him!' cried Myrtle incredulously. 'Who said I was crazy about him? I never was any more crazy about him than I was about that man there.'

She pointed suddenly at me, and everyone looked at me accusingly. I tried to show by my expression that I expected no affection.

'The only *crazy* I was was when I married him. I knew right away I made a mistake. He borrowed somebody's best suit to get married in, and never even told me about it, and the man came after it one day when he was out: "Oh, is that your suit?" I said. "This is the first I ever heard about it." But I gave it to him and then I lay down and cried to beat the band all afternoon.'

'She really ought to get away from him,' resumed Catherine to me. 'They've been living over that garage for eleven years. And Tom's the first sweetie she ever had.'

The bottle of whiskey – a second one – was now in constant demand by all present, excepting Catherine, who 'felt just as good on nothing at all'. Tom rang for the janitor and sent him for some celebrated sandwiches, which were a complete supper in themselves. I wanted to get out and walk eastward towards the park through the soft twilight, but each time I tried to go I became entangled in some wild, strident argument which pulled me back, as if with ropes, into my chair. Yet high over the city our line of yellow windows must have contributed their share of human secrecy to the casual watcher in the darkening streets, and I saw him too, looking up and wondering. I was within and without, simultaneously enchanted and repelled by the inexhaustible variety of life.

Myrtle pulled her chair close to mine, and suddenly her warm breath poured over me the story of her first meeting with Tom.

'It was on the two little seats facing each other that are always the last ones left on the train. I was going up to New York to see my sister and spend the night. He had on a dress suit and patent-leather shoes, and I couldn't keep my eyes off him, but every time he looked at me I had to pretend to be looking at the advertisement over his head. When we came into the station he was next to me, and his white shirt-front pressed against my arm, and so I told him I'd have to call a policeman, but he knew I lied. I was so excited that when I got into a taxi with him I didn't hardly know I wasn't getting into a subway train. All I kept thinking about, over and over, was, "You can't live for ever; you can't live for ever." '

She turned to Mrs McKee and the room rang full of her artificial laughter.

'My dear,' she cried, 'I'm going to give you this dress as soon as I'm through with it. I've got to get another one tomorrow. I'm going to make a list of all the things I've got to get. A massage and a wave, and a collar for the dog, and one of those cute little ashtrays where you touch a spring, and a wreath with a black silk bow for mother's grave that'll last all summer. I got to write down a list so I won't forget all the things I got to do.'

It was nine o'clock – almost immediately afterwards I looked at my watch and found it was ten. Mr McKee was asleep on a chair with his fists clenched in his lap, like a photograph of a man of action. Taking out my handkerchief I wiped from his cheek the spot of dried lather that had worried me all the afternoon.

The little dog was sitting on the table looking with blind eyes through the smoke, and from time to time groaning faintly. People disappeared, reappeared, made plans to go somewhere, and then lost each other, searched for each other, found each other a few feet away. Sometime towards midnight Tom Buchanan and Mrs

Wilson stood face to face discussing, in impassioned voices, whether Mrs Wilson had any right to mention Daisy's name.

'Daisy! Daisy! Daisy!' shouted Mrs Wilson. 'I'll say it whenever I want to! Daisy! Dai – '

Making a short deft movement, Tom Buchanan broke her nose with his open hand.

Then there were bloody towels upon the bathroom floor, and women's voices scolding, and high over the confusion a long broken wail of pain. Mr McKee awoke from his doze and started in a daze towards the door. When he had gone halfway he turned around and stared at the scene – his wife and Catherine scolding and consoling as they stumbled here and there among the crowded furniture with articles of aid, and the despairing figure on the couch, bleeding fluently, and trying to spread a copy of *Town Tattle* over the tapestry scenes of Versailles. Then Mr McKee turned and continued on out the door. Taking my hat from the chandelier, I followed.

'Come to lunch some day,' he suggested, as we groaned down in the elevator.

'Where?'

'Anywhere.'

'Keep your hands off the lever,' snapped the elevator boy.

'I beg your pardon,' said Mr McKee with dignity, 'I didn't know I was touching it.'

'All right,' I agreed, 'I'll be glad to.'

. . . I was standing beside his bed and he was sitting up between the sheets, clad in his underwear, with a great portfolio in his hands.

'Beauty and the Beast . . . Loneliness . . . Old Grocery Horse . . . Brook'n Bridge . . . '

Then I was lying half-asleep in the cold lower level of the Pennsylvania Station, staring at the morning *Tribune*, and waiting for the four o'clock train.

Three

There was music from my neighbour's house through the summer nights. In his blue gardens men and girls came and went like moths among the whisperings and the champagne and the stars. At high tide in the afternoon I watched his guests diving from the tower of his raft, or taking the sun on the hot sand of his beach while his two motorboats slit the waters of the Sound, drawing aquaplanes over cataracts of foam. On weekends his Rolls-Royce became an omnibus, bearing parties to and from the city between nine in the morning and long past midnight, while his station-wagon scampered like a brisk yellow bug to meet all trains. And on Mondays eight servants, including an extra gardener, toiled all day with mops and scrubbing-brushes and hammers and garden-shears, repairing the ravages of the night before.

Every Friday five crates of oranges and lemons arrived from a fruiterer in New York – every Monday these same oranges and lemons left his back door in a pyramid of pulpless halves. There was a machine in the kitchen which could extract the juice of two hundred oranges in half an hour if a little button was pressed two hundred times by a butler's thumb.

At least once a fortnight a corps of caterers came down with several hundred feet of canvas and enough coloured lights to make a Christmas tree of Gatsby's enormous garden. On buffet tables, garnished with glistening hors d'oeuvre, spiced baked hams crowded against salads of harlequin designs and pastry pigs and turkeys bewitched to a dark gold. In the main hall a bar with a real brass rail was set up, and stocked with gins and liquors and with cordials so long forgotten that most of his female guests were too young to know one from another.

By seven o'clock the orchestra has arrived, no thin five-piece affair, but a whole pitful of oboes and trombones and saxophones and viols and cornets and piccolos, and low and high drums. The last swimmers have come in from the beach now and are dressing upstairs; the cars from New York are parked five deep in the drive, and already the halls and salons and verandas are gaudy with primary colours, and hair bobbed in strange new ways, and shawls beyond the dreams of Castile. The bar is in full swing, and floating rounds of cocktails permeate the garden outside, until the air is alive with chatter and laughter, and casual innuendo and introductions forgotten on the spot, and enthusiastic meetings between women who never knew each other's names.

The lights grow brighter as the earth lurches away from the sun, and now the orchestra is playing yellow cocktail music, and the opera of voices pitches a key higher. Laughter is easier minute by minute, spilled with prodigality, tipped out at a cheerful word. The groups change more swiftly, swell with new arrivals, dissolve and form in the same breath; already there are wanderers, confident girls who weave here and there among the stouter and more stable, become for a sharp, joyous moment the centre of a group, and then, excited with triumph, glide on through the sea-change of faces and voices and colour under the constantly changing light.

Suddenly one of these gypsies, in trembling opal, seizes a cocktail out of the air, dumps it down for courage and, moving her hands like Frisco, dances out alone on the canvas platform. A momentary hush; the orchestra leader varies his rhythm obligingly for her, and there is a burst of chatter as the erroneous news goes around that she is Gilda Gray's understudy from the *Follies*. The party has begun.

I believe that on the first night I went to Gatsby's house I was one of the few guests who had actually been invited. People were not invited – they went there. They got into automobiles which bore them out to Long Island, and somehow they ended up at Gatsby's door. Once there they were introduced by somebody who knew Gatsby, and after that they conducted themselves according to the rules of behaviour associated with an amusement park. Sometimes they came and went without having met Gatsby at all, came for the party with a simplicity of heart that was its own ticket of admission.

I had been actually invited. A chauffeur in a uniform of robin's-egg blue crossed my lawn early that Saturday morning with a surprisingly formal note from his employer: the honour would be entirely Gatsby's, it said, if I would attend his 'little party' that night. He had seen me several times, and had intended to call on me long before, but a peculiar combination of circumstances had prevented it – signed Jay Gatsby, in a majestic hand.

Dressed up in white flannels I went over to his lawn a little while after seven, and wandered around rather ill at ease among swirls and eddies of people I didn't know – though here and there was a face I had noticed on the commuting train. I was immediately struck by the number of young Englishmen dotted about, all well dressed, all looking a little hungry, and all talking in low, earnest voices to solid and prosperous Americans. I was sure that they were selling something: bonds or insurance or automobiles. They were at least agonisingly aware of the easy money in the vicinity and convinced that it was theirs for a few words in the right key.

As soon as I arrived I made an attempt to find my host, but the two or three people of whom I asked his whereabouts stared at me in such an amazed way, and denied so vehemently any knowledge of his movements, that I slunk off in the direction of the cocktail table – the only place in the garden where a single man could linger without looking purposeless and alone.

I was on my way to getting roaring drunk from sheer embarrassment when Jordan Baker came out of the house and stood at the head of the marble steps, leaning a little backwards and looking with contemptuous interest down into the garden.

Welcome or not, I found it necessary to attach myself to someone before I could begin to address cordial remarks to the passers-by.

'Hello!' I roared, advancing towards her. My voice seemed unnaturally loud across the garden.

'I thought you might be here,' she responded absently as I came up. 'I remembered you lived next door to – '

She held my hand impersonally, as a promise that she'd take care of me in a minute, and gave ear to two girls in twin yellow dresses, who stopped at the foot of the steps.

'Hello!' they cried together. 'Sorry you didn't win.'

That was for the golf tournament she had lost in the finals the week before.

'You don't know who we are,' said one of the girls in yellow, 'but we met you here about a month ago.'

'You've dyed your hair since then,' remarked Jordan, and I started, but the girls had moved casually on and her remark was addressed to the premature moon, produced like the supper, no doubt, out of a caterer's basket. With Jordan's slender golden arm resting in mine, we descended the steps and sauntered about the garden. A tray of cocktails floated at us through the twilight, and we sat down at a table with the two girls in yellow and three men, each one introduced to us as Mr Mumble.

'Do you come to these parties often?' enquired Jordan of the girl beside her.

'The last one was the one I met you at,' answered the girl, in an alert confident voice. She turned to her companion: 'Wasn't it for you, Lucille?'

It was for Lucille, too.

'I like to come,' Lucille said. 'I never care what I do, so I always have a good time. When I was here last I tore my gown on a chair, and he asked me my name and address – inside of a week I got a package from Croirier's with a new evening gown in it.'

'Did you keep it?' asked Jordan.

'Sure I did. I was going to wear it tonight, but it was too big in the bust and had to be altered. It was gas blue with lavender beads. Two hundred and sixty-five dollars.'

'There's something funny about a fellow that'll do a thing like that,' said the other girl eagerly. 'He doesn't want any trouble with *any*body.'

'Who doesn't?' I enquired.

'Gatsby. Somebody told me – '

The two girls and Jordan leaned together confidentially.

'Somebody told me they thought he killed a man once.'

A thrill passed over all of us. The three Mr Mumbles bent forward and listened eagerly.

'I don't think it's so much *that*,' argued Lucille sceptically; 'it's more that he was a German spy during the war.'

One of the men nodded in confirmation.

'I heard that from a man who knew all about him, grew up with him in Germany,' he assured us positively.

'Oh, no,' said the first girl, 'it couldn't be that, because he was in the American army during the war.' As our credulity switched back to her she leaned forward with enthusiasm. 'You look at him sometimes when he thinks nobody's looking at him. I'll bet he killed a man.'

She narrowed her eyes and shivered. Lucille shivered. We all turned and looked around for Gatsby. It was testimony to the romantic speculation he inspired that there were whispers about him from those who had found little that it was necessary to whisper about in this world.

The first supper – there would be another one after midnight – was now being served, and Jordan invited me to join her own party, who were spread around a table on the other side of the garden. There were three married couples and Jordan's escort, a persistent undergraduate given to violent innuendo, and obviously under the impression that sooner or later Jordan was going to yield him up her person to a greater or lesser degree. Instead of rambling, this party had preserved a dignified homogeneity, and assumed to itself the function of representing the staid nobility of the countryside – East Egg condescending to West Egg, and carefully on guard against its spectroscopic gaiety.

'Let's get out,' whispered Jordan, after a somehow wasteful and inappropriate half-hour; 'this is much too polite for me.'

We got up, and she explained that we were going to find the host: I had never met him, she said, and it was making me uneasy. The undergraduate nodded in a cynical, melancholy way.

The bar, where we glanced first, was crowded, but Gatsby was not there. She couldn't find him from the top of the steps, and he wasn't on the veranda. On a chance we tried an important-looking door, and walked into a high Gothic library, panelled with carved English oak, and probably transported complete from some ruin overseas.

A stout, middle-aged man, with enormous owl-eyed spectacles, was sitting somewhat drunk on the edge of a great table, staring with unsteady concentration at the shelves of books. As we entered he wheeled excitedly around and examined Jordan from head to foot.

'What do you think?' he demanded impetuously.

'About what?'

He waved his hand towards the bookshelves.

'About that. As a matter of fact you needn't bother to ascertain. I ascertained. They're real.'

'The books?'

He nodded.

'Absolutely real – have pages and everything. I thought they'd be a nice durable cardboard. Matter of fact, they're absolutely real. Pages and – Here! Lemme show you.'

Taking our scepticism for granted, he rushed to the bookcases and returned with Volume One of the *Stoddard Lectures.*

'See!' he cried triumphantly. 'It's a bona-fide piece of printed matter. It fooled me. This fella's a regular Belasco. It's a triumph. What thoroughness! What realism! Knew when to stop, too – didn't cut the pages. But what do you want? What do you expect?'

He snatched the book from me and replaced it hastily on its shelf, muttering that if one brick was removed the whole library was liable to collapse.

'Who brought you?' he demanded. 'Or did you just come? I was brought. Most people were brought.'

Jordan looked at him alertly, cheerfully, without answering.

'I was brought by a woman named Roosevelt,' he continued. 'Mrs Claude Roosevelt. Do you know her? I met her somewhere last night. I've been drunk for about a week now, and I thought it might sober me up to sit in a library.'

'Has it?'

'A little bit, I think. I can't tell yet. I've only been here an hour. Did I tell you about the books? They're real. They're – '

'You told us.'

We shook hands with him gravely and went back outdoors.

There was dancing now on the canvas in the garden; old men pushing young girls backwards in eternal graceless circles, superior couples holding each other tortuously, fashionably, and keeping in the corners – and a great number of single girls dancing individualistically or relieving the orchestra for a moment of the burden of the banjo or the traps. By midnight the hilarity had increased. A celebrated tenor had sung in Italian, and a notorious contralto had sung in jazz, and between the numbers people were doing 'stunts' all over the garden, while happy, vacuous bursts of laughter rose towards the summer sky. A pair of stage twins, who turned out to be the girls in yellow, did a baby act in costume, and champagne was served in glasses bigger than finger-bowls. The moon had risen higher, and floating in the Sound was a triangle of silver scales, trembling a little to the stiff, tinny drip of the banjos on the lawn.

I was still with Jordan Baker. We were sitting at a table with a man of about my age and a rowdy little girl, who gave way upon the slightest provocation to uncontrollable laughter. I was enjoying myself now. I had taken two finger-bowls of champagne, and the scene had changed before my eyes into something significant, elemental and profound.

At a lull in the entertainment the man looked at me and smiled.

'Your face is familiar,' he said, politely. 'Weren't you in the First Division during the war?'

'Why, yes. I was in the Twenty-eighth Infantry.'

'I was in the Sixteenth until June 1918. I knew I'd seen you somewhere before.'

We talked for a moment about some wet, grey little villages in France. Evidently he lived in this vicinity, for he told me that he had just bought a hydroplane, and was going to try it out in the morning.

'Want to go with me, old sport? Just near the shore along the Sound.'

'What time?'

'Any time that suits you best.'

It was on the tip of my tongue to ask his name when Jordan looked around and smiled.

'Having a gay time now?' she enquired.

'Much better.' I turned again to my new acquaintance. 'This is an unusual party for me. I haven't even seen the host. I live over there – ' I waved my hand at the invisible hedge in the distance, 'and this man Gatsby sent over his chauffeur with an invitation.'

For a moment he looked at me as if he failed to understand.

'I'm Gatsby,' he said suddenly.

'What!' I exclaimed. 'Oh, I beg your pardon.'

'I thought you knew, old sport. I'm afraid I'm not a very good host.'

He smiled understandingly – much more than understandingly. It was one of those rare smiles with a quality of eternal reassurance in it, that you may come across four or five times in life. It faced – or seemed to face – the whole eternal world for an instant, and then concentrated on *you* with an irresistible prejudice in your favour. It understood you just as far as you wanted to be understood, believed in you as you would like to believe in yourself, and assured you that it had precisely the impression of you that, at your best, you hoped to convey. Precisely at that point it vanished – and I was looking at an elegant young roughneck, a year or two over thirty, whose elaborate formality of speech just missed being absurd. Sometime before he introduced himself I'd got a strong impression that he was picking his words with care.

Almost at the moment when Mr Gatsby identified himself, a butler hurried towards him with the information that Chicago was calling him on the wire. He excused himself with a small bow that included each of us in turn.

'If you want anything just ask for it, old sport,' he urged me. 'Excuse me. I will rejoin you later.'

When he was gone I turned immediately to Jordan – constrained to assure her of my surprise. I had expected that Mr Gatsby would be a florid and corpulent person in his middle years.

'Who is he?' I demanded. 'Do you know?'

'He's just a man named Gatsby.'

'Where is he from, I mean? And what does he do?'

'Now *you're* started on the subject,' she answered with a wan smile. 'Well, he told me once he was an Oxford man.'

A dim background started to take shape behind him, but at her next remark it faded away.

'However, I don't believe it.'

'Why not?'

'I don't know,' she insisted, 'I just don't think he went there.'

Something in her tone reminded me of the other girl's 'I think he killed a man', and had the effect of stimulating my curiosity. I would have accepted without question the information that Gatsby sprang from the swamps of Louisiana or from the lower East Side of New York. That was comprehensible. But young men didn't – at least in my provincial inexperience I believed they didn't – drift coolly out of nowhere and buy a palace on Long Island Sound.

'Anyhow, he gives large parties,' said Jordan, changing the subject with an urban taste for the concrete. 'And I like large parties. They're so intimate. At small parties there isn't any privacy.'

There was the boom of a bass drum, and the voice of the orchestra leader rang out suddenly above the echolalia of the garden.

'Ladies and gentlemen,' he cried. 'At the request of Mr Gatsby we are going to play for you Mr Vladimir Tostoff's latest work, which attracted so much attention at Carnegie Hall last May. If you read the papers, you know there was a big sensation.' He smiled with jovial condescension, and added: 'Some sensation!' Whereupon everybody laughed.

'The piece is known,' he concluded lustily, 'as Vladimir Tostoff's *Jazz History of the World*.'

The nature of Mr Tostoff's composition eluded me, because just as it began my eyes fell on Gatsby, standing alone on the marble steps and looking from one group to another with approving eyes. His tanned skin was drawn attractively tight on his face and his short hair looked as though it were trimmed every day. I could see nothing sinister about him. I wondered if the fact that he was not drinking helped to set him off from his guests, for it seemed to me that he grew more correct as the fraternal hilarity increased. When the *Jazz History of the World* was over, girls were putting their heads on men's shoulders in a puppyish, convivial way, girls were swooning backwards playfully into men's arms, even into groups, knowing that someone would arrest their falls – but no one swooned backwards on Gatsby, and no French bob touched Gatsby's shoulder, and no singing quartets were formed with Gatsby's head for one link.

'I beg your pardon.'

Gatsby's butler was suddenly standing beside us.

'Miss Baker?' he enquired. 'I beg your pardon, but Mr Gatsby would like to speak to you alone.'

'With me?' she exclaimed in surprise.

'Yes, madame.'

She got up slowly, raising her eyebrows at me in astonishment, and followed the butler towards the house. I noticed that she wore her evening-dress, all her dresses, like sports clothes – there was a jauntiness about her movements as if she had first learned to walk upon golf courses on clean, crisp mornings.

I was alone and it was almost two. For some time confused and intriguing sounds had issued from a long, many-windowed room which overhung the terrace. Eluding Jordan's undergraduate, who was now engaged in an obstetrical conversation with two chorus girls, and who implored me to join him, I went inside.

The large room was full of people. One of the girls in yellow was playing the piano, and beside her stood a tall, red-haired young lady from a famous chorus, engaged in song. She had drunk a quantity of champagne, and during the course of her song she had decided, ineptly, that everything was very, very sad – she was not only singing, she was weeping too. Whenever there was a pause in the song she filled it with gasping, broken sobs, and then took up the lyric again in a quavering soprano. The tears coursed down her cheeks – not freely, however, for when they came into contact with her heavily beaded eyelashes they assumed an inky colour, and pursued the rest of their way in slow black rivulets. A humorous suggestion was made that she sing the notes on her face, whereupon she threw up her hands, sank into a chair, and went off into a deep vinous sleep.

'She had a fight with a man who says he's her husband,' explained a girl at my elbow.

I looked around. Most of the remaining women were now having fights with men said to be their husbands. Even Jordan's party, the quartet from East Egg, were rent asunder by dissension. One of the men was talking with curious intensity to a young actress, and his wife, after attempting to laugh at the situation in a dignified and indifferent way, broke down entirely and resorted to flank attacks – at intervals she appeared suddenly at his side like an angry diamond, and hissed: 'You promised!' into his ear.

The reluctance to go home was not confined to wayward men. The hall was at present occupied by two deplorably sober men and their highly indignant wives. The wives were sympathising with each other in slightly raised voices.

'Whenever he sees I'm having a good time he wants to go home.'

'Never heard anything so selfish in my life.'

'We're always the first ones to leave.'

'So are we.'

'Well, we're almost the last tonight,' said one of the men sheepishly. 'The orchestra left half an hour ago.'

In spite of the wives' agreement that such malevolence was beyond credibility, the dispute ended in a short struggle, and both wives were lifted, kicking, into the night.

As I waited for my hat in the hall the door of the library opened and Jordan Baker and Gatsby came out together. He was saying some last word to her, but the eagerness in his manner tightened abruptly into formality as several people approached him to say goodbye.

Jordan's party were calling impatiently to her from the porch, but she lingered for a moment to shake hands.

'I've just heard the most amazing thing,' she whispered. 'How long were we in there?'

'Why, about an hour.'

'It was . . . simply amazing,' she repeated abstractedly. 'But I swore I wouldn't tell it and here I am tantalising you.' She yawned gracefully in my face. 'Please come and see me . . . Phone book . . . Under the name of Mrs Sigourney Howard . . . My aunt . . . ' She was hurrying off as she talked – her brown hand waved a jaunty salute as she melted into her party at the door.

Rather ashamed that on my first appearance I had stayed so late, I joined the last of Gatsby's guests, who were clustered around him. I wanted to explain that I'd hunted for him early in the evening and to apologise for not having known him in the garden.

'Don't mention it,' he enjoined me eagerly. 'Don't give it another thought, old sport.' The familiar expression held no more familiarity than the hand which reassuringly brushed my shoulder. 'And don't forget we're going up in the hydroplane tomorrow morning, at nine o'clock.'

Then the butler, behind his shoulder: 'Philadelphia wants you on the phone, sir.'

'All right, in a minute. Tell them I'll be right there . . . Good-night.'

'Good-night.'

'Good-night.' He smiled – and suddenly there seemed to be a pleasant significance in having been among the last to go, as if he had desired it all the time. 'Good-night, old sport . . . Good-night.'

But as I walked down the steps I saw that the evening was not quite over. Fifty feet from the door a dozen headlights illuminated a bizarre and tumultuous scene. In the ditch beside the road, right side up, but violently shorn of one wheel, rested a new coupé which had left Gatsby's drive not two minutes before. The sharp jut of a wall accounted for the detachment of the wheel, which was now getting considerable attention from half a dozen curious chauffeurs. However, as they had left their cars blocking the road, a harsh, discordant din from those in the rear had been audible for some time, and added to the already violent confusion of the scene.

A man in a long duster had dismounted from the wreck and now stood in the middle of the road, looking from the car to the tyre and from the tyre to the observers in a pleasant, puzzled way.

'See!' he explained. 'It went in the ditch.'

The fact was infinitely astonishing to him, and I recognised first the unusual quality of wonder, and then the man – it was the late patron of Gatsby's library.

'How'd it happen?'

He shrugged his shoulders.

'I know nothing whatever about mechanics,' he said decisively.

'But how did it happen? Did you run into the wall?'

'Don't ask me,' said Owl Eyes, washing his hands of the whole matter. 'I know very little about driving – next to nothing. It happened, and that's all I know.'

'Well, if you're a poor driver you oughtn't to try driving at night.'

'But I wasn't even trying,' he explained indignantly, 'I wasn't even trying.'

An awed hush fell upon the bystanders.

'Do you want to commit suicide?'

'You're lucky it was just a wheel! A bad driver and not even *try*ing!'

'You don't understand,' explained the criminal. 'I wasn't driving. There's another man in the car.'

The shock that followed this declaration found voice in a sustained 'Ah–h–h!' as the door of the coupé swung slowly open. The crowd – it was now a crowd – stepped back involuntarily, and when the door had opened wide there was a ghostly pause. Then, very gradually, part by part, a pale, dangling individual stepped out of the wreck, pawing tentatively at the ground with a large uncertain dancing shoe.

Blinded by the glare of the headlights and confused by the incessant groaning of the horns, the apparition stood swaying for a moment before he perceived the man in the duster.

'Wha's matter?' he enquired calmly. 'Did we run outa gas?'

'Look!'

Half a dozen fingers pointed at the amputated wheel – he stared at it for a moment, and then looked upward as though he suspected that it had dropped from the sky.

'It came off,' someone explained.

He nodded.

'At first I din' notice we'd stopped.'

A pause. Then, taking a long breath and straightening his shoulders, he remarked in a determined voice: 'Wonder'ff tell me where there's a gas'line station?'

At least a dozen men, some of them a little better off than he was, explained to him that wheel and car were no longer joined by any physical bond.

'Back out,' he suggested after a moment. 'Put her in reverse.'

'But the *wheel's* off!'

He hesitated.

'No harm in trying,' he said.

The caterwauling horns had reached a crescendo and I turned away and cut across the lawn towards home. I glanced back once. A wafer of a moon was shining over Gatsby's house, making the night fine as before, and surviving the laughter and the sound of his still glowing garden. A sudden emptiness seemed to flow now from the windows and the great doors, endowing with complete isolation the figure of the host, who stood on the porch, his hand up in a formal gesture of farewell.

Reading over what I have written so far, I see I have given the impression that the events of three nights several weeks apart were all that absorbed me. On the contrary, they were merely casual events in a crowded summer, and, until much later, they absorbed me infinitely less than my personal affairs.

Most of the time I worked. In the early morning the sun threw my shadow westward as I hurried down the white chasms of lower New York to the Probity Trust. I knew the other clerks and young bond-salesmen by their first names, and lunched with them in dark, crowded restaurants on little pig sausages and mashed potatoes and coffee. I even had a short affair with a girl who lived in Jersey City and worked in the accounting department, but her brother began throwing mean looks in my direction, so when she went on her vacation in July I let it blow quietly away.

I took dinner usually at the Yale Club – for some reason it was the gloomiest event of my day – and then I went upstairs to the library and studied investments and securities for a conscientious hour. There were generally a few rioters around, but they never came into the library, so it was a good place to work. After that, if the night was mellow, I strolled down Madison Avenue past the old Murray Hill Hotel, and over 33rd Street to the Pennsylvania Station.

I began to like New York, the racy, adventurous feel of it at night, and the satisfaction that the constant flicker of men and women and machines gives to the restless eye. I liked to walk up Fifth Avenue and pick out romantic women from the crowd and imagine that in a few minutes I was going to enter into their lives, and no one would ever know or disapprove. Sometimes, in my mind, I followed them to their apartments on the corners of hidden streets, and they turned and smiled back at me before they faded through a door into warm darkness. At the enchanted metropolitan twilight I felt a haunting loneliness sometimes, and felt it in others – poor young clerks who loitered in front of windows waiting until it was time for a solitary restaurant dinner – young clerks in the dusk, wasting the most poignant moments of night and life.

Again at eight o'clock, when the dark lanes of the Forties were lined five deep with throbbing taxicabs, bound for the theatre district, I felt a sinking in my heart. Forms leaned together in the taxis as they waited, and voices sang, and there was laughter from unheard jokes, and lighted cigarettes made unintelligible circles inside. Imagining that I, too, was hurrying towards gaiety and sharing their intimate excitement, I wished them well.

For a while I lost sight of Jordan Baker, and then in midsummer I found her again. At first I was flattered to go places with her, because she was a golf champion, and everyone knew her name. Then it was something more. I wasn't actually in love, but I felt a sort of tender curiosity. The bored haughty face that she turned to the world concealed something – most affectations conceal something eventually, even though they don't in the beginning – and one day I found what it was. When we were on a house-party together up in Warwick, she left a borrowed car out in the rain with the top down, and then lied about it – and suddenly I remembered the story about her that had eluded me that night at Daisy's. At her first big golf tournament there was a row that nearly reached the newspapers – a suggestion that she had moved her ball from a bad lie in the semi-final round. The thing approached the proportions of a scandal – then died away. A caddy retracted his statement, and the only other witness admitted that he might have been mistaken. The incident and the name had remained together in my mind.

Jordan Baker instinctively avoided clever, shrewd men, and now I saw that this was because she felt safer on a plane where any divergence from a code would be thought impossible. She was incurably dishonest. She wasn't able to endure being at a disadvantage and, given this unwillingness, I suppose she had begun dealing in subterfuges when she was very young in order to keep that cool, insolent smile turned to the world and yet satisfy the demands of her hard, jaunty body.

It made no difference to me. Dishonesty in a woman is a thing you never blame deeply – I was casually sorry, and then I forgot. It was on that same house-party that we had a curious conversation about driving a car. It started because she passed so close to some workmen that our fender flicked a button on one man's coat.

'You're a rotten driver,' I protested. 'Either you ought to be more careful, or you oughtn't to drive at all.'

'I am careful.'

'No, you're not.'

'Well, other people are,' she said lightly.

'What's that got to do with it?'

'They'll keep out of my way,' she insisted. 'It takes two to make an accident.'

'Suppose you met somebody just as careless as yourself.'

'I hope I never will,' she answered. 'I hate careless people. That's why I like you.'

Her grey, sun-strained eyes stared straight ahead, but she had deliberately shifted our relations, and for a moment I thought I loved her. But I am slow-thinking and full of interior rules that act as brakes on my desires, and I knew that first I had to get myself definitely out of that tangle back home. I'd been writing letters once a week and signing them: 'Love, Nick', and all I could think of was how, when that certain girl played tennis, a faint moustache of perspiration appeared on her upper lip. Nevertheless there was a vague understanding that had to be tactfully broken off before I was free.

Everyone suspects himself of at least one of the cardinal virtues, and this is mine: I am one of the few honest people that I have ever known.

Four

On Sunday morning while church bells rang in the villages alongshore, the world and its mistress returned to Gatsby's house and twinkled hilariously on his lawn.

'He's a bootlegger,' said the young ladies, moving somewhere between his cocktails and his flowers. 'One time he killed a man who had found out that he was nephew to Von Hindenburg and second cousin to the devil. Reach me a rose, honey, and pour me a last drop into that there crystal glass.'

Once I wrote down on the empty spaces of a timetable the names of those who came to Gatsby's house that summer. It is an old timetable now, disintegrating at its folds, and headed, 'This schedule in effect July 5th, 1922'. But I can still read the grey names, and they will give you a better impression than my generalities of those who accepted Gatsby's hospitality and paid him the subtle tribute of knowing nothing whatever about him.

From East Egg, then, came the Chester Beckers and the Leeches, and a man named Bunsen, whom I knew at Yale, and Dr Webster Civet, who was drowned last summer up in Maine. And the Hornbeams and the Willie Voltaires, and a whole clan named Blackbuck, who always gathered in a corner and flipped up their noses like goats at whomsoever came near. And the Ismays and the Chrysties (or rather Hubert Auerbach and Mr Chrystie's wife), and Edgar Beaver, whose hair, they say, turned cotton-white one winter afternoon for no good reason at all.

Clarence Endive was from East Egg, as I remember. He came only once, in white knickerbockers, and had a fight with a bum named Etty in the garden. From farther out on the Island came the Cheadles and the O. R. P. Schraeders, and the Stonewall Jackson Abrams of Georgia, and the Fishguards and the Ripley

Snells. Snell was there three days before he went to the penitentiary, so drunk out on the gravel drive that Mrs Ulysses Swett's automobile ran over his right hand. The Dancies came, too, and S. B. Whitebait, who was well over sixty, and Maurice A. Flink, and the Hammerheads, and Beluga the tobacco importer, and Beluga's girls.

From West Egg came the Poles and the Mulreadys and Cecil Roebuck and Cecil Schoen and Gulick the State senator and Newton Orchid, who controlled Films Par Excellence, and Eckhaust and Clyde Cohen and Don S. Schwartze (the son) and Arthur McCarty, all connected with the movies in one way or another. And the Catlips and the Bembergs and G. Earl Muldoon, brother to that Muldoon who afterwards strangled his wife. Da Fontano the promoter came there, and Ed Legros and James B. ('Rot-Gut') Ferret and the De Jongs and Ernest Lilly – they came to gamble, and when Ferret wandered into the garden it meant he was cleaned out and Associated Traction would have to fluctuate profitably next day.

A man named Klipspringer was there so often and so long that he became known as 'the boarder' – I doubt if he had any other home. Of theatrical people there were Gus Waize and Horace O'Donavan and Lester Myer and George Duckweed and Francis Bull. Also from New York were the Chromes and the Backhyssons and the Dennickers and Russell Betty and the Corrigans and the Kellehers and the Dewers and the Scullys and S. W. Belcher and the Smirkes and the young Quinns, divorced now, and Henry L. Palmetto, who killed himself by jumping in front of a subway train at Times Square.

Benny McClenahan arrived always with four girls. They were never quite the same ones in physical person, but they were so identical one with another that it inevitably seemed that they had been there before. I have forgotten their names – Jacqueline, I think, or else Consuela, or Gloria or Judy or June, and their last names were either the melodious names of flowers and months or the sterner ones of the great American capitalists whose cousins, if pressed, they would confess themselves to be.

In addition to all these I can remember that Faustina O'Brien came there at least once and the Baedeker girls and young Brewer, who had his nose shot off in the war, and Mr Albrucksburger and Miss Haag, his fiancée, and Ardita Fitz-Peters and Mr P. Jewett, once head of the American Legion, and Miss Claudia Hip, with a man reputed to be her chauffeur, and a prince of something, whom we called Duke, and whose name, if I ever knew it, I have forgotten.

All these people came to Gatsby's house in the summer.

At nine o'clock one morning late in July, Gatsby's gorgeous car lurched up the rocky drive to my door and gave out a burst of melody from its three-noted horn. It was the first time he had called on me, though I had gone to two of his parties, mounted in his hydroplane, and, at his urgent invitation, made frequent use of his beach.

'Good-morning, old sport. You're having lunch with me today and I thought we'd ride up together.'

He was balancing himself on the dashboard of his car with that resourcefulness of movement that is so peculiarly American – that comes, I suppose, with the absence of lifting work in youth and, even more, with the formless grace of our nervous, sporadic games. This quality was continually breaking through his punctilious manner in the shape of restlessness. He was never quite still; there was always a tapping foot somewhere or the impatient opening and closing of a hand.

He saw me looking with admiration at his car.

'It's pretty, isn't it, old sport?' He jumped off to give me a better view. 'Haven't you ever seen it before?'

I'd seen it. Everybody had seen it. It was a rich cream colour, bright with nickel, swollen here and there in its monstrous length with triumphant hatboxes and supper-boxes and tool-boxes, and terraced with a labyrinth of wind-shields that mirrored a dozen suns. Sitting down behind many layers of glass in a sort of green leather conservatory, we started to town.

I had talked with him perhaps half a dozen times in the past month and found, to my disappointment, that he had little to say. So my first impression, that he was a person of some undefined consequence, had gradually faded and he had become simply the proprietor of an elaborate roadhouse next door.

And then came that disconcerting ride. We hadn't reached West Egg Village before Gatsby began leaving his elegant sentences unfinished and slapping himself indecisively on the knee of his caramel-coloured suit.

'Look here, old sport,' he broke out surprisingly, 'what's your opinion of me, anyhow?'

A little overwhelmed, I began the generalised evasions which that question deserves.

'Well, I'm going to tell you something about my life,' he interrupted. 'I don't want you to get a wrong idea of me from all these stories you hear.'

So he was aware of the bizarre accusations that flavoured conversation in his halls.

'I'll tell you God's truth.' His right hand suddenly ordered divine retribution to stand by. 'I am the son of some wealthy people in the Middle West – all dead now. I was brought up in America but educated at Oxford, because all my ancestors have been educated there for many years. It is a family tradition.'

He looked at me sideways – and I knew why Jordan Baker had believed he was lying. He hurried the phrase 'educated at Oxford', or swallowed it, or choked on it, as though it had bothered him before. And with this doubt, his whole statement fell to pieces, and I wondered if there wasn't something a little sinister about him, after all.

'What part of the Middle West?' I enquired casually.

'San Francisco.'

'I see.'

'My family all died and I came into a good deal of money.'

His voice was solemn, as if the memory of that sudden extinction of a clan still haunted him. For a moment I suspected that he was pulling my leg, but a glance at him convinced me otherwise.

'After that I lived like a young rajah in all the capitals of Europe –

Paris, Venice, Rome – collecting jewels, chiefly rubies, hunting big game, painting a little, things for myself only, and trying to forget something very sad that had happened to me long ago.'

With an effort I managed to restrain my incredulous laughter. The very phrases were worn so threadbare that they evoked no image except that of a turbaned 'character' leaking sawdust at every pore as he pursued a tiger through the Bois de Boulogne.

'Then came the war, old sport. It was a great relief, and I tried very hard to die, but I seemed to bear an enchanted life. I accepted a commission as first lieutenant when it began. In the Argonne Forest I took the remains of my machine-gun battalion so far forward that there was a half-mile gap on either side of us where the infantry couldn't advance. We stayed there two days and two nights, a hundred and thirty men with sixteen Lewis guns, and when the infantry came up at last they found the insignia of three German divisions among the piles of dead. I was promoted to be a major, and every Allied government gave me a decoration – even Montenegro, little Montenegro down on the Adriatic Sea!'

Little Montenegro! He lifted up the words and nodded at them – with his smile. The smile comprehended Montenegro's troubled history and sympathised with the brave struggles of the Montenegrin people. It appreciated fully the chain of national circumstances which had elicited this tribute from Montenegro's warm little heart. My incredulity was submerged in fascination now; it was like skimming hastily through a dozen magazines.

He reached in his pocket, and a piece of metal, slung on a ribbon, fell into my palm.

'That's the one from Montenegro.'

To my astonishment, the thing had an authentic look. 'Orderi di Danilo', ran the circular legend, 'Montenegro, Nicolas Rex'.

'Turn it.'

'Major Jay Gatsby,' I read, 'For Valour Extraordinary.'

'Here's another thing I always carry. A souvenir of Oxford days. It was taken in Trinity Quad – the man on my left is now the Earl of Doncaster.'

It was a photograph of half a dozen young men in blazers loafing in an archway through which was visible a host of spires. There was Gatsby, looking a little, not much, younger – with a cricket bat in his hand.

Then it was all true. I saw the skins of tigers flaming in his palace on the Grand Canal; I saw him opening a chest of rubies to ease, with their crimson-lighted depths, the gnawings of his broken heart.

'I'm going to make a big request of you today,' he said, pocketing his souvenirs with satisfaction, 'so I thought you ought to know something about me. I didn't want you to think I was just some nobody. You see, I usually find myself among strangers because I drift here and there trying to forget the sad thing that happened to me.' He hesitated. 'You'll hear about it this afternoon.'

'At lunch?'

'No, this afternoon. I happened to find out that you're taking Miss Baker to tea.'

'Do you mean you're in love with Miss Baker?'

'No, old sport, I'm not. But Miss Baker has kindly consented to speak to you about this matter.'

I hadn't the faintest idea what 'this matter' was, but I was more annoyed than interested. I hadn't asked Jordan to tea in order to discuss Mr Jay Gatsby. I was sure the request would be something utterly fantastic, and for a moment I was sorry I'd ever set foot upon his overpopulated lawn.

He wouldn't say another word. His correctness grew on him as we neared the city. We passed Port Roosevelt, where there was a glimpse of red-belted ocean-going ships, and sped along a cobbled slum lined with the dark, undeserted saloons of the faded-gilt nineteen-hundreds. Then the valley of ashes opened out on both sides of us, and I had a glimpse of Mrs Wilson straining at the garage pump with panting vitality as we went by.

With fenders spread like wings we scattered light through half Astoria – only half, for as we twisted among the pillars of the elevated I heard the familiar 'jug–jug–*spat*!' of a motorcycle, and a frantic policeman rode alongside.

'All right, old sport,' called Gatsby. We slowed down. Taking a white card from his wallet, he waved it before the man's eyes.

'Right you are,' agreed the policeman, tipping his cap. 'Know you next time, Mr Gatsby. Excuse *me*!'

'What was that?' I enquired. 'The picture of Oxford?'

'I was able to do the commissioner a favour once, and he sends me a Christmas card every year.'

Over the great bridge, with the sunlight through the girders making a constant flicker upon the moving cars, with the city rising up across the river in white heaps and sugar lumps all built with a wish out of non-olfactory money. The city seen from the Queensboro Bridge is always the city seen for the first time, in its first wild promise of all the mystery and the beauty in the world.

A dead man passed us in a hearse heaped with blooms, followed by two carriages with drawn blinds, and by more cheerful carriages for friends. The friends looked out at us with the tragic eyes and short upper lips of south-eastern Europe, and I was glad that the sight of Gatsby's splendid car was included in their sombre holiday. As we crossed Blackwell's Island a limousine passed us, driven by a white chauffeur, in which sat three modish negroes, two bucks and a girl. I laughed aloud as the yolks of their eyeballs rolled towards us in haughty rivalry.

'Anything can happen now that we've slid over this bridge,' I thought; 'anything at all . . . '

Even Gatsby could happen, without any particular wonder.

Roaring noon. In a well-fanned Forty-second Street cellar I met Gatsby for lunch. Blinking away the brightness of the street outside, my eyes picked him out obscurely in the ante-room, talking to another man.

'Mr Carraway, this is my friend Mr Wolfsheim.'

A small, flat-nosed Jew raised his large head and regarded me with two fine growths of hair which luxuriated in either nostril. After a moment I discovered his tiny eyes in the half-darkness.

' – So I took one look at him,' said Mr Wolfsheim, shaking my hand earnestly, 'and what do you think I did?'

'What?' I enquired politely.

But evidently he was not addressing me, for he dropped my hand

and covered Gatsby with his expressive nose.

'I handed the money to Katspaugh and I said: "All right, Katspaugh, don't pay him a penny till he shuts his mouth." He shut it then and there.'

Gatsby took an arm of each of us and moved forward into the restaurant, whereupon Mr Wolfsheim swallowed a new sentence he was starting and lapsed into a somnambulatory abstraction.

'Highballs?' asked the head waiter.

'This is a nice restaurant here,' said Mr Wolfsheim, looking at the Presbyterian nymphs on the ceiling. 'But I like across the street better!'

'Yes, highballs,' agreed Gatsby, and then to Mr Wolfsheim: 'It's too hot over there.'

'Hot and small – yes,' said Mr Wolfsheim, 'but full of memories.'

'What place is that?' I asked.

'The old Metropole.'

'The old Metropole,' brooded Mr Wolfsheim gloomily. 'Filled with faces dead and gone. Filled with friends gone now for ever. I can't forget so long as I live the night they shot Rosy Rosenthal there. It was six of us at the table, and Rosy had ate and drunk a lot all evening. When it was almost morning the waiter came up to him with a funny look and says somebody wants to speak to him outside. "All right," says Rosy, and begins to get up, and I pulled him down in his chair.

' "Let the bastards come in here if they want you, Rosy, but don't you, so help me, move outside this room."

'It was four o'clock in the morning then, and if we'd of raised the blinds we'd of seen daylight.'

'Did he go?' I asked innocently.

'Sure he went.' Mr Wolfsheim's nose flashed at me indignantly. 'He turned around in the door and says: "Don't let that waiter take away my coffee!" Then he went out on the sidewalk, and they shot him three times in his full belly and drove away.'

'Four of them were electrocuted,' I said, remembering.

'Five, with Becker.' His nostrils turned to me in an interested way. 'I understand you're looking for a business gonnegtion.'

The juxtaposition of these two remarks was startling.

Gatsby answered for me: 'Oh, no,' he exclaimed, 'this isn't the man.'

'No?' Mr Wolfsheim seemed disappointed.

'This is just a friend. I told you we'd talk about that some other time.'

'I beg your pardon,' said Mr Wolfsheim, 'I had a wrong man.'

A succulent hash arrived, and Mr Wolfsheim, forgetting the more sentimental atmosphere of the old Metropole, began to eat with ferocious delicacy. His eyes, meanwhile, roved very slowly all around the room – he completed the arc by turning to inspect the people directly behind. I think that, except for my presence, he would have taken one short glance beneath our own table.

'Look here, old sport,' said Gatsby leaning towards me, 'I'm afraid I made you a little angry this morning in the car.'

There was the smile again, but this time I held out against it.

'I don't like mysteries,' I answered, 'and I don't understand why you won't come out frankly and tell me what you want. Why has it all got to come through Miss Baker?'

'Oh, it's nothing underhand,' he assured me. 'Miss Baker's a great sportswoman, you know, and she'd never do anything that wasn't all right.'

Suddenly he looked at his watch, jumped up, and hurried from the room, leaving me with Mr Wolfsheim at the table.

'He has to telephone,' said Mr Wolfsheim, following him with his eyes. 'Fine fellow, isn't he? Handsome to look at and a perfect gentleman.'

'Yes.'

'He's an Oggsford man.'

'Oh!'

'He went to Oggsford College in England. You know Oggsford College?'

'I've heard of it.'

'It's one of the most famous colleges in the world.'

'Have you known Gatsby for a long time?' I enquired.

'Several years,' he answered in a gratified way. 'I made the pleasure of his acquaintance just after the war. But I knew I had discovered a man of fine breeding after I talked with him an hour. I said to myself: "There's the kind of man you'd like to take home and introduce to your mother and sister." ' He paused. 'I see you're looking at my cuff buttons.'

I hadn't been looking at them, but I did now. They were composed of oddly familiar pieces of ivory.

'Finest specimens of human molars,' he informed me.

'Well!' I inspected them. 'That's a very interesting idea.'

'Yeah.' He flipped his sleeves up under his coat. 'Yeah, Gatsby's very careful about women. He would never so much as look at a friend's wife.'

When the subject of this instinctive trust returned to the table and sat down, Mr Wolfsheim drank his coffee with a jerk and got to his feet.

'I have enjoyed my lunch,' he said, 'and I'm going to run off from you two young men before I outstay my welcome.'

'Don't hurry, Meyer,' said Gatsby, without enthusiasm. Mr Wolfsheim raised his hand in a sort of benediction.

'You're very polite, but I belong to another generation,' he announced solemnly. 'You sit here and discuss your sports and your young ladies and your – ' He supplied an imaginary noun with another wave of his hand. 'As for me, I am fifty years old, and I won't impose myself on you any longer.'

As he shook hands and turned away his tragic nose was trembling. I wondered if I had said anything to offend him.

'He becomes very sentimental sometimes,' explained Gatsby. 'This is one of his sentimental days. He's quite a character around New York – a denizen of Broadway.'

'Who is he, anyhow, an actor?'

'No.'

'A dentist?'

'Meyer Wolfsheim? No, he's a gambler.' Gatsby hesitated, then added coolly: 'He's the man who fixed the World's Series back in 1919.'

'Fixed the World's Series?' I repeated.

The idea staggered me. I remembered, of course, that the World's Series had been fixed in 1919, but if I had thought of it at all I would have thought of it as a thing that merely *happened*, the end of some inevitable chain. It never occurred to me that one man could start to play with the faith of fifty million people – with the single-mindedness of a burglar blowing a safe.

'How did he happen to do that?' I asked after a minute.

'He just saw the opportunity.'

'Why isn't he in jail?'

'They can't get him, old sport. He's a smart man.'

I insisted on paying the check. As the waiter brought my change I caught sight of Tom Buchanan across the crowded room.

'Come along with me for a minute,' I said; 'I've got to say hello to someone.'

When he saw us Tom jumped up and took half a dozen steps in our direction.

'Where've you been?' he demanded eagerly. 'Daisy's furious because you haven't called up.'

'This is Mr Gatsby, Mr Buchanan.'

They shook hands briefly, and a strained, unfamiliar look of embarrassment came over Gatsby's face.

'How've you been, anyhow?' demanded Tom of me. 'How'd you happen to come up this far to eat?'

'I've been having lunch with Mr Gatsby.'

I turned towards Mr Gatsby, but he was no longer there.

One October day in 1917 – (said Jordan Baker that afternoon, sitting up very straight on a straight chair in the tea-garden at the Plaza Hotel) – I was walking along from one place to another, half on the sidewalks and half on the lawns. I was happier on the lawns because I had on shoes from England with rubber nobs on the soles that bit into the soft ground. I had on a new plaid skirt also that blew a little in the wind, and whenever this happened the red-white-and-blue banners in front of all the houses stretched out stiff and said *tut-tut-tut-tut*, in a disapproving way.

The largest of the banners and the largest of the lawns belonged to Daisy Fay's house. She was just eighteen, two years older than me, and by far the most popular of all the young girls in Louisville. She dressed in white, and had a little white roadster, and all day long the telephone rang in her house and excited young officers from Camp Taylor demanded the privilege of monopolising her that night. 'Anyways, for an hour!'

When I came opposite her house that morning her white roadster was beside the curb, and she was sitting in it with a lieutenant I had never seen before. They were so engrossed in each other that she didn't see me until I was five feet away.

'Hello, Jordan,' she called unexpectedly. 'Please come here.'

I was flattered that she wanted to speak to me, because of all the older girls I admired her most. She asked me if I was going to the Red Cross and make bandages. I was. Well, then, would I tell them that she couldn't come that day? The officer looked at Daisy while she was speaking, in a way that every young girl wants to be looked at sometime, and because it seemed romantic to me I have remembered the incident ever since. His name was Jay Gatsby, and I didn't lay eyes on him again for over four years – even after I'd met him on Long Island I didn't realise it was the same man.

That was 1917. By the next year I had a few beaux myself, and I began to play in tournaments, so I didn't see Daisy very often. She went with a slightly older crowd – when she went with anyone at all. Wild rumours were circulating about her – how her mother had found her packing her bag one winter night to go to New York and say goodbye to a soldier who was going overseas. She was effectually prevented, but she wasn't on speaking terms with her family for several weeks. After that she didn't play around with the soldiers any more, but only with a few flat-footed, short-sighted young men in town, who couldn't get into the army at all.

By the next autumn she was gay again, gay as ever. She had a début after the Armistice, and in February she was presumably engaged to a man from New Orleans. In June she married Tom Buchanan of Chicago, with more pomp and circumstance than Louisville ever knew before. He came down with a hundred people in four private cars, and hired a whole floor of the Muhlbach Hotel, and the day before the wedding he gave her a string of pearls valued at three hundred and fifty thousand dollars.

I was a bridesmaid. I came into her room half an hour before the bridal dinner, and found her lying on her bed as lovely as the June night in her flowered dress – and as drunk as a monkey. She had a bottle of Sauterne in one hand and a letter in the other.

' 'Gratulate me,' she muttered. 'Never had a drink before, but oh how I do enjoy it.'

'What's the matter, Daisy?'

I was scared, I can tell you; I'd never seen a girl like that before.

'Here, deares'.' She groped around in a waste-basket she had with her on the bed and pulled out the string of pearls. 'Take 'em downstairs and give 'em back to whoever they belong to. Tell 'em all Daisy's change' her mine. Say: "Daisy's change' her mine!" '

She began to cry – she cried and cried. I rushed out and found her mother's maid, and we locked the door and got her into a cold bath. She wouldn't let go of the letter. She took it into the tub with her and squeezed it up into a wet ball, and only let me leave it in the soap-dish when she saw that it was coming to pieces like snow.

But she didn't say another word. We gave her spirits of ammonia and put ice on her forehead and hooked her back into her dress, and half an hour later, when we walked out of the room, the pearls were around her neck and the incident was over. Next day at five o'clock she married Tom Buchanan without so much as a shiver, and started off on a three months' trip to the South Seas.

I saw them in Santa Barbara when they came back, and I thought I'd never seen a girl so mad about her husband. If he left the room for a minute she'd look around uneasily, and say: 'Where's Tom gone?' and wear the most abstracted expression until she saw him coming in the door. She used to sit on the sand with his head in her lap by the hour, rubbing her fingers over his eyes and looking at him with unfathomable delight. It was touching to see them together – it made you laugh in a hushed, fascinated way. That was in August. A week after I left Santa Barbara, Tom ran into a wagon on the Ventura road one night, and ripped a front wheel off his car. The girl who was with him got into the papers, too, because her arm was broken – she was one of the chambermaids in the Santa Barbara Hotel.

The next April Daisy had her little girl, and they went to France for a year. I saw them one spring in Cannes, and later in Deauville, and then they came back to Chicago to settle down. Daisy was popular in Chicago, as you know. They moved with a fast crowd, all of them young and rich and wild, but she came out with an absolutely perfect reputation. Perhaps because she doesn't drink. It's a great advantage not to drink among hard-drinking people. You can hold your tongue, and, moreover, you can time any little irregularity of your own so that everybody else is so blind that they don't see or care. Perhaps Daisy never went in for amour at all – and yet there's something in that voice of hers . . .

Well, about six weeks ago, she heard the name Gatsby for the first time in years. It was when I asked you – do you remember? – if you knew Gatsby in West Egg. After you had gone home she came into my room and woke me up, and said: 'What Gatsby?' and when I described him – I was half-asleep – she said in the strangest voice that it must be the man she used to know. It wasn't until then that I connected this Gatsby with the officer in her white car.

When Jordan Baker had finished telling all this we had left the Plaza for half an hour and were driving in a victoria through Central Park. The sun had gone down behind the tall apartments of the movie stars in the West Fifties, and the clear voices of children, already gathered like crickets on the grass, rose through the hot twilight:

'I'm the Sheik of Araby.
Your love belongs to me.
At night when you're asleep
Into your tent I'll creep – '

'It was a strange coincidence,' I said.

'But it wasn't a coincidence at all.'

'Why not?'

'Gatsby bought that house so that Daisy would be just across the bay.'

Then it had not been merely the stars to which he had aspired on that June night. He came alive to me, delivered suddenly from the womb of his purposeless splendour.

'He wants to know,' continued Jordan, 'if you'll invite Daisy to your house some afternoon and then let him come over.'

The modesty of the demand shook me. He had waited five years and bought a mansion where he dispensed starlight to casual moths – so that he could 'come over' some afternoon to a stranger's garden.

'Did I have to know all this before he could ask such a little thing?'

'He's afraid, he's waited so long. He thought you might be offended. You see, he's regular tough underneath it all.'

Something worried me.

'Why didn't he ask you to arrange a meeting?'

'He wants her to see his house,' she explained. 'And your house is right next door.'

'Oh!'

'I think he half expected her to wander into one of his parties, some night,' went on Jordan, 'but she never did. Then he began asking people casually if they knew her, and I was the first one he found. It was that night he sent for me at his dance, and you should have heard the elaborate way he worked up to it. Of course, I immediately suggested a luncheon in New York – and I thought he'd go mad: ' "I don't want to do anything out of the way!" he kept saying. "I want to see her right next door."

'When I said you were a particular friend of Tom's, he started to abandon the whole idea. He doesn't know very much about Tom, though he says he's read a Chicago paper for years just on the chance of catching a glimpse of Daisy's name.'

It was dark now, and as we dipped under a little bridge I put my arm around Jordan's golden shoulder and drew her towards me and asked her to dinner. Suddenly I wasn't thinking of Daisy and Gatsby any more, but of this clean, hard, limited person, who dealt in universal scepticism, and who leaned back jauntily just within the circle of my arm. A phrase began to beat in my ears with a sort of heady excitement: 'There are only the pursued, the pursuing, the busy and the tired.'

'And Daisy ought to have something in her life,' murmured Jordan to me.

'Does she want to see Gatsby?'

'She's not to know about it. Gatsby doesn't want her to know. You're just supposed to invite her to tea.'

We passed a barrier of dark trees, and then the façade of Fifty-ninth Street, a block of delicate pale light, beamed down into the park. Unlike Gatsby and Tom Buchanan, I had no girl whose disembodied face floated along the dark cornices and blinding signs, and so I drew up the girl beside me, tightening my arms. Her wan, scornful mouth smiled, and so I drew her up again closer, this time to my face.

Five

When I came home to West Egg that night I was afraid for a moment that my house was on fire. Two o'clock and the whole corner of the peninsula was blazing with light, which fell unreal on the shrubbery and made thin elongating glints upon the roadside wires. Turning a corner, I saw that it was Gatsby's house, lit from tower to cellar.

At first I thought it was another party, a wild rout that had resolved itself into 'hide-and-seek' or 'sardines-in-the-box', with all the house thrown open to the game. But there wasn't a sound. Only wind in the trees, which blew the wires and made the lights go off and on again as if the house had winked into the darkness. As my taxi groaned away I saw Gatsby walking towards me across his lawn.

'Your place looks like the World's Fair,' I said.

'Does it?' He turned his eyes towards it absently. 'I have been glancing into some of the rooms. Let's go to Coney Island, old sport. In my car.'

'It's too late.'

'Well, suppose we take a plunge in the swimming-pool? I haven't made use of it all summer.'

'I've got to go to bed.'

'All right.'

He waited, looking at me with suppressed eagerness.

'I talked with Miss Baker,' I said after a moment. 'I'm going to call up Daisy tomorrow and invite her over here to tea.'

'Oh, that's all right,' he said carelessly. 'I don't want to put you to any trouble.'

'What day would suit you?'

'What day would suit *you*?' he corrected me quickly. 'I don't want to put you to any trouble, you see.'

'How about the day after tomorrow?'

He considered for a moment. Then, with reluctance: 'I want to get the grass cut,' he said.

We both looked down at the grass – there was a sharp line where my ragged lawn ended and the darker, well-kept expanse of his began. I suspected that he meant my grass.

'There's another little thing,' he said uncertainly, and hesitated.

'Would you rather put it off for a few days?' I asked.

'Oh, it isn't about that. At least – ' He fumbled with a series of beginnings. 'Why, I thought – why, look here, old sport, you don't make much money, do you?'

'Not very much.'

This seemed to reassure him and he continued more confidently.

'I thought you didn't, if you'll pardon my – you see, I carry on a little business on the side, a sort of sideline, you understand. And I thought that if you don't make very much – You're selling bonds, aren't you, old sport?'

'Trying to.'

'Well, this would interest you. It wouldn't take up much of your time and you might pick up a nice bit of money. It happens to be a rather confidential sort of thing.'

I realise now that under different circumstances that conversation might have been one of the crises of my life. But, because the offer was obviously and tactlessly for a service to be rendered, I had no choice except to cut him off there.

'I've got my hands full,' I said. 'I'm much obliged but I couldn't take on any more work.'

'You wouldn't have to do any business with Wolfsheim.' Evidently he thought that I was shying away from the 'gonnegtion' mentioned at lunch, but I assured him he was wrong. He waited a moment longer, hoping I'd begin a conversation, but I was too absorbed to be responsive, so he went unwillingly home.

The evening had made me light-headed and happy; I think I walked into a deep sleep as I entered my front door. So I don't know whether or not Gatsby went to Coney Island, or for how many hours he 'glanced into rooms' while his house blazed gaudily on. I called up Daisy from the office next morning, and invited her to come to tea.

'Don't bring Tom,' I warned her.

'What?'

'Don't bring Tom.'

'Who is "Tom"?' she asked innocently.

The day agreed upon was pouring rain. At eleven o'clock a man in a raincoat, dragging a lawn-mower, tapped at my front door and said that Mr Gatsby had sent him over to cut my grass. This reminded me that I had forgotten to tell my Finn to come back, so I drove into West Egg Village to search for her among soggy whitewashed alleys and to buy some cups and lemons and flowers.

The flowers were unnecessary, for at two o'clock a greenhouse arrived from Gatsby's, with innumerable receptacles to contain it. An hour later the front door opened nervously, and Gatsby, in a white flannel suit, silver shirt and gold-coloured tie, hurried in. He was pale, and there were dark signs of sleeplessness beneath his eyes.

'Is everything all right?' he asked immediately.

'The grass looks fine, if that's what you mean.'

'What grass?' he enquired blankly. 'Oh, the grass in the yard.' He looked out the window at it, but, judging from his expression, I don't believe he saw a thing.

'Looks very good,' he remarked vaguely. 'One of the papers said they thought the rain would stop about four. I think it was the *Journal*. Have you got everything you need in the shape of – of tea?'

I took him into the pantry, where he looked a little reproachfully at the Finn. Together we scrutinised the twelve lemon cakes from the delicatessen shop.

'Will they do?' I asked.

'Of course, of course! They're fine!' and he added hollowly, ' . . . old sport.'

The rain cooled about half-past three to a damp mist, through which occasional thin drops swam like dew. Gatsby looked with vacant eyes through a copy of Clay's *Economics*, starting at the Finnish tread that shook the kitchen floor and peering towards the bleared windows from time to time as if a series of invisible but alarming happenings were taking place outside. Finally he got up and informed me, in an uncertain voice, that he was going home.

'Why's that?'

'Nobody's coming to tea. It's too late!' He looked at his watch as if there was some pressing demand on his time elsewhere. 'I can't wait all day.'

'Don't be silly; it's just two minutes to four.'

He sat down miserably, as if I had pushed him, and simultaneously there was the sound of a motor turning into my lane. We both jumped up, and, a little harrowed myself, I went out into the yard.

Under the dripping bare lilac trees a large open car was coming up the drive. It stopped. Daisy's face, tipped sideways beneath a three-cornered lavender hat, looked at me with a bright ecstatic smile.

'Is this absolutely where you live, my dearest one?'

The exhilarating ripple of her voice was a wild tonic in the rain. I had to follow the sound of it for a moment, up and down, with my ear alone, before any words came through. A damp streak of hair lay like a dash of blue paint across her cheek, and her hand was wet with glistening drops as I took it to help her from the car.

'Are you in love with me,' she said low in my ear, 'or why did I have to come alone?'

'That's the secret of Castle Rackrent. Tell your chauffeur to go far away and spend an hour.'

'Come back in an hour, Ferdie.' Then in a grave murmur: 'His name is Ferdie.'

'Does the gasoline affect his nose?'

'I don't think so,' she said innocently. 'Why?'

We went in. To my overwhelming surprise the living-room was deserted.

'Well, that's funny,' I exclaimed.

'What's funny?'

She turned her head as there was a light dignified knocking at the front door. I went out and opened it. Gatsby, pale as death, with his hands plunged like weights in his coat pockets, was standing in a puddle of water glaring tragically into my eyes.

With his hands still in his coat pockets he stalked by me into the hall, turned sharply as if he were on a wire, and disappeared into the living-room. It wasn't a bit funny. Aware of the loud beating of my own heart I pulled the door to against the increasing rain.

For half a minute there wasn't a sound. Then from the living-room I heard a sort of choking murmur and part of a laugh, followed by Daisy's voice on a clear artificial note: 'I certainly am awfully glad to see you again.'

A pause; it endured horribly. I had nothing to do in the hall, so I went into the room.

Gatsby, his hands still in his pockets, was reclining against the mantelpiece in a strained counterfeit of perfect ease, even of boredom. His head leaned back so far that it rested against the face of a defunct mantelpiece clock, and from this position his distraught eyes stared down at Daisy, who was sitting, frightened but graceful, on the edge of a stiff chair.

'We've met before,' muttered Gatsby. His eyes glanced momentarily at me, and his lips parted with an abortive attempt at a laugh. Luckily the clock took this moment to tilt dangerously at the pressure of his head, whereupon he turned and caught it with trembling fingers and set it back in place. Then he sat down, rigidly, his elbow on the arm of the sofa and his chin in his hand.

'I'm sorry about the clock,' he said.

My own face had now assumed a deep tropical burn. I couldn't muster up a single commonplace out of the thousand in my head.

'It's an old clock,' I told them idiotically.

I think we all believed for a moment that it had smashed in pieces on the floor.

'We haven't met for many years,' said Daisy, her voice as matter-of-fact as it could ever be.

'Five years next November.'

The automatic quality of Gatsby's answer set us all back at least another minute. I had them both on their feet with the desperate suggestion that they help me make tea in the kitchen when the demoniac Finn brought it in on a tray.

Amid the welcome confusion of cups and cakes a certain physical decency established itself. Gatsby got himself into a shadow and, while Daisy and I talked, looked conscientiously from one to the other of us with tense, unhappy eyes. However, as calmness wasn't an end in itself, I made an excuse at the first possible moment, and got to my feet.

'Where are you going?' demanded Gatsby in immediate alarm.

'I'll be back.'

'I've got to speak to you about something before you go.'

He followed me wildly into the kitchen, closed the door, and whispered: 'Oh, God!' in a miserable way.

'What's the matter?'

'This is a terrible mistake,' he said, shaking his head from side to side, 'a terrible, terrible mistake.'

'You're just embarrassed, that's all,' and luckily I added: 'Daisy's embarrassed too.'

'She's embarrassed?' he repeated incredulously.

'Just as much as you are.'

'Don't talk so loud.'

'You're acting like a little boy,' I broke out impatiently. 'Not only that, but you're rude. Daisy's sitting in there all alone.'

He raised his hand to stop my words, looked at me with

unforgettable reproach, and, opening the door cautiously, went back into the other room.

I walked out the back way – just as Gatsby had when he had made his nervous circuit of the house half an hour before – and ran for a huge black knotted tree, whose massed leaves made a fabric against the rain. Once more it was pouring, and my irregular lawn, well shaved by Gatsby's gardener, abounded in small muddy swamps and prehistoric marshes. There was nothing to look at from under the tree except Gatsby's enormous house, so I stared at it, like Kant at his church steeple, for half an hour. A brewer had built it early in the 'period' craze a decade before, and there was a story that he'd agreed to pay five years' taxes on all the neighbouring cottages if the owners would have their roofs thatched with straw. Perhaps their refusal took the heart out of his plan to Found a Family – he went into an immediate decline. His children sold his house with the black wreath still on the door. Americans, while willing, even eager, to be serfs, have always been obstinate about being peasantry.

After half an hour, the sun shone again, and the grocer's automobile rounded Gatsby's drive with the raw material for his servants' dinner – I felt sure he wouldn't eat a spoonful. A maid began opening the upper windows of his house, appeared momentarily in each, and, leaning from the large central bay, spat meditatively into the garden. It was time I went back. While the rain continued it had seemed like the murmur of their voices, rising and swelling a little now and then with gusts of emotion. But in the new silence I felt that silence had fallen within the house too.

I went in – after making every possible noise in the kitchen, short of pushing over the stove – but I don't believe they heard a sound. They were sitting at either end of the couch, looking at each other as if some question had been asked, or was in the air, and every vestige of embarrassment was gone. Daisy's face was smeared with tears, and when I came in she jumped up and began wiping at it with her handkerchief before a mirror. But there was a change in Gatsby that was simply confounding. He literally glowed; without a word or a gesture of exultation a new well-being radiated from him and filled the little room.

'Oh hello, old sport,' he said, as if he hadn't seen me for years. I thought for a moment he was going to shake hands.

'It's stopped raining.'

'Has it?' When he realised what I was talking about, that there were twinkle-bells of sunshine in the room, he smiled like a weather man, like an ecstatic patron of recurrent light, and repeated the news to Daisy. 'What do you think of that? It's stopped raining.'

'I'm glad, Jay.' Her throat, full of aching, grieving beauty, told only of her unexpected joy.

'I want you and Daisy to come over to my house,' he said, 'I'd like to show her around.'

'You're sure you want me to come?'

'Absolutely, old sport.'

Daisy went upstairs to wash her face – too late, I thought with humiliation of my towels – while Gatsby and I waited on the lawn.

'My house looks well, doesn't it?' he demanded. 'See how the whole front of it catches the light.'

I agreed that it was splendid.

'Yes.' His eyes went over it, every arched door and square tower. 'It took me just three years to earn the money that bought it.'

'I thought you inherited your money.'

'I did, old sport,' he said automatically, 'but I lost most of it in the big panic – the panic of the war.'

I think he hardly knew what he was saying, for when I asked him what business he was in he answered: 'That's my affair,' before he realised that it wasn't an appropriate reply.

'Oh, I've been in several things,' he corrected himself. 'I was in the drug business and then I was in the oil business. But I'm not in either one now.' He looked at me with more attention. 'Do you mean you've been thinking over what I proposed the other night?'

Before I could answer, Daisy came out of the house and two rows of brass buttons on her dress gleamed in the sunlight.

'That huge place *there*?' she cried pointing.

'Do you like it?'

'I love it, but I don't see how you live there all alone.'

'I keep it always full of interesting people, night and day. People who do interesting things. Celebrated people.'

Instead of taking the short cut along the Sound we went down to the road and entered by the big postern. With enchanting murmurs, Daisy admired this aspect or that of the feudal silhouette against the sky, admired the gardens, the sparking odour of jonquils and the frothy odour of hawthorn and plum blossoms and the pale gold odour of kiss-me-at-the-gate. It was strange to reach the marble steps and find no stir of bright dresses in and out of the door, and hear no sound but bird voices in the trees.

And inside, as we wandered through Marie Antoinette music-rooms and Restoration salons, I felt that there were guests concealed behind every couch and table, under orders to be breathlessly silent until we had passed through. As Gatsby closed the door of 'the Merton College Library' I could have sworn I heard the owl-eyed man break into ghostly laughter.

We went upstairs, through period bedrooms swathed in rose and lavender silk and vivid with new flowers, through dressing-rooms and poolrooms and bathrooms with sunken baths – intruding into one chamber where a dishevelled man in pyjamas was doing liver exercises on the floor. It was Mr Klipspringer, the 'boarder'. I had seen him wandering hungrily about the beach that morning. Finally we came to Gatsby's own apartment, a bedroom and a bath, and an Adam study, where we sat down and drank a glass of some Chartreuse he took from a cupboard in the wall.

He hadn't once ceased looking at Daisy, and I think he revalued everything in his house according to the measure of response it drew from her well-loved eyes. Sometimes, too, he stared around at his possessions in a dazed way, as though in her actual and astounding presence none of it was any longer real. Once he nearly toppled down a flight of stairs.

His bedroom was the simplest room of all – except where the dresser was garnished with a toilet set of pure dull gold. Daisy took the brush with delight, and smoothed her hair, whereupon Gatsby sat down and shaded his eyes and began to laugh.

'It's the funniest thing, old sport,' he said hilariously. 'I can't – When I try to – '

He had passed visibly through two states and was entering upon a third. After his embarrassment and his unreasoning joy he was consumed with wonder at her presence. He had been full of the idea so long, dreamed it right through to the end, waited with his teeth set, so to speak, at an inconceivable pitch of intensity. Now, in the reaction, he was running down like an overwound clock.

Recovering himself in a minute he opened for us two hulking patent cabinets which held his massed suits and dressing-gowns and ties, and his shirts, piled like bricks in stacks a dozen high.

'I've got a man in England who buys me clothes. He sends over a selection of things at the beginning of each season, spring and fall.'

He took out a pile of shirts and began throwing them, one by one, before us, shirts of sheer linen and thick silk and fine flannel, which lost their folds as they fell and covered the table in many-coloured disarray. While we admired he brought more and the soft rich heap mounted higher – shirts with stripes and scrolls and plaids in coral and apple-green and lavender and faint orange, with monograms of Indian blue. Suddenly, with a strained sound, Daisy bent her head into the shirts and began to cry stormily.

'They're such beautiful shirts,' she sobbed, her voice muffled in the thick folds. 'It makes me sad because I've never seen such – such beautiful shirts before.'

After the house, we were to see the grounds and the swimming-pool, and the hydroplane and the midsummer flowers – but outside Gatsby's window it began to rain again, so we stood in a row looking at the corrugated surface of the Sound.

'If it wasn't for the mist we could see your home across the bay,' said Gatsby. 'You always have a green light that burns all night at the end of your dock.'

Daisy put her arm through his abruptly, but he seemed absorbed in what he had just said. Possibly it had occurred to him that the colossal significance of that light had now vanished for ever. Compared to the great distance that had separated him from Daisy it had seemed very near to her, almost touching her. It had seemed as close as a star to the moon. Now it was again a green light on a dock. His count of enchanted objects had diminished by one.

I began to walk about the room, examining various indefinite objects in the half darkness. A large photograph of an elderly man in yachting costume attracted me, hung on the wall over his desk.

'Who's this?'

'That? That's Mr Dan Cody, old sport.'

The name sounded faintly familiar.

'He's dead now. He used to be my best friend years ago.'

There was a small picture of Gatsby, also in yachting costume, on the bureau – Gatsby with his head thrown back defiantly – taken apparently when he was about eighteen.

'I adore it,' exclaimed Daisy. 'The pompadour. You never told me you had a pompadour – or a yacht.'

'Look at this,' said Gatsby quickly. 'Here's a lot of clippings – about you.'

They stood side by side examining them. I was going to ask to see the rubies when the phone rang, and Gatsby took up the receiver.

'Yes . . . Well, I can't talk now . . . I can't talk now, old sport . . . I said a *small* town . . . He must know what a *small* town is . . . Well, he's no use to us if Detroit is his idea of a small town . . . '

He rang off.

'Come here *quick*!' cried Daisy at the window.

The rain was still falling, but the darkness had parted in the west, and there was a pink and golden billow of foamy clouds above the sea.

'Look at that,' she whispered, and then after a moment: 'I'd like to just get one of those pink clouds and put you in it and push you around.'

I tried to go then, but they wouldn't hear of it; perhaps my presence made them feel more satisfactorily alone.

'I know what we'll do,' said Gatsby, 'we'll have Klipspringer play the piano.'

He went out of the room calling, 'Ewing!' and returned in a few minutes accompanied by an embarrassed, slightly worn young man, with shell-rimmed glasses and scanty blond hair. He was now decently clothed, in a 'sport shirt', open at the neck, sneakers and duck trousers of a nebulous hue.

'Did we interrupt your exercises?' enquired Daisy politely.

'I was asleep,' cried Mr Klipspringer, in a spasm of embarrassment. 'That is, I'd *been* asleep. Then I got up . . . '

'Klipspringer plays the piano,' said Gatsby, cutting him off. 'Don't you, Ewing, old sport?'

'I don't play well. I don't – I hardly play at all, I'm all out of prac – '

'We'll go downstairs,' interrupted Gatsby. He flipped a switch. The grey windows disappeared as the house glowed full of light.

In the music-room Gatsby turned on a solitary lamp beside the piano. He lit Daisy's cigarette from a trembling match, and sat down with her on a couch far across the room, where there was no light save what the gleaming floor bounced in from the hall.

When Klipspringer had played *The Love Nest* he turned around on the bench and searched unhappily for Gatsby in the gloom.

'I'm all out of practice, you see. I told you I couldn't play. I'm all out of prac – '

'Don't talk so much, old sport,' commanded Gatsby. 'Play!'

In the morning,
In the evening,
Ain't we got fun –

Outside the wind was loud and there was a faint flow of thunder along the Sound. All the lights were going on in West Egg now; the electric trains, men-carrying, were plunging home through the rain from New York. It was the hour of a profound human change, and excitement was generating on the air.

One thing's sure and nothing's surer
The rich get richer and the poor get – children.
In the meantime,
In between time –

As I went over to say goodbye I saw that the expression of bewilderment had come back into Gatsby's face, as though a faint doubt had occurred to him as to the quality of his present happiness. Almost five years! There must have been moments even that afternoon when Daisy tumbled short of his dreams – not through her own fault, but because of the colossal vitality of his illusion. It had gone beyond her, beyond everything. He had thrown himself into it with a creative passion, adding to it all the time, decking it out with every bright feather that drifted his way. No amount of fire or freshness can challenge what a man can store up in his ghostly heart.

As I watched him he adjusted himself a little, visibly. His hand took hold of hers, and as she said something low in his ear he turned towards her with a rush of emotion. I think that voice held him most, with its fluctuating, feverish warmth, because it couldn't be over-dreamed – that voice was a deathless song.

They had forgotten me, but Daisy glanced up and held out her hand; Gatsby didn't know me now at all. I looked once more at them and they looked back at me, remotely, possessed by intense life. Then I went out of the room and down the marble steps into the rain, leaving them there together.

Six

About this time an ambitious young reporter from New York arrived one morning at Gatsby's door and asked him if he had anything to say.

'Anything to say about what?' enquired Gatsby politely.

'Why – any statement to give out.'

It transpired after a confused five minutes that the man had heard Gatsby's name around his office in a connection which he either wouldn't reveal or didn't fully understand. This was his day off and with laudable initiative he had hurried out 'to see'.

It was a random shot, and yet the reporter's instinct was right. Gatsby's notoriety, spread about by the hundreds who had accepted his hospitality and so become authorities upon his past, had increased all summer until he fell just short of being news. Contemporary legends such as the 'underground pipeline to Canada' attached themselves to him, and there was one persistent story that he didn't live in a house at all, but in a boat that looked like a house and was moved secretly up and down the Long Island shore. Just why these inventions were a source of satisfaction to James Gatz of North Dakota isn't easy to say.

James Gatz – that was really, or at least legally, his name. He had changed it at the age of seventeen and at the specific moment that witnessed the beginning of his career – when he saw Dan Cody's yacht drop anchor over the most insidious flat on Lake Superior. It was James Gatz who had been loafing along the beach that afternoon in a torn green jersey and a pair of canvas pants, but it was already Jay Gatsby who borrowed a rowboat, pulled out to the *Tuolomee* and informed Cody that a wind might catch him and break him up in half an hour.

I suppose he'd had the name ready for a long time, even then. His parents were shiftless and unsuccessful farm people – his imagination had never really accepted them as his parents at all. The truth was that Jay Gatsby of West Egg, Long Island, sprang from his Platonic conception of himself. He was a son of God – a phrase which, if it means anything, means just that – and he must be about His Father's business, the service of a vast, vulgar and meretricious beauty. So he invented just the sort of Jay Gatsby that a seventeen-year-old boy would be likely to invent, and to this conception he was faithful to the end.

For over a year he had been beating his way along the south shore of Lake Superior as a clam-digger and a salmon-fisher or in any other capacity that brought him food and bed. His brown, hardening body lived naturally through the half-fierce, half-lazy work of the bracing days. He knew women early, and since they spoiled him he became contemptuous of them, of young virgins because they were ignorant, of the others because they were hysterical about things which in his overwhelming self-absorption he took for granted.

But his heart was in a constant, turbulent riot. The most grotesque and fantastic conceits haunted him in his bed at night. A universe of ineffable gaudiness spun itself out in his brain while the clock ticked on the washstand and the moon soaked with wet light his tangled clothes upon the floor. Each night he added to the pattern of his fancies until drowsiness closed down upon some vivid scene with an oblivious embrace. For a while these reveries provided an outlet for his imagination; they were a satisfactory hint of the unreality of reality, a promise that the rock of the world was founded securely on a fairy's wing.

An instinct towards his future glory had led him, some months before, to the small Lutheran College of St Olaf's in southern Minnesota. He stayed there two weeks, dismayed at its ferocious indifference to the drums of his destiny, to destiny itself, and despising the janitor's work with which he was to pay his way through. Then he drifted back to Lake Superior, and he was still searching for something to do on the day that Dan Cody's yacht dropped anchor in the shallows alongshore.

Cody was fifty years old then, a product of the Nevada silver fields, of the Yukon, of every rush for metal since 1875. The transactions in Montana copper that made him many times a millionaire found him physically robust but on the verge of soft-mindedness, and, suspecting this, an infinite number of women tried to separate him from his money. The none too savoury ramifications by which Ella Kaye, the newspaper woman, played Madame de Maintenon to his weakness and sent him to sea in a yacht, were common property of the turgid journalism of 1902. He had been coasting along all too hospitable shores for five years when he turned up as James Gatz's destiny in Little Girl Bay.

To young Gatz, resting on his oars and looking up at the railed deck, that yacht represented all the beauty and glamour in the world. I suppose he smiled at Cody – he had probably discovered that people liked him when he smiled. At any rate Cody asked him a few questions (one of them elicited the brand new name) and found that he was quick and extravagantly ambitious. A few days later he took him to Duluth and bought him a blue coat, six pairs of white duck trousers, and a yachting cap. And when the *Tuolomee* left for the West Indies and the Barbary Coast, Gatsby left too.

He was employed in a vague personal capacity – while he remained with Cody he was in turn steward, mate, skipper, secretary and even jailor, for Dan Cody sober knew what lavish doings Dan Cody drunk might soon be about, and he provided for such contingencies by reposing more and more trust in Gatsby. The arrangement lasted five years, during which the boat went three times around the Continent. It might have lasted indefinitely except for the fact that Ella Kaye came on board one night in Boston and a week later Dan Cody inhospitably died.

I remember the portrait of him up in Gatsby's bedroom, a grey, florid man with a hard, empty face – the pioneer debauchee, who during one phase of American life brought back to the Eastern seaboard the savage violence of the frontier brothel and saloon. It was indirectly due to Cody that Gatsby drank so little. Sometimes in the course of gay parties women used to rub champagne into his hair; for himself he formed the habit of letting liquor alone.

And it was from Cody that he inherited money – a legacy of twenty-five thousand dollars. He didn't get it. He never understood the legal device that was used against him, but what remained of the millions went intact to Ella Kaye. He was left with his singularly appropriate education; the vague contour of Jay Gatsby had filled out to the substantiality of a man.

He told me all this very much later, but I've put it down here with the idea of exploding those first wild rumours about his antecedents, which weren't even faintly true. Moreover he told it to me at a time of confusion, when I had reached the point of believing everything and nothing about him. So I take advantage of this short halt, while Gatsby, so to speak, caught his breath, to clear this set of misconceptions away.

It was a halt, too, in my association with his affairs. For several weeks I didn't see him or hear his voice on the phone – mostly I was in New York, trotting around with Jordan and trying to ingratiate myself with her senile aunt – but finally I went over to his house one Sunday afternoon. I hadn't been there two minutes when somebody brought Tom Buchanan in for a drink. I was startled, naturally, but the really surprising thing was that it hadn't happened before.

They were a party of three on horseback – Tom and a man named Sloane and a pretty woman in a brown riding-habit, who had been there previously.

'I'm delighted to see you,' said Gatsby, standing on his porch. 'I'm delighted that you dropped in.'

As though they cared!

'Sit right down. Have a cigarette or a cigar.' He walked around the room quickly, ringing bells. 'I'll have something to drink for you in just a minute.'

He was profoundly affected by the fact that Tom was there. But he would be uneasy anyhow until he had given them something, realising in a vague way that that was all they came for. Mr Sloane wanted nothing. A lemonade? No, thanks. A little champagne? Nothing at all, thanks . . . I'm sorry –

'Did you have a nice ride?'

'Very good roads around here.'

'I suppose the automobiles – '

'Yeah.'

Moved by an irresistible impulse, Gatsby turned to Tom, who had accepted the introduction as a stranger.

'I believe we've met somewhere before, Mr Buchanan.'

'Oh, yes,' said Tom, gruffly polite, but obviously not remembering. 'So we did. I remember very well.'

'About two weeks ago.'

'That's right. You were with Nick here.'

'I know your wife,' continued Gatsby, almost aggressively.

'That so?'

Tom turned to me.

'You live near here, Nick?'

'Next door.'

'That so?'

Mr Sloane didn't enter into the conversation, but lounged back haughtily in his chair; the woman said nothing either – until unexpectedly, after two highballs, she became cordial.

'We'll all come over to your next party, Mr Gatsby,' she suggested. 'What do you say?'

'Certainly; I'd be delighted to have you.'

'Be ver' nice,' said Mr Sloane, without gratitude. 'Well – think ought to be starting home.'

'Please don't hurry,' Gatsby urged them. He had control of himself now, and he wanted to see more of Tom. 'Why don't you – why don't you stay for supper? I wouldn't be surprised if some other people dropped in from New York.'

'You come to supper with *me*,' said the lady enthusiastically. 'Both of you.'

This included me. Mr Sloane got to his feet.

'Come along,' he said – but to her only.

'I mean it,' she insisted. 'I'd love to have you. Lots of room.'

Gatsby looked at me questioningly. He wanted to go, and he didn't see that Mr Sloane had determined he shouldn't.

'I'm afraid I won't be able to,' I said.

'Well, you come,' she urged, concentrating on Gatsby.

Mr Sloane murmured something close to her ear.

'We won't be late if we start now,' she insisted aloud.

'I haven't got a horse,' said Gatsby. 'I used to ride in the army, but I've never bought a horse. I'll have to follow you in my car. Excuse me for just a minute.'

The rest of us walked out on the porch, where Sloane and the lady began an impassioned conversation aside.

'My God, I believe the man's coming,' said Tom. 'Doesn't he know she doesn't want him?'

'She says she does want him.'

'She has a big dinner party and he won't know a soul there.' He frowned. 'I wonder where in the devil he met Daisy. By God, I may be old-fashioned in my ideas, but women run around too much these days to suit me. They meet all kinds of crazy fish.'

Suddenly Mr Sloane and the lady walked down the steps and mounted their horses.

'Come on,' said Mr Sloane to Tom, 'we're late. We've got to go.' And then to me: 'Tell him we couldn't wait, will you?'

Tom and I shook hands, the rest of us exchanged a cool nod, and they trotted quickly down the drive, disappearing under the August foliage just as Gatsby, with hat and light overcoat in hand, came out the front door.

Tom was evidently perturbed at Daisy's running around alone, for on the following Saturday night he came with her to Gatsby's party. Perhaps his presence gave the evening its peculiar quality of oppressiveness – it stands out in my memory from Gatsby's other parties that summer. There were the same people, or at least the same sort of people, the same profusion of champagne, the same many-coloured, many-keyed commotion, but I felt an unpleasantness in the air, a pervading harshness that hadn't been there before. Or perhaps I had merely grown used to it, grown to accept West Egg as a world complete in itself, with its own standards and its own great figures, second to nothing because it had no consciousness of being so, and now I was looking at it again, through Daisy's eyes. It is invariably saddening to look through new eyes at things upon which you have expended your own powers of adjustment.

They arrived at twilight, and, as we strolled out among the sparkling hundreds, Daisy's voice was playing murmurous tricks in her throat.

'These things excite me *so*,' she whispered. 'If you want to kiss me any time during the evening, Nick, just let me know and I'll be glad to arrange it for you. Just mention my name. Or present a green card. I'm giving out green – '

'Look around,' suggested Gatsby.

'I'm looking around. I'm having a marvellous – '

'You must see the faces of many people you've heard about.'

Tom's arrogant eyes roamed the crowd.

'We don't go around very much,' he said; 'in fact, I was just thinking I don't know a soul here.'

'Perhaps you know that lady,' Gatsby indicated a gorgeous, scarcely human orchid of a woman who sat in state under a white-plum tree. Tom and Daisy stared, with that particularly unreal feeling that accompanies the recognition of a hitherto ghostly celebrity of the movies.

'She's lovely,' said Daisy.

'The man bending over her is her director.'

He took them ceremoniously from group to group: 'Mrs Buchanan . . . and Mr Buchanan – ' After an instant's hesitation he added: 'the polo player.'

'Oh, no,' objected Tom quickly, 'not me.'

But evidently the sound of it pleased Gatsby, for Tom remained 'the polo player' for the rest of the evening.

'I've never met so many celebrities,' Daisy exclaimed. 'I liked that man – what was his name? – with the sort of blue nose.'

Gatsby identified him, adding that he was a small producer.

'Well, I liked him anyhow.'

'I'd a little rather not be the polo player,' said Tom pleasantly. 'I'd rather look at all these famous people in – in oblivion.'

Daisy and Gatsby danced. I remember being surprised by his graceful, conservative foxtrot – I had never seen him dance before. Then they sauntered over to my house and sat on the steps for half an hour, while, at her request, I remained watchfully in the garden. 'In case there's a fire, or a flood,' she explained, 'or any act of God.'

Tom appeared from his oblivion as we were sitting down to supper together. 'Do you mind if I eat with some people over here?' he said. 'A fellow's getting off some funny stuff.'

'Go ahead,' answered Daisy genially, 'and if you want to take down any addresses here's my little gold pencil.' . . . She looked around after a moment and told me the girl was 'common but pretty', and I knew that except for the half-hour she'd been alone with Gatsby she wasn't having a good time.

We were at a particularly tipsy table. That was my fault – Gatsby had been called to the phone, and I'd enjoyed these same people only two weeks before. But what had amused me then turned septic on the air now.

'How do you feel, Miss Baedeker?'

The girl addressed was trying, unsuccessfully, to slump against my shoulder. At this enquiry she sat up and opened her eyes.

'Wha'?'

A massive and lethargic woman, who had been urging Daisy

to play golf with her at the local club tomorrow, spoke in Miss Baedeker's defence: 'Oh, she's all right now. When she's had five or six cocktails she always starts screaming like that. I tell her she ought to leave it alone.'

'I do leave it alone,' affirmed the accused hollowly.

'We heard you yelling, so I said to Doc Civet here: "There's somebody that needs your help, Doc." '

'She's much obliged, I'm sure,' said another friend, without gratitude, 'but you got her dress all wet when you stuck her head in the pool.'

'Anything I hate is to get my head stuck in a pool,' mumbled Miss Baedeker. 'They almost drowned me once over in New Jersey.'

'Then you ought to leave it alone,' countered Dr Civet.

'Speak for yourself!' cried Miss Baedeker violently. 'Your hand shakes. I wouldn't let you operate on me!'

It was like that. Almost the last thing I remember was standing with Daisy and watching the moving-picture director and his Star. They were still under the white-plum tree and their faces were touching except for a pale, thin ray of moonlight between. It occurred to me that he had been very slowly bending towards her all evening to attain this proximity, and even while I watched I saw him stoop one ultimate degree and kiss at her cheek.

'I like her,' said Daisy, 'I think she's lovely.'

But the rest offended her – and inarguably, because it wasn't a gesture but an emotion. She was appalled by West Egg, this unprecedented 'place' that Broadway had begotten upon a Long Island fishing village – appalled by its raw vigour that chafed under the old euphemisms and by the too obtrusive fate that herded its inhabitants along a short-cut from nothing to nothing. She saw something awful in the very simplicity she failed to understand.

I sat on the front steps with them while they waited for their car. It was dark here; only the bright door sent ten square feet of light volleying out into the soft black morning. Sometimes a shadow moved against a dressing-room blind above, gave way to another shadow, an indefinite procession of shadows, that rouged and powdered in an invisible glass.

'Who is this Gatsby anyhow?' demanded Tom suddenly. 'Some big bootlegger?'

'Where'd you hear that?' I enquired.

'I didn't hear it. I imagined it. A lot of these newly rich people are just big bootleggers, you know.'

'Not Gatsby,' I said shortly.

He was silent for a moment. The pebbles of the drive crunched under his feet.

'Well, he certainly must have strained himself to get this menagerie together.'

A breeze stirred the grey haze of Daisy's fur collar.

'At least they are more interesting than the people we know,' she said with an effort.

'You didn't look so interested.'

'Well, I was.'

Tom laughed and turned to me.

'Did you notice Daisy's face when that girl asked her to put her under a cold shower?'

Daisy began to sing with the music in a husky, rhythmic whisper, bringing out a meaning in each word that it had never had before and would never have again. When the melody rose, her voice broke up sweetly, following it, in a way contralto voices have, and each change tipped out a little of her warm human magic upon the air.

'Lots of people come who haven't been invited,' she said suddenly. 'That girl hadn't been invited. They simply force their way in and he's too polite to object.'

'I'd like to know who he is and what he does,' insisted Tom. 'And I think I'll make a point of finding out.'

'I can tell you right now,' she answered. 'He owned some drugstores, a lot of drugstores. He built them up himself.'

The dilatory limousine came rolling up the drive.

'Good-night, Nick,' said Daisy.

Her glance left me and sought the lighted top of the steps, where *Three O'Clock in the Morning*, a neat, sad little waltz of that year, was drifting out the open door. After all, in the very casualness of

Gatsby's party there were romantic possibilities totally absent from her world. What was it up there in the song that seemed to be calling her back inside? What would happen now in the dim, incalculable hours? Perhaps some unbelievable guest would arrive, a person infinitely rare and to be marvelled at, some authentically radiant young girl who with one fresh glance at Gatsby, one moment of magical encounter, would blot out those five years of unwavering devotion.

I stayed late that night. Gatsby asked me to wait until he was free, and I lingered in the garden until the inevitable swimming party had run up, chilled and exalted, from the black beach, until the lights were extinguished in the guest-rooms overhead. When he came down the steps at last the tanned skin was drawn unusually tight on his face, and his eyes were bright and tired.

'She didn't like it,' he said immediately.

'Of course she did.'

'She didn't like it,' he insisted. 'She didn't have a good time.'

He was silent, and I guessed at his unutterable depression. 'I feel far away from her,' he said. 'It's hard to make her understand.'

'You mean about the dance?'

'The dance?' He dismissed all the dances he had given with a snap of his fingers. 'Old sport, the dance is unimportant.'

He wanted nothing less of Daisy than that she should go to Tom and say: 'I never loved you.' After she had obliterated four years with that sentence they could decide upon the more practical measures to be taken. One of them was that, after she was free, they were to go back to Louisville and be married from her house – just as if it were five years ago.

'And she doesn't understand,' he said. 'She used to be able to understand. We'd sit for hours – '

He broke off and began to walk up and down a desolate path of fruit rinds and discarded favours and crushed flowers.

'I wouldn't ask too much of her,' I ventured. 'You can't repeat the past.'

'Can't repeat the past?' he cried incredulously. 'Why of course you can!'

He looked around him wildly, as if the past were lurking here in the shadow of his house, just out of reach of his hand.

'I'm going to fix everything just the way it was before,' he said, nodding determinedly. 'She'll see.'

He talked a lot about the past, and I gathered that he wanted to recover something, some idea of himself perhaps, that had gone into loving Daisy. His life had been confused and disordered since then, but if he could once return to a certain starting place and go over it all slowly, he could find out what that thing was . . .

. . . One autumn night, five years before, they had been walking down the street when the leaves were falling, and they came to a place where there were no trees and the sidewalk was white with moonlight. They stopped here and turned towards each other. Now it was a cool night with that mysterious excitement in it which comes at the two changes of the year. The quiet lights in the houses were burning out into the darkness and there was a stir and bustle among the stars. Out of the corner of his eye Gatsby saw that the blocks of the sidewalks really formed a ladder and mounted to a secret place above the trees – he could climb to it, if he climbed alone, and once there he could suck on the pap of life, gulp down the incomparable milk of wonder.

His heart beat faster and faster as Daisy's white face came up to his own. He knew that when he kissed this girl, and forever wed his unutterable visions to her perishable breath, his mind would never romp again like the mind of God. So he waited, listening for a moment longer to the tuning-fork that had been struck upon a star. Then he kissed her. At his lips' touch she blossomed for him like a flower and the incarnation was complete.

Through all he said, even through his appalling sentimentality, I was reminded of something – an elusive rhythm, a fragment of lost words, that I had heard somewhere a long time ago. For a moment a phrase tried to take shape in my mouth and my lips parted like a dumb man's, as though there was more struggling upon them than a wisp of startled air. But they made no sound, and what I had almost remembered was uncommunicable for ever.

Seven

It was when curiosity about Gatsby was at its highest that the lights in his house failed to go on one Saturday night – and, as obscurely as it had begun, his career as Trimalchio was over. Only gradually did I become aware that the automobiles which turned expectantly into his drive stayed for just a minute and then drove sulkily away. Wondering if he were sick I went over to find out – an unfamiliar butler with a villainous face squinted at me suspiciously from the door.

'Is Mr Gatsby sick?'

'Nope.' After a pause he added 'sir' in a dilatory, grudging way.

'I hadn't seen him around, and I was rather worried. Tell him Mr Carraway came over.'

'Who?' he demanded rudely.

'Carraway.'

'Carraway. All right, I'll tell him.'

Abruptly he slammed the door.

My Finn informed me that Gatsby had dismissed every servant in his house a week ago and replaced them with half a dozen others, who never went into West Egg Village to be bribed by the tradesmen, but ordered moderate supplies over the telephone. The grocery boy reported that the kitchen looked like a pigsty, and the general opinion in the village was that the new people weren't servants at all.

Next day Gatsby called me on the phone.

'Going away?' I enquired.

'No, old sport.'

'I hear you fired all your servants.'

'I wanted somebody who wouldn't gossip. Daisy comes over quite often – in the afternoons.'

So the whole caravansarai had fallen in like a card house at the disapproval in her eyes.

'They're some people Wolfsheim wanted to do something for. They're all brothers and sisters. They used to run a small hotel.'

'I see.'

He was calling up at Daisy's request – would I come to lunch at her house tomorrow? Miss Baker would be there. Half an hour later Daisy herself telephoned and seemed relieved to find that I was coming. Something was up. And yet I couldn't believe that they would choose this occasion for a scene – especially for the rather harrowing scene that Gatsby had outlined in the garden.

The next day was broiling, almost the last, certainly the warmest, of the summer. As my train emerged from the tunnel into sunlight, only the hot whistles of the National Biscuit Company broke the simmering hush at noon. The straw seats of the car hovered on the edge of combustion; the woman next to me perspired delicately for a while into her white shirtwaist, and then, as her newspaper dampened under her fingers, lapsed despairingly into deep heat with a desolate cry. Her pocketbook slapped to the floor.

'Oh, my!' she gasped.

I picked it up with a weary bend and handed it back to her, holding it at arm's length and by the extreme tip of the corners to indicate that I had no designs upon it – but everyone near by, including the woman, suspected me just the same.

'Hot!' said the conductor to familiar faces. 'Some weather . . . Hot! . . . Hot! . . . Hot! . . . Is it hot enough for you? Is it hot? Is it . . . ?'

My commutation ticket came back to me with a dark stain from his hand. That anyone should care in this heat whose flushed lips he kissed, whose head made damp the pyjama pocket over his heart!

. . . Through the hall of the Buchanans' house blew a faint wind, carrying the sound of the telephone bell out to Gatsby and me as we waited at the door.

'The master's body!' roared the butler into the mouthpiece. 'I'm sorry, madame, but we can't furnish it – it's far too hot to touch this noon!'

What he really said was: 'Yes . . . Yes . . . I'll see.'

He set down the receiver and came towards us, glistening slightly, to take our stiff straw hats.

'Madame expects you in the salon!' he cried, needlessly indicating the direction. In this heat every extra gesture was an affront to the common store of life.

The room, shadowed well with awnings, was dark and cool. Daisy and Jordan lay upon an enormous couch, like silver idols weighing down their own white dresses against the singing breeze of the fans.

'We can't move,' they said together.

Jordan's fingers, powdered white over their tan, rested for a moment in mine.

'And Mr Thomas Buchanan, the athlete?' I enquired.

Simultaneously I heard his voice, gruff, muffled, husky, at the hall telephone.

Gatsby stood in the centre of the crimson carpet and gazed around with fascinated eyes. Daisy watched him and laughed her sweet, exciting laugh; a tiny gust of powder rose from her bosom into the air.

'The rumour is,' whispered Jordan, 'that that's Tom's girl on the telephone.'

We were silent. The voice in the hall rose high with annoyance: 'Very well, then, I won't sell you the car at all . . . I'm under no obligations to you at all . . . and as for your bothering me about it at lunchtime, I won't stand that at all!'

'Holding down the receiver,' said Daisy cynically.

'No, he's not,' I assured her. 'It's a bona-fide deal. I happen to know about it.'

Tom flung open the door, blocked out its space for a moment with his thick body, and hurried into the room.

'Mr Gatsby!' He put out his broad, flat hand with well-concealed dislike. 'I'm glad to see you, sir . . . Nick . . . '

'Make us a cold drink,' cried Daisy.

As he left the room again she got up and went over to Gatsby and pulled his face down, kissing him on the mouth.

'You know I love you,' she murmured.

'You forget there's a lady present,' said Jordan.

Daisy looked around doubtfully.

'You kiss Nick too.'

'What a low, vulgar girl!'

'I don't care!' cried Daisy, and began to clog on the brick fireplace. Then she remembered the heat and sat down guiltily on the couch just as a freshly laundered nurse leading a little girl came into the room.

'Bles–sed pre–cious,' she crooned, holding out her arms. 'Come to your own mother that loves you.'

The child, relinquished by the nurse, rushed across the room and rooted shyly into her mother's dress.

'The bles–sed pre–cious! Did mother get powder on your old yellowy hair? Stand up now, and say – How-de-do.'

Gatsby and I in turn leaned down and took the small reluctant hand. Afterwards he kept looking at the child with surprise. I don't think he had ever really believed in its existence before.

'I got dressed before luncheon,' said the child, turning eagerly to Daisy.

'That's because your mother wanted to show you off.' Her face bent into the single wrinkle of the small white neck. 'You dream, you. You absolute little dream.'

'Yes,' admitted the child calmly. 'Aunt Jordan's got on a white dress, too.'

'How do you like mother's friends?' Daisy turned her around so that she faced Gatsby. 'Do you think they're pretty?'

'Where's Daddy?'

'She doesn't look like her father,' explained Daisy. 'She looks like me. She's got my hair and shape of the face.'

Daisy sat back upon the couch. The nurse took a step forward and held out her hand.

'Come, Pammy.'

'Goodbye, sweetheart!'

With a reluctant backward glance the well-disciplined child held to her nurse's hand and was pulled out of the door, just as Tom came back, preceding four gin rickeys that clicked full of ice.

Gatsby took up his drink.

'They certainly look cool,' he said, with visible tension.

We drank in long, greedy swallows.

'I read somewhere that the sun's getting hotter every year,' said Tom genially. 'It seems that pretty soon the earth's going to fall into the sun – or wait a minute – it's just the opposite – the sun's getting colder every year.

'Come outside,' he suggested to Gatsby, 'I'd like you to have a look at the place.'

I went with them out to the veranda. On the green Sound, stagnant in the heat, one small sail crawled slowly towards the fresher sea. Gatsby's eyes followed it momentarily; he raised his hand and pointed across the bay.

'I'm right across from you.'

'So you are.'

Our eyes lifted over the rose-beds and the hot lawn and the weedy refuse of the dog-days alongshore. Slowly the white wings of the boat moved against the blue cool limit of the sky. Ahead lay the scalloped ocean and the abounding blessed isles.

'There's sport for you,' said Tom, nodding. 'I'd like to be out there with him for about an hour.'

We had luncheon in the dining-room, darkened too against the heat, and drank down nervous gaiety with the cold ale.

'What'll we do with ourselves this afternoon?' cried Daisy, 'and the day after that, and the next thirty years?'

'Don't be morbid,' Jordan said. 'Life starts all over again when it gets crisp in the fall.'

'But it's so hot,' insisted Daisy, on the verge of tears, 'and everything's so confused. Let's all go to town!'

Her voice struggled on through the heat, beating against it, moulding its senselessness into forms.

'I've heard of making a garage out of a stable,' Tom was saying to Gatsby, 'but I'm the first man who ever made a stable out of a garage.'

'Who wants to go to town?' demanded Daisy insistently. Gatsby's eyes floated towards her. 'Ah,' she cried, 'you look so cool.'

Their eyes met, and they stared together at each other, alone in space. With an effort she glanced down at the table.

'You always look so cool,' she repeated.

She had told him that she loved him, and Tom Buchanan saw. He was astounded. His mouth opened a little, and he looked at Gatsby, and then back at Daisy as if he had just recognised her as someone he knew a long time ago.

'You resemble the advertisement of the man,' she went on innocently. 'You know the advertisement of the man – '

'All right,' broke in Tom quickly, 'I'm perfectly willing to go to town. Come on – we're all going to town.'

He got up, his eyes still flashing between Gatsby and his wife. No one moved.

'Come on!' His temper cracked a little. 'What's the matter, anyhow? If we're going to town, let's start.'

His hand, trembling with his effort at self-control, bore to his lips the last of his glass of ale. Daisy's voice got us to our feet and out on to the blazing gravel drive.

'Are we just going to go?' she objected. 'Like this? Aren't we going to let anyone smoke a cigarette first?'

'Everybody smoked all through lunch.'

'Oh, let's have fun,' she begged him. 'It's too hot to fuss.'

He didn't answer.

'Have it your own way,' she said. 'Come on, Jordan.'

They went upstairs to get ready while we three men stood there shuffling the hot pebbles with our feet. A silver curve of the moon hovered already in the western sky. Gatsby started to speak, changed his mind, but not before Tom wheeled and faced him expectantly.

'Have you got your stables here?' asked Gatsby with an effort.

'About a quarter of a mile down the road.'

'Oh.'

A pause.

'I don't see the idea of going to town,' broke out Tom savagely. 'Women get these notions in their heads – '

'Shall we take anything to drink?' called Daisy from an upper window.

'I'll get some whiskey,' answered Tom. He went inside.

Gatsby turned to me rigidly: 'I can't say anything in his house, old sport.'

'She's got an indiscreet voice,' I remarked. 'It's full of – ' I hesitated.

'Her voice is full of money,' he said suddenly.

That was it. I'd never understood before. It was full of money – that was the inexhaustible charm that rose and fell in it, the jingle of it, the cymbals' song of it . . . High in a white palace the king's daughter, the golden girl . . .

Tom came out of the house wrapping a quart bottle in a towel, followed by Daisy and Jordan wearing small tight hats of metallic cloth and carrying light capes over their arms.

'Shall we all go in my car?' suggested Gatsby. He felt the hot, green leather of the seat. 'I ought to have left it in the shade.'

'Is it standard shift?' demanded Tom.

'Yes.'

'Well, you take my coupé and let me drive your car to town.'

The suggestion was distasteful to Gatsby.

'I don't think there's much gas,' he objected.

'Plenty of gas,' said Tom boisterously. He looked at the gauge. 'And if it runs out I can stop at a drugstore. You can buy anything at a drugstore nowadays.'

A pause followed this apparently pointless remark. Daisy looked at Tom frowning, and an indefinable expression, at once definitely unfamiliar and vaguely recognisable, as if I had only heard it described in words, passed over Gatsby's face.

'Come on, Daisy,' said Tom, pressing her with his hand towards Gatsby's car. 'I'll take you in this circus wagon.'

He opened the door, but she moved out from the circle of his arm.

'You take Nick and Jordan. We'll follow you in the coupé.'

She walked close to Gatsby, touching his coat with her hand. Jordan and Tom and I got into the front seat of Gatsby's car, Tom pushed the unfamiliar gears tentatively, and we shot off into the oppressive heat, leaving them out of sight behind.

'Did you see that?' demanded Tom.

'See what?'

He looked at me keenly, realising that Jordan and I must have known all along.

'You think I'm pretty dumb, don't you?' he suggested. 'Perhaps I am, but I have a – almost a second sight, sometimes, that tells me what to do. Maybe you don't believe that, but science – '

He paused. The immediate contingency overtook him, pulled him back from the edge of the theoretical abyss.

'I've made a small investigation of this fellow,' he continued. 'I could have gone deeper if I'd known – '

'Do you mean you've been to a medium?' enquired Jordan humorously.

'What?' Confused, he stared at us as we laughed. 'A medium?'

'About Gatsby.'

'About Gatsby! No, I haven't. I said I'd been making a small investigation of his past.'

'And you found he was an Oxford man,' said Jordan helpfully.

'An Oxford man!' He was incredulous. 'Like hell he is! He wears a pink suit.'

'Nevertheless he's an Oxford man.'

'Oxford, New Mexico,' snorted Tom contemptuously, 'or something like that.'

'Listen, Tom. If you're such a snob, why did you invite him to lunch?' demanded Jordan crossly.

'Daisy invited him; she knew him before we were married – God knows where!'

We were all irritable now with the fading ale, and aware of it we drove for a while in silence. Then as Dr T. J. Eckleburg's faded eyes came into sight down the road, I remembered Gatsby's caution about gasoline.

'We've got enough to get us to town,' said Tom.

'But there's a garage right here,' objected Jordan. 'I don't want to get stalled in this baking heat.'

Tom threw on both brakes impatiently, and we slid to an abrupt dusty stop under Wilson's sign. After a moment the proprietor emerged from the interior of his establishment and gazed hollow-eyed at the car.

'Let's have some gas!' cried Tom roughly. 'What do you think we stopped for – to admire the view?'

'I'm sick,' said Wilson without moving. 'Been sick all day.'

'What's the matter?'

'I'm all run down.'

'Well, shall I help myself?' Tom demanded. 'You sounded well enough on the phone.'

With an effort Wilson left the shade and support of the doorway and, breathing hard, unscrewed the cap of the tank. In the sunlight his face was green.

'I didn't mean to interrupt your lunch,' he said. 'But I need money pretty bad, and I was wondering what you were going to do with your old car.'

'How do you like this one?' enquired Tom. 'I bought it last week.'

'It's a nice yellow one,' said Wilson, as he strained at the handle.

'Like to buy it?'

'Big chance,' Wilson smiled faintly. 'No, but I could make some money on the other.'

'What do you want money for, all of a sudden?'

'I've been here too long. I want to get away. My wife and I want to go West.'

'Your wife does?' exclaimed Tom, startled.

'She's been talking about it for ten years.' He rested for a moment against the pump, shading his eyes. 'And now she's going whether she wants to or not. I'm going to get her away.'

The coupé flashed by us with a flurry of dust and the flash of a waving hand.

'What do I owe you?' demanded Tom harshly.

'I just got wised up to something funny the last two days,' remarked Wilson. 'That's why I want to get away. That's why I been bothering you about the car.'

'What do I owe you?'

'Dollar twenty.'

The relentless beating heat was beginning to confuse me and I had a bad moment there before I realised that so far his suspicions hadn't alighted on Tom. He had discovered that Myrtle had some sort of life apart from him in another world, and the shock had made him physically sick. I stared at him and then at Tom, who had made a parallel discovery less than an hour before – and it occurred to me that there was no difference between men, in intelligence or race, so profound as the difference between the sick and the well. Wilson was so sick that he looked guilty, unforgivably guilty – as if he had just got some poor girl with child.

'I'll let you have that car,' said Tom. 'I'll send it over tomorrow afternoon.'

That locality was always vaguely disquieting, even in the broad glare of afternoon, and now I turned my head as though I had been warned of something behind. Over the ash heaps the giant eyes of Dr T. J. Eckleburg kept their vigil, but I perceived, after a moment, that other eyes were regarding us less than twenty feet away.

In one of the windows over the garage the curtains had been moved aside a little, and Myrtle Wilson was peering down at the car. So engrossed was she that she had no consciousness of being observed, and one emotion after another crept into her face like objects into a slowly developing picture. Her expression was curiously familiar – it was an expression I had often seen on women's faces, but on Myrtle Wilson's face it seemed purposeless and inexplicable until I realised that her eyes, wide with jealous terror, were fixed not on Tom, but on Jordan Baker, whom she took to be his wife.

There is no confusion like the confusion of a simple mind, and as we drove away Tom was feeling the hot whips of panic. His wife and his mistress, until an hour ago secure and inviolate, were slipping precipitately from his control. Instinct made him step on the accelerator with the double purpose of overtaking Daisy and leaving Wilson behind, and we sped along towards Astoria at fifty miles an hour, until, among the spidery girders of the elevated, we came in sight of the easy-going blue coupé.

'Those big movies around Fiftieth Street are cool,' suggested

Jordan. 'I love New York on summer afternoons when everyone's away. There's something very sensuous about it – overripe, as if all sorts of funny fruits were going to fall into your hands.'

The word 'sensuous' had the effect of further disquieting Tom, but before he could invent a protest the coupé came to a stop, and Daisy signalled us to draw up alongside.

'Where are we going?' she cried.

'How about the movies?'

'It's so hot,' she complained. 'You go. We'll ride around and meet you after.' With an effort her wit rose faintly, 'We'll meet you on some corner. I'll be the man smoking two cigarettes.'

'We can't argue about it here,' Tom said impatiently, as a truck gave out a cursing whistle behind us. 'You follow me to the south side of Central Park, in front of the Plaza.'

Several times he turned his head and looked back for their car, and if the traffic delayed them he slowed up until they came into sight. I think he was afraid they would dart down a side street and out of his life for ever.

But they didn't. And we all took the less explicable step of engaging the parlour of a suite in the Plaza Hotel.

The prolonged and tumultuous argument that ended by herding us into that room eludes me, though I have a sharp physical memory that, in the course of it, my underwear kept climbing like a damp snake around my legs and intermittent beads of sweat raced cool across my back. The notion originated with Daisy's suggestion that we hire five bathrooms and take cold baths, and then assumed more tangible form as 'a place to have a mint julep'. Each of us said over and over that it was a 'crazy idea' – we all talked at once to a baffled clerk and thought, or pretended to think, that we were being very funny . . .

The room was large and stifling, and, though it was already four o'clock, opening the windows admitted only a gust of hot shrubbery from the Park. Daisy went to the mirror and stood with her back to us, fixing her hair.

'It's a swell suite,' whispered Jordan respectfully, and everyone laughed.

'Open another window,' commanded Daisy, without turning around.

'There aren't any more.'

'Well, we'd better telephone for an axe – '

'The thing to do is to forget about the heat,' said Tom impatiently. 'You make it ten times worse by crabbing about it.'

He unrolled the bottle of whiskey from the towel and put it on the table.

'Why not let her alone, old sport?' remarked Gatsby. 'You're the one that wanted to come to town.'

There was a moment of silence. The telephone book slipped from its nail and splashed to the floor, whereupon Jordan whispered, 'Excuse me' – but this time no one laughed.

'I'll pick it up,' I offered.

'I've got it.' Gatsby examined the parted string, muttered, 'Hum!' in an interested way, and tossed the book on a chair.

'That's a great expression of yours, isn't it?' said Tom sharply.

'What is?'

'All this "old sport" business. Where'd you pick that up?'

'Now see here, Tom,' said Daisy, turning around from the mirror, 'if you're going to make personal remarks I won't stay here a minute. Call up and order some ice for the mint julep.'

As Tom took up the receiver the compressed heat exploded into sound and we were listening to the portentous chords of Mendelssohn's Wedding March from the ballroom below.

'Imagine marrying anybody in this heat!' cried Jordan dismally.

'Still – I was married in the middle of June,' Daisy remembered. 'Louisville in June! Somebody fainted. Who was it fainted, Tom?'

'Biloxi,' he answered shortly.

'A man named Biloxi. "Blocks" Biloxi, and he made boxes – that's a fact – and he was from Biloxi, Tennessee.'

'They carried him into my house,' appended Jordan, 'because we lived just two doors from the church. And he stayed three weeks, until Daddy told him he had to get out. The day after he left Daddy died.' After a moment she added, 'There wasn't any connection.'

'I used to know a Bill Biloxi from Memphis,' I remarked.

'That was his cousin. I knew his whole family history before he left. He gave me an aluminium putter that I use today.'

The music had died down as the ceremony began and now a long cheer floated in at the window, followed by intermittent cries of 'Yea–ea–ea!' and finally by a burst of jazz as the dancing began.

'We're getting old,' said Daisy. 'If we were young we'd rise and dance.'

'Remember Biloxi,' Jordan warned her. 'Where'd you know him, Tom?'

'Biloxi?' He concentrated with an effort. 'I didn't know him. He was a friend of Daisy's.'

'He was not,' she denied. 'I'd never seen him before. He came down in the private car.'

'Well, he said he knew you. He said he was raised in Louisville. Asa Bird brought him around at the last minute and asked if we had room for him.'

Jordan smiled.

'He was probably bumming his way home. He told me he was president of your class at Yale.'

Tom and I looked at each other blankly.

'Bil*ox*i?'

'First place, we didn't have any president – '

Gatsby's foot beat a short, restless tattoo and Tom eyed him suddenly.

'By the way, Mr Gatsby, I understand you're an Oxford man.'

'Not exactly.'

'Oh, yes, I understand you went to Oxford.'

'Yes – I went there.'

A pause. Then Tom's voice incredulous and insulting: 'You must have gone there about the time Biloxi went to New Haven.'

Another pause. A waiter knocked and came in with crushed mint and ice, but the silence was unbroken by his 'thank you' and the soft closing of the door. This tremendous detail was to be cleared up at last.

'I told you I went there,' said Gatsby.

'I heard you, but I'd like to know when.'

'It was in 1919. I only stayed five months. That's why I can't really call myself an Oxford man.'

Tom glanced around to see if we mirrored his unbelief. But we were all looking at Gatsby.

'It was an opportunity they gave to some of the officers after the Armistice,' he continued. 'We could go to any of the universities in England or France.'

I wanted to get up and slap him on the back. I had one of those renewals of complete faith in him that I'd experienced before.

Daisy rose, smiling faintly, and went to the table.

'Open the whiskey, Tom,' she ordered, 'and I'll make you a mint julep. Then you won't seem so stupid to yourself . . . Look at the mint!'

'Wait a minute,' snapped Tom, 'I want to ask Mr Gatsby one more question.'

'Go on,' Gatsby said politely.

'What kind of a row are you trying to cause in my house anyhow?'

They were out in the open at last and Gatsby was content.

'He isn't causing a row,' Daisy looked desperately from one to the other. 'You're causing a row. Please have a little self-control.'

'Self-control!' repeated Tom incredulously. 'I suppose the latest thing is to sit back and let Mr Nobody from Nowhere make love to your wife. Well, if that's the idea you can count me out . . . Nowadays people begin by sneering at family life and family institutions, and next they'll throw everything overboard and have intermarriage between black and white.'

Flushed with his impassioned gibberish, he saw himself standing alone on the last barrier of civilisation.

'We're all white here,' murmured Jordan.

'I know I'm not very popular. I don't give big parties. I suppose you've got to make your house into a pigsty in order to have any friends – in the modern world.'

Angry as I was, as we all were, I was tempted to laugh whenever he opened his mouth. The transition from libertine to prig was so complete.

'I've got something to tell *you*, old sport – ' began Gatsby. But Daisy guessed at his intention.

'Please don't!' she interrupted helplessly. 'Please let's all go home. Why don't we all go home?'

'That's a good idea.' I got up. 'Come on, Tom. Nobody wants a drink.'

'I want to know what Mr Gatsby has to tell me.'

'Your wife doesn't love you,' said Gatsby. 'She's never loved you. She loves me.'

'You must be crazy!' exclaimed Tom automatically.

Gatsby sprang to his feet, vivid with excitement.

'She never loved you, do you hear?' he cried. 'She only married you because I was poor and she was tired of waiting for me. It was a terrible mistake, but in her heart she never loved anyone except me!'

At this point Jordan and I tried to go, but Tom and Gatsby insisted with competitive firmness that we remain – as though neither of them had anything to conceal and it would be a privilege to partake vicariously of their emotions.

'Sit down, Daisy,' Tom's voice groped unsuccessfully for the paternal note. 'What's been going on? I want to hear all about it.'

'I told you what's been going on,' said Gatsby. 'Going on for five years – and you didn't know.'

Tom turned to Daisy sharply.

'You've been seeing this fellow for five years?'

'Not seeing,' said Gatsby. 'No, we couldn't meet. But both of us loved each other all that time, old sport, and you didn't know. I used to laugh sometimes' – but there was no laughter in his eyes – 'to think that you didn't know.'

'Oh – that's all.' Tom tapped his thick fingers together like a clergyman and leaned back in his chair. 'You're crazy!' he exploded. 'I can't speak about what happened five years ago because I didn't know Daisy then – and I'll be damned if I see how you got within a mile of her unless you brought the groceries to the back door. But all the rest of that's a God-damned lie. Daisy loved me when she married me and she loves me now.'

'No,' said Gatsby, shaking his head.

'She does, though. The trouble is that sometimes she gets foolish ideas in her head and doesn't know what she's doing.' He nodded sagely. 'And what's more I love Daisy too. Once in a while I go off on a spree and make a fool of myself, but I always come back, and in my heart I love her all the time.'

'You're revolting,' said Daisy. She turned to me, and her voice, dropping an octave lower, filled the room with thrilling scorn: 'Do you know why we left Chicago? I'm surprised that they didn't treat you to the story of that little spree.'

Gatsby walked over and stood beside her.

'Daisy, that's all over now,' he said earnestly. 'It doesn't matter any more. Just tell him the truth – that you never loved him – and it's all wiped out for ever.'

She looked at him blindly. 'Why – how could I love him – possibly?'

'You never loved him.'

She hesitated. Her eyes fell on Jordan and me with a sort of appeal, as though she realised at last what she was doing – and as though she had never, all along, intended doing anything at all. But it was done now. It was too late.

'I never loved him,' she said, with perceptible reluctance.

'Not at Kapiolani?' demanded Tom suddenly.

'No.'

From the ballroom beneath, muffled and suffocating chords were drifting up on hot waves of air.

'Not that day I carried you down from the Punch Bowl to keep your shoes dry?' There was a husky tenderness in his tone . . . 'Daisy?'

'Please don't.' Her voice was cold, but the rancour was gone from it. She looked at Gatsby. 'There, Jay,' she said – but her hand as she tried to light a cigarette was trembling. Suddenly she threw the cigarette and the burning match on the carpet.

'Oh, you want too much!' she cried to Gatsby. 'I love you now – isn't that enough? I can't help what's past.' She began to sob helplessly. 'I did love him once – but I loved you too.'

Gatsby's eyes opened and closed.

'You loved me *too*?' he repeated.

'Even that's a lie,' said Tom savagely. 'She didn't know you were alive. Why – there're things between Daisy and me that you'll never know, things that neither of us can ever forget.'

The words seemed to bite physically into Gatsby.

'I want to speak to Daisy alone,' he insisted. 'She's all excited now – '

'Even alone I can't say I never loved Tom,' she admitted in a pitiful voice. 'It wouldn't be true.'

'Of course it wouldn't,' agreed Tom.

She turned to her husband. 'As if it mattered to you,' she said.

'Of course it matters. I'm going to take better care of you from now on.'

'You don't understand,' said Gatsby, with a touch of panic. 'You're not going to take care of her any more.'

'I'm not?' Tom opened his eyes wide and laughed. He could afford to control himself now. 'Why's that?'

'Daisy's leaving you.'

'Nonsense.'

'I am, though,' she said with a visible effort.

'She's not leaving me!' Tom's words suddenly leaned down over Gatsby. 'Certainly not for a common swindler who'd have to steal the ring he put on her finger.'

'I won't stand this!' cried Daisy. 'Oh, please let's get out.'

'Who are you, anyhow?' broke out Tom. 'You're one of that bunch that hangs around with Meyer Wolfsheim – that much I happen to know. I've made a little investigation into your affairs – and I'll carry it further tomorrow.'

'You can suit yourself about that, old sport,' said Gatsby steadily.

'I found out what your "drugstores" were.' He turned to us and spoke rapidly. 'He and this Wolfsheim bought up a lot of side-street drugstores here and in Chicago and sold grain alcohol over the counter. That's one of his little stunts. I picked him for a bootlegger the first time I saw him, and I wasn't far wrong.'

'What about it?' said Gatsby politely. 'I guess your friend Walter Chase wasn't too proud to come in on it.'

'And you left him in the lurch, didn't you? You let him go to jail for a month over in New Jersey. God! You ought to hear Walter on the subject of *you*.'

'He came to us dead broke. He was very glad to pick up some money, old sport.'

'Don't you call me "old sport"!' cried Tom. Gatsby said nothing. 'Walter could have you up on the betting laws too, but Wolfsheim scared him into shutting his mouth.'

That unfamiliar yet recognisable look was back again in Gatsby's face.

'That drugstore business was just small change,' continued Tom slowly, 'but you've got something on now that Walter's afraid to tell me about.'

I glanced at Daisy, who was staring terrified between Gatsby and her husband, and at Jordan, who had begun to balance an invisible but absorbing object on the tip of her chin. Then I turned back to Gatsby – and was startled at his expression. He looked – and this is said in all contempt for the babbled slander of his garden – as if he had 'killed a man'. For a moment the set of his face could be described in just that fantastic way.

It passed, and he began to talk excitedly to Daisy, denying everything, defending his name against accusations that had not been made. But with every word she was drawing further and further into herself, so he gave that up, and only the dead dream fought on as the afternoon slipped away, trying to touch what was no longer tangible, struggling unhappily, undespairingly, towards that lost voice across the room.

The voice begged again to go.

'*Please*, Tom! I can't stand this any more.'

Her frightened eyes told that whatever intentions, whatever courage she had had, were definitely gone.

'You two start on home, Daisy,' said Tom. 'In Mr Gatsby's car.'

She looked at Tom, alarmed now, but he insisted with magnanimous scorn.

'Go on. He won't annoy you. I think he realises that his presumptuous little flirtation is over.'

They were gone, without a word, snapped out, made accidental, isolated, like ghosts, even from our pity.

After a moment Tom got up and began wrapping the unopened bottle of whiskey in the towel.

'Want any of this stuff? Jordan? . . . Nick?'

I didn't answer.

'Nick?' He asked again.

'What?'

'Want any?'

'No . . . I just remembered that today's my birthday.'

I was thirty. Before me stretched the portentous, menacing road of a new decade.

It was seven o'clock when we got into the coupé with him and started for Long Island. Tom talked incessantly, exulting and laughing, but his voice was as remote from Jordan and me as the foreign clamour on the sidewalk or the tumult of the elevated overhead. Human sympathy has its limits, and we were content to let all their tragic arguments fade with the city lights behind. Thirty – the promise of a decade of loneliness, a thinning list of single men to know, a thinning briefcase of enthusiasm, thinning hair. But there was Jordan beside me, who, unlike Daisy, was too wise ever to carry well-forgotten dreams from age to age. As we passed over the dark bridge her wan face fell lazily against my coat's shoulder and the formidable stroke of thirty died away with the reassuring pressure of her hand.

So we drove on towards death through the cooling twilight.

The young Greek, Michaelis, who ran the coffee joint beside the ash heaps was the principal witness at the inquest. He had slept through the heat until after five, when he strolled over to the garage, and found George Wilson sick in his office – really sick, pale as his own pale hair and shaking all over. Michaelis advised him to go to bed, but Wilson refused, saying that he'd miss a lot of business if he did. While his neighbour was trying to persuade him a violent racket broke out overhead.

'I've got my wife locked in up there,' explained Wilson calmly.

'She's going to stay there till the day after tomorrow, and then we're going to move away.'

Michaelis was astonished; they had been neighbours for four years, and Wilson had never seemed faintly capable of such a statement. Generally he was one of these worn-out men: when he wasn't working, he sat on a chair in the doorway and stared at the people and the cars that passed along the road. When anyone spoke to him he invariably laughed in an agreeable, colourless way. He was his wife's man and not his own.

So naturally Michaelis tried to find out what had happened, but Wilson wouldn't say a word – instead he began to throw curious suspicious glances at his visitor and ask him what he'd been doing at certain times on certain days. Just as the latter was getting uneasy, some workmen came past the door bound for his restaurant, and Michaelis took the opportunity to get away, intending to come back later. But he didn't. He supposed he forgot to, that's all. When he came outside again, a little after seven, he was reminded of the conversation because he heard Mrs Wilson's voice, loud and scolding, downstairs in the garage.

'Beat me!' he heard her cry. 'Throw me down and beat me, you dirty little coward!'

A moment later she rushed out into the dusk, waving her hands and shouting – before he could move from his door the business was over.

The 'death car' as the newspapers called it, didn't stop; it came out of the gathering darkness, wavered tragically for a moment, and then disappeared around the next bend. Mavromichaelis wasn't even sure of its colour – he told the first policeman that it was light green. The other car, the one going towards New York, came to rest a hundred yards beyond, and its driver hurried back to where Myrtle Wilson, her life violently extinguished, knelt in the road and mingled her thick dark blood with the dust.

Michaelis and this man reached her first, but when they had torn open her shirtwaist, still damp with perspiration, they saw that her left breast was swinging loose like a flap, and there was no need to listen for the heart beneath. The mouth was wide open and ripped a little at the corners, as though she had choked a little in giving up the tremendous vitality she had stored so long.

We saw the three or four automobiles and the crowd when we were still some distance away.

'Wreck!' said Tom. 'That's good. Wilson'll have a little business at last.'

He slowed down, but still without any intention of stopping, until, as we came nearer, the hushed, intent faces of the people at the garage door made him automatically put on his brakes.

'We'll take a look,' he said doubtfully, 'just a look.'

I became aware now of a hollow, wailing sound which issued incessantly from the garage, a sound which as we got out of the coupé and walked towards the door resolved itself into the words, 'Oh, my God!' uttered over and over in a gasping moan.

'There's some bad trouble here,' said Tom excitedly.

He reached up on tiptoes and peered over a circle of heads into the garage, which was lit only by a yellow light in a swinging metal basket overhead. Then he made a harsh sound in his throat, and with a violent thrusting movement of his powerful arms pushed his way through.

The circle closed up again with a running murmur of expostulation; it was a minute before I could see anything at all. Then new arrivals deranged the line, and Jordan and I were pushed suddenly inside.

Myrtle Wilson's body, wrapped in a blanket, and then in another blanket, as though she suffered from a chill in the hot night, lay on a work-table by the wall, and Tom, with his back to us, was bending over it, motionless. Next to him stood a motorcycle policeman taking down names with much sweat and correction in a little book. At first I couldn't find the source of the high, groaning words that echoed clamorously through the bare garage – then I saw Wilson standing on the raised threshold of his office, swaying back and forth and holding to the doorposts with both hands. Some man was talking to him in a low voice and attempting, from time to time, to lay a hand on his shoulder, but

Wilson neither heard nor saw. His eyes would drop slowly from the swinging light to the laden table by the wall, and then jerk back to the light again, and he gave out incessantly his high, horrible call: 'Oh, my Ga–od! Oh, my Ga–od! Oh, Ga–od! Oh, my Ga–od!'

Presently Tom lifted his head with a jerk and, after staring around the garage with glazed eyes, addressed a mumbled incoherent remark to the policeman.

'M, a, v – ' the policeman was saying, 'o – '

'No, r,' corrected the man, 'M, a, v, r, o – '

'Listen to me!' muttered Tom fiercely.

'r,' said the policeman, 'o – '

'g.'

'g – ' He looked up as Tom's broad hand fell sharply on his shoulder. 'What you want, fella?'

'What happened? – that's what I want to know.'

'Auto hit her. Ins'antly killed.'

'Instantly killed,' repeated Tom, staring.

'She ran out ina road. Son-of-a-bitch didn't even stopus car.'

'There was two cars,' said Michaelis, 'one comin', one goin', see?'

'Going where?' asked the policeman keenly.

'One goin' each way. Well, she – ' his hand rose towards the blankets but stopped halfway and fell to his side – 'she ran out there an' the one comin' from N'York knock right into her, goin' thirty or forty miles an hour.'

'What's the name of this place here?' demanded the officer.

'Hasn't got any name.'

A pale well-dressed negro stepped near.

'It was a yellow car,' he said, 'big yellow car. New.'

'See the accident?' asked the policeman.

'No, but the car passed me down the road, going faster'n forty. Going fifty, sixty.'

'Come here and let's have your name. Look out now. I want to get his name.'

Some words of this conversation must have reached Wilson, swaying in the office door, for suddenly a new theme found voice among his gasping cries: 'You don't have to tell me what kind of car it was! I know what kind of car it was!'

Watching Tom, I saw the wad of muscle back of his shoulder tighten under his coat. He walked quickly over to Wilson and, standing in front of him, seized him firmly by the upper arms.

'You've got to pull yourself together,' he said with soothing gruffness.

Wilson's eyes fell upon Tom; he started up on his tiptoes and then would have collapsed to his knees had not Tom held him upright.

'Listen,' said Tom, shaking him a little. 'I just got here a minute ago, from New York. I was bringing you that coupé we've been talking about. That yellow car I was driving this afternoon wasn't mine – do you hear? I haven't seen it all afternoon.'

Only the negro and I were near enough to hear what he said, but the policeman caught something in the tone and looked over with truculent eyes.

'What's all that?' he demanded.

'I'm a friend of his.' Tom turned his head but kept his hands firm on Wilson's body. 'He says he knows the car that did it . . . It was a yellow car.'

Some dim impulse moved the policeman to look suspiciously at Tom.

'And what colour's your car?'

'It's a blue car, a coupé.'

'We've come straight from New York,' I said.

Someone who had been driving a little behind us confirmed this, and the policeman turned away.

'Now, if you'll let me have that name again correct – '

Picking up Wilson like a doll, Tom carried him into the office, set him down in a chair, and came back.

'If somebody'll come here and sit with him – ' he snapped authoritatively. He watched while the two men standing closest glanced at each other and went unwillingly into the room. Then Tom shut the door on them and came down the single step, his eyes avoiding the table. As he passed close to me he whispered: 'Let's get out.'

Self-consciously, with his authoritative arms breaking the way, we pushed through the still-gathering crowd, passing a hurried doctor, case in hand, who had been sent for in wild hope half an hour ago.

Tom drove slowly until we were beyond the bend – then his foot came down hard, and the coupé raced along through the night. In a little while I heard a low husky sob, and saw that the tears were overflowing down his face.

'The God-damned coward!' he whimpered. 'He didn't even stop his car.'

The Buchanans' house floated suddenly towards us through the dark rustling trees. Tom stopped beside the porch and looked up at the second floor, where two windows bloomed with light among the vines.

'Daisy's home,' he said. As we got out of the car he glanced at me and frowned slightly.

'I ought to have dropped you in West Egg, Nick. There's nothing we can do tonight.'

A change had come over him, and he spoke gravely, and with decision. As we walked across the moonlight gravel to the porch he disposed of the situation in a few brisk phrases.

'I'll telephone for a taxi to take you home, and while you're waiting you and Jordan better go in the kitchen and have them get you some supper – if you want any.' He opened the door. 'Come in.'

'No, thanks. But I'd be glad if you'd order me the taxi. I'll wait outside.'

Jordan put her hand on my arm.

'Won't you come in, Nick?'

'No, thanks.'

I was feeling a little sick and I wanted to be alone. But Jordan lingered for a moment more.

'It's only half-past nine,' she said.

I'd be damned if I'd go in; I'd had enough of all of them for one day, and suddenly that included Jordan too. She must have seen something of this in my expression, for she turned abruptly away and ran up the porch steps into the house. I sat down for a few minutes with my head in my hands, until I heard the phone taken up inside and the butler's voice calling a taxi. Then I walked slowly down the drive away from the house, intending to wait by the gate.

I hadn't gone twenty yards when I heard my name and Gatsby stepped from between two bushes into the path. I must have felt pretty weird by that time, because I could think of nothing except the luminosity of his pink suit under the moon.

'What are you doing?' I enquired.

'Just standing here, old sport.'

Somehow, that seemed a despicable occupation. For all I knew he was going to rob the house in a moment; I wouldn't have been surprised to see sinister faces, the faces of 'Wolfsheim's people', behind him in the dark shrubbery.

'Did you see any trouble on the road?' he asked after a minute.

'Yes.'

He hesitated.

'Was she killed?'

'Yes.'

'I thought so; I told Daisy I thought so. It's better that the shock should all come at once. She stood it pretty well.'

He spoke as if Daisy's reaction was the only thing that mattered.

'I got to West Egg by a side road,' he went on, 'and left the car in my garage. I don't think anybody saw us, but of course I can't be sure.'

I disliked him so much by this time that I didn't find it necessary to tell him he was wrong.

'Who was the woman?' he enquired.

'Her name was Wilson. Her husband owns the garage. How the devil did it happen?'

'Well, I tried to swing the wheel – ' He broke off, and suddenly I guessed at the truth.

'Was Daisy driving?'

'Yes,' he said after a moment, 'but of course I'll say I was. You see, when we left New York she was very nervous and she thought it would steady her to drive – and this woman rushed out at us just as we were passing a car coming the other way. It all happened in a minute, but it seemed to me that she wanted to speak to us, thought we were somebody she knew. Well, first Daisy turned away from the woman towards the other car, and then she lost her nerve and turned back. The second my hand reached the wheel I felt the shock – it must have killed her instantly.'

'It ripped her open – '

'Don't tell me, old sport.' He winced. 'Anyhow – Daisy stepped on it. I tried to make her stop, but she couldn't, so I pulled on the emergency brake. Then she fell over into my lap and I drove on.

'She'll be all right tomorrow,' he said presently. 'I'm just going to wait here and see if he tries to bother her about that unpleasantness this afternoon. She's locked herself into her room, and if he tries any brutality she's going to turn the light out and on again.'

'He won't touch her,' I said. 'He's not thinking about her.'

'I don't trust him, old sport.'

'How long are you going to wait?'

'All night, if necessary. Anyhow, till they all go to bed.'

A new point of view occurred to me. Suppose Tom found out that Daisy had been driving. He might think he saw a connection in it – he might think anything. I looked at the house; there were two or three bright windows downstairs and the pink glow from Daisy's room on the second floor.

'You wait here,' I said. 'I'll see if there's any sign of a commotion.'

I walked back along the border of the lawn, traversed the gravel softly, and tiptoed up the veranda steps. The drawing-room curtains were open, and I saw that the room was empty. Crossing the porch where we had dined that June night three months before, I came to a small rectangle of light which I guessed was the pantry window. The blind was drawn, but I found a rift at the sill.

Daisy and Tom were sitting opposite each other at the kitchen table, with a plate of cold fried chicken between them, and two bottles of ale. He was talking intently across the table at her, and in his earnestness his hand had fallen upon and covered her own. Once in a while she looked up at him and nodded in agreement.

They weren't happy, and neither of them had touched the chicken or the ale – and yet they weren't unhappy either. There was an unmistakable air of natural intimacy about the picture, and anybody would have said that they were conspiring together.

As I tiptoed from the porch I heard my taxi feeling its way along the dark drive towards the house. Gatsby was waiting where I had left him in the drive.

'Is it all quiet up there?' he asked anxiously.

'Yes, it's all quiet.' I hesitated. 'You'd better come home and get some sleep.'

He shook his head.

'I want to wait here till Daisy goes to bed. Good-night, old sport.'

He put his hands in his coat pockets and turned back eagerly to his scrutiny of the house, as though my presence marred the sacredness of the vigil. So I walked away and left him standing there in the moonlight – watching over nothing.

Eight

I couldn't sleep all night; a foghorn was groaning incessantly on the Sound, and I tossed half-sick between grotesque reality and savage, frightening dreams. Towards dawn I heard a taxi go up Gatsby's drive, and immediately I jumped out of bed and began to dress – I felt that I had something to tell him, something to warn him about, and morning would be too late.

Crossing his lawn, I saw that his front door was still open and he was leaning against a table in the hall, heavy with dejection or sleep.

'Nothing happened,' he said wanly. 'I waited, and about four o'clock she came to the window and stood there for a minute and then turned out the light.'

His house had never seemed so enormous to me as it did that night when we hunted through the great rooms for cigarettes. We pushed aside curtains that were like pavilions, and felt over innumerable feet of dark wall for electric-light switches – once I tumbled with a sort of splash upon the keys of a ghostly piano. There was an inexplicable amount of dust everywhere, and the rooms were musty, as though they hadn't been aired for many days. I found the humidor on an unfamiliar table, with two stale, dry cigarettes inside. Throwing open the French windows of the drawing-room, we sat smoking out into the darkness.

'You ought to go away,' I said. 'It's pretty certain they'll trace your car.'

'Go away *now*, old sport?'

'Go to Atlantic City for a week, or up to Montreal.'

He wouldn't consider it. He couldn't possibly leave Daisy until he knew what she was going to do. He was clutching at some last hope and I couldn't bear to shake him free.

It was this night that he told me the strange story of his youth with Dan Cody – told it to me because 'Jay Gatsby' had broken up like glass against Tom's hard malice, and the long secret extravaganza was played out. I think that he would have acknowledged anything now, without reserve, but he wanted to talk about Daisy.

She was the first 'nice girl' he had ever known. In various unrevealed capacities he had come in contact with such people, but always with indiscernible barbed wire between. He found her excitingly desirable. He went to her house, at first with other officers from Camp Taylor, then alone. It amazed him – he had never been in such a beautiful house before. But what gave it an air of breathless intensity was that Daisy lived there – it was as casual a thing to her as his tent out at camp was to him. There was a ripe mystery about it, a hint of bedrooms upstairs more beautiful and cool than other bedrooms, of gay and radiant activities taking place through its corridors, and of romances that were not musty and laid away already in lavender but fresh and breathing and redolent of this year's shining motor cars and of dances whose flowers were scarcely withered. It excited him, too, that many men had already loved Daisy – it increased her value in his eyes. He felt their presence all about the house, pervading the air with the shades and echoes of still vibrant emotions.

But he knew that he was in Daisy's house by a colossal accident. However glorious might be his future as Jay Gatsby, he was at present a penniless young man without a past, and at any moment the invisible cloak of his uniform might slip from his shoulders. So he made the most of his time. He took what he could get, ravenously and unscrupulously – eventually he took Daisy one still October night, took her because he had no real right to touch her hand.

He might have despised himself, for he had certainly taken her under false pretences. I don't mean that he had traded on his phantom millions, but he had deliberately given Daisy a sense of security; he let her believe that he was a person from much the same strata as herself – that he was fully able to take care of her. As a matter of fact, he had no such facilities – he had no comfortable family standing behind him, and he was liable at the whim of an impersonal government to be blown anywhere about the world.

But he didn't despise himself and it didn't turn out as he had imagined. He had intended, probably, to take what he could and go – but now he found that he had committed himself to the following of a grail. He knew that Daisy was extraordinary, but he didn't realise just how extraordinary a 'nice' girl could be. She vanished into her rich house, into her rich, full life, leaving Gatsby – nothing. He felt married to her, that was all.

When they met again, two days later, it was Gatsby who was breathless, who was, somehow, betrayed. Her porch was bright with the bought luxury of star-shine; the wicker of the settee squeaked fashionably as she turned towards him and he kissed her curious and lovely mouth. She had caught a cold, and it made her voice huskier and more charming than ever, and Gatsby was overwhelmingly aware of the youth and mystery that wealth imprisons and preserves, of the freshness of many clothes, and of Daisy, gleaming like silver, safe and proud above the hot struggles of the poor.

'I can't describe to you how surprised I was to find out I loved her, old sport. I even hoped for a while that she'd throw me over, but she didn't, because she was in love with me too. She thought I knew a lot because I knew different things from her . . . Well, there I was, 'way off my ambitions, getting deeper in love every minute, and all of a sudden I didn't care. What was the use of doing great things if I could have a better time telling her what I was going to do?'

On the last afternoon before he went abroad, he sat with Daisy in his arms for a long, silent time. It was a cold fall day, with fire in the room and her cheeks flushed. Now and then she moved and he changed his arm a little, and once he kissed her dark shining hair. The afternoon had made them tranquil for a while, as if to give them a deep memory for the long parting the next day promised. They had never been closer in their month of love, nor communicated more profoundly one with another, than when she brushed silent lips against his coat's shoulder or when he touched the end of her fingers, gently, as though she were asleep.

He did extraordinarily well in the war. He was a captain before he went to the front, and following the Argonne battles he got his majority and the command of the divisional machine-guns. After the Armistice he tried frantically to get home, but some complication or misunderstanding sent him to Oxford instead. He was worried now – there was a quality of nervous despair in Daisy's letters. She didn't see why he couldn't come. She was feeling the pressure of the world outside, and she wanted to see him and feel his presence beside her and be reassured that she was doing the right thing after all.

For Daisy was young and her artificial world was redolent of orchids and pleasant, cheerful snobbery and orchestras which set the rhythm of the year, summing up the sadness and suggestiveness of life in new tunes. All night the saxophones wailed the hopeless comment of the *Beale Street Blues* while a hundred pairs of golden and silver slippers shuffled the shining dust. At the grey tea hour there were always rooms that throbbed incessantly with this low, sweet fever, while fresh faces drifted here and there like rose petals blown by the sad horns around the floor.

Through this twilight universe Daisy began to move again with the season; suddenly she was again keeping half a dozen dates a day with half a dozen men, and drowsing asleep at dawn with the beads and chiffon of an evening dress tangled among dying orchids on the floor beside her bed. And all the time something within her was crying for a decision. She wanted her life shaped now, immediately – and the decision must be made by some force – of love, of money, of unquestionable practicality – that was close at hand.

That force took shape in the middle of spring with the arrival of Tom Buchanan. There was a wholesome bulkiness about his person and his position, and Daisy was flattered. Doubtless there was a certain struggle and a certain relief. The letter reached Gatsby while he was still at Oxford.

It was dawn now on Long Island and we went about opening the rest of the windows downstairs, filling the house with grey-turning, gold-turning light. The shadow of a tree fell abruptly across the dew and ghostly birds began to sing among the blue leaves. There was a slow, pleasant movement in the air, scarcely a wind, promising a cool, lovely day.

'I don't think she ever loved him,' Gatsby turned around from a window and looked at me challengingly. 'You must remember, old sport, she was very excited this afternoon. He told her those things in a way that frightened her – that made it look as if I was some kind of cheap sharper. And the result was she hardly knew what she was saying.'

He sat down gloomily.

'Of course she might have loved him just for a minute, when they were first married – and loved me more even then, do you see?'

Suddenly he came out with a curious remark.

'In any case,' he said, 'it was just personal.'

What could you make of that, except to suspect some intensity in his conception of the affair that couldn't be measured?

He came back from France when Tom and Daisy were still on their wedding trip, and made a miserable but irresistible journey to Louisville on the last of his army pay. He stayed there a week, walking the streets where their footsteps had clicked together through the November night and revisiting the out-of-the-way places to which they had driven in her white car. Just as Daisy's house had always seemed to him more mysterious and gay than other houses, so his idea of the city itself, even though she was gone from it, was pervaded with a melancholy beauty.

He left, feeling that if he had searched harder, he might have found her – that he was leaving her behind. The day-coach – he was penniless now – was hot. He went out to the open vestibule and sat down on a folding-chair, and the station slid away and the backs of unfamiliar buildings moved by. Then out into the spring fields, where a yellow trolley raced them for a minute with people in it who might once have seen the pale magic of her face along the casual street.

The track curved and now it was going away from the sun, which, as it sank lower, seemed to spread itself in benediction over the vanishing city where she had drawn her breath. He stretched out his hand desperately as if to snatch only a wisp of air, to save a fragment of the spot that she had made lovely for him. But it was all going by too fast now for his blurred eyes and he knew that he had lost that part of it, the freshest and the best, for ever.

It was nine o'clock when we finished breakfast and went out on the porch. The night had made a sharp difference in the weather and there was an autumn flavour in the air. The gardener, the last one of Gatsby's former servants, came to the foot of the steps.

'I'm going to drain the pool today, Mr Gatsby. Leaves'll start falling pretty soon, and then there's always trouble with the pipes.'

'Don't do it today,' Gatsby answered. He turned to me apologetically. 'You know, old sport, I've never used that pool all summer.'

I looked at my watch and stood up. 'Twelve minutes to my train.'

I didn't want to go to the city. I wasn't worth a decent stroke of work, but it was more than that – I didn't want to leave Gatsby. I missed that train, and then another, before I could get myself away.

'I'll call you up,' I said finally.

'Do, old sport.'

'I'll call you about noon.'

We walked slowly down the steps.

'I suppose Daisy'll call too.' He looked at me anxiously, as if he hoped I'd corroborate this.

'I suppose so.'

'Well, goodbye.'

We shook hands and I started away. Just before I reached the hedge I remembered something and turned around.

'They're a rotten crowd,' I shouted across the lawn. 'You're worth the whole damn bunch put together.'

I've always been glad I said that. It was the only compliment I ever gave him, because I disapproved of him from beginning to end. First he nodded politely, and then his face broke into that radiant and understanding smile, as if we'd been in ecstatic cahoots on that fact all the time. His gorgeous pink rag of a suit made a bright spot of colour against the white steps, and I thought of the night when I first came to his ancestral home, three months before. The lawn and drive had been crowded with the faces of those who guessed at his corruption – and he had stood on those steps, concealing his incorruptible dream, as he waved them goodbye.

I thanked him for his hospitality. We were always thanking him for that – I and the others.

'Goodbye,' I called. 'I enjoyed breakfast, Gatsby.'

Up in the city, I tried for a while to list the quotations on an interminable amount of stock, then I fell asleep in my swivel-chair. Just before noon the phone woke me, and I started up with sweat breaking out on my forehead. It was Jordan Baker; she often called me up at this hour because the uncertainty of her own movements between hotels and clubs and private houses made her hard to find in any other way. Usually her voice came over the wire as something fresh and cool, as if a divot from a green golf-links had come sailing in at the office window, but this morning it seemed harsh and dry.

'I've left Daisy's house,' she said. 'I'm at Hempstead, and I'm going down to Southampton this afternoon.'

Probably it had been tactful to leave Daisy's house, but the act annoyed me, and her next remark made me rigid.

'You weren't so nice to me last night.'

'How could it have mattered then?'

Silence for a moment. Then: 'However – I want to see you.'

'I want to see you, too.'

'Suppose I don't go to Southampton, and come into town this afternoon?'

'No – I don't think this afternoon.'

'Very well.'

'It's impossible this afternoon. Various – '

We talked like that for a while, and then abruptly we weren't talking any longer. I don't know which of us hung up with a sharp click, but I know I didn't care. I couldn't have talked to her across a tea-table that day if I never talked to her again in this world.

I called Gatsby's house a few minutes later, but the line was busy. I tried four times; finally an exasperated central told me the wire was being kept open for long distance from Detroit. Taking out my timetable, I drew a small circle around the three-fifty train. Then I leaned back in my chair and tried to think. It was just noon.

When I passed the ash heaps on the train that morning I had crossed deliberately to the other side of the car. I supposed there'd be a curious crowd around there all day, with little boys searching for dark spots in the dust and some garrulous man telling over and over what had happened, until it became less and less real even to him and he could tell it no longer, and Myrtle Wilson's tragic achievement was forgotten. Now I want to go back a little and tell what happened at the garage after we left there the night before.

They had difficulty in locating the sister, Catherine. She must have broken her rule against drinking that night, for when she arrived she was stupid with liquor and unable to understand that the ambulance had already gone to Flushing. When they convinced her of this, she immediately fainted, as if that was the intolerable part of the affair. Someone, kind or curious, took her in his car and drove her in the wake of her sister's body.

Until long after midnight a changing crowd lapped up against the front of the garage, while George Wilson rocked himself back and forth on the couch inside. For a while the door of the office was open, and everyone who came into the garage glanced irresistibly through it. Finally someone said it was a shame, and closed the door. Michaelis and several other men were with him; first, four or five men, later two or three men. Still later Michaelis had to ask the last stranger to wait there fifteen minutes longer while he went back to his own place and made a pot of coffee. After that, he stayed there alone with Wilson until dawn.

About three o'clock the quality of Wilson's incoherent muttering changed – he grew quieter and began to talk about the yellow car. He announced that he had a way of finding out whom the yellow car belonged to, and then he blurted out that a couple of months ago his wife had come from the city with her face bruised and her nose swollen.

But when he heard himself say this, he flinched and began to cry, 'Oh, my God!' again in his groaning voice. Michaelis made a clumsy attempt to distract him.

'How long have you been married, George? Come on there, try and sit still a minute and answer my question. How long have you been married?'

'Twelve years.'

'Ever had any children? Come on, George, sit still – I asked you a question. Did you ever have any children?'

The hard brown beetles kept thudding against the dull light, and whenever Michaelis heard a car go tearing along the road outside it sounded to him like the car that hadn't stopped a few hours before. He didn't like to go into the garage, because the work bench was stained where the body had been lying, so he moved uncomfortably around the office – he knew every object in it before morning – and from time to time sat down beside Wilson, trying to keep him more quiet.

'Have you got a church you go to sometimes, George? Maybe even if you haven't been there for a long time? Maybe I could call up the church and get a priest to come over and he could talk to you, see?'

'Don't belong to any.'

'You ought to have a church, George, for times like this. You must have gone to church once. Didn't you get married in a church? Listen, George, listen to me. Didn't you get married in a church?'

'That was a long time ago.'

The effort of answering broke the rhythm of his rocking – for a moment he was silent. Then the same half-knowing, half-bewildered look came back into his faded eyes.

'Look in the drawer there,' he said, pointing at the desk.

'Which drawer?'

'That drawer – that one.'

Michaelis opened the drawer nearest his hand. There was nothing in it but a small, expensive dog-leash, made of leather and braided silver. It was apparently new.

'This?' he enquired, holding it up.

Wilson stared and nodded. 'I found it yesterday afternoon. She tried to tell me about it, but I knew it was something funny.'

'You mean your wife bought it?'

'She had it wrapped in tissue paper on her bureau.'

Michaelis didn't see anything odd in that, and he gave Wilson a dozen reasons why his wife might have bought the dog-leash. But conceivably Wilson had heard some of these same explanations before, from Myrtle, because he began saying, 'Oh, my God!' again in a whisper – his comforter left several explanations in the air.

'Then he killed her,' said Wilson. His mouth dropped open suddenly.

'Who did?'

'I have a way of finding out.'

'You're morbid, George,' said his friend. 'This has been a strain to you and you don't know what you're saying. You'd better try and sit quiet till morning.'

'He murdered her.'

'It was an accident, George.'

Wilson shook his head. His eyes narrowed and his mouth widened slightly with the ghost of a superior, 'Hm!'

'I know,' he said definitely. 'I'm one of these trusting fellas and I don't think any harm to *no*body, but when I get to know a thing I know it. It was the man in that car. She ran out to speak to him and he wouldn't stop.'

Michaelis had seen this too, but it hadn't occurred to him that there was any special significance in it. He believed that Mrs Wilson had been running away from her husband, rather than trying to stop any particular car.

'How could she of been like that?'

'She's a deep one,' said Wilson, as if that answered the question. 'Ah–h–h – '

He began to rock again, and Michaelis stood twisting the leash in his hand.

'Maybe you got some friend that I could telephone for, George?'

This was a forlorn hope – he was almost sure that Wilson had no friend: there was not enough of him for his wife. He was glad a little later when he noticed a change in the room, a blue quickening by the window, and realised that dawn wasn't far off. About five o'clock it was blue enough outside to snap off the light.

Wilson's glazed eyes turned out to the ash heaps, where small grey clouds took on fantastic shapes and scurried here and there in the faint dawn wind.

'I spoke to her,' he muttered, after a long silence. 'I told her she might fool me but she couldn't fool God. I took her to the window' – with an effort he got up and walked to the rear window and leaned with his face pressed against it – 'and I said, "God knows what you've been doing, everything you've been doing. You may fool me, but you can't fool God!" '

Standing behind him, Michaelis saw with a shock that he was looking at the eyes of Dr T. J. Eckleburg, which had just emerged, pale and enormous, from the dissolving night.

'God sees everything,' repeated Wilson.

'That's an advertisement,' Michaelis assured him. Something made him turn away from the window and look back into the room. But Wilson stood there a long time, his face close to the window pane, nodding into the twilight.

By six o'clock Michaelis was worn out, and grateful for the sound of a car stopping outside. It was one of the watchers of the night before who had promised to come back, so he cooked breakfast for three, which he and the other man ate together. Wilson was quieter now, and Michaelis went home to sleep; when he awoke four hours later and hurried back to the garage, Wilson was gone.

His movements – he was on foot all the time – were afterwards traced to Port Roosevelt and then to Gad's Hill, where he bought a sandwich, that he didn't eat, and a cup of coffee. He must have been tired and walking slowly, for he didn't reach Gad's Hill until noon. Thus far there was no difficulty in accounting for his time – there were boys who had seen a man 'acting sort of crazy', and motorists at whom he stared oddly from the side of the road. Then for three hours he disappeared from view. The police, on the strength of what he had said to Michaelis, that he 'had a way of finding out', supposed that he spent that time going from garage to garage thereabouts, enquiring for a yellow car. On the other hand, no garage man who had seen him ever came forward, and perhaps he had an easier, surer way of finding out what he wanted to know. By half-past two he was in West Egg, where he asked someone the way to Gatsby's house. So by that time he knew Gatsby's name.

At two o'clock Gatsby put on his bathing-suit and left word with the butler that if anyone phoned word was to be brought to him at the pool. He stopped at the garage for a pneumatic mattress that had amused his guests during the summer, and the chauffeur helped him pump it up. Then he gave instructions that the open car wasn't to be taken out under any circumstances – and this was strange, because the front right fender needed repair.

Gatsby shouldered the mattress and started for the pool. Once he stopped and shifted it a little, and the chauffeur asked him if he needed help, but he shook his head and in a moment disappeared among the yellowing trees.

No telephone message arrived, but the butler went without his sleep and waited for it until four o'clock – until long after there was anyone to give it to if it came. I have an idea that Gatsby himself didn't believe it would come, and perhaps he no longer cared. If that was true he must have felt that he had lost the old warm world, paid a high price for living too long with a single dream. He must have looked up at an unfamiliar sky through frightening leaves and shivered as he found what a grotesque thing a rose is and how raw the sunlight was upon the scarcely created grass. A new world, material without being real, where poor ghosts, breathing dreams like air, drifted fortuitously about . . . like that ashen, fantastic figure gliding towards him through the amorphous trees.

The chauffeur – he was one of Wolfsheim's protégés – heard the shots – afterwards he could only say that he hadn't thought anything much about them. I drove from the station directly to Gatsby's house and my rushing anxiously up the front steps was the first thing that alarmed anyone. But they knew then, I firmly believe. With scarcely a word said, four of us, the chauffeur, butler, gardener and I, hurried down to the pool.

There was a faint, barely perceptible movement of the water as the fresh flow from one end urged its way towards the drain at the other. With little ripples that were hardly the shadows of waves, the laden mattress moved irregularly down the pool. A small gust of wind that scarcely corrugated the surface was enough to disturb its accidental course with its accidental burden. The touch of a cluster of leaves revolved it slowly, tracing, like the leg of transit, a thin red circle in the water.

It was after we started with Gatsby towards the house that the gardener saw Wilson's body a little way off in the grass, and the holocaust was complete.

Nine

After two years I remember the rest of that day, and that night and the next day, only as an endless drill of police and photographers and newspaper men in and out of Gatsby's front door. A rope stretched across the main gate and a policeman by it kept out the curious, but little boys soon discovered that they could enter through my yard, and there were always a few of them clustered open-mouthed about the pool. Someone with a positive manner, perhaps a detective, used the expression 'madman' as he bent over Wilson's body that afternoon, and the adventitious authority of his voice set the key for the newspaper reports next morning.

Most of those reports were a nightmare – grotesque, circumstantial, eager and untrue. When Michaelis's testimony at the inquest brought to light Wilson's suspicions of his wife I thought the whole tale would shortly be served up in racy pasquinade – but Catherine, who might have said anything, didn't say a word. She showed a surprising amount of character about it too – looked at the coroner with determined eyes under that corrected brow of hers, and swore that her sister had never seen Gatsby, that her sister was completely happy with her husband, that her sister had been into no mischief whatever. She convinced herself of it, and cried into her handkerchief, as if the very suggestion was more than she could endure. So Wilson was reduced to a man 'deranged by grief' in order that the case might remain in its simplest form. And it rested there.

But all this part of it seemed remote and unessential. I found myself on Gatsby's side, and alone. From the moment I telephoned news of the catastrophe to West Egg village, every surmise about him, and every practical question, was referred to me. At first I was surprised and confused; then, as he lay in his house and didn't move or breathe or speak, hour upon hour, it grew upon me that I was responsible, because no one else was interested – interested, I mean, with that intense personal interest to which everyone has some vague right at the end.

I called up Daisy half an hour after we found him, called her instinctively and without hesitation. But she and Tom had gone away early that afternoon, and taken baggage with them.

'Left no address?'

'No.'

'Say when they'd be back?'

'No.'

'Any idea where they are? How I could reach them?'

'I don't know. Can't say.'

I wanted to get somebody for him. I wanted to go into the room where he lay and reassure him: 'I'll get somebody for you, Gatsby. Don't worry. Just trust me and I'll get somebody for you – '

Meyer Wolfsheim's name wasn't in the phone book. The butler gave me his once address on Broadway, and I called Information, but by the time I had the number it was long after five, and no one answered the phone.

'Will you ring again?'

'I've rung them three times.'

'It's very important.'

'Sorry. I'm afraid no one's there.'

I went back to the drawing-room and thought for an instant that they were chance visitors, all these official people who suddenly filled it. But, though they drew back the sheet and looked at Gatsby with shocked eyes, his protest continued in my brain: 'Look here, old sport, you've got to get somebody for me. You've got to try hard. I can't go through this alone.'

Someone started to ask me questions, but I broke away and going upstairs looked hastily through the unlocked parts of his desk – he'd never told me definitely that his parents were dead. But there was nothing – only the picture of Dan Cody, a token of forgotten violence, staring down from the wall.

Next morning I sent the butler to New York with a letter to Wolfsheim, which asked for information and urged him to come out on the next train. That request seemed superfluous when I wrote it. I was sure he'd start when he saw the newspapers, just as I was sure there'd be a wire from Daisy before noon – but neither a wire nor Mr Wolfsheim arrived; no one arrived except more police and photographers and newspaper men. When the butler brought back Wolfsheim's answer I began to have a feeling of defiance, of scornful solidarity between Gatsby and me against them all.

> DEAR MR CARRAWAY – This has been one of the most terrible shocks of my life to me I hardly can believe it that it is true at all. Such a mad act as that man did should make us all think. I cannot come down now as I am tied up in some very important business and cannot get mixed up in this thing now. If there is anything I can do a little later let me know in a letter by Edgar. I hardly know where I am when I hear about a thing like this and am completely knocked down and out.
>
> Yours truly MEYER WOLFSHEIM

and then hasty addenda beneath:

> Let me know about the funeral etc. Do not know his family at all.

When the phone rang that afternoon and Long Distance said Chicago was calling I thought this would be Daisy at last. But the connection came through as a man's voice, very thin and far away.

'This is Slagle speaking . . . '

'Yes?' The name was unfamiliar.

'Hell of a note, isn't it? Get my wire?'

'There haven't been any wires.'

'Young Parke's in trouble,' he said rapidly. 'They picked him up when he handed the bonds over the counter. They got a circular from New York giving 'em the numbers just five minutes before. What d'you know about that, hey? You never can tell in these hick towns – '

'Hello!' I interrupted breathlessly. 'Look here – this isn't Mr Gatsby. Mr Gatsby's dead.'

There was a long silence on the other end of the wire, followed by an exclamation . . . then a quick squawk as the connection was broken.

I think it was on the third day that a telegram signed Henry C. Gatz arrived from a town in Minnesota. It said only that the sender was leaving immediately and to postpone the funeral until he came.

It was Gatsby's father, a solemn old man, very helpless and dismayed, bundled up in a long cheap ulster against the warm September day. His eyes leaked continuously with excitement, and when I took the bag and umbrella from his hands he began to pull so incessantly at his sparse grey beard that I had difficulty in getting off his coat. He was on the point of collapse, so I took him into the music-room and made him sit down while I sent for something to eat. But he wouldn't eat, and the glass of milk spilled from his trembling hand.

'I saw it in the Chicago newspaper,' he said. 'It was all in the Chicago newspaper. I started right away.'

'I didn't know how to reach you.'

His eyes, seeing nothing, moved ceaselessly about the room.

'It was a madman,' he said. 'He must have been mad.'

'Wouldn't you like some coffee?' I urged him.

'I don't want anything. I'm all right now, Mr – '

'Carraway.'

'Well, I'm all right now. Where have they got Jimmy?'

I took him into the drawing-room, where his son lay, and left him there. Some little boys had come up on the steps and were looking into the hall; when I told them who had arrived, they went reluctantly away.

After a little while Mr Gatz opened the door and came out, his mouth ajar, his face flushed slightly, his eyes leaking isolated and unpunctual tears. He had reached an age where death no longer has the quality of ghastly surprise, and when he looked around him now for the first time and saw the height and splendour of the hall and the great rooms opening out from it into other rooms, his grief began to be mixed with an awed pride. I helped him to a bedroom upstairs; while he took off his coat and vest I told him that all arrangements had been deferred until he came.

'I didn't know what you'd want, Mr Gatsby – '

'Gatz is my name.'

' – Mr Gatz. I thought you might want to take the body West.'

He shook his head.

'Jimmy always liked it better down East. He rose up to his position in the East. Were you a friend of my boy's, Mr – ?'

'We were close friends.'

'He had a big future before him, you know. He was only a young man, but he had a lot of brain power here.'

He touched his head impressively, and I nodded.

'If he'd of lived, he'd of been a great man. A man like James J. Hill. He'd of helped build up the country.'

'That's true,' I said, uncomfortably.

He fumbled at the embroidered coverlet, trying to take it from the bed, and lay down stiffly – and was instantly asleep.

That night an obviously frightened person called up, and demanded to know who I was before he would give his name.

'This is Mr Carraway,' I said.

'Oh!' He sounded relieved. 'This is Klipspringer.'

I was relieved too, for that seemed to promise another friend at Gatsby's grave. I didn't want it to be in the papers and draw a sightseeing crowd, so I'd been calling up a few people myself. They were hard to find.

'The funeral's tomorrow,' I said. 'Three o'clock, here at the house. I wish you'd tell anybody who'd be interested.'

'Oh, I will,' he broke out hastily. 'Of course I'm not likely to see anybody, but if I do – '

His tone made me suspicious.

'Of course you'll be there yourself.'

'Well, I'll certainly try. What I called up about is – '

'Wait a minute,' I interrupted. 'How about saying you'll come?'

'Well, the fact is – the truth of the matter is that I'm staying with some people up here in Greenwich, and they rather expect me to be with them tomorrow. In fact, there's a sort of picnic or something. Of course I'll do my very best to get away.'

I ejaculated an unrestrained 'Huh' and he must have heard me, for he went on nervously: 'What I called up about was a pair of shoes I left there. I wonder if it'd be too much trouble to have the butler send them on. You see, they're tennis shoes, and I'm sort of helpless without them. My address is care of B. F. – '

I didn't hear the rest of the name, because I hung up the receiver.

After that I felt a certain shame for Gatsby – one gentleman to whom I telephoned implied that he had got what he deserved. However, that was my fault, for he was one of those who used to sneer most bitterly at Gatsby on the courage of Gatsby's liquor, and I should have known better than to call him.

The morning of the funeral I went up to New York to see Meyer Wolfsheim; I couldn't seem to reach him any other way. The door that I pushed open, on the advice of an elevator boy, was marked 'The Swastika Holding Company', and at first there didn't seem to be anyone inside. But when I'd shouted, 'Hello,' several times in vain, an argument broke out behind a partition, and presently a lovely Jewess appeared at an interior door and scrutinised me with black hostile eyes.

'Nobody's in,' she said. 'Mr Wolfsheim's gone to Chicago.'

The first part of this was obviously untrue, for someone had begun to whistle 'The Rosary', tunelessly, inside.

'Please say that Mr Carraway wants to see him.'

'I can't get him back from Chicago, can I?'

At this moment a voice, unmistakably Wolfsheim's, called 'Stella!' from the other side of the door.

'Leave your name on the desk,' she said quickly. 'I'll give it to him when he gets back.'

'But I know he's there.'

She took a step towards me and began to slide her hands indignantly up and down her hips.

'You young men think you can force your way in here any time,' she scolded. 'We're getting sickantired of it. When I say he's in Chicago, he's in Chi*ca*go.'

I mentioned Gatsby.

'Oh–h!' She looked at me over again. 'Will you just – What was your name?'

She vanished. In a moment Meyer Wolfsheim stood solemnly in the doorway, holding out both hands. He drew me into his office, remarking in a reverent voice that it was a sad time for all of us, and offered me a cigar.

'My memory goes back to when first I met him,' he said. 'A young major just out of the army and covered over with medals he got in the war. He was so hard up he had to keep on wearing his uniform because he couldn't buy some regular clothes. First time I saw him was when he come into Winebrenner's poolroom at Forty-third Street and asked for a job. He hadn't ate anything for a couple of days. "Come on have some lunch with me," I said. He ate more than four dollars' worth of food in half an hour.'

'Did you start him in business?' I enquired.

'Start him! I made him.'

'Oh.'

'I raised him up out of nothing, right out of the gutter. I saw right away he was a fine-appearing, gentlemanly young man, and when he told me he was an Oggsford I knew I could use him good. I got him to join up in the American Legion and he used to stand high there. Right off he did some work for a client of mine up to Albany. We were so thick like that in everything' – he held up two bulbous fingers – 'always together.'

I wondered if this partnership had included the World's Series transaction in 1919.

'Now he's dead,' I said after a moment. 'You were his closest friend, so I know you'll want to come to his funeral this afternoon.'

'I'd like to come.'

'Well, come then.'

The hair in his nostrils quivered slightly, and as he shook his head his eyes filled with tears.

'I can't do it – I can't get mixed up in it,' he said.

'There's nothing to get mixed up in. It's all over now.'

'When a man gets killed I never like to get mixed up in it in any way. I keep out. When I was a young man it was different – if a friend of mine died, no matter how, I stuck with them to the end. You may think that's sentimental, but I mean it – to the bitter end.'

I saw that for some reason of his own he was determined not to come, so I stood up.

'Are you a college man?' he enquired suddenly.

For a moment I thought he was going to suggest a 'gonnegtion', but he only nodded and shook my hand.

'Let us learn to show our friendship for a man when he is alive and not after he is dead,' he suggested. 'After that, my own rule is to let everything alone.'

When I left his office the sky had turned dark and I got back to West Egg in a drizzle. After changing my clothes I went next door and found Mr Gatz walking up and down excitedly in the hall. His pride in his son and in his son's possessions was continually increasing and now he had something to show me.

'Jimmy sent me this picture.' He took out his wallet with trembling fingers. 'Look there.'

It was a photograph of the house, cracked in the corners and dirty with many hands. He pointed out every detail to me eagerly. 'Look there!' and then sought admiration from my eyes. He had shown it so often that I think it was more real to him now than the house itself.

'Jimmy sent it to me. I think it's a very pretty picture. It shows up well.'

'Very well. Had you seen him lately?'

'He came out to see me two years ago and bought me the house I live in now. Of course we was broke up when he run off from home, but I see now there was a reason for it. He knew he had a big future in front of him. And ever since he made a success he was very generous with me.'

He seemed reluctant to put away the picture, held it for another minute, lingeringly, before my eyes. Then he returned the wallet and pulled from his pocket a ragged old copy of a book called *Hopalong Cassidy*.

'Look here, this is a book he had when he was a boy. It just shows you.'

He opened it at the back cover and turned it around for me to see. On the last flyleaf was printed the word Schedule, and the date September 12, 1906. And underneath:

Rise from bed	6.00	a.m.
Dumb-bell exercise and wall-scaling	6.15 – 6.30	"
Study electricity, etc.	7.15 – 8.15	"
Work	8.30 – 4.30	p.m.
Baseball and sports	4.30 – 5.00	"
Practise elocution, poise and how to attain it	1.00 – 6.00	"
Study needed inventions	7.00 – 9.00	"

GENERAL RESOLVES

No wasting time at Shafters or [a name, indecipherable]
No more smoking or chewing
Bath every other day
Read one improving book or magazine per week
Save $5.00 [crossed out] $3.00 per week
Be better to parents

'I come across this book by accident,' said the old man. 'It just shows you, don't it?

'Jimmy was bound to get ahead. He always had some resolves like this or something. Do you notice what he's got about improving his mind? He was always great for that. He told me I et like a hog once, and I beat him for it.'

He was reluctant to close the book, reading each item aloud and then looking eagerly at me. I think he rather expected me to copy down the list for my own use.

A little before three the Lutheran minister arrived from Flushing, and I began to look involuntarily out the windows for other cars. So did Gatsby's father. And as the time passed and the servants came in and stood waiting in the hall, his eyes began to blink anxiously, and he spoke of the rain in a worried, uncertain way. The minister glanced several times at his watch, so I took him aside and asked him to wait for half an hour. But it wasn't any use. Nobody came.

About five o'clock our procession of three cars reached the cemetery and stopped in a thick drizzle beside the gate – first a motor hearse, horribly black and wet, then Mr Gatz and the minister and I in the limousine, and a little later four or five servants and the postman from West Egg, in Gatsby's station-wagon, all wet to the skin. As we started through the gate into the cemetery I heard a car stop and then the sound of someone splashing after us over the soggy ground. I looked around. It was the man with owl-eyed glasses whom I had found marvelling over Gatsby's books in the library one night three months before.

I'd never seen him since then. I don't know how he knew about the funeral, or even his name. The rain poured down his thick glasses, and he took them off and wiped them to see the protecting canvas unrolled from Gatsby's grave.

I tried to think about Gatsby then for a moment, but he was already too far away, and I could only remember, without resentment, that Daisy hadn't sent a message or a flower. Dimly I heard someone murmur, 'Blessed are the dead that the rain falls on,' and then the owl-eyed man said, 'Amen to that,' in a brave voice.

We straggled down quickly through the rain to the cars. Owl-eyes spoke to me by the gate.

'I couldn't get to the house,' he remarked.

'Neither could anybody else.'

'Go on!' He started. 'Why, my God! they used to go there by the hundreds.' He took off his glasses and wiped them again, outside and in. 'The poor son-of-a-bitch,' he said.

One of my most vivid memories is of coming back West from prep school and later from college at Christmastime. Those who went farther than Chicago would gather in the old dim Union Station at six o'clock of a December evening, with a few Chicago friends, already caught up into their own holiday gaieties, to bid them a hasty goodbye. I remember the fur coats of the girls returning from Miss This-or-That's and the chatter of frozen breath and the hands waving overhead as we caught sight of old acquaintances, and the matchings of invitations: 'Are you going to the Ordways'? the Herseys'? the Schultzes'?' and the long green tickets clasped tight in our gloved hands. And last the murky yellow cars of the Chicago, Milwaukee & St Paul Railroad looking cheerful as Christmas itself on the tracks beside the gate.

When we pulled out into the winter night and the real snow, our snow, began to stretch out beside us and twinkle against the windows, and the dim lights of small Wisconsin stations moved by, a sharp wild brace came suddenly into the air. We drew in deep breaths of it as we walked back from dinner through the cold vestibules, unutterably aware of our identity with this country for one strange hour, before we melted indistinguishably into it again.

That's my Middle West – not the wheat or the prairies or the lost Swede towns, but the thrilling returning trains of my youth, and the street lamps and sleigh bells in the frosty dark and the shadows of holly wreaths thrown by lighted windows on the snow. I am part of that, a little solemn with the feel of those long winters, a little complacent from growing up in the Carraway house in a city where dwellings are still called through decades by a family's name. I see now that this has been a story of the West, after all – Tom and

Gatsby, Daisy and Jordan and I were all Westerners, and perhaps we possessed some deficiency in common which made us subtly unadaptable to Eastern life.

Even when the East excited me most, even when I was most keenly aware of its superiority to the bored, sprawling, swollen towns beyond the Ohio, with their interminable inquisitions which spared only the children and the very old – even then it had always for me a quality of distortion. West Egg, especially, still figures in my more fantastic dreams. I see it as a night scene by El Greco: a hundred houses, at once conventional and grotesque, crouching under a sullen, overhanging sky and a lustreless moon. In the foreground four solemn men in dress suits are walking long the sidewalk with a stretcher on which lies a drunken woman in a white evening dress. Her hand, which dangles over the side, sparkles cold with jewels. Gravely the men turn in at a house – the wrong house. But no one knows the woman's name, and no one cares.

After Gatsby's death the East was haunted for me like that, distorted beyond my eyes' power of correction. So when the blue smoke of brittle leaves was in the air and the wind blew the wet laundry stiff on the line I decided to come back home.

There was one thing to be done before I left, an awkward, unpleasant thing that perhaps had better have been let alone. But I wanted to leave things in order and not just trust that obliging and indifferent sea to sweep my refuse away. I saw Jordan Baker and talked over and around what had happened to us together, and what had happened afterwards to me, and she lay perfectly still, listening, in a big chair.

She was dressed to play golf, and I remember thinking she looked like a good illustration, her chin raised a little jauntily, her hair the colour of an autumn leaf, her face the same brown tint as the fingerless glove on her knee. When I had finished she told me without comment that she was engaged to another man. I doubted that, though there were several she could have married at a nod of her head, but I pretended to be surprised. For just a minute I wondered if I wasn't making a mistake, then I thought it all over again quickly and got up to say goodbye.

'Nevertheless you did throw me over,' said Jordan suddenly. 'You threw me over on the telephone. I don't give a damn about you now, but it was a new experience for me, and I felt a little dizzy for a while.'

We shook hands.

'Oh, and do you remember' – she added – 'a conversation we had once about driving a car?'

'Why – not exactly.'

'You said a bad driver was only safe until she met another bad driver? Well, I met another bad driver, didn't I? I mean it was careless of me to make such a wrong guess. I thought you were rather an honest, straightforward person. I thought it was your secret pride.'

'I'm thirty,' I said. 'I'm five years too old to lie to myself and call it honour.'

She didn't answer. Angry, and half in love with her, and tremendously sorry, I turned away.

One afternoon late in October I saw Tom Buchanan. He was walking ahead of me along Fifth Avenue in his alert, aggressive way, his hands out a little from his body as if to fight off interference, his head moving sharply here and there, adapting itself to his restless eyes. Just as I slowed up to avoid overtaking him he stopped and began frowning into the windows of a jewellery store. Suddenly he saw me and walked back, holding out his hand.

'What's the matter, Nick? Do you object to shaking hands with me?'

'Yes. You know what I think of you.'

'You're crazy, Nick,' he said quickly. 'Crazy as hell. I don't know what's the matter with you.'

'Tom,' I enquired, 'what did you say to Wilson that afternoon?'

He stared at me without a word, and I knew I had guessed right about those missing hours. I started to turn away, but he took a step after me and grabbed my arm.

'I told him the truth,' he said. 'He came to the door while we were getting ready to leave, and when I sent down word that we weren't in he tried to force his way upstairs. He was crazy enough to kill me if I hadn't told him who owned the car. His hand was on a revolver in his pocket every minute he was in the house – ' He broke off defiantly. 'What if I did tell him? That fellow had it coming to him. He threw dust into your eyes just like he did in Daisy's, but he was a tough one. He ran over Myrtle like you'd run over a dog and never even stopped his car.'

There was nothing I could say, except the one unutterable fact that it wasn't true.

'And if you think I didn't have my share of suffering – look here, when I went to give up that flat and saw that damn box of dog biscuits sitting there on the sideboard, I sat down and cried like a baby. By God, it was awful – '

I couldn't forgive him or like him, but I saw that what he had done was, to him, entirely justified. It was all very careless and confused. They were careless people, Tom and Daisy – they smashed up things and creatures and then retreated back into their money or their vast carelessness, or whatever it was that kept them together, and let other people clean up the mess they had made . . .

I shook hands with him; it seemed silly not to for I felt suddenly as though I were talking to a child. Then he went into the jewellery store to buy a pearl necklace – or perhaps only a pair of cuff buttons – rid of my provincial squeamishness for ever.

Gatsby's house was still empty when I left – the grass on his lawn had grown as long as mine. One of the taxi drivers in the village never took a fare past the entrance gate without stopping for a minute and pointing inside; perhaps it was he who drove Daisy and Gatsby over to East Egg the night of the accident, and perhaps he had made a story about it all his own. I didn't want to hear it and I avoided him when I got off the train.

I spent my Saturday nights in New York, because those gleaming, dazzling parties of his were with me so vividly that I could still hear the music and the laughter, faint and incessant, from his garden, and the cars going up and down his drive. One night I did hear a material car there, and saw its lights stop at his front steps. But I didn't investigate. Probably it was some final guest who had been away at the ends of the earth and didn't know that the party was over.

On the last night, with my trunk packed and my car sold to the grocer, I went over and looked at that huge incoherent failure of a house once more. On the white steps an obscene word, scrawled by some boy with a piece of brick, stood out clearly in the moonlight, and I erased it, drawing my shoe raspingly along the stone. Then I wandered down to the beach and sprawled out on the sand.

Most of the big shore places were closed now and there were hardly any lights except the shadowy, moving glow of a ferryboat across the Sound. And as the moon rose higher the inessential houses began to melt away until gradually I became aware of the old island here that flowered once for Dutch sailors' eyes – a fresh, green breast of the new world. Its vanished trees, the trees that had made way for Gatsby's house, had once pandered in whispers to the last and greatest of all human dreams; for a transitory enchanted moment man must have held his breath in the presence of this continent, compelled into an aesthetic contemplation he neither understood nor desired, face to face for the last time in history with something commensurate to his capacity for wonder.

And as I sat there brooding on the old, unknown world, I thought of Gatsby's wonder when he first picked out the green light at the end of Daisy's dock. He had come a long way to this blue lawn, and his dream must have seemed so close that he could hardly fail to grasp it. He did not know that it was already behind him, somewhere back in that vast obscurity beyond the city, where the dark fields of the republic rolled on under the night.

Gatsby believed in the green light, the orgastic future that year by year recedes before us. It eluded us then, but that's no matter – tomorrow we will run faster, stretch out our arms farther . . . And one fine morning –

So we beat on, boats against the current, borne back ceaselessly into the past.

TEN SHORT STORIES

Absolution

1

There was once a priest with cold, watery eyes, who, in the still of the night, wept cold tears. He wept because the afternoons were warm and long, and he was unable to attain a complete mystical union with our Lord. Sometimes, near four o'clock, there was a rustle of Swede girls along the path by his window, and in their shrill laughter he found a terrible dissonance that made him pray aloud for the twilight to come. At twilight the laughter and the voices were quieter, but several times he had walked past Romberg's Drugstore when it was dusk and the yellow lights shone inside and the nickel taps of the soda-fountain were gleaming, and he had found the scent of cheap toilet soap desperately sweet upon the air. He passed that way when he returned from hearing confessions on Saturday nights, and he grew careful to walk on the other side of the street so that the smell of the soap would float upwards before it reached his nostrils as it drifted, rather like incense, towards the summer moon.

But there was no escape from the hot madness of four o'clock. From his window, as far as he could see, the Dakota wheat thronged the valley of the Red River. The wheat was terrible to look upon and the carpet pattern to which in agony he bent his eyes sent his thoughts brooding through grotesque labyrinths, open always to the unavoidable sun.

One afternoon when he had reached the point where the mind runs down like an old clock, his housekeeper brought into his study a beautiful, intense little boy of eleven named Rudolph Miller. The little boy sat down in a patch of sunshine, and the priest, at his walnut desk, pretended to be very busy. This was to conceal his relief that someone had come into his haunted room.

Presently he turned around and found himself staring into two enormous, staccato eyes, lit with gleaming points of cobalt light.

For a moment their expression startled him – then he saw that his visitor was in a state of abject fear.

'Your mouth is trembling,' said Father Schwartz, in a haggard voice.

The little boy covered his quivering mouth with his hand.

'Are you in trouble?' asked Father Schwartz, sharply. 'Take your hand away from your mouth and tell me what's the matter.'

The boy – Father Schwartz recognised him now as the son of a parishioner, Mr Miller the freight-agent – moved his hand reluctantly off his mouth and became articulate in a despairing whisper.

'Father Schwartz – I've committed a terrible sin.'

'A sin against purity?'

'No, father . . . worse.'

Father Schwartz's body jerked sharply.

'Have you killed somebody?'

'No – but I'm afraid – ' the voice rose to a shrill whimper.

'Do you want to go to confession?'

The little boy shook his head miserably. Father Schwartz cleared his throat so that he could make his voice soft and say some quiet, kind thing. In this moment he should forget his own agony, and try to act like God. He repeated to himself a devotional phrase, hoping that in return God would help him to act correctly.

'Tell me what you've done,' said his new soft voice.

The little boy looked at him through his tears, and was reassured by the impression of moral resiliency which the distraught priest had created. Abandoning as much of himself as he was able to this man, Rudolph Miller began to tell his story.

'On Saturday, three days ago, my father he said I had to go to confession, because I hadn't been for a month, and the family they go every week, and I hadn't been. So I knew I had to go, I didn't care. But I put it off till after supper because I was playing with a bunch of kids and father asked me if I went, and I said, "No," and he took me by the neck and he said, "You go now," so I said, "All right," so I went over to church. And he yelled after me: "Don't come back till you go" . . .

2

'On Saturday, Three Days Ago . . .'

The plush curtain of the confessional rearranged its dismal creases, leaving exposed only the bottom of an old man's old shoe. Behind the curtain an immortal soul was alone with God and the Revd Adolphus Schwartz, priest of the parish. Sound began, a laboured whispering, sibilant and discreet, broken at intervals by the voice of the priest in audible question.

Rudolph Miller knelt in the pew beside the confessional and waited, straining nervously to hear and yet not to hear what was being said within. The fact that the priest was audible alarmed him. His own turn came next, and the three or four others who waited might listen unscrupulously while he admitted his violations of the Sixth and Ninth Commandments.

Rudolph had never committed adultery, nor even coveted his neighbour's wife – but it was the confession of the associate sins that was particularly hard to contemplate. In comparison he relished the less shameful fallings away – they formed a greyish background which relieved the ebony mark of sexual offences upon his soul.

He had been covering his ears with his hands, hoping that his refusal to hear would be noticed, and a like courtesy rendered to him in turn, when a sharp movement of the penitent in the confessional made him sink his face precipitately into the crook of his elbow. Fear assumed solid form, and pressed out a lodging between his heart and his lungs. He must try now with all his might to be sorry for his sins – not because he was afraid, but because he had offended God. He must convince God that he was sorry and to do so he must first convince himself. After a tense emotional struggle he achieved a tremulous self-pity, and decided that he was now ready. If, by allowing no other thought to enter his head, he could preserve this state of emotion unimpaired until he went into that large coffin set on end, he would have survived another crisis in his religious life.

For some time, however, a demoniac notion had partially possessed him. He could go home now, before his turn came, and tell his mother that he had arrived too late, and found the priest gone. This, unfortunately, involved the risk of being caught in a lie. As an alternative he could say that he *had* gone to confession, but this meant that he must avoid communion next day, for communion taken upon an uncleansed soul would turn to poison in his mouth, and he would crumple limp and damned from the altar-rail.

Again Father Schwartz's voice became audible.

'And for your – '

The words blurred to a husky mumble, and Rudolph got excitedly to his feet. He felt that it was impossible for him to go to confession this afternoon. He hesitated tensely. Then from the confessional came a tap, a creak and a sustained rustle. The slide had fallen and the plush curtain trembled. Temptation had come to him too late . . .

'Bless me, father, for I have sinned . . . I confess to Almighty God and to you, father, that I have sinned . . . Since my last confession it has been one month and three days . . . I accuse myself of – taking the Name of the Lord in vain . . . '

This was an easy sin. His curses had been but bravado – telling of them was little less than a brag.

' . . . of being mean to an old lady.'

The wan shadow moved a little on the latticed slat.

'How, my child?'

'Old lady Swenson,' Rudolph's murmur soared jubilantly. 'She got our baseball that we knocked in her window, and she wouldn't give it back, so we yelled, "Twenty-three, Skidoo," at her all afternoon. Then about five o'clock she had a fit, and they had to have the doctor.'

'Go on, my child.'

'Of – of not believing I was the son of my parents.'

'What?' The interrogator was distinctly startled.

'Of not believing that I was the son of my parents.'

'Why not?'

'Oh, just pride,' answered the penitent airily.

'You mean you thought you were too good to be the son of your parents?'

'Yes, father.' On a less jubilant note.

'Go on.'

'Of being disobedient and calling my mother names. Of slandering people behind their back. Of smoking – '

Rudolph had now exhausted the minor offences, and was approaching the sins it was agony to tell. He held his fingers against his face like bars as if to press out between them the shame in his heart.

'Of dirty words and immodest thoughts and desires,' he whispered very low.

'How often?'

'I don't know.'

'Once a week? Twice a week?'

'Twice a week.'

'Did you yield to these desires?'

'No, father.'

'Were you alone when you had them?'

'No, father. I was with two boys and a girl.'

'Don't you know, my child, that you should avoid the occasions of sin as well as the sin itself? Evil companionship leads to evil desires and evil desires to evil actions. Where were you when this happened?'

'In a barn in back of – '

'I don't want to hear any names,' interrupted the priest sharply.

'Well, it was up in the loft of this barn and this girl and – a fella, they were saying things – saying immodest things, and I stayed.'

'You should have gone – you should have told the girl to go.'

He should have gone! He could not tell Father Schwartz how his pulse had bumped in his wrist, how a strange, romantic excitement had possessed him when those curious things had been said. Perhaps in the houses of delinquency among the dull and hard-eyed incorrigible girls can be found those for whom has burned the whitest fire.

'Have you anything else to tell me?'

'I don't think so, father.'

Rudolph felt a great relief. Perspiration had broken out under his tight-pressed fingers.

'Have you told any lies?'

The question startled him. Like all those who habitually and instinctively lie, he had an enormous respect and awe for the truth. Something almost exterior to himself dictated a quick, hurt answer.

'Oh, no, father, I never tell lies.'

For a moment, like the commoner in the king's chair, he tasted the pride of the situation. Then as the priest began to murmur conventional admonitions he realised that in heroically denying he had told lies, he had committed a terrible sin – he had told a lie in confession.

In automatic response to Father Schwartz's, 'Make an act of contrition,' he began to repeat aloud meaninglessly: 'Oh, my God, I am heartily sorry for having offended Thee . . . '

He must fix this now – it was a bad mistake – but as his teeth shut on the last words of his prayer there was a sharp sound, and the slat was closed.

A minute later when he emerged into the twilight the relief in coming from the muggy church into an open world of wheat and sky postponed the full realisation of what he had done. Instead of worrying he took a deep breath of the crisp air and began to say over and over to himself the words 'Blatchford Sarnemington, Blatchford Sarnemington!'

Blatchford Sarnemington was himself, and these words were in effect a lyric. When he became Blatchford Sarnemington a suave nobility flowed from him. Blatchford Sarnemington lived in great sweeping triumphs. When Rudolph half closed his eyes it meant that Blatchford had established dominance over him and, as he went by, there were envious mutters in the air: 'Blatchford Sarnemington! There goes Blatchford Sarnemington.'

He was Blatchford now for a while as he strutted homewards along the staggering road, but when the road braced itself in macadam in order to become the main street of Ludwig, Rudolph's exhilaration faded out and his mind cooled, and he felt the horror of his lie. God, of course, already knew of it – but Rudolph reserved a corner of his mind where he was safe from God, where he prepared the subterfuges with which he often tricked God. Hiding now in this corner he considered how he could best avoid the consequences of his misstatement.

At all costs he must avoid communion next day. The risk of angering God to such an extent was too great. He would have to drink water 'by accident' in the morning, and thus, in accordance with a church law, render himself unfit to receive communion that day. In spite of its flimsiness, this subterfuge was the most feasible that occurred to him. He accepted its risks, and was concentrating on how best to put it into effect as he turned the corner by Romberg's Drugstore and came in sight of his father's house.

3

Rudolph's father, the local freight-agent, had floated with the second wave of German and Irish stock to the Minnesota-Dakota country. Theoretically, great opportunities lay ahead of a young man of energy in that day and place, but Carl Miller had been incapable of establishing either with his superiors or his subordinates the reputation for approximate immutability which is essential to success in a hierarchic industry. Somewhat gross, he was, nevertheless, insufficiently hard-headed and unable to take fundamental relationships for granted, and this inability made him suspicious, unrestful, and continually dismayed.

His two bonds with the colourful life were his faith in the Roman Catholic Church and his mystical worship of the Empire Builder, James J. Hill. Hill was the apotheosis of that quality in which Miller himself was deficient – the sense of things, the feel of things, the hint of rain in the wind on the cheek. Miller's mind worked late on the old decisions of other men, and he had never in his life felt the balance of any single thing in his hands. His weary, sprightly, undersized body was growing old in Hill's gigantic shadow. For twenty years he had lived alone with Hill's name and God.

On Sunday morning Carl Miller awoke in the dustless quiet of six o'clock. Kneeling by the side of the bed he bent his yellow-grey hair and the full dapple bangs of his moustache into the pillow, and prayed for several minutes. Then he drew off his nightshirt – like the rest of his generation he had never been able to endure pyjamas – and clothed his thin, white, hairless body in woollen underwear.

He shaved. Silence in the other bedroom where his wife lay nervously asleep. Silence from the screened-off corner of the hall where his son's cot stood, and his son slept among his Alger books, his collection of cigar-bands, his mothy pennants – 'Cornell', 'Hamlin', and 'Greetings from Pueblo, New Mexico' – and the other possessions of his private life. From outside Miller could hear the shrill birds and the whirring movement of the poultry, and, as an undertone, the low, swelling click-a-tick of the six-fifteen through-train for Montana and the green coast beyond. Then as the cold water dripped from the wash-rag in his hand he raised his head suddenly – he had heard a furtive sound from the kitchen below.

He dried his razor hastily, slipped his dangling suspenders to his shoulder, and listened. Someone was walking in the kitchen, and he knew by the light footfall that it was not his wife. With his mouth faintly ajar he ran quickly down the stairs and opened the kitchen door.

Standing by the sink, with one hand on the still dripping faucet and the other clutching a full glass of water, stood his son. The boy's eyes, still heavy with sleep, met his father's with a frightened, reproachful beauty. He was barefooted, and his pyjamas were rolled up at the knees and sleeves.

For a moment they both remained motionless – Carl Miller's brow went down and his son's went up, as though they were striking a balance between the extremes of emotion which filled them. Then the bangs of the parent's moustache descended portentously until they obscured his mouth, and he gave a short glance around to see if anything had been disturbed.

The kitchen was garnished with sunlight which beat on the pans and made the smooth boards of the floor and table yellow and clean as wheat. It was the centre of the house where the fire burned and the tins fitted into tins like toys, and the steam whistled all day on a thin pastel note. Nothing was moved, nothing touched –

except the faucet where beads of water still formed and dripped with a white flash into the sink below.

'What are you doing?'

'I got awful thirsty, so I thought I'd just come down and get – '

'I thought you were going to communion.'

A look of vehement astonishment spread over his son's face.

'I forgot all about it.'

'Have you drunk any water?'

'No – '

As the word left his mouth Rudolph knew it was the wrong answer, but the faded indignant eyes facing him had signalled up the truth before the boy's will could act. He realised, too, that he should never have come downstairs; some vague necessity for verisimilitude had made him want to leave a wet glass as evidence by the sink; the honesty of his imagination had betrayed him.

'Pour it out,' commanded his father, 'that water!'

Rudolph despairingly inverted the tumbler.

'What's the matter with you, anyways?' demanded Miller angrily.

'Nothing.'

'Did you go to confession yesterday?'

'Yes.'

'Then why were you going to drink water?'

'I don't know – I forgot.'

'Maybe you care more about being a little bit thirsty than you do about your religion.'

'I forgot.' Rudolph could feel the tears straining in his eyes.

'That's no answer.'

'Well, I did.'

'You better look out!' His father held to a high, persistent, inquisitory note: 'If you're so forgetful that you can't remember your religion something better be done about it.'

Rudolph filled a sharp pause with: 'I can remember it all right.'

'First you begin to neglect your religion,' cried his father, fanning his own fierceness, 'the next thing you'll begin to lie and steal, and the *next* thing is the *reform* school!'

Not even this familiar threat could deepen the abyss that Rudolph saw before him. He must either tell all now, offering his body for what he knew would be a ferocious beating, or else tempt the thunderbolts by receiving the Body and Blood of Christ with sacrilege upon his soul. And of the two the former seemed more terrible – it was not so much the beating he dreaded as the savage ferocity, outlet of the ineffectual man, which would lie behind it.

'Put down that glass and go upstairs and dress!' his father ordered, 'and when we get to church, before you go to communion, you better kneel down and ask God to forgive you for your carelessness.'

Some accidental emphasis in the phrasing of this command acted like a catalytic agent on the confusion and terror of Rudolph's mind. A wild, proud anger rose in him, and he dashed the tumbler passionately into the sink.

His father uttered a strained, husky sound, and sprang for him. Rudolph dodged to the side, tipped over a chair, and tried to get beyond the kitchen table. He cried out sharply when a hand grasped his pajama shoulder, then he felt the dull impact of a fist against the side of his head, and glancing blows on the upper part of his body. As he slipped here and there in his father's grasp, dragged or lifted when he clung instinctively to an arm, aware of sharp smarts and strains, he made no sound except that he laughed hysterically several times. Then in less than a minute the blows abruptly ceased. After a lull during which Rudolph was tightly held, and during which they both trembled violently and uttered strange, truncated words, Carl Miller half dragged, half threatened his son upstairs.

'Put on your clothes!'

Rudolph was now both hysterical and cold. His head hurt him, and there was a long, shallow scratch on his neck from his father's fingernail, and he sobbed and trembled as he dressed. He was aware of his mother standing at the doorway in a wrapper, her wrinkled face compressing and squeezing and opening out into new series of wrinkles which floated and eddied from neck to brow. Despising her nervous ineffectuality and avoiding her rudely when she tried to touch his neck with witch-hazel, he made a hasty, choking toilet. Then he followed his father out of the house and along the road towards the Catholic church.

4

They walked without speaking except when Carl Miller acknowledged automatically the existence of passers-by. Rudolph's uneven breathing alone ruffled the hot Sunday silence.

His father stopped decisively at the door of the church.

'I've decided you'd better go to confession again. Go in and tell Father Schwartz what you did and ask God's pardon.'

'You lost your temper, too!' said Rudolph quickly.

Carl Miller took a step towards his son, who moved cautiously backwards.

'All right, I'll go.'

'Are you going to do what I say?' cried his father in a hoarse whisper.

'All right.'

Rudolph walked into the church, and for the second time in two days entered the confessional and knelt down. The slat went up almost at once.

'I accuse myself of missing my morning prayers.'

'Is that all?'

'That's all.'

A maudlin exultation filled him. Not easily ever again would he be able to put an abstraction before the necessities of his ease and pride. An invisible line had been crossed, and he had become aware of his isolation – aware that it applied not only to those moments when he was Blatchford Sarnemington but that it applied to all his inner life. Hitherto such phenomena as 'crazy' ambitions and petty shames and fears had been but private reservations, unacknowledged before the throne of his official soul. Now he realised unconsciously that his private reservations were himself – and all the rest a garnished front and a conventional flag. The pressure of his environment had driven him into the lonely secret road of adolescence.

He knelt in the pew beside his father. Mass began. Rudolph knelt up – when he was alone he slumped his posterior back against the seat – and tasted the consciousness of a sharp, subtle revenge. Beside him his father prayed that God would forgive Rudolph, and asked also that his own outbreak of temper would be pardoned. He glanced sidewise at his son, and was relieved to see that the strained, wild look had gone from his face and that he had ceased sobbing. The Grace of God, inherent in the Sacrament, would do the rest, and perhaps after Mass everything would be better. He was proud of Rudolph in his heart, and beginning to be truly as well as formally sorry for what he had done.

Usually, the passing of the collection box was a significant point for Rudolph in the services. If, as was often the case, he had no money to drop in he would be furiously ashamed and bow his head and pretend not to see the box, lest Jeanne Brady in the pew behind should take notice and suspect an acute family poverty. But today he glanced coldly into it as it skimmed under his eyes, noting with casual interest the large number of pennies it contained.

When the bell rang for communion, however, he quivered. There was no reason why God should not stop his heart. During the past twelve hours he had committed a series of mortal sins increasing in gravity, and he was now to crown them all with a blasphemous sacrilege.

'Domine, non sum dignus; ut interes sub tectum meum; sed tantum dic verbo, et sanabitur anima mea . . . '

There was a rustle in the pews, and the communicants worked their ways into the aisle with downcast eyes and joined hands. Those of larger piety pressed together their fingertips to form steeples. Among these latter was Carl Miller. Rudolph followed him towards the altar-rail and knelt down, automatically taking up the napkin under his chin. The bell rang sharply, and the priest turned from the altar with the white Host held above the chalice: 'Corpus Domini nostri Jesu Christi custodiat animam meam in vitam aeternam.'

A cold sweat broke out on Rudolph's forehead as the communion began. Along the line Father Schwartz moved, and with gathering nausea Rudolph felt his heart-valves weakening at the will of God. It seemed to him that the church was darker and that a great quiet had fallen, broken only by the inarticulate mumble which announced the approach of the Creator of Heaven and Earth. He dropped his head down between his shoulders and waited for the blow.

Then he felt a sharp nudge in his side. His father was poking him to sit up, not to slump against the rail; the priest was only two places away.

'Corpus Domini nostri Jesu Christi custodiat animam meam in vitam aeternam.'

Rudolph opened his mouth. He felt the sticky wax taste of the wafer on his tongue. He remained motionless for what seemed an interminable period of time, his head still raised, the wafer un-dissolved in his mouth. Then again he started at the pressure of his father's elbow, and saw that the people were falling away from the altar like leaves and turning with blind downcast eyes to their pews, alone with God.

Rudolph was alone with himself, drenched with perspiration and deep in mortal sin. As he walked back to his pew the sharp taps of his cloven hoofs were loud upon the floor, and he knew that it was a dark poison he carried in his heart.

5

'Sagitta Volante in Dei'

The beautiful little boy with eyes like blue stones, and lashes that sprayed open from them like flower-petals had finished telling his sin to Father Schwartz – and the square of sunshine in which he sat had moved forward half an hour into the room. Rudolph had become less frightened now; once eased of the story a reaction had set in. He knew that as long as he was in the room with this priest God would not stop his heart, so he sighed and sat quietly, waiting for the priest to speak.

Father Schwartz's cold watery eyes were fixed upon the carpet pattern on which the sun had brought out the swastikas and the flat bloomless vines and the pale echoes of flowers. The hall-clock ticked insistently towards sunset, and from the ugly room and from the afternoon outside the window arose a stiff monotony, shattered now and then by the reverberate clapping of a faraway hammer on the dry air. The priest's nerves were strung thin and the beads of his rosary were crawling and squirming like snakes upon the green felt of his table top. He could not remember now what it was he should say.

Of all the things in this lost Swede town he was most aware of this little boy's eyes – the beautiful eyes, with lashes that left them reluctantly and curved back as though to meet them once more.

For a moment longer the silence persisted while Rudolph waited, and the priest struggled to remember something that was slipping further and further away from him, and the clock ticked in the broken house. Then Father Schwartz stared hard at the little boy and remarked in a peculiar voice: 'When a lot of people get together in the best places things go glimmering.'

Rudolph started and looked quickly at Father Schwartz's face.

'I said – ' began the priest, and paused, listening. 'Do you hear the hammer and the clock ticking and the bees? Well, that's no good. The thing is to have a lot of people in the centre of the world, wherever that happens to be. Then' – his watery eyes widened knowingly – 'things go glimmering.'

'Yes, father,' agreed Rudolph, feeling a little frightened.

'What are you going to be when you grow up?'

'Well, I was going to be a baseball-player for a while,' answered Rudolph nervously, 'but I don't think that's a very good ambition, so I think I'll be an actor or a navy officer.'

Again the priest stared at him.

'I see *exactly* what you mean,' he said, with a fierce air.

Rudolph had not meant anything in particular, and at the implication that he had, he became more uneasy.

'This man is crazy,' he thought, 'and I'm scared of him. He wants me to help him out some way, and I don't want to.'

'You look as if things went glimmering,' cried Father Schwartz wildly. 'Did you ever go to a party?'

'Yes, father.'

'And did you notice that everybody was properly dressed? That's what I mean. Just as you went into the party there was a moment when everybody was properly dressed. Maybe two little girls were standing by the door and some boys were leaning over the banisters, and there were bowls around full of flowers.'

'I've been to a lot of parties,' said Rudolph, rather relieved that the conversation had taken this turn.

'Of course,' continued Father Schwartz triumphantly, 'I knew you'd agree with me. But my theory is that when a whole lot of people get together in the best places things go glimmering all the time.'

Rudolph found himself thinking of Blatchford Sarnemington.

'Please listen to me!' commanded the priest impatiently. 'Stop worrying about last Saturday. Apostasy implies an absolute damnation only on the supposition of a previous perfect faith. Does that fix it?'

Rudolph had not the faintest idea what Father Schwartz was talking about, but he nodded and the priest nodded back at him and returned to his mysterious preoccupation.

'Why,' he cried, 'they have lights now as big as stars – do you realise that? I heard of one light they had in Paris or somewhere that was as big as a star. A lot of people had it – a lot of gay people. They have all sorts of things now that you never dreamed of.

'Look here – ' He came nearer to Rudolph, but the boy drew away, so Father Schwartz went back and sat down in his chair, his eyes dried out and hot. 'Did you ever see an amusement park?'

'No, father.'

'Well, go and see an amusement park.' The priest waved his hand vaguely. 'It's a thing like a fair, only much more glittering. Go to one at night and stand a little way off from it in a dark place – under dark trees. You'll see a big wheel made of lights turning in the air, and a long slide shooting boats down into the water. A band playing somewhere, and a smell of peanuts – and everything will twinkle. But it won't remind you of anything, you see. It will all just hang out there in the night like a coloured balloon – like a big yellow lantern on a pole.'

Father Schwartz frowned as he suddenly thought of something.

'But don't get up close,' he warned Rudolph, 'because if you do you'll only feel the heat and the sweat and the life.'

All this talking seemed particularly strange and awful to Rudolph because this man was a priest. He sat there, half terrified, his beautiful eyes open wide and staring at Father Schwartz. But underneath his terror he felt that his own inner convictions were confirmed. There was something ineffably gorgeous somewhere that had nothing to do with God. He no longer thought that God was angry at him about the original lie, because He must have understood that Rudolph had done it to make things finer in the confessional, brightening up the dinginess of his admissions by saying a thing radiant and proud. At the moment when he had affirmed immaculate honour a silver pennon had flapped out into the breeze somewhere and there had been the crunch of leather and the shine of silver spurs and a troop of horsemen waiting for dawn on a low green hill. The sun had made stars of light on their breastplates like the picture at home of the German cuirassiers at Sedan.

But now the priest was muttering inarticulate and heart-broken words, and the boy became wildly afraid. Horror entered suddenly in at the open window, and the atmosphere of the room changed. Father Schwartz collapsed precipitously down on his knees, and let his body settle back against a chair.

'Oh, my God!' he cried out, in a strange voice, and wilted to the floor.

Then a human oppression rose from the priest's worn clothes, and mingled with the faint smell of old food in the corners. Rudolph gave a sharp cry and ran in a panic from the house – while the collapsed man lay there quite still, filling his room, filling it with voices and faces until it was crowded with echolalia, and rang loud with a steady, shrill note of laughter.

Outside the window the blue sirocco trembled over the wheat, and girls with yellow hair walked sensuously along roads that bounded the fields, calling innocent, exciting things to the young men who were working in the lines between the grain. Legs were shaped under starchless gingham, and rims of the necks of dresses were warm and damp. For five hours now hot fertile life had burned in the afternoon. It would be night in three hours, and all along the land there would be these blonde Northern girls and the tall young men from the farms lying out beside the wheat, under the moon.

Love in the Night

1

The words thrilled Val. They had come into his mind sometime during the fresh gold April afternoon and he kept repeating them to himself over and over: 'Love in the night; love in the night.' He tried them in three languages – Russian, French and English – and decided that they were best in English. In each language they meant a different sort of love and a different sort of night – the English night seemed the warmest and softest with the thinnest and most crystalline sprinkling of stars. The English love seemed the most fragile and romantic – a white dress and a dim face above it and eyes that were pools of light. And when I add that it was a French night he was thinking about, after all, I see I must go back and begin over.

Val was half Russian and half American. His mother was the daughter of that Morris Hasylton who helped finance the Chicago World's Fair in 1892, and his father was – see the *Almanach de Gotha*, issue of 1910 – Prince Paul Serge Boris Rostoff, son of Prince Vladimir Rostoff, grandson of a grand duke – 'Jimber-Jawed Serge' – and third-cousin-once-removed to the Tsar. It was all very impressive, you see, on that side – house in St Petersburg, shooting lodge near Riga, and swollen villa, more like a palace, overlooking the Mediterranean. It was at this villa in Cannes that the Rostoffs passed the winter – and it wasn't at all the thing to remind Princess Rostoff that this Riviera villa, from the marble fountain – after Bernini – to the gold cordial glasses – after dinner – was paid for with American gold.

The Russians, of course, were gay people on the Continent in the gala days before the war. Of the three races that used Southern France for a pleasure ground they were easily the most adept at the grand manner. The English were too practical, and the Americans, though they spent freely, had no tradition of romantic conduct. But the Russians – there was a people as gallant as the Latins, and rich besides! When the Rostoffs arrived at Cannes late in January the restaurateurs telegraphed north for the prince's favourite labels to paste on their champagne, and the jewellers put incredibly gorgeous articles aside to show to him – but not to the princess – and the Russian Church was swept and garnished for the season that the prince might beg Orthodox forgiveness for his sins. Even the Mediterranean turned obligingly to a deep wine colour in the spring evenings, and fishing boats with robin-breasted sails loitered exquisitely offshore.

In a vague way young Val realised that this was all for the benefit of him and his family. It was a privileged paradise, this white little city on the water, in which he was free to do what he liked because he was rich and young and the blood of Peter the Great ran indigo in his veins. He was only seventeen in 1914, when this history begins, but he had already fought a duel with a young man four years his senior, and he had a small hairless scar to show for it on top of his handsome head.

But the question of love in the night was the thing nearest his heart. It was a vague pleasant dream he had, something that was going to happen to him someday that would be unique and incomparable. He could have told no more about it than that there was a lovely unknown girl concerned in it, and that it ought to take place beneath the Riviera moon.

The odd thing about all this was not that he had this excited and yet almost spiritual hope of romance, for all boys of any imagination have just such hopes, but that it actually came true. And when it happened, it happened so unexpectedly; it was such a jumble of impressions and emotions, of curious phrases that sprang to his lips, of sights and sounds and moments that were here, were lost, were past, that he scarcely understood it at all. Perhaps its very vagueness preserved it in his heart and made him for ever unable to forget.

There was an atmosphere of love all about him that spring – his father's loves, for instance, which were many and indiscreet, and which Val became aware of gradually from overhearing the gossip of servants, and definitely from coming on his American mother unexpectedly one afternoon, to find her storming hysterically at his father's picture on the salon wall. In the picture his father wore a white uniform with a furred dolman and looked back impassively at his wife as if to say, 'Were you under the impression, my dear, that you were marrying into a family of clergymen?'

Val tiptoed away, surprised, confused – and excited. It didn't shock him as it would have shocked an American boy of his age. He had known for years what life was among the Continental rich, and he condemned his father only for making his mother cry.

Love went on around him – reproachless love and illicit love alike. As he strolled along the seaside promenade at nine o'clock, when the stars were bright enough to compete with the bright lamps, he was aware of love on every side. From the open-air cafés, vivid with dresses just down from Paris, came a sweet pungent odour of flowers and chartreuse and fresh black coffee and cigarettes – and mingled with them all he caught another scent, the mysterious thrilling scent of love. Hands touched jewel-sparkling hands upon the white tables. Gay dresses and white shirt-fronts swayed together, and matches were held, trembling a little, for slow-lighting cigarettes. On the other side of the boulevard lovers less fashionable, young Frenchmen who worked in the stores of Cannes, sauntered with their fiancées under the dim trees, but Val's young eyes seldom turned that way. The luxury of music and bright colours and low voices – they were all part of his dream. They were the essential trappings of love in the night.

But assume as he might the rather fierce expression that was expected from a young Russian gentleman who walked the streets alone, Val was beginning to be unhappy. April twilight had succeeded March twilight, the season was almost over, and he had found no use to make of the warm spring evenings. The girls of sixteen and seventeen whom he knew, were chaperoned with care between dusk and bedtime – this, remember, was before the war – and the others who might gladly have walked beside him were an affront to his romantic desire. So April passed by – one week, two weeks, three weeks –

He had played tennis until seven and loitered at the courts for another hour, so it was half-past eight when a tired cab horse accomplished the hill on which gleamed the façade of the Rostoff villa. The lights of his mother's limousine were yellow in the drive, and the princess, buttoning her gloves, was just coming out of the glowing door. Val tossed two francs to the cabman and went to kiss her on the cheek.

'Don't touch me,' she said quickly. 'You've been handling money.'

'But not in my mouth, mother,' he protested humorously.

The princess looked at him impatiently.

'I'm angry,' she said. 'Why must you be so late tonight? We're dining on a yacht and you were to have come along too.'

'What yacht?'

'Americans.' There was always a faint irony in her voice when she mentioned the land of her nativity. Her America was the Chicago of the nineties which she still thought of as the vast upstairs of a butcher's shop. Even the irregularities of Prince Paul were not too high a price to have paid for her escape.

'Two yachts,' she continued; 'in fact we don't know which one. The note was very indefinite. Very careless indeed.'

Americans. Val's mother had taught him to look down on Americans, but she hadn't succeeded in making him dislike them. American men noticed you, even if you were seventeen. He liked Americans. Although he was thoroughly Russian he wasn't immaculately so – the exact proportion, like that of a celebrated soap, was about ninety-nine and three-quarters per cent.

'I want to come,' he said. 'I'll hurry up, mother. I'll – '

'We're late now.' The princess turned as her husband appeared in the door. 'Now Val says he wants to come.'

'He can't,' said Prince Paul shortly. 'He's too outrageously late.'

Val nodded. Russian aristocrats, however indulgent about themselves, were always admirably Spartan with their children. There were no arguments.

'I'm sorry,' he said.

Prince Paul grunted. The footman, in red and silver livery, opened the limousine door. But the grunt decided the matter for

Val, because Princess Rostoff at that day and hour had certain grievances against her husband which gave her command of the domestic situation.

'On second thoughts you'd better come, Val,' she announced coolly. 'It's too late now, but come after dinner. The yacht is either the *Minnehaha* or the *Privateer*.' She got into the limousine. 'The one to come to will be the gayer one, I suppose – the Jacksons' yacht – '

'Find got sense,' muttered the Prince cryptically, conveying that Val would find it if he had any sense. 'Have my man take a look at you 'fore you start. Wear tie of mine 'stead of that outrageous string you affected in Vienna. Grow up. High time.'

As the limousine crawled crackling down the pebbled drive Val's face was burning.

2

It was dark in Cannes harbour, rather it seemed dark after the brightness of the promenade that Val had just left behind. Three frail dock lights glittered dimly upon innumerable fishing boats heaped like shells along the beach. Farther out in the water there were other lights where a fleet of slender yachts rode the tide with slow dignity, and farther still a full ripe moon made the water bosom into a polished dancing floor. Occasionally there was a swish! creak! drip! as a rowboat moved about in the shallows, and its blurred shape threaded the labyrinth of hobbled fishing skiffs and launches. Val, descending the velvet slope of sand, stumbled over a sleeping boatman and caught the rank savour of garlic and plain wine. Taking the man by the shoulders he shook open his startled eyes.

'Do you know where the *Minnehaha* is anchored, and the *Privateer*?'

As they slid out into the bay he lay back in the stern and stared with vague discontent at the Riviera moon. That was the right moon, all right. Frequently, five nights out of seven, there was the right moon. And here was the soft air, aching with enchantment, and here was the music, many strains of music from many orchestras, drifting out from the shore. Eastward lay the dark Cape of Antibes, and then Nice, and beyond that Monte Carlo, where the night rang chinking full of gold. Someday he would enjoy all that, too, know its every pleasure and success – when he was too old and wise to care.

But tonight – tonight, that stream of silver that waved like a wide strand of curly hair towards the moon; those soft romantic lights of Cannes behind him, the irresistible ineffable love in this air – that was to be wasted for ever.

'Which one?' asked the boatman suddenly.

'Which what?' demanded Val, sitting up.

'Which boat?'

He pointed. Val turned; above hovered the grey, sword-like prow of a yacht. During the sustained longing of his wish they had covered half a mile.

He read the brass letters over his head. It was the *Privateer*, but there were only dim lights on board, and no music and no voices, only a murmurous k-plash at intervals as the small waves leaped at the sides.

'The other one,' said Val; 'the *Minnehaha*.'

'Don't go yet.'

Val started. The voice, low and soft, had dropped down from the darkness overhead.

'What's the hurry?' said the soft voice. 'Thought maybe somebody was coming to see me, and have suffered terrible disappointment.'

The boatman lifted his oars and looked hesitatingly at Val. But Val was silent, so the man let the blades fall into the water and swept the boat out into the moonlight.

'Wait a minute!' cried Val sharply.

'Goodbye,' said the voice. 'Come again when you can stay longer.'

'But I am going to stay now,' he answered breathlessly.

He gave the necessary order and the rowboat swung back to the foot of the small companionway. Someone young, someone in a misty white dress, someone with a lovely low voice, had actually called to him out of the velvet dark. 'If she has eyes!' Val murmured to himself. He liked the romantic sound of it and repeated it under his breath – 'If she has eyes.'

'What are you?' She was directly above him now; she was looking down and he was looking up as he climbed the ladder, and as their eyes met they both began to laugh.

She was very young, slim, almost frail, with a dress that accentuated her youth by its blanched simplicity. Two wan dark spots on her cheeks marked where the colour was by day.

'What are you?' she repeated, moving back and laughing again as his head appeared on the level of the deck. 'I'm frightened now and I want to know.'

'I am a gentleman,' said Val, bowing.

'What sort of a gentleman? There are all sorts of gentlemen. There was a – there was a coloured gentleman at the table next to ours in Paris, and so – ' She broke off. 'You're not American, are you?'

'I'm Russian,' he said, as he might have announced himself to be an archangel. He thought quickly and then added, 'And I am the most fortunate of Russians. All this day, all this spring I have dreamed of falling in love on such a night, and now I see that heaven has sent me to you.'

'Just one moment!' she said, with a little gasp. 'I'm sure now that this visit is a mistake. I don't go in for anything like that. Please!'

'I beg your pardon.' He looked at her in bewilderment, unaware that he had taken too much for granted. Then he drew himself up formally.

'I have made an error. If you will excuse me I will say good-night.'

He turned away. His hand was on the rail.

'Don't go,' she said, pushing a strand of indefinite hair out of her eyes. 'On second thoughts you can talk any nonsense you like if you'll only not go. I'm miserable and I don't want to be left alone.'

Val hesitated; there was some element in this that he failed to understand. He had taken it for granted that a girl who called to a strange man at night, even from the deck of a yacht, was certainly in a mood for romance. And he wanted intensely to stay. Then he remembered that this was one of the two yachts he had been seeking.

'I imagine that the dinner's on the other boat,' he said.

'The dinner? Oh, yes, it's on the *Minnehaha.* Were you going there?'

'I was going there – a long time ago.'

'What's your name?'

He was on the point of telling her when something made him ask a question instead.

'And you? Why are you not at the party?'

'Because I preferred to stay here. Mrs Jackson said there would be some Russians there – I suppose that's you.' She looked at him with interest. 'You're a very young man, aren't you?'

'I am much older than I look,' said Val stiffly. 'People always comment on it. It's considered rather a remarkable thing.'

'How old are you?'

'Twenty-one,' he lied.

She laughed.

'What nonsense! You're not more than nineteen.'

His annoyance was so perceptible that she hastened to reassure him. 'Cheer up! I'm only seventeen myself. I might have gone to the party if I'd thought there'd be anyone under fifty there.'

He welcomed the change of subject.

'You preferred to sit and dream here beneath the moon.'

'I've been thinking of mistakes.' They sat down side by side in two canvas deckchairs. 'It's a most engrossing subject – the subject of mistakes. Women very seldom brood about mistakes – they're much more willing to forget than men are. But when they do brood – '

'You have made a mistake?' enquired Val.

She nodded.

'Is it something that cannot be repaired?'

'I think so,' she answered. 'I can't be sure. That's what I was considering when you came along.'

'Perhaps I can help in some way,' said Val. 'Perhaps your mistake is not irreparable, after all.'

'You can't,' she said unhappily. 'So let's not think about it. I'm very tired of my mistake and I'd much rather you'd tell me about all the gay, cheerful things that are going on in Cannes tonight.'

They glanced shoreward at the line of mysterious and alluring lights, the big toy banks with candles inside that were really the great fashionable hotels, the lighted clock in the old town, the blurred glow of the Café de Paris, the pricked-out points of villa windows rising on slow hills towards the dark sky.

'What is everyone doing there?' she whispered. 'It looks as though something gorgeous was going on, but what it is I can't quite tell.'

'Everyone there is making love,' said Val quietly.

'Is that it?' She looked for a long time, with a strange expression in her eyes. 'Then I want to go home to America,' she said. 'There is too much love here. I want to go home tomorrow.'

'You are afraid of being in love then?'

She shook her head.

'It isn't that. It's just because – there is no love here for me.'

'Or for me either,' added Val quietly. 'It is sad that we two should be at such a lovely place on such a lovely night and have – nothing.'

He was leaning towards her intently, with a sort of inspired and chaste romance in his eyes – and she drew back.

'Tell me more about yourself,' she enquired quickly. 'If you are Russian where did you learn to speak such excellent English?'

'My mother is American,' he admitted. 'My grandfather was American also, so she had no choice in the matter.'

'Then you're American too!'

'I am Russian,' said Val with dignity.

She looked at him closely, smiled and decided not to argue. 'Well then,' she said diplomatically, 'I suppose you must have a Russian name.'

But he had no intention now of telling her his name. A name, even the Rostoff name, would be a desecration of the night. They were their own low voices, their two white faces – and that was enough. He was sure, without any reason for being sure but with a sort of instinct that sang triumphantly through his mind, that in a little while, a minute or an hour, he was going to undergo an initiation into the life of romance. His name had no reality beside what was stirring in his heart.

'You are beautiful,' he said suddenly.

'How do you know?'

'Because for women moonlight is the hardest light of all.'

'Am I nice in the moonlight?'

'You are the loveliest thing that I have ever known.'

'Oh.' She thought this over. 'Of course I had no business to let you come on board. I might have known what we'd talk about – in this moon. But I can't sit here and look at the shore – for ever. I'm too young for that. Don't you think I'm too young for that?'

'Much too young,' he agreed solemnly.

Suddenly they both became aware of new music that was close at hand, music that seemed to come out of the water not a hundred yards away.

'Listen!' she cried. 'It's from the *Minnehaha*. They've finished dinner.'

For a moment they listened in silence.

'Thank you,' said Val suddenly.

'For what?'

He hardly knew he had spoken. He was thanking the deep low horns for singing in the breeze, the sea for its warm murmurous complaint against the bow, the milk of the stars for washing over them until he felt buoyed up in a substance more taut than air.

'So lovely,' she whispered.

'What are we going to do about it?'

'Do we have to do something about it? I thought we could just sit and enjoy – '

'You didn't think that,' he interrupted quietly. 'You know that we must do something about it. I am going to make love to you – and you are going to be glad.'

'I can't,' she said very low. She wanted to laugh now, to make some light cool remark that would bring the situation back into the safe waters of a casual flirtation. But it was too late now. Val knew that the music had completed what the moon had begun.

'I will tell you the truth,' he said. 'You are my first love. I am seventeen – the same age as you, no more.'

There was something utterly disarming about the fact that they were the same age. It made her helpless before the fate that had thrown them together. The deckchairs creaked and he was conscious of a faint illusive perfume as they swayed suddenly and childishly together.

3

Whether he kissed her once or several times he could not afterwards remember, though it must have been an hour that they sat there close together and he held her hand. What surprised him most about making love was that it seemed to have no element of wild passion – regret, desire, despair – but a delirious promise of such happiness in the world, in living, as he had never known. First love – this was only first love! What must love itself in its fullness, its perfection be. He did not know that what he was experiencing then, that unreal, undesirous medley of ecstasy and peace, would be unrecapturable for ever.

The music had ceased for some time when presently the murmurous silence was broken by the sound of a rowboat disturbing the quiet waves. She sprang suddenly to her feet and her eyes strained out over the bay.

'Listen!' she said quickly. 'I want you to tell me your name.'

'No.'

'Please,' she begged him. 'I'm going away tomorrow.'

He didn't answer.

'I don't want you to forget me,' she said. 'My name is – '

'I won't forget you. I will promise to remember you always. Whoever I may love I will always compare her to you, my first love. So long as I live you will always have that much freshness in my heart.'

'I want you to remember,' she murmured brokenly. 'Oh, this has meant more to me than it has to you – much more.'

She was standing so close to him that he felt her warm young breath on his face. Once again they swayed together. He pressed her hands and wrists between his as it seemed right to do, and kissed her lips. It was the right kiss, he thought, the romantic kiss – not too little or too much. Yet there was a sort of promise in it of other kisses he might have had, and it was with a slight sinking of his heart that he heard the rowboat close to the yacht and realised that her family had returned. The evening was over.

'And this is only the beginning,' he told himself. 'All my life will be like this night.'

She was saying something in a low quick voice and he was listening tensely.

'You must know one thing – I am married. Three months ago. That was the mistake that I was thinking about when the moon brought you out here. In a moment you will understand.'

She broke off as the boat swung against the companionway and a man's voice floated up out of the darkness.

'Is that you, my dear?'

'Yes.'

'What is this other rowboat waiting?'

'One of Mrs Jackson's guests came here by mistake and I made him stay and amuse me for an hour.'

A moment later the thin white hair and weary face of a man of sixty appeared above the level of the deck. And then Val saw and realised too late how much he cared.

4

When the Riviera season ended in May the Rostoffs and all the other Russians closed their villas and went north for the summer. The Russian Orthodox Church was locked up and so were the bins of rarer wine, and the fashionable spring moonlight was put away, so to speak, to wait for their return.

'We'll be back next season,' they said as a matter of course.

But this was premature, for they were never coming back any more. Those few who straggled south again after five tragic years were glad to get work as chambermaids or *valets de chambre* in the great hotels where they had once dined. Many of them, of course, were killed in the war or in the revolution; many of them faded out as spongers and small cheats in the big capitals, and not a few ended their lives in a sort of stupefied despair.

When the Kerensky government collapsed in 1917, Val was a lieutenant on the eastern front, trying desperately to enforce authority in his company long after any vestige of it remained. He was still trying when Prince Paul Rostoff and his wife gave up their lives one rainy morning to atone for the blunders of the Romanoffs – and the enviable career of Morris Hasylton's daughter ended in a city that bore even more resemblance to a butcher shop's than had Chicago in 1892.

After that Val fought with Denikin's army for a while until he realised that he was participating in a hollow farce and the glory of Imperial Russia was over. Then he went to France and was suddenly confronted with the astounding problem of keeping his body and soul together.

It was, of course, natural that he should think of going to America. Two vague aunts with whom his mother had quarrelled many years ago still lived there in comparative affluence. But the idea was repugnant to the prejudices his mother had implanted in him, and besides he hadn't sufficient money left to pay for his passage over. Until a possible counter-revolution should restore to him the Rostoff properties in Russia he must somehow keep alive in France.

So he went to the little city he knew best of all. He went to Cannes. His last two hundred francs bought him a third-class ticket and when he arrived he gave his dress suit to an obliging party who dealt in such things and received in return money for food and bed. He was sorry afterwards that he had sold the dress suit, because it might have helped him to a position as a waiter. But he obtained work as a taxi driver instead and was quite as happy, or rather quite as miserable, at that.

Sometimes he carried Americans to look at villas for rent, and when the front glass of the automobile was up, curious fragments of conversation drifted out to him from within.

' – heard this fellow was a Russian prince.' . . . 'Sh!' . . . 'No, this one right here.' . . . 'Be quiet, Esther!' – followed by subdued laughter.

When the car stopped, his passengers would edge around to have a look at him. At first he was desperately unhappy when girls did this; after a while he didn't mind any more. Once a cheerfully intoxicated American asked him if it were true and invited him to lunch, and another time an elderly woman seized his hand as she got out of the taxi, shook it violently and then pressed a hundred-franc note into his palm.

'Well, Florence, now I can tell 'em back home I shook hands with a Russian prince.'

The inebriated American who had invited him to lunch thought at first that Val was a son of the czar, and it had to be explained to him that a prince in Russia was simply the equivalent of a British courtesy lord. But he was puzzled that a man of Val's personality didn't go out and make some real money.

'This is Europe,' said Val gravely. 'Here money is not made. It is inherited or else it is slowly saved over a period of many years and maybe in three generations a family moves up into a higher class.'

'Think of something people want – like we do.'

'That is because there is more money to want with in America. Everything that people want here has been thought of long ago.'

But after a year and with the help of a young Englishman he had played tennis with before the war, Val managed to get into the Cannes branch of an English bank. He forwarded mail and bought railroad tickets and arranged tours for impatient sightseers. Sometimes a familiar face came to his window; if Val was recognised he shook hands; if not he kept silence. After two years he was no longer pointed out as a former prince, for the Russians were an old story now – the splendour of the Rostoffs and their friends was forgotten.

He mixed with people very little. In the evenings he walked for a while on the promenade, took a slow glass of beer in a café, and went early to bed. He was seldom invited anywhere because people thought that his sad, intent face was depressing – and he never accepted anyhow. He wore cheap French clothes now instead of the rich tweeds and flannels that had been ordered with his father's from England. As for women, he knew none at all. Of the many things he had been certain about at seventeen, he had been most certain about this – that his life would be full of romance. Now after eight years he knew that it was not to be. Somehow he had never had time for love – the war, the revolution, and now his poverty had conspired against his expectant heart. The springs of his emotion which had first poured forth one April night had dried up immediately and only a faint trickle remained.

His happy youth had ended almost before it began. He saw himself growing older and more shabby, and living always more and more in the memories of his gorgeous boyhood. Eventually he would become absurd, pulling out an old heirloom of a watch and showing it to amused young fellow clerks who would listen with winks to his tales of the Rostoff name.

He was thinking these gloomy thoughts one April evening in 1922 as he walked beside the sea and watched the never-changing magic of the awakening lights. It was no longer for his benefit, that magic, but it went on, and he was somehow glad. Tomorrow he was going away on his vacation, to a cheap hotel farther down the shore where he could bathe and rest and read; then he would come back and work some more. Every year for three years he had taken his vacation during the last two weeks in April, perhaps because it was then that he felt the most need for remembering. It was in April that what was destined to be the best part of his life had come to a culmination under a romantic moonlight. It was sacred to him – for what he had thought of as an initiation and a beginning had turned out to be the end.

He paused now in front of the Café des Étrangers and after a moment crossed the street on impulse and sauntered down to the shore. A dozen yachts, already turned to a beautiful silver colour, rode at anchor in the bay. He had seen them that afternoon, and read the names painted on their bows – but only from habit. He had done it for three years now, and it was almost a natural function of his eye.

'Un beau soir,' remarked a French voice at his elbow. It was a boatman who had often seen Val here before. 'Monsieur finds the sea beautiful?'

'Very beautiful.'

'I too. But a bad living except in the season. Next week, though, I earn something special. I am paid well for simply waiting here and doing nothing more from eight o'clock until midnight.'

'That's very nice,' said Val politely.

'A widowed lady, very beautiful, from America, whose yacht always anchors in the harbour for the last two weeks in April. If the *Privateer* comes tomorrow it will make three years.'

5

All night Val didn't sleep – not because there was any question in his mind as to what he should do, but because his long stupefied emotions were suddenly awake and alive. Of course he must not see her – not he, a poor failure with a name that was now only a shadow – but it would make him a little happier always to know that she remembered. It gave his own memory another dimension, raised it like those stereopticon glasses that bring out a picture from the flat paper. It made him sure that he had not deceived himself – he had been charming once upon a time to a lovely woman, and she did not forget.

An hour before train time next day he was at the railway station with his grip, so as to avoid any chance encounter in the street. He found himself a place in a third-class carriage of the waiting train.

Somehow as he sat there he felt differently about life – a sort of hope, faint and illusory, that he hadn't felt twenty-four hours before. Perhaps there was some way in those next few years in which he could make it possible to meet her once again – if he worked hard, threw himself passionately into whatever was at hand. He knew of at least two Russians in Cannes who had started over again with nothing except good manners and ingenuity and were now doing surprisingly well. The blood of Morris Hasylton began to throb a little in Val's temples and made him remember something he had never before cared to remember – that Morris Hasylton, who had built his daughter a palace in St Petersburg, had also started from nothing at all.

Simultaneously another emotion possessed him, less strange, less dynamic but equally American – the emotion of curiosity. In case he did – well, in case life should ever make it possible for him to seek her out, he should at least know her name.

He jumped to his feet, fumbled excitedly at the carriage handle and jumped from the train. Tossing his valise into the check room he started at a run for the American consulate.

'A yacht came in this morning,' he said hurriedly to a clerk, 'an American yacht – the *Privateer*. I want to know who owns it.'

'Just a minute,' said the clerk, looking at him oddly. 'I'll try to find out.'

After what seemed to Val an interminable time he returned.

'Why, just a minute,' he repeated hesitantly. 'We're – it seems we're finding out.'

'Did the yacht come?'

'Oh, yes – it's here all right. At least I think so. If you'll just wait in that chair.'

After another ten minutes Val looked impatiently at his watch. If they didn't hurry he'd probably miss his train. He made a nervous movement as if to get up from his chair.

'Please sit still,' said the clerk, glancing at him quickly from his desk. 'I ask you. Just sit down in that chair.'

Val stared at him. How could it possibly matter to the clerk whether or not he waited?

'I'll miss my train,' he said impatiently. 'I'm sorry to have given you all this bother – '

'Please sit still! We're glad to get it off our hands. You see, we've been waiting for your enquiry for – ah – three years.'

Val jumped to his feet and jammed his hat on his head.

'Why didn't you tell me that?' he demanded angrily.

'Because we had to get word to our – our client. Please don't go! It's – ah, it's too late.'

Val turned. Someone slim and radiant with dark frightened eyes was standing behind him, framed against the sunshine of the doorway.

'Why – '

Val's lips parted, but no words came through. She took a step towards him.

'I – ' She looked at him helplessly, her eyes filling with tears. 'I just wanted to say hello,' she murmured. 'I've come back for three years just because I wanted to say hello.'

Still Val was silent.

'You might answer,' she said impatiently. 'You might answer when I'd – when I'd just about begun to think you'd been killed in the war.' She turned to the clerk. 'Please introduce us!' she cried. 'You see, I can't say hello to him when we don't even know each other's names.'

It's the thing to distrust these international marriages, of course. It's an American tradition that they always turn out badly, and we are accustomed to such headlines as: ' "Would Trade Coronet for True American Love," says Duchess', and 'Claims Count Mendicant Tortured Toledo Wife'. The other sort of headlines are never printed, for who would want to read: ' "Castle is Love Nest," Asserts Former Georgia Belle', or 'Duke and Packer's Daughter Celebrate Golden Honeymoon'.

So far there have been no headlines at all about the young Rostoffs. Prince Val is much too absorbed in that string of moonlight-blue taxicabs which he manipulates with such unusual efficiency, to give out interviews. He and his wife only leave New York once a year – but there is still a boatman who rejoices when the *Privateer* steams into Cannes harbour on a mid-April night.

At Your Age

1

Tom Squires came into the drugstore to buy a toothbrush, a can of talcum, a gargle, Castile soap, Epsom salts and a box of cigars. Having lived alone for many years, he was methodical, and while waiting to be served he held the list in his hand. It was Christmas week and Minneapolis was under two feet of exhilarating, constantly refreshed snow; with his cane Tom knocked two clean crusts of it from his overshoes. Then, looking up, he saw the blonde girl.

She was a rare blonde, even in that Promised Land of Scandinavians, where pretty blondes are not rare. There was warm colour in her cheeks, lips and pink little hands that folded powders into papers; her hair, in long braids twisted about her head, was shining and alive. She seemed to Tom suddenly the cleanest person he knew of, and he caught his breath as he stepped forward and looked into her grey eyes.

'A can of talcum.'

'What kind?'

'Any kind . . . That's fine.'

She looked back at him apparently without self-consciousness, and, as the list melted away, his heart raced with it wildly.

'I am not old,' he wanted to say. 'At fifty I'm younger than most men of forty. Don't I interest you at all?'

But she only said, 'What kind of gargle?'

And he answered, 'What can you recommend? . . . That's fine.'

Almost painfully he took his eyes from her, went out and got into his coupé.

'If that young idiot only knew what an old imbecile like me could do for her,' he thought humorously – 'what worlds I could open out to her!'

As he drove away into the winter twilight he followed this train of thought to a totally unprecedented conclusion. Perhaps the time of day was the responsible stimulant, for the shop windows glowing into the cold, the tinkling bells of a delivery sleigh, the white gloss left by shovels on the sidewalks, the enormous distance of the stars, brought back the feel of other nights thirty years ago. For an instant the girls he had known then slipped like phantoms out of their dull matronly selves of today and fluttered past him with frosty, seductive laughter, until a pleasant shiver crawled up his spine.

'Youth! Youth! Youth!' he apostrophised with conscious lack of originality, and, as a somewhat ruthless and domineering man of no morals whatsoever, he considered going back to the drugstore to seek the blonde girl's address. It was not his sort of thing, so the half-formed intention passed; the idea remained.

'Youth, by heaven – youth!' he repeated under his breath. 'I want it near me, all around me, just once more before I'm too old to care.'

He was tall, lean and handsome, with the ruddy, bronzed face of a sportsman and a just faintly greying moustache. Once he had been among the city's best beaus, organiser of cotillions and charity balls, popular with men and women, and with several generations of them. After the war he had suddenly felt poor, gone into business, and in ten years accumulated nearly a million dollars. Tom Squires was not introspective, but he perceived now that the wheel of his life had revolved again, bringing up forgotten, yet familiar, dreams and yearnings. Entering his house, he turned suddenly to a pile of disregarded invitations to see whether or not he had been bidden to a dance tonight.

Throughout his dinner, which he ate alone at the Downtown Club, his eyes were half closed and on his face was a faint smile. He was practising so that he would be able to laugh at himself painlessly, if necessary.

'I don't even know what they talk about,' he admitted. 'They pet – prominent broker goes to petting party with débutante. What is a petting party? Do they serve refreshments? Will I have to learn to play a saxophone?'

These matters, lately as remote as China in a newsreel, came alive to him. They were serious questions. At ten o'clock he walked up the steps of the College Club to a private dance with the same sense of entering a new world as when he had gone into a training camp back in 1917. He spoke to a hostess of his generation and to her daughter, overwhelmingly of another, and sat down in a corner to acclimate himself.

He was not alone long. A silly young man named Leland Jaques, who lived across the street from Tom, remarked him kindly and came over to brighten his life. He was such an exceedingly fatuous young man that, for a moment, Tom was annoyed, but he perceived craftily that he might be of service.

'Hello, Mr Squires. How are you, sir?'

'Fine, thanks, Leland. Quite a dance.'

As one man of the world with another, Mr Jaques sat, or lay, down on the couch and lit – or so it seemed to Tom – three or four cigarettes at once.

'You should of been here last night, Mr Squires. Oh, boy, that was a party and a half! The Caulkins. Hap-past five!'

'Who's that girl who changes partners every minute?' Tom asked . . . 'No, the one in white passing the door.'

'That's Annie Lorry.'

'Arthur Lorry's daughter?'

'Yes.'

'She seems popular.'

'About the most popular girl in town – anyway, at a dance.'

'Not popular except at dances?'

'Oh, sure, but she hangs around with Randy Cambell all the time.'

'What Cambell?'

'D. B.'

There were new names in town in the last decade.

'It's a boy-and-girl affair.' Pleased with this phrase, Jaques tried to repeat it: 'One of those boy-and-girls affair – boys-and-girl affairs – ' He gave it up and lit several more cigarettes, crushing out the first series on Tom's lap.

'Does she drink?'

'Not especially. At least I never saw her passed out . . . That's Randy Cambell just cut in on her now.'

They were a nice couple. Her beauty sparkled bright against his strong, tall form, and they floated hoveringly, delicately, like two people in a nice, amusing dream. They came near and Tom admired the faint dust of powder over her freshness, the guarded sweetness of her smile, the fragility of her body calculated by nature to a millimetre to suggest a bud, yet guarantee a flower. Her innocent, passionate eyes were brown, perhaps; but almost violet in the silver light.

'Is she out this year?'

'Who?'

'Miss Lorry.'

'Yes.'

Although the girl's loveliness interested Tom, he was unable to picture himself as one of the attentive, grateful queue that pursued her around the room. Better meet her when the holidays were over and most of these young men were back in college 'where they belonged'. Tom Squires was old enough to wait.

He waited a fortnight while the city sank into the endless Northern midwinter, where grey skies were friendlier than metallic blue skies, and dusk, whose lights were a reassuring glimpse into the continuity of human cheer, was warmer than the afternoons of bloodless sunshine. The coat of snow lost its press and became soiled and shabby, and ruts froze in the street; some of the big houses on Crest Avenue began to close as their occupants went South. In those cold days Tom asked Annie and her parents to go as his guests to the last Bachelors' Ball.

The Lorrys were an old family in Minneapolis, grown a little harassed and poor since the war. Mrs Lorry, a contemporary of Tom's, was not surprised that he should send mother and daughter orchids and dine them luxuriously in his apartment on fresh caviare, quail and champagne. Annie saw him only dimly – he lacked vividness, as the old do for the young – but she perceived his interest in her and performed for him the traditional ritual of young beauty – smiles, polite, wide-eyed attention, a profile held obligingly in this light or in that. At the ball he danced with her twice, and, though she was teased about it, she was flattered that such a man of the world – he had become that instead of a mere old man – had singled her out. She accepted his invitation to the symphony the following week, with the idea that it would be uncouth to refuse.

There were several 'nice invitations' like that. Sitting beside him, she dozed in the warm shadow of Brahms and thought of Randy Cambell and other romantic nebulosities who might appear tomorrow. Feeling casually mellow one afternoon, she deliberately provoked Tom to kiss her on the way home, but she wanted to laugh when he took her hands and told her fervently he was falling in love.

'But how could you?' she protested. 'Really, you musn't say such crazy things. I won't go out with you any more, and then you'll be sorry.'

A few days later her mother spoke to her as Tom waited outside in his car: 'Who's that, Annie?'

'Mr Squires.'

'Shut the door a minute. You're seeing him quite a bit.'

'Why not?'

'Well, dear, he's fifty years old.'

'But, mother, there's hardly anybody else in town.'

'But you musn't get any silly ideas about him.'

'Don't worry. Actually, he bores me to extinction most of the time.' She came to a sudden decision: 'I'm not going to see him any more. I just couldn't get out of going with him this afternoon.'

And that night, as she stood by her door in the circle of Randy Cambell's arm, Tom and his single kiss had no existence for her.

'Oh, I do love you so,' Randy whispered. 'Kiss me once more.'

Their cool cheeks and warm lips met in the crisp darkness, and, watching the icy moon over his shoulder, Annie knew that she was his surely and, pulling his face down, kissed him again, trembling with emotion.

'When'll you marry me then?' he whispered.

'When can you – we afford it?'

'Couldn't you announce our engagement? If you knew the misery of having you out with somebody else and then making love to you.'

'Oh, Randy, you ask so much.'

'It's so awful to say good-night. Can't I come in for a minute?'

'Yes.'

Sitting close together in a trance before the flickering, lessening fire, they were oblivious that their common fate was being coolly weighed by a man of fifty who lay in a hot bath some blocks away.

2

Tom Squires had guessed from Annie's extremely kind and detached manner of the afternoon that he had failed to interest her. He had promised himself that in such an eventuality he would drop the matter, but now he found himself in no such humour. He did not want to marry her; he simply wanted to see her and be with her a little; and up to the moment of her sweetly casual, half passionate, yet wholly unemotional kiss, giving her up would have been easy, for he was past the romantic age; but since that kiss the thought of her made his heart move up a few inches in his chest and beat there steady and fast.

'But this is the time to get out,' he said to himself. 'My age; no possible right to force myself into her life.'

He rubbed himself dry, brushed his hair before the mirror, and, as he laid down the comb, said decisively: 'That is that.' And after reading for an hour he turned out the lamp with a snap and repeated aloud: 'That is that.'

In other words, that was not that at all, and the click of material things did not finish off Annie Lorry as a business decision might be settled by the tap of a pencil on the table.

'I'm going to carry this matter a little further,' he said to himself about half-past four; on that acknowledgement he turned over and found sleep.

In the morning she had receded somewhat, but by four o'clock in the afternoon she was all around him – the phone was for calling her, a woman's footfalls passing his office were her footfalls, the snow outside the window was blowing, perhaps, against her rosy face.

'There is always the little plan I thought of last night,' he said to himself. 'In ten years I'll be sixty, and then no youth, no beauty for me ever any more.'

In a sort of panic he took a sheet of notepaper and composed a carefully phrased letter to Annie's mother, asking permission to pay court to her daughter. He took it himself into the hall, but before the letter slide he tore it up and dropped the pieces in a cuspidor.

'I couldn't do such an underhand trick,' he told himself, 'at my age.' But this self-congratulation was premature, for he rewrote the letter and mailed it before he left his office that night.

Next day the reply he had counted on arrived – he could have guessed its very words in advance. It was a curt and indignant refusal.

It ended:

I think it best that you and my daughter meet no more.
Very sincerely yours,

MABEL TOLLMAN LORRY

'And now,' Tom thought coolly, 'we'll see what the girl says to that.' He wrote a note to Annie. Her mother's letter had surprised him, it said, but perhaps it was best that they should meet no more, in view of her mother's attitude.

By return post came Annie's defiant answer to her mother's fiat: 'This isn't the Dark Ages. I'll see you whenever I like.' She named a rendezvous for the following afternoon. Her mother's short-sightedness brought about what he had failed to achieve directly; for where Annie had been on the point of dropping him, she was now determined to do nothing of the sort. And the secrecy engendered by disapproval at home simply contributed the missing excitement. As February hardened into deep, solemn, interminable winter, she met him frequently and on a new basis. Sometimes they drove over to St Paul to see a picture or to have dinner; sometimes they parked far out on a boulevard in his coupé, while the bitter sleet glazed the windshield to opacity and furred his lamps with ermine. Often he brought along something special to drink – enough to make her gay, but, carefully, never more; for mingled with his other emotions about her was something paternally concerned.

Laying his cards on the table, he told her that it was her mother who had unwittingly pushed her towards him, but Annie only laughed at his duplicity.

She was having a better time with him than with anyone else she had ever known. In place of the selfish exigency of a younger man, he showed her a never-failing consideration. What if his eyes were tired, his cheeks a little leathery and veined, if his will was masculine and strong. Moreover, his experience was a window looking out upon a wider, richer world; and with Randy Cambell next day she would feel less taken care of, less valued, less rare.

It was Tom now who was vaguely discontented. He had what he wanted – her youth at his side – and he felt that anything further would be a mistake. His liberty was precious to him and he could offer her only a dozen years before he would be old, but she had become something precious to him and he perceived that drifting wasn't fair. Then one day late in February the matter was decided out of hand.

They had ridden home from St Paul and dropped into the College Club for tea, breaking together through the drifts that masked the walk and rimmed the door. It was a revolving door; a young man came around in it, and stepping into his space, they smelt onions and whiskey. The door revolved again after them, and he was back within, facing them. It was Randy Cambell; his face was flushed, his eyes dull and hard.

'Hello, beautiful,' he said, approaching Annie.

'Don't come so close,' she protested lightly. 'You smell of onions.'

'You're particular all of a sudden.'

'Always. I'm always particular.' Annie made a slight movement back towards Tom.

'Not always,' said Randy unpleasantly. Then, with increased emphasis and a fractional glance at Tom: 'Not always.' With his remark he seemed to join the hostile world outside. 'And I'll just give you a tip,' he continued: 'Your mother's inside.'

The jealous ill-temper of another generation reached Tom only faintly, like the protest of a child, but at this impertinent warning he bristled with annoyance.

'Come on, Annie,' he said brusquely. 'We'll go in.'

With her glance uneasily averted from Randy, Annie followed Tom into the big room.

It was sparsely populated; three middle-aged women sat near the fire. Momentarily Annie drew back, then she walked towards them.

'Hello, mother . . . Mrs Trumble . . . Aunt Caroline.'

The two latter responded; Mrs Trumble even nodded faintly at Tom. But Annie's mother got to her feet without a word, her eyes frozen, her mouth drawn. For a moment she stood staring at her daughter; then she turned abruptly and left the room.

Tom and Annie found a table across the room.

'Wasn't she terrible?' said Annie, breathing aloud. He didn't answer.

'For three days she hasn't spoken to me.' Suddenly she broke out: 'Oh, people can be so small! I was going to sing the leading part in the Junior League show, and yesterday Cousin Mary Betts, the president, came to me and said I couldn't.'

'Why not?'

'Because a representative Junior League girl mustn't defy her mother. As if I were a naughty child!'

Tom stared at a row of cups on the mantelpiece – two or three of them bore his name. 'Perhaps she was right,' he said suddenly. 'When I begin to do harm to you it's time to stop.'

'What do you mean?'

At her shocked voice his heart poured a warm liquid forth into his body, but he answered quietly: 'You remember I told you I was going South? Well, I'm going tomorrow.'

There was an argument, but he had made up his mind. At the station next evening she wept and clung to him.

'Thank you for the happiest month I've had in years,' he said.

'But you'll come back, Tom.'

'I'll be two months in Mexico; then I'm going East for a few weeks.'

He tried to sound fortunate, but the frozen city he was leaving seemed to be in blossom. Her frozen breath was a flower on the air, and his heart sank as he realised that some young man was waiting outside to take her home in a car hung with blooms.

'Goodbye, Annie. Goodbye, sweet!'

Two days later he spent the morning in Houston with Hal Meigs, a classmate at Yale.

'You're in luck for such an old fella,' said Meigs at luncheon, 'because I'm going to introduce you to the cutest little travelling companion you ever saw, who's going all the way to Mexico City.'

The lady in question was frankly pleased to learn at the station that she was not returning alone. She and Tom dined together on the train and later played rummy for an hour; but when, at ten o'clock, standing in the door of the stateroom, she turned back to him suddenly with a certain look, frank and unmistakable, and stood there holding that look for a long moment, Tom Squires was suddenly in the grip of an emotion that was not the one in question. He wanted desperately to see Annie, call her for a second on the phone, and then fall asleep, knowing she was young and pure as a star, and safe in bed.

'Good-night,' he said, trying to keep any repulsion out of his voice.

'Oh! Good-night.'

Arriving in El Paso next day, he drove over the border to Juarez. It was bright and hot, and after leaving his bags at the station he went into a bar for an iced drink; as he sipped it a girl's voice addressed him thickly from the table behind: 'You'n American?'

He had noticed her slumped forward on her elbows as he came in; now, turning, he faced a young girl of about seventeen, obviously drunk, yet with gentility in her unsteady, sprawling voice.

The American bartender leaned confidentially forward. 'I don't know what to do about her,' he said. 'She come in about three o'clock with two young fellows – one of them her sweetie. They had a fight and the men went off, and this one's been here ever since.'

A spasm of distaste passed over Tom – the rules of his generation were outraged and defiled. That an American girl should be drunk and deserted in a tough foreign town – that such things happened, might happen to Annie. He looked at his watch, hesitated.

'Has she got a bill?' he asked.

'She owes for five gins. But suppose her boyfriends come back?'

'Tell them she's at the Roosevelt Hotel in El Paso.'

Approaching, he put his hand on her shoulder. She looked up.

'You look like Santa Claus,' she said vaguely. 'You couldn't possibly be Santa Claus, could you?'

'I'm going to take you to El Paso.'

'Well,' she considered, 'you look perfectly safe to me.'

She was so young – a drenched little rose. He could have wept for her wretched unconsciousness of the old facts, the old penalties of life. Jousting at nothing in an empty tilt yard with a shaking spear. The taxi moved too slowly through the suddenly poisonous night.

Having explained things to a reluctant night clerk, he went out and found a telegraph office.

'Have given up Mexican trip,' he wired. 'Leaving here tonight. Please meet train in the St Paul station at three o'clock and ride with me to Minneapolis, as I can't spare you for another minute. All my love.'

He could at least keep an eye on her, advise her, see what she did with her life. That silly mother of hers!

On the train, as the baked tropical lands and green fields fell away and the North swept near again with patches of snow, then fields of it, fierce winds in the vestibule and bleak, hibernating farms, he paced the corridors with intolerable restlessness. When they drew into the St Paul station he swung himself off like a young man and searched the platform eagerly, but his eyes failed to find her. He had counted on those few minutes between the cities; they had become a symbol of her fidelity to their friendship, and as the train started again he searched it desperately from smoker to observation car. But he could not find her, and now he knew that he was mad for her; at the thought that she had taken his advice and plunged into affairs with other men, he grew weak with fear.

Drawing into Minneapolis, his hands fumbled so that he must call the porter to fasten his baggage. Then there was an interminable wait in the corridor while the baggage was taken off and he was pressed up against a girl in a squirrel-trimmed coat.

'Tom!'

'Well, I'll be – '

Her arms went up around his neck. 'But, Tom,' she cried, 'I've been right here in this car since St Paul!'

His cane fell in the corridor, he drew her very tenderly close and their lips met like starved hearts.

3

The new intimacy of their definite engagement brought Tom a feeling of young happiness. He awoke on winter mornings with the sense of undeserved joy hovering in the room; meeting young men, he found himself matching the vigour of his mind and body against theirs. Suddenly his life had a purpose and a background; he felt rounded and complete. On grey March afternoons when she wandered familiarly in his apartment the warm sureties of his youth flooded back – ecstasy and poignancy, the mortal and the eternal posed in their immemorially tragic juxtaposition and, a little astounded, he found himself relishing the very terminology of young romance. But he was more thoughtful than a younger lover; and to Annie he seemed to 'know everything', to stand holding open the gates for her passage into the truly golden world.

'We'll go to Europe first,' he said.

'Oh, we'll go there a lot, won't we? Let's spend our winters in Italy and the spring in Paris.'

'But, little Annie, there's business.'

'Well, we'll stay away as much as we can anyhow. I hate Minneapolis.'

'Oh, no.' He was a little shocked. 'Minneapolis is all right.'

'When you're here it's all right.'

Mrs Lorry yielded at length to the inevitable. With ill grace she acknowledged the engagement, asking only that the marriage should not take place until fall.

'Such a long time,' Annie sighed.

'After all, I'm your mother. It's so little to ask.'

It was a long winter, even in a land of long winters. March was full of billowy drifts, and when it seemed at last as though the cold must be defeated, there was a series of blizzards, desperate as last stands. The people waited; their first energy to resist was spent, and man, like weather, simply hung on. There was less to do now and the general restlessness was expressed by surliness in daily contacts. Then, early in April, with a long sigh the ice cracked, the snow ran into the ground and the green, eager spring broke up through.

One day, riding along a slushy road in a fresh, damp breeze with a little starved, smothered grass in it, Annie began to cry. Sometimes she cried for nothing, but this time Tom suddenly stopped the car and put his arm around her.

'Why do you cry like that? Are you unhappy?'

'Oh, no, no!' she protested.

'But you cried yesterday the same way. And you wouldn't tell me why. You must always tell me.'

'Nothing, except the spring. It smells so good, and it always has so many sad thoughts and memories in it.'

'It's our spring, my sweetheart,' he said. 'Annie, don't let's wait. Let's be married in June.'

'I promised mother, but if you like we can announce our engagement in June.'

The spring came fast now. The sidewalks were damp, then dry, and the children roller-skated on them and boys played baseball in the soft, vacant lots. Tom got up elaborate picnics of Annie's contemporaries and encouraged her to play golf and tennis with them. Abruptly, with a final, triumphant lurch of nature, it was full summer.

On a lovely May evening Tom came up the Lorrys' walk and sat down beside Annie's mother on the porch.

'It's so pleasant,' he said, 'I thought Annie and I would walk instead of driving this evening. I want to show her the funny old house I was born in.'

'On Chambers Street, wasn't it? Annie'll be home in a few minutes. She went riding with some young people after dinner.'

'Yes, on Chambers Street.'

He looked at his watch presently, hoping Annie would come while it was still light enough to see. Quarter of nine. He frowned. She had kept him waiting the night before, kept him waiting an hour yesterday afternoon.

'If I was twenty-one,' he said to himself, 'I'd make scenes and we'd both be miserable.'

He and Mrs Lorry talked; the warmth of the night precipitated the vague evening lassitude of the fifties and softened them both, and for the first time since his attentions to Annie began, there was no unfriendliness between them. By and by long silences fell, broken only by the scratch of a match or the creak of her swinging settee. When Mr Lorry came home, Tom threw away his second cigar in surprise and looked at his watch; it was after ten.

'Annie's late,' Mrs Lorry said.

'I hope there's nothing wrong,' said Tom anxiously. 'Who is she with?'

'There were four when they started out. Randy Cambell and another couple – I didn't notice who. They were only going for a soda.'

'I hope there hasn't been any trouble. Perhaps – Do you think I ought to go and see?'

'Ten isn't late nowadays. You'll find – ' Remembering that Tom Squires was marrying Annie, not adopting her, she kept herself from adding: 'You'll get used to it.'

Her husband excused himself and went up to bed, and the conversation became more forced and desultory. When the church clock over the way struck eleven they both broke off and listened to the beats. Twenty minutes later, just as Tom impatiently crushed out his last cigar, an automobile drifted down the street and came to rest in front of the door.

For a minute no one moved on the porch or in the auto. Then Annie, with a hat in her hand, got out and came quickly up the walk. Defying the tranquil night, the car snorted away.

'Oh, hello!' she cried. 'I'm so sorry! What time is it? Am I terribly late?'

Tom didn't answer. The street lamp threw wine colour upon her face and expressed with a shadow the heightened flush of her cheek. Her dress was crushed, her hair was in brief, expressive disarray. But it was the strange little break in her voice that made him afraid to speak, made him turn his eyes aside.

'What happened?' Mrs Lorry asked casually.

'Oh, a blow-out and something wrong with the engine – and we lost our way. Is it terribly late?'

And then, as she stood before them, her hat still in her hand, her breast rising and falling a little, her eyes wide and bright, Tom realised with a shock that he and her mother were people of the same age looking at a person of another. Try as he might, he could not separate himself from Mrs Lorry. When she excused herself he suppressed a frantic tendency to say, 'But why should you go now? After sitting here all evening?'

They were alone. Annie came up to him and pressed his hand. He had never been so conscious of her beauty; her damp hands were touched with dew.

'You were out with young Cambell,' he said.

'Yes. Oh, don't be mad. I feel – I feel so upset tonight.'

'Upset?'

She sat down, whimpering a little.

'I couldn't help it. Please don't be mad. He wanted so for me to take a ride with him and it was such a wonderful night, so I went just for an hour. And we began talking and I didn't realise the time. I felt so sorry for him.'

'How do you think I felt?' He scorned himself, but it was said now.

'Don't, Tom. I told you I was terribly upset. I want to go to bed.'

'I understand. Good-night, Annie.'

'Oh, please don't act that way, Tom. Can't you understand?'

But he could, and that was just the trouble. With the courteous bow of another generation, he walked down the steps and off into the obliterating moonlight. In a moment he was just a shadow passing the street lamps and then a faint footfall up the street.

4

All through that summer he often walked abroad in the evenings. He liked to stand for a minute in front of the house where he was born, and then in front of another house where he had been a little boy. On his customary routes there were other sharp landmarks of the 90s, converted habitats of gaieties that no longer existed – the shell of Jansen's Livery Stables and the old Nushka Rink, where every winter his father had curled on the well-kept ice.

'And it's a darn pity,' he would mutter. 'A darn pity.'

He had a tendency, too, to walk past the lights of a certain drugstore, because it seemed to him that it had contained the seed of another and nearer branch of the past. Once he went in, and enquiring casually about the blonde clerk, found that she had married and departed several months before. He obtained her name and on an impulse sent her a wedding present 'from a dumb admirer', for he felt he owed something to her for his happiness and pain. He had lost the battle against youth and spring, and with his grief paid the penalty for age's unforgivable sin – refusing to die. But he could not have walked down wasted into the darkness without being used up a little; what he had wanted, after all, was only to break his strong old heart. Conflict itself has a value beyond victory and defeat, and those three months – he had them for ever.

Family in the Wind

1

The two men drove up the hill towards the blood-red sun. The cotton fields bordering the road were thin and withered, and no breeze stirred in the pines.

'When I am totally sober,' the doctor was saying – 'I mean when I am totally sober – I don't see the same world that you do. I'm like a friend of mine who had one good eye and got glasses made to correct his bad eye; the result was that he kept seeing elliptical suns and falling off tilted curbs, until he had to throw the glasses away. Granted that I am thoroughly anaesthetised the greater part of the day – well, I only undertake work that I know I can do when I am in that condition.'

'Yeah,' agreed his brother Gene uncomfortably. The doctor was a little tight at the moment and Gene could find no opening for what he had to say. Like so many Southerners of the humbler classes, he had a deep-seated courtesy, characteristic of all violent and passionate lands – he could not change the subject until there was a moment's silence, and Forrest would not shut up.

'I'm very happy,' he continued, 'or very miserable. I chuckle or I weep alcoholically and, as I continue to slow up, life accommodatingly goes faster, so that the less there is of myself inside, the more diverting becomes the moving picture without. I have cut myself off from the respect of my fellow man, but I am aware of a compensatory cirrhosis of the emotions. And because my sensitivity, my pity, no longer has direction, but fixes itself on whatever is at hand, I have become an exceptionally good fellow – much more so than when I was a good doctor.'

As the road straightened after the next bend and Gene saw his house in the distance, he remembered his wife's face as she had made him promise, and he could wait no longer: 'Forrest, I got a thing – '

But at that moment the doctor brought his car to a sudden stop in front of a small house just beyond a grove of pines. On the front steps a girl of eight was playing with a grey cat.

'This is the sweetest little kid I ever saw,' the doctor said to Gene, and then to the child, in a grave voice: 'Helen, do you need any pills for kitty?'

The little girl laughed.

'Well, I don't know,' she said doubtfully. She was playing another game with the cat now and this came as rather an interruption.

'Because kitty telephoned me this morning,' the doctor continued, 'and said her mother was neglecting her and couldn't I get her a trained nurse from Montgomery.'

'She did not.' The little girl grabbed the cat close indignantly; the doctor took a nickel from his pocket and tossed it to the steps.

'I recommend a good dose of milk,' he said as he put the car into gear. 'Good-night, Helen.'

'Good-night, doctor.'

As they drove off, Gene tried again: 'Listen; stop,' he said. 'Stop here a little way down . . . Here.'

The doctor stopped the car and the brothers faced each other. They were alike as to robustness of figure and a certain asceticism of feature and they were both in their middle forties; they were unlike in that the doctor's glasses failed to conceal the veined, weeping eyes of a soak, and that he wore corrugated city wrinkles; Gene's wrinkles bounded fields, followed the lines of roof trees, of poles propping up sheds. His eyes were a fine, furry blue. But the sharpest contrast lay in the fact that Gene Janney was a country man while Dr Forrest Janney was obviously a man of education.

'Well?' the doctor asked.

'You know Pinky's at home,' Gene said, looking down the road.

'So I hear,' the doctor answered noncommittally.

'He got in a row in Birmingham and somebody shot him in the head.' Gene hesitated. 'We got Doc Behrer because we thought maybe you wouldn't – maybe you wouldn't – '

'I wouldn't,' agreed Dr Janney blandly.

'But look, Forrest; here's the thing,' Gene insisted. 'You know how it is – you often say Doc Behrer doesn't know nothing. Shucks, I never thought he was much either. He says the bullet's pressing on the – pressing on the brain, and he can't take it out without causin' a hemmering, and he says he doesn't know whether we could get him to Birmingham or Montgomery or not, he's so low. Doc wasn't no help. What we want – '

'No,' said his brother, shaking his head. 'No.'

'I just want you to look at him and tell us what to do,' Gene begged. 'He's unconscious, Forrest. He wouldn't know you; you'd hardly know him. Thing is his mother's about crazy.'

'She's in the grip of a purely animal instinct.' The doctor took from his hip a flask containing half water and half Alabama corn, and drank. 'You and I know that boy ought to been drowned the day he was born.'

Gene flinched. 'He's bad,' he admitted, 'but I don't know – You see him lying there – '

As the liquor spread over the doctor's insides he felt an instinct to do something, not to violate his prejudices but simply to make some gesture, to assert his own moribund but still struggling will to power.

'All right, I'll see him,' he said. 'I'll do nothing myself to help him, because he ought to be dead. And even his death wouldn't make up for what he did to Mary Decker.'

Gene Janney pursed his lips. 'Forrest, you sure about that?'

'Sure about it!' exclaimed the doctor. 'Of course I'm sure. She died of starvation; she hadn't had more than a couple cups of coffee in a week. And if you looked at her shoes, you could see she'd walked for miles.'

'Doc Behrer says – '

'What does he know? I performed the autopsy the day they found her on the Birmingham Highway. There was nothing the matter with her but starvation. That – that' – his voice shook with feeling – 'that Pinky got tired of her and turned her out, and she was trying to get home. It suits me fine that he was invalided home himself a couple of weeks later.'

As he talked, the doctor had plunged the car savagely into gear and let the clutch out with a jump; in a moment they drew up before Gene Janney's home.

It was a square frame house with a brick foundation and a well-kept lawn blocked off from the farm, a house rather superior to the buildings that composed the town of Bending and the surrounding agricultural area, yet not essentially different in type or in its interior economy. The last of the plantation houses in this section of Alabama had long disappeared, the proud pillars yielding to poverty, rot and rain.

Gene's wife, Rose, got up from her rocking-chair on the porch.

'Hello, doc.' She greeted him a little nervously and without meeting his eyes. 'You been a stranger here lately.'

The doctor met her eyes for several seconds. 'How do you do, Rose,' he said. 'Hi, Edith . . . Hi, Eugene' – this to the little boy and girl who stood beside their mother; and then: 'Hi, Butch!' to the stocky youth of nineteen who came around the corner of the house hugging a round stone.

'Goin to have a sort of low wall along the front here – kind of neater,' Gene explained.

All of them had a lingering respect for the doctor. They felt reproachful towards him because they could no longer refer to him as their celebrated relative – 'one of the bess surgeons up in Montgomery, yes, suh' – but there was his learning and the position he had once occupied in the larger world, before he had committed professional suicide by taking to cynicism and drink. He had come home to Bending and bought a half interest in the local drugstore two years ago, keeping up his licence, but practising only when sorely needed.

'Rose,' said Gene, 'doc says he'll take a look at Pinky.'

Pinky Janney, his lips curved mean and white under a new beard, lay in bed in a darkened room. When the doctor removed the bandage from his head, his breath blew into a low groan, but his paunchy body did not move. After a few minutes, the doctor replaced the bandage and, with Gene and Rose, returned to the porch.

'Behrer wouldn't operate?' he asked.

'No.'

'Why didn't they operate in Birmingham?'

'I don't know.'

'H'm.' The doctor put on his hat. 'That bullet ought to come out, and soon. It's pressing against the carotid sheath. That's the – anyhow, you can't get him to Montgomery with that pulse.'

'What'll we do?' Gene's question carried a little tail of silence as he sucked his breath back.

'Get Behrer to think it over. Or else get somebody in Montgomery. There's about a twenty-five-per-cent chance that the operation would save him; without the operation he hasn't any chance at all.'

'Who'll we get in Montgomery?' asked Gene.

'Any good surgeon would do it. Even Behrer could do it if he had any nerve.'

Suddenly Rose Janney came close to him, her eyes straining and burning with an animal maternalism. She seized his coat where it hung open.

'Doc, you do it! You can do it. You know you were as good a surgeon as any of 'em once. Please, doc, you go on do it.'

He stepped back a little so that her hands fell from his coat, and held out his own hands in front of him.

'See how they tremble?' he said with elaborate irony. 'Look close and you'll see. I wouldn't dare operate.'

'You could do it all right,' said Gene hastily, 'with a drink to stiffen you up.'

The doctor shook his head and said, looking at Rose: 'No. You see, my decisions are not reliable, and if anything went wrong, it would seem to be my fault.' He was acting a little now – he chose his words carefully. 'I hear that when I found that Mary Decker died of starvation, my opinion was questioned on the ground that I was a drunkard.'

'I didn't say that,' lied Rose breathlessly.

'Certainly not. I just mention it to show how careful I've got to be.' He moved down the steps. 'Well, my advice is to see Behrer again, or, failing that, get somebody from the city. Good-night.'

But before he had reached the gate, Rose came tearing after him, her eyes white with fury.

'I did say you were a drunkard!' she cried. 'When you said Mary Decker died of starvation, you made it out as if it was Pinky's fault – you, swilling yourself full of corn all day! How can anybody tell whether you know what you're doing or not? Why did you think so much about Mary Decker, anyhow – a girl half your age? Everybody saw how she used to come in your drugstore and talk to you – '

Gene, who had followed, seized her arms. 'Shut up now, Rose . . . Drive along, Forrest.'

Forrest drove along, stopping at the next bend to drink from his flask. Across the fallow cotton fields he could see the house where Mary Decker had lived, and had it been six months before, he might have detoured to ask her why she hadn't come into the store that day for her free soda, or to delight her with a sample cosmetic left by a salesman that morning. He had not told Mary Decker how he felt about her; never intended to – she was seventeen, he was forty-five, and he no longer dealt in futures – but only after she ran away to Birmingham with Pinky Janney did he realise how much his love for her had counted in his lonely life.

His thoughts went back to his brother's house.

'Now, if I were a gentleman,' he thought, 'I wouldn't have done like that. And another person might have been sacrificed to that dirty dog, because if he died afterwards Rose would say I killed him.'

Yet he felt pretty bad as he put his car away; not that he could have acted differently, but just that it was all so ugly.

He had been home scarcely ten minutes when a car creaked to rest outside and Butch Janney came in. His mouth was set tight and his eyes were narrowed as though to permit of no escape to the temper that possessed him until it should be unleashed upon its proper objective.

'Hi, Butch.'

'I want to tell you, Uncle Forrest, you can't talk to my mother thataway. I'll kill you, you talk to my mother like that!'

'Now shut up, Butch, and sit down,' said the doctor sharply.

'She's already bout sick on account of Pinky, and you come over and talk to her like that.'

'Your mother did all the insulting that was done, Butch. I just took it.'

'She doesn't know what she's saying and you ought to understand that.'

The doctor thought a minute. 'Butch, what do you think of Pinky?'

Butch hesitated uncomfortably. 'Well, I can't say I ever thought so much of him' – his tone changed defiantly – 'but after all, he's my own brother – '

'Wait a minute, Butch. What do you think of the way he treated Mary Decker?'

But Butch had shaken himself free, and now he let go the artillery of his rage: 'That ant the point; the point is anybody that doesn't do right to my mother has me to answer to. It's only fair when you got all the education – '

'I got my education myself, Butch.'

'I don't care. We're going to try again to get Doc Behrer to operate or get us some fellow from the city. But if we can't, I'm coming and get you, and you're going to take that bullet out if I have to hold a gun to you while you do it.' He nodded, panting a little; then he turned and went out and drove away.

'Something tells me,' said the doctor to himself, 'that there's no more peace for me in Chilton County.' He called to his coloured boy to put supper on the table. Then he rolled himself a cigarette and went out on the back stoop.

The weather had changed. The sky was now overcast and the grass stirred restlessly and there was a sudden flurry of drops without a sequel. A minute ago it had been warm, but now the moisture on his forehead was suddenly cool, and he wiped it away with his handkerchief. There was a buzzing in his ears and he swallowed and shook his head. For a moment he thought he must be sick; then suddenly the buzzing detached itself from him, grew into a swelling sound, louder and ever nearer, that might have been the roar of an approaching train.

2

Butch Janney was halfway home when he saw it – a huge, black, approaching cloud whose lower edge bumped the ground. Even as he stared at it vaguely, it seemed to spread until it included the whole southern sky, and he saw pale electric fire in it and heard an increasing roar. He was in a strong wind now; blown débris, bits of broken branches, splinters, larger objects unidentifiable in the growing darkness, flew by him. Instinctively he got out of his car and, by now hardly able to stand against the wind, ran for a bank, or rather found himself thrown and pinned against a bank. Then for a minute, two minutes, he was in the black centre of pandemonium.

First there was the sound, and he was part of the sound, so engulfed in it and possessed by it that he had no existence apart from it. It was not a collection of sounds, it was just Sound itself; a great screeching bow drawn across the chords of the universe. The sound and force were inseparable. The sound as well as the force held him to what he felt was the bank like a man crucified. Somewhere in this first moment his face, pinned sideways, saw his automobile make a little jump, spin halfway around and then go bobbing off over a field in a series of great helpless leaps. Then began the bombardment, the sound dividing its sustained cannon note into the cracks of a gigantic machine-gun. He was only half-conscious as he felt himself become part of one of those cracks, felt himself lifted away from the bank to tear through space, through a blinding, lacerating mass of twigs and branches, and then, for an incalculable time, he knew nothing at all.

His body hurt him. He was lying between two branches in the top of a tree; the air was full of dust and rain, and he could hear nothing; it was a long time before he realised that the tree he was in had been blown down and that his involuntary perch among the pine needles was only five feet from the ground.

'Say, man!' he cried aloud, outraged. 'Say, man! Say, what a wind! Say, man!'

Made acute by pain and fear, he guessed that he had been standing on the tree's root and had been catapulted by the terrific wrench as the big pine was torn from the earth. Feeling over himself, he found that his left ear was caked full of dirt, as if someone had wanted to take an impression of the inside. His clothes were in rags, his coat had torn on the back seam, and he could feel where, as some stray gust tried to undress him, it had cut into him under the arms.

Reaching the ground, he set off in the direction of his father's house, but it was a new and unfamiliar landscape he traversed. The Thing – he did not know it was a tornado – had cut a path a quarter of a mile wide, and he was confused, as the dust slowly settled, by vistas he had never seen before. It was unreal that Bending church tower should be visible from here; there had been groves of trees between.

But where was here? For he should be close to the Baldwin house; only as he tripped over great piles of boards, like a carelessly kept lumber yard, did Butch realise that there was no more a Baldwin house, and then, looking around wildly, that there was no Necrawney house on the hill, no Peltzer house below it. There was not a light, not a sound, save the rain falling on the fallen trees.

He broke into a run. When he saw the bulk of his father's house in the distance, he gave a 'Hey!' of relief, but coming closer, he realised that something was missing. There were no outhouses and the built-on wing that held Pinky's room had been sheared completely away.

'Mother!' he called. 'Dad!' There was no answer; a dog bounded out of the yard and licked his hand . . .

. . . It was full dark twenty minutes later when Doc Janney stopped his car in front of his own drugstore in Bending. The electric lights had gone out, but there were men with lanterns in the street, and in a minute a small crowd had collected around him. He unlocked the door hurriedly.

'Somebody break open the old Wiggins Hospital.' He pointed across the street. 'I've got six badly injured in my car. I want some fellows to carry 'em in. Is Doc Behrer here?'

'Here he is,' offered eager voices out of the darkness as the doctor, case in hand, came through the crowd. The two men stood face to face by lantern light, forgetting that they disliked each other.

'God knows how many more there's going to be,' said Doc Janney. 'I'm getting dressing and disinfectant. There'll be a lot of fractures – ' He raised his voice, 'Somebody bring me a barrel!'

'I'll get started over there,' said Doc Behrer. 'There's about half a dozen more crawled in.'

'What's been done?' demanded Doc Janney of the men who followed him into the drugstore. 'Have they called Birmingham and Montgomery?'

'The telephone wires are down, but the telegraph got through.'

'Well, somebody get Dr Cohen from Wettala, and tell any people who have automobiles to go up the Willard Pike and cut across towards Corsica and all through those roads there. There's not a house left at the crossroads by the nigger store. I passed a lot of folks walking in, all of them hurt, but I didn't have room for anybody else.' As he talked he was throwing bandages, disinfectant and drugs into a blanket. 'I thought I had a lot more stuff than this in stock! And wait!' he called. 'Somebody drive out and look down in that hollow where the Wooleys live. Drive right across the fields – the road's blocked . . . Now, you with the cap – Ed Jenks, ain't it?'

'Yes, doc.'

'You see what I got here? You collect everything in the store that looks like this and bring it across the way, understand?'

'Yes, doc.'

As the doctor went out into the street, the victims were streaming into town – a woman on foot with a badly injured child, a buckboard full of groaning Negroes, frantic men gasping terrible stories. Everywhere confusion and hysteria mounted in the dimly illumined darkness. A mud-covered reporter from Birmingham drove up in a sidecar, the wheels crossing the fallen wires and brushwood that clogged the street, and there was the siren of a police car from Cooper, thirty miles away.

Already a crowd pressed around the doors of the hospital, closed these three months for lack of patients. The doctor squeezed past the *mêlée* of white faces and established himself in the nearest ward, grateful for the waiting row of old iron beds. Dr Behrer was already at work across the hall.

'Get me half a dozen lanterns,' he ordered.

'Dr Behrer wants idodine and adhesive.'

'All right, there it is . . . Here, you, Shinkey, stand by the door and keep everybody out except cases that can't walk. Somebody run over and see if there ain't some candles in the grocery store.'

The street outside was full of sound now – the cries of women, the contrary directions of volunteer gangs trying to clear the highway, the tense staccato of people rising to an emergency. A little before midnight arrived the first unit of the Red Cross. But the three doctors, presently joined by two others from nearby villages, had lost track of time long before that. The dead began to be brought in by ten o'clock; there were twenty, twenty-five, thirty, forty – the list grew. Having no more needs, these waited, as became simple husbandmen, in a garage behind, while the stream of injured – hundreds of them – flowed through the old hospital built to house only a score. The storm had dealt out fractures of the leg, collarbone, ribs and hip, lacerations of the back, elbows, ears, eyelids, nose; there were wounds from flying planks, and odd splinters in odd places, and a scalped man, who would recover to grow a new head of hair. Living or dead, Doc Janney knew every face, almost every name.

'Don't you fret now. Billy's all right. Hold still and let me tie this. People are drifting in every minute, but it's so consarned dark they can't find 'em – All right, Mrs Oakey. That's nothing. Ev here'll touch it with iodine . . . Now let's see this man.'

Two o'clock. The old doctor from Wettala gave out, but now there were fresh men from Montgomery to take his place. Upon the air of the room, heavy with disinfectant, floated the ceaseless babble of human speech reaching the doctor dimly through layer after layer of increasing fatigue: ' . . . Over and over – just rolled me over and over. Got hold of a bush and the bush came along too.'

'*Jeff! Where's Jeff?*

' . . . I bet that pig sailed a hundred yards – '

' – just stopped the train in time. All the passengers got out and helped pull the poles – '

'Where's Jeff?'

'He says, "Let's get down the cellar," and I says, "We ain't got no cellar – " '

' – If there's no more stretchers, find some light doors.'

' . . . Five seconds? Say, it was more like five minutes!'

At some time he heard that Gene and Rose had been seen with their two youngest children. He had passed their house on the way in and, seeing it standing, hurried on. The Janney family had been lucky; the doctor's own house was outside the sweep of the storm.

Only as he saw the electric lights go on suddenly in the streets and glimpsed the crowd waiting for hot coffee in front of the Red Cross did the doctor realise how tired he was.

'You better go rest,' a young man was saying. 'I'll take this side of the room. I've got two nurses with me.'

'All right – all right. I'll finish this row.'

The injured were being evacuated to the cities by train as fast as their wounds were dressed, and their places taken by others. He had only two beds to go – in the first one he found Pinky Janney.

He put his stethoscope to the heart. It was beating feebly. That he, so weak, so nearly gone, had survived this storm at all was remarkable. How he had got there, who had found him and carried him, was a mystery in itself. The doctor went over the body; there were small contusions and lacerations, two broken fingers, the dirt-filled ears that marked every case – nothing else. For a moment the doctor hesitated, but even when he closed his eyes, the image of Mary Decker seemed to have receded, eluding him. Something purely professional that had nothing to do with human sensibilities had been set in motion inside him, and he was powerless to head it off. He held out his hands before him; they were trembling slightly.

'Hell's bells!' he muttered.

He went out of the room and around the corner of the hall, where he drew from his pocket the flask containing the last of the corn and water he had had in the afternoon. He emptied it.

Returning to the ward, he disinfected two instruments and applied a local anaesthetic to a square section at the base of Pinky's skull where the wound had healed over the bullet. He called a nurse to his side and then, scalpel in hand, knelt on one knee beside his nephew's bed.

3

Two days later the doctor drove slowly around the mournful countryside. He had withdrawn from the emergency work after the first desperate night, feeling that his status as a pharmacist might embarrass his collaborators. But there was much to be done in bringing the damage to outlying sections under the aegis of the Red Cross, and he devoted himself to that.

The path of the demon was easy to follow. It had pursued an irregular course in its seven-league boots, cutting cross-country, through woods, or even urbanely keeping to roads until they curved, when it went off on its own again. Sometimes the trail could be traced by cotton fields, apparently in full bloom, but this cotton came from the insides of hundreds of quilts and mattresses redistributed in the fields by the storm.

At a lumber pile that had lately been a Negro cabin, he stopped a moment to listen to a dialogue between two reporters and two shy piccaninnies. The old grandmother, her head bandaged, sat among the ruins, gnawing some vague meat and moving her rocker ceaselessly.

'But where is the river you were blown across?' one of the reporters demanded.

'There.'

'Where?'

The piccaninnies looked to their grandmother for aid.

'Right there behind y'all,' spoke up the old woman.

The newspapermen looked disgustedly at a muddy stream four yards wide.

'That's no river.'

'That's a Menada River, we always calls it ever since I was a gull. Yes, suh, that's a Menada River. An' them two boys was blowed right across it an set down on the othah side just as pretty, 'thout any hurt at all. Chimney fell on me,' she concluded, feeling her head.

'Do you mean to say that's all it was?' demanded the younger reporter indignantly. 'That's the river they were blown across! And one hundred and twenty million people have been led to believe – '

'That's all right, boys,' interrupted Doc Janney. 'That's a right good river for these parts. And it'll get bigger as those little fellahs get older.'

He tossed a quarter to the old woman and drove on.

Passing a country church, he stopped and counted the new brown mounds that marred the graveyard. He was nearing the centre of the holocaust now. There was the Howden house where three had been killed; there remained a gaunt chimney, a rubbish heap and a scarecrow surviving ironically in the kitchen garden. In the ruins of the house across the way a rooster strutted on top of a piano, reigning vociferously over an estate of trunks, boots, cans, books, calendars, rugs, chairs and window frames, a twisted radio and a legless sewing machine. Everywhere there was bedding – blankets, mattresses, bent springs, shredded padding – he had not realised how much of people's lives was spent in bed. Here and there, cows and horses, often stained with disinfectant, were grazing again in the fields. At intervals there were Red Cross tents, and sitting by one of these, with the grey cat in her arms, the doctor came upon little Helen Kilrain. The usual lumber pile, like a child's building game knocked down in a fit of temper, told the story.

'Hello, dear,' he greeted her, his heart sinking. 'How did kitty like the tornado?'

'She didn't.'

'What did she do?'

'She meowed.'

'Oh.'

'She wanted to get away, but I hanged on to her and she scratched me – see?'

He glanced at the Red Cross tent. 'Who's taking care of you?'

'The lady from the Red Cross and Mrs Wells,' she answered.

'My father got hurt. He stood over me so it wouldn't fall on me, and I stood over kitty. He's in the hospital in Birmingham. When he comes back, I guess he'll build our house again.'

The doctor winced. He knew that her father would build no more houses; he had died that morning. She was alone, and she did not know she was alone. Around her stretched the dark universe, impersonal, inconscient. Her lovely little face looked up at him confidently as he asked: 'You got any kin anywhere, Helen?'

'I don't know.'

'You've got kitty, anyhow, haven't you?'

'It's just a cat,' she admitted calmly, but anguished by her own betrayal of her love, she hugged it closer.

'Taking care of a cat must be pretty hard.'

'Oh, no,' she said hurriedly. 'It isn't any trouble at all. It doesn't eat hardly anything.'

He put his hand in his pocket, and then changed his mind suddenly.

'Dear, I'm coming back and see you later – later today. You take good care of kitty now, won't you?'

'Oh, yes,' she answered lightly.

The doctor drove on. He stopped next at a house that had escaped damage. Walt Cupps, the owner, was cleaning a shotgun on his front porch.

'What's that, Walt? Going to shoot up the next tornado?'

'Ain't going to be a next tornado.'

'You can't tell. Just take a look at that sky now. It's getting mighty dark.'

Walt laughed and slapped his gun. 'Not for a hundred years, anyhow. This here is for looters. There's a lot of 'em around, and not all black either. Wish when you go to town that you'd tell 'em to scatter some militia out here.'

'I'll tell 'em now. You come out all right?'

'I did, thank God. With six of us in the house. It took off one hen, and probably it's still carrying it around somewhere.'

The doctor drove on towards town, overcome by a feeling of uneasiness he could not define.

'It's the weather,' he thought. 'It's the same kind of feel in the air there was last Saturday.'

For a month the doctor had felt an urge to go away permanently. Once this countryside had seemed to promise peace. When the impetus that had lifted him temporarily out of tired old stock was exhausted, he had come back here to rest, to watch the earth put forth, and live on simple, pleasant terms with his neighbours. Peace! He knew that the present family quarrel would never heal, nothing would ever be the same; it would all be bitter for ever. And he had seen the placid countryside turned into a land of mourning. There was no peace here. Move on!

On the road he overtook Butch Janney walking to town.

'I was coming to see you,' said Butch, frowning. 'You operated on Pinky after all, didn't you?'

'Jump in . . . Yes, I did. How did you know?'

'Doc Behrer told us.' He shot a quick look at the doctor, who did not miss the quality of suspicion in it. 'They don't think he'll last out the day.'

'I'm sorry for your mother.'

Butch laughed unpleasantly. 'Yes, you are.'

'I said I'm sorry for your mother,' said the doctor sharply.

'I heard you.'

They drove for a moment in silence.

'Did you find your automobile?'

'Did I?' Butch laughed ruefully. 'I found something – I don't know whether you'd call it a car any more. And, you know, I could of had tornado insurance for twenty-five cents.' His voice trembled indignantly: 'Twenty-five cents – but who would ever of thought of getting tornado insurance?'

It was growing darker; there was a thin crackle of thunder far to the southward.

'Well, all I hope,' said Butch with narrowed glance, 'is that you hadn't been drinking anything when you operated on Pinky.'

'You know, Butch,' the doctor said slowly, 'that was a pretty dirty trick of mine to bring that tornado here.'

He had not expected the sarcasm to hit home, but he expected a retort – when suddenly he caught sight of Butch's face. It was fish-white, the mouth was open, the eyes fixed and staring, and from the throat came a mewling sound. Limply he raised one hand before him, and then the doctor saw.

Less than a mile away, an enormous, top-shaped black cloud filled the sky and bore towards them, dipping and swirling, and in front of it sailed already a heavy, singing wind.

'It's come back!' the doctor yelled.

Fifty yards ahead of them was the old iron bridge spanning Bilby Creek. He stepped hard on the accelerator and drove for it. The fields were full of running figures headed in the same direction. Reaching the bridge, he jumped out and yanked Butch's arm.

'Get out, you fool! Get out!'

A nerveless mass stumbled from the car; in a moment they were in a group of half a dozen, huddled in the triangular space that the bridge made with the shore.

'Is it coming here?'

'No, it's turning!'

'We had to leave grampa!'

'Oh, save me, save me! Jesus save me! Help me!'

'Jesus save my soul!'

There was a quick rush of wind outside, sending little tentacles under the bridge with a curious tension in them that made the doctor's skin crawl. Then immediately there was a vacuum, with no more wind, but a sudden thresh of rain. The doctor crawled to the edge of the bridge and put his head up cautiously.

'It's passed,' he said. 'We only felt the edge; the centre went way to the right of us.'

He could see it plainly; for a second he could even distinguish objects in it – shrubbery and small trees, planks and loose earth. Crawling farther out, he produced his watch and tried to time it, but the thick curtain of rain blotted it from sight.

Soaked to the skin, he crawled back underneath. Butch lay shivering in the farthest corner, and the doctor shook him.

'It went in the direction of your house!' the doctor cried. 'Pull yourself together! Who's there?'

'No one,' Butch groaned. 'They're all down with Pinky.'

The rain had changed to hail now; first small pellets, then larger ones, and larger, until the sound of their fall upon the iron bridge was an ear-splitting tattoo.

The spared wretches under the bridge were slowly recovering, and in the relief there were titters of hysterical laughter. After a certain point of strain, the nervous system makes its transitions without dignity or reason. Even the doctor felt the contagion.

'This is worse than a calamity,' he said dryly. 'It's getting to be a nuisance.'

4

There were to be no more tornadoes in Alabama that spring. The second one – it was popularly thought to be the first one come back; for to the people of Chilton County it had become a personified force, definite as a pagan god – took a dozen houses, Gene Janney's among them, and injured about thirty people. But this time – perhaps because everyone had developed some scheme of self-protection – there were no fatalities. It made its last dramatic bow by sailing down the main street of Bending, prostrating the telephone poles and crushing in the fronts of three shops, including Doc Janney's drugstore.

At the end of a week, houses were going up again, made of the old boards; and before the end of the long, lush Alabama summer the grass would be green on all the graves. But it will be years before the people of the country cease to reckon events as happening 'before the tornado' or 'after the tornado' – and for many families things will never be the same.

Dr Janney decided that this was as good a time to leave as any. He sold the remains of his drugstore, gutted alike by charity and catastrophe, and turned over his house to his brother until Gene could rebuild his own. He was going up to the city by train, for his car had been rammed against a tree and couldn't be counted on for much more than the trip to the station.

Several times on the way in he stopped by the roadside to say goodbye – once it was to Walter Cupps.

'So it hit you, after all,' he said, looking at the melancholy back house which alone marked the site.

'It's pretty bad,' Walter answered. 'But just think; they was six of us in or about the house and not one was injured. I'm content to give thanks to God for that.'

'You were lucky there, Walt,' the doctor agreed. 'Do you happen to have heard whether the Red Cross took little Helen Kilrain to Montgomery or to Birmingham?'

'To Montgomery. Say, I was there when she came into town with that cat, tryin' to get somebody to bandage up its paw. She must of walked miles through that rain and hail, but all that mattered to her was her kitty. Bad as I felt, I couldn't help laughin' at how spunky she was.'

The doctor was silent for a moment. 'Do you happen to recollect if she has any people left?'

'I don't, suh,' Walter replied, 'but I think as not.'

At his brother's place, the doctor made his last stop. They were all there, even the youngest, working among the ruins; already Butch had a shed erected to house the salvage of their goods. Save for this the most orderly thing surviving was the pattern of round white stones which was to have enclosed the garden.

The doctor took a hundred dollars in bills from his pocket and handed it to Gene.

'You can pay it back sometime, but don't strain yourself,' he said. 'It's money I got from the store.' He cut off Gene's thanks: 'Pack up my books carefully when I send for 'em.'

'You reckon to practice medicine up there, Forrest?'

'I'll maybe try it.'

The brothers held on to each other's hands for a moment; the two youngest children came up to say goodbye. Rose stood in the background in an old blue dress – she had no money to wear black for her eldest son.

'Goodbye, Rose,' said the doctor.

'Goodbye,' she responded, and then added in a dead voice, 'Good luck to you, Forrest.'

For a moment he was tempted to say something conciliatory, but he saw it was no use. He was up against the maternal instinct, the same force that had sent little Helen through the storm with her injured cat.

At the station he bought a one-way ticket to Montgomery. The village was drab under the sky of a retarded spring, and as the train pulled out, it was odd to think that six months ago it had seemed to him as good a place as any other.

He was alone in the white section of the day coach; presently he felt for a bottle on his hip and drew it forth. 'After all, a man of forty-five is entitled to more artificial courage when he starts over again.' He began thinking of Helen. 'She hasn't got any kin. I guess she's my little girl now.'

He patted the bottle, then looked down at it as if in surprise.

'Well, we'll have to put you aside for a while, old friend. Any cat that's worth all that trouble and care is going to need a lot of grade-B milk.'

He settled down in his seat, looking out the window. In his memory of that terrible week the winds still sailed about him, came in as draughts through the corridor of the car – winds of the world – cyclones, hurricanes, tornadoes – grey and black, expected or unforeseen, some from the sky, some from the caves of hell.

But he would not let them touch Helen again – if he could help it.

He dozed momentarily, but a haunting dream woke him: *'Daddy stood over me and I stood over kitty.'*

'All right, Helen,' he said aloud, for he often talked to himself, 'I guess the old brig can keep afloat a little longer – in any wind.'

Three Hours Between Planes

It was a wild chance but Donald was in the mood, healthy and bored, with a sense of tiresome duty done. He was now rewarding himself. Maybe.

When the plane landed he stepped out into a mid-western summer night and headed for the isolated pueblo airport, conventionalised as an old red 'railway depot'. He did not know whether she was alive, or living in this town, or what was her present name. With mounting excitement he looked through the phone book for her father, who might be dead too, somewhere in these twenty years.

No. Judge Harmon Holmes – Hillside 3194.

A woman's amused voice answered his enquiry for Miss Nancy Holmes.

'Nancy is Mrs Walter Gifford now. Who is this?'

But Donald hung up without answering. He had found out what he wanted to know and had only three hours. He did not remember any Walter Gifford and there was another suspended moment while he scanned the phone book. She might have married out of town. No. Walter Gifford – Hillside 1191. Blood flowed back into his fingertips.

'Hello?'

'Hello. Is Mrs Gifford there – this is an old friend of hers.'

'This is Mrs Gifford.'

He remembered, or thought he remembered, the funny magic in the voice. 'This is Donald Plant. I haven't seen you since I was twelve years old.'

'Oh–h–h!' The note was utterly surprised, very polite, but he could distinguish in it neither joy nor certain recognition.

' – Donald!' added the voice. This time there was something more in it than struggling memory.

' . . . when did you come back to town?' Then cordially, 'Where *are* you?'

'I'm out at the airport – for just a few hours.'

'Well, come up and see me.'

'Sure you're not just going to bed?'

'Heavens, no!' she exclaimed. 'I was sitting here – having a highball by myself. Just tell your taxi man . . . '

On his way Donald analysed the conversation. His words 'at the airport' established that he had retained his position in the upper bourgeoisie. Nancy's aloneness might indicate that she had matured into an unattractive woman without friends. Her husband might be either away or in bed. And – because she was always ten years old in his dreams – the highball shocked him. But he adjusted himself with a smile – she was very close to thirty.

At the end of a curved drive he saw a dark-haired little beauty standing against the lighted door, a glass in her hand. Startled by her final materialisation, Donald got out of the cab, saying: 'Mrs Gifford?'

She turned on the porch light and stared at him, wide-eyed and tentative. A smile broke through the puzzled expression.

'Donald – it is you – we all change so. Oh, this is remarkable!'

As they walked inside, their voices jingled the words 'all these years', and Donald felt a sinking in his stomach. This derived in part from a vision of their last meeting – when she rode past him on a bicycle, cutting him dead – and in part from fear lest they have nothing to say. It was like a college reunion – but there the failure to find the past was disguised by the hurried boisterous occasion. Aghast, he realised that this might be a long and empty hour. He plunged in desperately.

'You always were a lovely person. But I'm a little shocked to find you as beautiful as you are.'

It worked. The immediate recognition of their changed state, the bold compliment, made them interesting strangers instead of fumbling childhood friends.

'Have a highball?' she asked. 'No? Please don't think I've become a secret drinker, but this was a blue night. I expected my husband but he wired he'd be two days longer. He's very nice, Donald, and very attractive. Rather your type and colouring.' She hesitated, ' –

and I think he's interested in someone in New York – and I don't know.'

'After seeing you it sounds impossible,' he assured her. 'I was married for six years, and there was a time I tortured myself that way. Then one day I just put jealousy out of my life for ever. After my wife died I was very glad of that. It left a very rich memory – nothing marred or spoiled or hard to think over.'

She looked at him attentively, then sympathetically as he spoke.

'I'm very sorry,' she said. And after a proper moment, 'You've changed a lot. Turn your head. I remember father saying, "That boy has a brain." '

'You probably argued against it.'

'I was impressed. Up to then I thought everybody had a brain. That's why it sticks in my mind.'

'What else sticks in your mind?' he asked smiling.

Suddenly Nancy got up and walked quickly a little away.

'Ah, now,' she reproached him. 'That isn't fair! I suppose I was a naughty girl.'

'You were not,' he said stoutly. 'And I *will* have a drink now.'

As she poured it, her face still turned from him, he continued: 'Do you think you were the only little girl who was ever kissed?'

'Do you like the subject?' she demanded. Her momentary irritation melted and she said: 'What the hell! We *did* have fun. Like in the song.'

'On the sleigh-ride.'

'Yes – and somebody's picnic – Trudy James's. And at Frontenac that – those summers.'

It was the sleigh-ride he remembered most and kissing her cool cheeks in the straw in one corner while she laughed up at the cold white stars. The couple next to them had their backs turned and he kissed her little neck and her ears and never her lips.

'And the Macks' party where they played post office and I couldn't go because I had the mumps,' he said.

'I don't remember that.'

'Oh, you were there. And you were kissed and I was crazy with jealousy like I never have been since.'

'Funny I don't remember. Maybe I wanted to forget.'

'But why?' he asked in amusement. 'We were two perfectly innocent kids. Nancy, whenever I talked to my wife about the past, I told her you were the girl I loved almost as much as I loved her. But I think I really loved you just as much. When we moved out of town I carried you like a cannon ball in my insides.'

'Were you *that* much – stirred up?'

'My God, yes! I – ' He suddenly realised that they were standing just two feet from each other, that he was talking as if he loved her in the present, that she was looking up at him with her lips half-parted and a clouded look in her eyes.

'Go on,' she said, 'I'm ashamed to say – I like it. I didn't know you were so upset *then*. I thought it was *me* who was upset.'

'You!' he exclaimed. 'Don't you remember throwing me over at the drugstore.' He laughed. 'You stuck out your tongue at me.'

'I don't remember at all. It seemed to me you did the throwing over.' Her hand fell lightly, almost consolingly on his arm. 'I've got a photograph book upstairs I haven't looked at for years. I'll dig it out.'

Donald sat for five minutes with two thoughts – first the hopeless impossibility of reconciling what different people remembered about the same event – and secondly that in a frightening way Nancy moved him as a woman as she had moved him as a child. Half an hour had developed an emotion that he had not known since the death of his wife – that he had never hoped to know again.

Side by side on a couch they opened the book between them. Nancy looked at him, smiling and very happy.

'Oh, this is *such* fun,' she said. 'Such fun that you're so nice, that you remember me so – beautifully. Let me tell you – I wish I'd known it then! After you'd gone I hated you.'

'What a pity,' he said gently.

'But not now,' she reassured him, and then impulsively, 'Kiss and make up – '

' . . . that isn't being a good wife,' she said after a minute. 'I really don't think I've kissed two men since I was married.'

He was excited – but most of all confused. Had he kissed Nancy?

or a memory? or this lovely trembly stranger who looked away from him quickly and turned a page of the book?

'Wait!' he said. 'I don't think I could *see* a picture for a few seconds.'

'We won't do it again. I don't feel so very calm myself.'

Donald said one of those trivial things that cover so much ground.

'Wouldn't it be awful if we fell in love again?'

'Stop it!' She laughed, but very breathlessly. 'It's all over. It was a moment. A moment I'll have to forget.'

'Don't tell your husband.'

'Why not? Usually I tell him everything.'

'It'll hurt him. Don't ever tell a man such things.'

'All right, I won't.'

'Kiss me once more,' he said inconsistently, but Nancy had turned a page and was pointing eagerly at a picture.

'Here's you,' she cried. 'Right away!'

He looked. It was a little boy in shorts standing on a pier with a sailboat in the background.

'I remember – ' she laughed triumphantly, ' – the very day it was taken. Kitty took it and I stole it from her.'

For a moment Donald failed to recognise himself in the photo – then, bending closer – he failed utterly to recognise himself.

'That's not me,' he said.

'Oh yes. It was at Frontenac – the summer we – we used to go to the cave.'

'What cave? I was only three days in Frontenac.' Again he strained his eyes at the slightly yellowed picture. 'And that isn't me. That's Donald Bowers. We did look rather alike.'

Now she was staring at him – leaning back, seeming to lift away from him.

'But you're Donald Bowers!' she exclaimed; her voice rose a little. 'No, you're not. You're Donald *Plant*.'

'I told you on the phone.'

She was on her feet – her face faintly horrified.

'Plant! Bowers! I must be crazy. Or it was that drink? I was mixed up a little when I first saw you. Look here! What have I told you?'

He tried for a monkish calm as he turned a page of the book.

'Nothing at all,' he said. Pictures that did not include him formed and re-formed before his eyes – Frontenac – a cave – Donald Bowers – 'You threw *me* over!'

Nancy spoke from the other side of the room. 'You'll never tell this story,' she said. 'Stories have a way of getting around.'

'There isn't any story,' he hesitated. But he thought: So she was a bad little girl.

And now suddenly he was filled with wild raging jealousy of little Donald Bowers – he who had banished jealousy from his life for ever. In the five steps he took across the room he crushed out twenty years and the existence of Walter Gifford with his stride.

'Kiss me again, Nancy,' he said, sinking to one knee beside her chair, putting his hand upon her shoulder. But Nancy strained away.

'You said you had to catch a plane.'

'It's nothing. I can miss it. It's of no importance.'

'Please go,' she said in a cool voice. 'And please try to imagine how I feel.'

'But you act as if you don't remember me,' he cried, ' – as if you don't remember Donald *Plant*!'

'I do. I remember you too . . . But it was all so long ago.' Her voice grew hard again. 'The taxi number is Crestwood 8484.'

On his way to the airport Donald shook his head from side to side. He was completely himself now but he could not digest the experience. Only as the plane roared up into the dark sky and its passengers became a different entity from the corporate world below did he draw a parallel from the fact of its flight. For five blinding minutes he had lived like a madman in two worlds at once. He had been a boy of twelve and a man of thirty-two, indissolubly and helplessly commingled.

Donald had lost a good deal, too, in those hours between the planes – but since the second half of life is a long process of getting rid of things, that part of the experience probably didn't matter.

The Lees of Happiness

1

If you should look through the files of old magazines for the first years of the present century you would find, sandwiched in between the stories of Richard Harding Davis and Frank Norris and others long since dead, the work of one Jeffrey Curtain: a novel or two, and perhaps three or four dozen short stories. You could, if you were interested, follow them along until, say, 1908, when they suddenly disappeared.

When you had read them all you would have been quite sure that here were no masterpieces – here were passably amusing stories, a bit out of date now, but doubtless the sort that would then have whiled away a dreary half-hour in a dental office. The man who did them was of good intelligence, talented, glib, probably young. In the samples of his work you found there would have been nothing to stir you to more than a faint interest in the whims of life – no deep interior laughs, no sense of futility or hint of tragedy.

After reading them you would yawn and put the number back in the files, and perhaps, if you were in some library reading-room, you would decide that by way of variety you would look at a newspaper of the period and see whether the Japs had taken Port Arthur. But if by any chance the newspaper you had chosen was the right one and had crackled open at the theatrical page, your eyes would have been arrested and held, and for at least a minute you would have forgotten Port Arthur as quickly as you forgot Château Thierry. For you would, by this fortunate chance, be looking at the portrait of an exquisite woman.

Those were the days of 'Florodora' and of sextets, of pinched-in waists and blown-out sleeves, of almost bustles and absolute ballet skirts, but here, without doubt, disguised as she might be by the unaccustomed stiffness and old fashion of her costume, was a butterfly of butterflies. Here was the gaiety of the period – the soft wine of eyes, the songs that flurried hearts, the toasts and the bouquets, the dances and the dinners. Here was a Venus of the hansom cab, the Gibson girl in her glorious prime. Here was . . .

. . . here was, you find by looking at the name beneath, one Roxanne Milbank, who had been chorus girl and understudy in *The Daisy Chain*, but who, by reason of an excellent performance when the star was indisposed, had gained a leading part.

You would look again – and wonder. Why you had never heard of her. Why did her name not linger in popular songs and vaudeville jokes and cigar bands, and the memory of that gay old uncle of yours along with Lillian Russell and Stella Mayhew and Anna Held? Roxanne Milbank – whither had she gone? What dark trapdoor had opened suddenly and swallowed her up? Her name was certainly not in last Sunday's supplement on the list of actresses married to English noblemen. No doubt she was dead – poor beautiful young lady – and quite forgotten.

I am hoping too much. I am having you stumble on Jeffrey Curtains's stories and Roxanne Milbank's picture. It would be incredible that you should find a newspaper item six months later, a single item two inches by four, which informed the public of the marriage, very quietly, of Miss Roxanne Milbank, who had been on tour with *The Daisy Chain*, to Mr Jeffrey Curtain, the popular author. 'Mrs Curtain,' it added dispassionately, 'will retire from the stage.'

It was a marriage of love. He was sufficiently spoiled to be charming; she was ingenuous enough to be irresistible. Like two floating logs they met in a head-on rush, caught, and sped along together. Yet had Jeffrey Curtain kept at scrivening for two-score years he could not have put a quirk into one of his stories weirder than the quirk that came into his own life. Had Roxanne Milbank played three dozen parts and filled five thousand houses she could never have had a role with more happiness and more despair than were in the fate prepared for Roxanne Curtain.

For a year they lived in hotels, travelled to California, to Alaska, to Florida, to Mexico, loved and quarrelled gently, and gloried in the golden triflings of his wit with her beauty – they were young and gravely passionate; they demanded everything and then yielded everything again in ecstasies of unselfishness and pride. She loved the swift tones of his voice and his frantic, if unfounded jealousy. He loved her dark radiance, the white irises of her eyes, the warm, lustrous enthusiasm of her smile.

'Don't you like her?' he would demand rather excitedly and shyly. 'Isn't she wonderful? Did you ever see – '

'Yes,' they would answer, grinning. 'She's a wonder. You're lucky.'

The year passed. They tired of hotels. They bought an old house and twenty acres near the town of Marlowe, half an hour from Chicago; bought a little car, and moved out riotously with a pioneering hallucination that would have confounded Balboa.

'Your room will be here!' they cried in turn.

– And then: 'And my room here!'

'And the nursery here when we have children.'

'And we'll build a sleeping porch – oh, next year.'

They moved out in April. In July Jeffrey's closest friend, Harry Cromwell, came to spend a week – they met him at the end of the long lawn and hurried him proudly to the house.

Harry was married also. His wife had had a baby some six months before and was still recuperating at her mother's in New York. Roxanne had gathered from Jeffrey that Harry's wife was not as attractive as Harry – Jeffrey had met her once and considered her – 'shallow'. But Harry had been married nearly two years and was apparently happy, so Jeffrey guessed that she was probably all right.

'I'm making biscuits,' chattered Roxanne gravely. 'Can your wife make biscuits? The cook is showing me how. I think every woman should know how to make biscuits. It sounds so utterly disarming. A woman who can make biscuits can surely do no – '

'You'll have to come out here and live,' said Jeffrey. 'Get a place out in the country like us, for you and Kitty.'

'You don't know Kitty. She hates the country. She's got to have her theatres and vaudevilles.'

'Bring her out,' repeated Jeffrey. 'We'll have a colony. There's an awfully nice crowd here already. Bring her out!'

They were at the porch steps now and Roxanne made a brisk gesture towards a dilapidated structure on the right.

'The garage,' she announced. 'It will also be Jeffrey's writing-room within the month. Meanwhile dinner is at seven. Meanwhile to that I will mix a cocktail.'

The two men ascended to the second floor – that is, they ascended halfway, for at the first landing Jeffrey dropped his guest's suitcase and in a cross between a query and a cry exclaimed: 'For God's sake, Harry, how do you like her?'

'We will go upstairs,' answered his guest, 'and we will shut the door.'

Half an hour later as they were sitting together in the library Roxanne reissued from the kitchen, bearing before her a pan of biscuits. Jeffrey and Harry rose.

'They're beautiful, dear,' said the husband, intensely.

'Exquisite,' murmured Harry.

Roxanne beamed. 'Taste one. I couldn't bear to touch them before you'd seen them all and I can't bear to take them back until I find what they taste like.'

'Like manna, darling.'

Simultaneously the two men raised the biscuits to their lips, nibbled tentatively. Simultaneously they tried to change the subject. But Roxanne, undeceived, set down the pan and seized a biscuit. After a second her comment rang out with lugubrious finality: 'Absolutely bum!'

'Really – '

'Why, I didn't notice – '

Roxanne roared.

'Oh, I'm useless,' she cried laughing. 'Turn me out, Jeffrey – I'm a parasite; I'm no good – '

Jeffrey put his arm around her.

'Darling, I'll eat your biscuits.'

'They're beautiful, anyway,' insisted Roxanne.

'They're – they're decorative,' suggested Harry.

Jeffrey took him up wildly. 'That's the word. They're decorative; they're masterpieces. We'll use them.'

He rushed to the kitchen and returned with a hammer and a handful of nails.

'We'll use them, by golly, Roxanne! We'll make a frieze out of them.'

'Don't!' wailed Roxanne. 'Our beautiful house.'

'Never mind. We're going to have the library repapered in October. Don't you remember?'

'Well – '

Bang! The first biscuit was impaled to the wall, where it quivered for a moment like a live thing.

Bang! . . .

When Roxanne returned with a second round of cocktails the biscuits were in a perpendicular row, twelve of them, like a collection of primitive spearheads.

'Roxanne,' exclaimed Jeffrey, 'you're an artist! Cook? – nonsense! You shall illustrate my books!'

During dinner the twilight faltered into dusk, and later it was a starry dark outside, filled and permeated with the frail gorgeousness of Roxanne's white dress and her tremulous, low laugh.

– Such a little girl she is, thought Harry. Not as old as Kitty.

He compared the two. Kitty – nervous without being sensitive, temperamental without temperament, a woman who seemed to flit and never light – and Roxanne, who was as young as spring night, and summed up in her own adolescent laughter.

– A good match for Jeffrey, he thought again. Two very young people, the sort who'll stay very young until they suddenly find themselves old.

Harry thought these things between his constant thoughts about Kitty. He was depressed about Kitty. It seemed to him that she was well enough to come back to Chicago and bring his little son. He was thinking vaguely of Kitty when he said good-night to his friend's wife and his friend at the foot of the stairs.

'You're our first real house guest,' called Roxanne after him. 'Aren't you thrilled and proud?'

When he was out of sight around the stair corner she turned to Jeffrey, who was standing beside her resting his hand on the end of the bannister.

'Are you tired, my dearest?'

Jeffrey rubbed the centre of his forehead with his fingers.

'A little. How did you know?'

'Oh, how could I help knowing about you?'

'It's a headache,' he said moodily. 'Splitting. I'll take some aspirin.'

She reached over and snapped out the light, and with his arm tight about her waist they walked up the stairs together.

2

Harry's week passed. They drove about the dreaming lanes or idled in cheerful inanity upon lake or lawn. In the evening Roxanne, sitting inside, played to them while the ashes whitened on the glowing ends of their cigars. Then came a telegram from Kitty saying that she wanted Harry to come East and get her, so Roxanne and Jeffrey were left alone in that privacy of which they never seemed to tire.

'Alone' thrilled them again. They wandered about the house, each feeling intimately the presence of the other; they sat on the same side of the table like honeymooners; they were intensely absorbed, intensely happy.

The town of Marlowe, though a comparatively old settlement, had only recently acquired a 'society'. Five or six years before, alarmed at the smoky swelling of Chicago, two or three young married couples, 'bungalow people', had moved out; their friends had followed. The Jeffrey Curtains found an already formed 'set' prepared to welcome them; a country club, ballroom and golf links yawned for them, and there were bridge parties, and poker parties, and parties where they drank beer, and parties where they drank nothing at all.

It was at a poker party that they found themselves a week after Harry's departure. There were two tables, and a good proportion of the young wives were smoking and shouting their bets, and being very daringly mannish for those days.

Roxanne had left the game early and taken to perambulation; she wandered into the pantry and found herself some grape juice – beer gave her a headache – and then passed from table to table, looking over shoulders at the hands, keeping an eye on Jeffrey and being pleasantly unexcited and content. Jeffrey, with intense concentration, was raising a pile of chips of all colours, and Roxanne knew by the deepened wrinkle between his eyes that he was interested. She liked to see him interested in small things.

She crossed over quietly and sat down on the arm of his chair.

She sat there five minutes, listening to the sharp intermittent comments of the men and the chatter of the women, which rose from the table like soft smoke – and yet scarcely hearing either. Then quite innocently she reached out her hand, intending to place it on Jeffrey's shoulder – as it touched him he started of a sudden, gave a short grunt, and, sweeping back his arm furiously, caught her a glancing blow on her elbow.

There was a general gasp. Roxanne regained her balance, gave a little cry, and rose quickly to her feet. It had been the greatest shock of her life. This, from Jeffrey, the heart of kindness, of consideration – this instinctively brutal gesture.

The gasp became a silence. A dozen eyes were turned on Jeffrey, who looked up as though seeing Roxanne for the first time. An expression of bewilderment settled on his face.

'Why – Roxanne – ' he said haltingly.

Into a dozen minds entered a quick suspicion, a rumour of scandal. Could it be that behind the scenes with this couple, apparently so in love, lurked some curious antipathy? Why else this streak of fire, across such a cloudless heaven?

'Jeffrey!' – Roxanne's voice was pleading – startled and horrified, she yet knew that it was a mistake. Not once did it occur to her to blame him or to resent it. Her word was a trembling supplication – 'Tell me, Jeffrey,' it said, 'tell Roxanne, your own Roxanne.'

'Why, Roxanne – ' began Jeffrey again. The bewildered look changed to pain. He was clearly as startled as she. 'I didn't intend that,' he went on; 'you startled me. You – I felt as if someone were attacking me. I – how – why, how idiotic!'

'Jeffrey!' Again the word was a prayer, incense offered up to a high God through this new and unfathomable darkness.

They were both on their feet, they were saying goodbye, faltering, apologising, explaining. There was no attempt to pass it off easily. That way lay sacrilege. Jeffrey had not been feeling well, they said. He had become nervous. Back of both their minds was the unexplained horror of that blow – the marvel that there had been for an instant something between them – his anger and her fear – and now to both a sorrow, momentary, no doubt, but to be bridged at once, at once, while there was yet time. Was that swift water lashing under their feet – the fierce glint of some uncharted chasm?

Out in their car under the harvest moon he talked brokenly. It was just – incomprehensible to him, he said. He had been thinking of the poker game – absorbed – and the touch on his shoulder had seemed like an attack. An attack! He clung to that word, flung it up as a shield. He had hated what touched him. With the impact of his hand it had gone, that – nervousness. That was all he knew.

Both their eyes filled with tears and they whispered love there under the broad night as the serene streets of Marlowe sped by. Later, when they went to bed, they were quite calm. Jeffrey was to take a week off all work – was simply to loll, and sleep, and go on long walks until this nervousness left him. When they had decided this safety settled down upon Roxanne. The pillows underhead became soft and friendly; the bed on which they lay seemed wide, and white, and sturdy beneath the radiance that streamed in at the window.

Five days later, in the first cool of late afternoon, Jeffrey picked up an oak chair and sent it crashing through his own front window. Then he lay down on the couch like a child, weeping piteously and begging to die. A blood clot the size of a marble had broken in his brain.

3

There is a sort of waking nightmare that sets in sometimes when one has missed a sleep or two, a feeling that comes with extreme fatigue and a new sun that the quality of the life around has changed. It is a fully articulate conviction that somehow the existence one is then leading is a branch shoot of life and is related to life only as a moving picture or a mirror – that the people, and streets, and houses are only projections from a very dim and chaotic past. It was in such a state that Roxanne found herself during the first months of Jeffrey's illness. She slept only when she was utterly exhausted; she awoke under a cloud. The long, sober-voiced consultations, the faint aura of medicine in the halls, the sudden tiptoeing in a house that had echoed to many cheerful footsteps, and most of all Jeffrey's white face amid the pillows of the bed they had shared – these things subdued her and made her indelibly older. The doctors held out hope, but that was all. A long rest, they said, and quiet. So responsibility came to Roxanne. It was she who paid the bills, pored over his bank book, corresponded with his publishers. She was in the kitchen constantly. She learned from the nurse how to prepare his meals and after the first month took complete charge of the sickroom. She had had to let the nurse go for reasons of economy. One of the two coloured girls left at the same time. Roxanne was realising that they had been living from short story to short story.

The most frequent visitor was Harry Cromwell. He had been shocked and depressed by the news, and though his wife was now living with him in Chicago he found time to come out several times a month. Roxanne found his sympathy welcome – there was some quality of suffering in the man, some inherent pitifulness that made her comfortable when he was near. Roxanne's nature had suddenly deepened. She felt sometimes that with Jeffrey she was losing her children also, those children that now most of all she needed and should have had.

It was six months after Jeffrey's collapse and when the nightmare had faded, leaving not the old world but a new one, greyer and colder, that she went to see Harry's wife. Finding herself in Chicago with an extra hour before train time, she decided out of courtesy to call.

As she stepped inside the door she had an immediate impression that the apartment was very like some place she had seen before – and almost instantly she remembered a round-the-corner bakery of her childhood, a bakery full of rows and rows of pink frosted cakes – a stuffy pink, pink as a food, pink triumphant, vulgar and odious.

And this apartment was like that. It was pink. It smelled pink!

Mrs Cromwell, attired in a wrapper of pink and black, opened the door. Her hair was yellow, heightened, Roxanne imagined, by a dash of peroxide in the rinsing water every week. Her eyes were a thin waxen blue – she was pretty and too consciously graceful. Her cordiality was strident and intimate, hostility melted so quickly to hospitality that it seemed they were both merely in the face and voice – never touching nor touched by the deep core of egotism beneath.

But to Roxanne these things were secondary; her eyes were caught and held in uncanny fascination by the wrapper. It was vilely unclean. From its lowest hem up four inches it was sheerly dirty with the blue dust of the floor; for the next three inches it was grey, then it shaded off into its natural colour, which was – pink. It was dirty at the sleeves, too, and at the collar, and when the woman turned to lead the way into the parlour, Roxanne was sure that her neck was dirty.

A one-sided rattle of conversation began. Mrs Cromwell became explicit about her likes and dislikes, her head, her stomach, her teeth, her apartment – avoiding with a sort of insolent meticulousness any inclusion of Roxanne with life, as if presuming that Roxanne, having been dealt a blow, wished life to be carefully skirted.

Roxanne smiled. That kimono! That neck!

After five minutes a little boy toddled into the parlour – a dirty little boy clad in dirty pink rompers. His face was smudgy – Roxanne wanted to take him into her lap and wipe his nose; other parts in the vicinity of his head needed attention; his tiny shoes were kicked out at the toes. Unspeakable!

'What a darling little boy!' exclaimed Roxanne, smiling radiantly. 'Come here to me.'

Mrs Cromwell looked coldly at her son.

'He will get dirty. Look at that face!' She held her head on one side and regarded it critically.

'Isn't he a *darling*?' repeated Roxanne.

'Look at his rompers,' frowned Mrs Cromwell. 'He needs a change, don't you, George?'

George stared at her curiously. To his mind the word rompers connotated a garment extraneously smeared, as this one.

'I tried to make him look respectable this morning,' complained Mrs Cromwell as one whose patience had been sorely tried, 'and I found he didn't have any more rompers – so rather than have him go round without any I put him back in those – and his face – '

'How many pairs has he?' Roxanne's voice was pleasantly curious, 'How many feather fans have you?' she might have asked.

'Oh – ' Mrs Cromwell considered, wrinkling her pretty brow. 'Five, I think. Plenty, I know.'

'You can get them for fifty cents a pair.'

Mrs Cromwell's eyes showed surprise – and the faintest superiority. The price of rompers!

'Can you really? I had no idea. He ought to have plenty, but I haven't had a minute all week to send the laundry out.' Then, dismissing the subject as irrelevant – 'I must show you some things – '

They rose and Roxanne followed her past an open bathroom door whose garment-littered floor showed indeed that the laundry hadn't been sent out for some time, into another room that was, so to speak, the quintessence of pinkness. This was Mrs Cromwell's room.

Here the hostess opened a closet door and displayed before Roxanne's eyes an amazing collection of lingerie.

There were dozens of filmy marvels of lace and silk, all clean, unruffled, seemingly not yet touched. On hangers beside them were three new evening dresses.

'I have some beautiful things,' said Mrs Cromwell, 'but not much of a chance to wear them. Harry doesn't care about going out.' Spite crept into her voice. 'He's perfectly content to let me play nursemaid and housekeeper all day and loving wife in the evening.'

Roxanne smiled again.

'You've got some beautiful clothes here.'

'Yes, I have. Let me show you – '

'Beautiful,' repeated Roxanne, interrupting, 'but I'll have to run if I'm going to catch my train.'

She felt that her hands were trembling. She wanted to put them on this woman and shake her – shake her. She wanted her locked up somewhere and set to scrubbing floors.

'Beautiful,' she repeated, 'and I just came in for a moment.'

'Well, I'm sorry Harry isn't here.'

They moved towards the door.

' – and, oh,' said Roxanne with an effort – yet her voice was still gentle and her lips were smiling – 'I think it's Argile's where you can get those rompers. Goodbye.'

It was not until she had reached the station and bought her ticket to Marlowe that Roxanne realised it was the first five minutes in six months that her mind had been off Jeffrey.

4

A week later Harry appeared at Marlowe, arrived unexpectedly at five o'clock, and coming up the walk sank into a porch chair in a state of exhaustion. Roxanne herself had had a busy day and was worn out. The doctors were coming at five-thirty, bringing a celebrated nerve specialist from New York. She was excited and thoroughly depressed, but Harry's eyes made her sit down beside him.

'What's the matter?'

'Nothing, Roxanne,' he denied. 'I came to see how Jeff was doing. Don't you bother about me.'

'Harry,' insisted Roxanne, 'there's something the matter.'

'Nothing,' he repeated. 'How's Jeff?'

Anxiety darkened her face.

'He's a little worse, Harry. Dr Jewett has come on from New York. They thought he could tell me something definite. He's going to try and find whether this paralysis has anything to do with the original blood clot.'

Harry rose.

'Oh, I'm sorry,' he said jerkily. 'I didn't know you expected a consultation. I wouldn't have come. I thought I'd just rock on your porch for an hour – '

'Sit down,' she commanded.

Harry hesitated.

'Sit down, Harry, dear boy.' Her kindness flooded out now – enveloped him. 'I know there's something the matter. You're white as a sheet. I'm going to get you a cool bottle of beer.'

All at once he collapsed into his chair and covered his face with his hands.

'I can't make her happy,' he said slowly. 'I've tried and I've tried. This morning we had some words about breakfast – I'd been getting my breakfast down town – and – well, just after I went to the office she left the house, went East to her mother's with George and a suitcase full of lace underwear.'

'Harry!'

'And I don't know – '

There was a crunch on the gravel, a car turning into the drive. Roxanne uttered a little cry.

'It's Dr Jewett.'

'Oh, I'll – '

'You'll wait, won't you?' she interrupted abstractedly. He saw that his problem had already died on the troubled surface of her mind.

There was an embarrassing minute of vague, elided introductions and then Harry followed the party inside and watched them disappear up the stairs. He went into the library and sat down on the big sofa.

For an hour he watched the sun creep up the patterned folds of the chintz curtains. In the deep quiet a trapped wasp buzzing on the inside of the window pane assumed the proportions of a clamour. From time to time another buzzing drifted down from upstairs, resembling several more larger wasps caught on larger windowpanes. He heard low footfalls, the clink of bottles, the clamour of pouring water.

What had he and Roxanne done that life should deal these crashing blows to them? Upstairs there was taking place a living inquest on the soul of his friend; he was sitting here in a quiet room listening to the plaint of a wasp, just as when he was a boy he had been compelled by a strict aunt to sit hour-long on a chair and atone for some misbehaviour. But who had put him here? What ferocious aunt had leaned out of the sky to make him atone for – what?

About Kitty he felt a great hopelessness. She was too expensive – that was the irremediable difficulty. Suddenly he hated her. He wanted to throw her down and kick at her – to tell her she was a cheat and a leech – that she was dirty. Moreover, she must give him his boy.

He rose and began pacing up and down the room. Simultaneously he heard someone begin walking along the hallway upstairs in exact time with him. He found himself wondering if they would walk in time until the person reached the end of the hall.

Kitty had gone to her mother. God help her, what a mother to go to! He tried to imagine the meeting: the abused wife collapsing upon the mother's breast. He could not. That Kitty was capable of any deep grief was unbelievable. He had gradually grown to think of her as something unapproachable and callous. She would get a divorce, of course, and eventually she would marry again. He began to consider this. Whom would she marry? He laughed bitterly, stopped; a picture flashed before him – of Kitty's arms around some man whose face he could not see, of Kitty's lips pressed close to other lips in what was surely passion.

'God!' he cried aloud. 'God! God! God!'

Then the pictures came thick and fast. The Kitty of this morning faded; the soiled kimono rolled up and disappeared; the pouts, and rages, and tears all were washed away. Again she was Kitty Carr – Kitty Carr with yellow hair and great baby eyes. Ah, she had loved him, she had loved him.

After a while he perceived that something was amiss with him, something that had nothing to do with Kitty or Jeff, something of a different genre. Amazingly it burst on him at last; he was hungry. Simple enough! He would go into the kitchen in a moment and ask the coloured cook for a sandwich. After that he must go back to the city.

He paused at the wall, jerked at something round, and fingering it absently, put it to his mouth and tasted it as a baby tastes a bright toy. His teeth closed on it – Ah!

She'd left that damn kimono, that dirty pink kimono. She might have had the decency to take it with her, he thought. It would hang in the house like the corpse of their sick alliance. He would try to throw it away, but he would never be able to bring himself to move it. It would be like Kitty, soft and pliable, withal impervious. You couldn't move Kitty; you couldn't reach Kitty. There was nothing there to reach. He understood that perfectly – he had understood it all along.

He reached to the wall for another biscuit and with an effort pulled it out, nail and all. He carefully removed the nail from the centre, wondering idly if he had eaten the nail with the first biscuit. Preposterous! He would have remembered – it was a huge nail. He felt his stomach. He must be very hungry. He considered – remembered – yesterday he had had no dinner. It was the girl's day out and Kitty had lain in her room eating chocolate drops. She had said she felt 'smothery' and couldn't bear having him near her. He had given George a bath and put him to bed, and then lain down on the couch intending to rest a minute before getting his own dinner. There he had fallen asleep and awakened about eleven, to find that there was nothing in the ice-box except a spoonful of potato salad. This he had eaten, together with some chocolate drops that he found on Kitty's bureau. This morning he had breakfasted hurriedly downtown before going to the office. But at noon, beginning to worry about Kitty, he had decided to go home and take her out to lunch. After that there had been the note on his pillow. The pile of lingerie in the closet was gone – and she had left instructions for sending her trunk.

He had never been so hungry, he thought.

At five o'clock, when the visiting nurse tiptoed downstairs, he was sitting on the sofa staring at the carpet.

'Mr Cromwell?'

'Yes?'

'Oh, Mrs Curtain won't be able to see you at dinner. She's not well. She told me to tell you that the cook will fix you something and that there's a spare bedroom.'

'She's sick, you say?'

'She's lying down in her room. The consultation is just over.'

'Did they – did they decide anything?'

'Yes,' said the nurse softly. 'Dr Jewett says there's no hope. Mr Curtain may live indefinitely, but he'll never see again or move again or think. He'll just breathe.'

'Just breathe?'

'Yes.'

For the first time the nurse noted that beside the writing-desk where she remembered that she had seen a line of a dozen curious round objects she had vaguely imagined to be some exotic form of decoration there was now only one. Where the others had been, there was now a series of little nail-holes.

Harry followed her glance dazedly and then rose to his feet.

'I don't believe I'll stay. I believe there's a train.'

She nodded. Harry picked up his hat.

'Goodbye,' she said pleasantly.

'Goodbye,' he answered, as though talking to himself, and, evidently moved by some involuntary necessity, he paused on his way to the door and she saw him pluck the last object from the wall and drop it into his pocket.

Then he opened the screen door and, descending the porch steps, passed out of her sight.

5

After a while the coat of clean white paint on the Jeffrey Curtain house made a definite compromise with the suns of many Julys and showed its good faith by turning grey. It scaled – huge peelings of very brittle old paint leaned over backwards like aged men practising grotesque gymnastics and finally dropped to a mouldy death in the overgrown grass beneath. The paint on the front pillars became streaky; the white ball was knocked off the left-hand door-post; the green blinds darkened, then lost all pretence of colour.

It began to be a house that was avoided by the tender-minded – some church bought a lot diagonally opposite for a graveyard, and this, combined with 'the place where Mrs Curtain stays with that living corpse', was enough to throw a ghostly aura over that quarter of the road. Not that she was left alone. Men and women came to see her, met her downtown, where she went to do her marketing, brought her home in their cars – and came in for a moment to talk and to rest in the glamour that still played in her smile. But men who did not know her no longer followed her with admiring glances in the street; a diaphanous veil had come down over her beauty, destroying its vividness, yet bringing neither wrinkles nor fat.

She acquired a character in the village – a group of little stories were told of her: how when the country was frozen over one winter so that no wagons nor automobiles could travel, she taught herself to skate so that she could make quick time to the grocer and druggist, and not leave Jeffrey alone for long. It was said that every night since his paralysis she slept in a small bed beside his bed, holding his hand.

Jeffrey Curtain was spoken of as though he were already dead. As the years dropped by those who had known him died or moved away – there were but half a dozen of the old crowd who had drunk cocktails together, called each other's wives by their first names, and thought that Jeff was about the wittiest and most talented fellow that Marlowe had ever known. Now, to the casual visitor, he was merely the reason that Mrs Curtain excused herself sometimes and hurried upstairs; he was a groan or a sharp cry borne to the silent parlour on the heavy air of a Sunday afternoon.

He could not move; he was stone blind, dumb and totally unconscious. All day he lay in his bed, except for a shift to his wheelchair every morning while she straightened the room. His paralysis was creeping slowly towards his heart. At first – for the first year – Roxanne had received the faintest answering pressure sometimes when she held his hand – then it had gone, ceased one evening and never come back, and through two nights Roxanne lay wide-eyed, staring into the dark and wondering what had gone, what fraction of his soul had taken flight, what last grain of comprehension those shattered broken nerves still carried to the brain.

After that hope died. Had it not been for her unceasing care the last spark would have gone long before. Every morning she shaved and bathed him, shifted him with her own hands from bed to chair and back to bed. She was in his room constantly, bearing medicine, straightening a pillow, talking to him almost as one talks to a nearly human dog, without hope of response or appreciation, but with the dim persuasion of habit, a prayer when faith has gone.

Not a few people, one celebrated nerve specialist among them, gave her a plain impression that it was futile to exercise so much care, that if Jeffrey had been conscious he would have wished to die, that if his spirit were hovering in some wider air it would agree to no such sacrifice from her, it would fret only for the prison of its body to give it full release.

'But you see,' she replied, shaking her head gently, 'when I married Jeffrey it was – until I ceased to love him.'

'But,' was protested, in effect, 'you can't love that.'

'I can love what it once was. What else is there for me to do?'

The specialist shrugged his shoulders and went away to say that Mrs Curtain was a remarkable woman and just about as sweet as an angel – but, he added, it was a terrible pity.

'There must be some man, or a dozen, just crazy to take care of her . . . '

Casually – there were. Here and there someone began in hope – and ended in reverence. There was no love in the woman except, strangely enough, for life, for the people in the world, from the tramp to whom she gave food she could ill afford to the butcher who sold her a cheap cut of steak across the meaty board. The other phase was sealed up somewhere in that expressionless mummy who lay with his face turned ever towards the light as mechanically as a compass needle and waited dumbly for the last wave to wash over his heart.

After eleven years he died in the middle of a May night, when the scent of the syringa hung upon the window-sill and a breeze wafted in the shrillings of the frogs and cicadas outside. Roxanne awoke at two, and realised with a start she was alone in the house at last.

6

After that she sat on her weather-beaten porch through many afternoons, gazing down across the fields that undulated in a slow descent to the white and green town. She was wondering what she would do with her life. She was thirty-six – handsome, strong and free. The years had eaten up Jeffrey's insurance; she had reluctantly parted with the acres to right and left of her, and had even placed a small mortgage on the house.

With her husband's death had come a great physical restlessness. She missed having to care for him in the morning, she missed her rush to town, and the brief and therefore accentuated neighbourly meetings in the butcher's and grocer's; she missed the cooking for two, the preparation of delicate liquid food for him. One day, consumed with energy, she went out and spaded up the whole garden, a thing that had not been done for years.

And she was alone at night in the room that had seen the glory of her marriage and then the pain. To meet Jeff again she went back in spirit to that wonderful year, that intense, passionate absorption and companionship, rather than looked forward to a problematical meeting hereafter; she awoke often to lie and wish for that presence beside her – inanimate yet breathing – still Jeff.

One afternoon six months after his death she was sitting on the porch, in a black dress which took away the faintest suggestion of plumpness from her figure. It was Indian summer – golden brown all about her; a hush broken by the sighing of leaves; westward a four o'clock sun dripping streaks of red and yellow over a flaming sky. Most of the birds had gone – only a sparrow that had built itself a nest on the cornice of a pillar kept up an intermittent cheeping varied by occasional fluttering sallies overhead. Roxanne moved her chair to where she could watch him and her mind idled drowsily on the bosom of the afternoon.

Harry Cromwell was coming out from Chicago to dinner. Since his divorce over eight years before he had been a frequent visitor. They had kept up what amounted to a tradition between them: when he arrived they would go to look at Jeff; Harry would sit down on the edge of the bed and in a hearty voice ask: 'Well, Jeff, old man, how do you feel today?'

Roxanne, standing beside, would look intently at Jeff, dreaming that some shadowy recognition of this former friend had passed across that broken mind – but the head, pale, carven, would only move slowly in its sole gesture towards the light as if something behind the blind eyes were groping for another light long since gone out.

These visits stretched over eight years – at Easter, Christmas, Thanksgiving and on many a Sunday, Harry had arrived, paid his call on Jeff, and then talked for a long while with Roxanne on the porch. He was devoted to her. He made no pretence of hiding, no attempt to deepen, this relation. She was his best friend as the mass of flesh on the bed there had been his best friend. She was peace, she was rest; she was the past. Of his own tragedy she alone knew.

He had been at the funeral, but since then the company for which he worked had shifted him to the East and only a business trip had brought him to the vicinity of Chicago. Roxanne had written him to come when he could – after a night in the city he had caught a train out.

They shook hands and he helped her move two rockers together.

'How's George?'

'He's fine, Roxanne. Seems to like school.'

'Of course it was the only thing to do, to send him.'

'Of course – '

'You miss him horribly, Harry?'

'Yes – I do miss him. He's a funny boy – '

He talked a lot about George. Roxanne was interested. Harry must bring him out on his next vacation. She had only seen him once in her life – a child in dirty rompers.

She left him with the newspaper while she prepared dinner – she had four chops tonight and some late vegetables from her own garden. She put it all on and then called him, and sitting down together they continued their talk about George.

'If I had a child – ' she would say.

Afterwards, Harry having given her what slender advice he could about investments, they walked through the garden, pausing here and there to recognise what had once been a cement bench or where the tennis court had lain . . .

'Do you remember – '

Then they were off on a flood of reminiscences: the day they had taken all the snapshots and Jeff had been photographed astride the calf; and the sketch Harry had made of Jeff and Roxanne, lying sprawled in the grass, their heads almost touching. There was to have been a covered lattice connecting the barn-studio with the house, so that Jeff could get there on wet days – the lattice had been started, but nothing remained except a broken triangular piece that still adhered to the house and resembled a battered chicken coop.

'And those mint juleps!'

'And Jeff's notebook! Do you remember how we'd laugh, Harry, when we'd get it out of his pocket and read aloud a page of material. And how frantic he used to get?'

'Wild! He was such a kid about his writing.'

They were both silent a moment, and then Harry said: 'We were to have a place out here, too. Do you remember? We were to buy the adjoining twenty acres. And the parties we were going to have!'

Again there was a pause, broken this time by a low question from Roxanne.

'Do you ever hear of her, Harry?'

'Why – yes,' he admitted placidly. 'She's in Seattle. She's married again to a man named Horton, a sort of lumber king. He's a great deal older than she is, I believe.'

'And she's behaving?'

'Yes – that is, I've heard so. She has everything, you see. Nothing much to do except dress up for this fellow at dinner-time.'

'I see.'

Without effort he changed the subject.

'Are you going to keep the house?'

'I think so,' she said, nodding. 'I've lived here so long, Harry, it'd seem terrible to move. I thought of trained nursing, but of course that'd mean leaving. I've about decided to be a boarding-house lady.'

'Live in one?'

'No. Keep one. Is there such an anomaly as a boarding-house lady? Anyway I'd have a negress and keep about eight people in the summer and two or three, if I can get them, in the winter. Of course I'll have to have the house repainted and gone over inside.'

Harry considered.

'Roxanne, why – naturally you know best what you can do, but it does seem a shock, Roxanne. You came here as a bride.'

'Perhaps,' she said, 'that's why I don't mind remaining here as a boarding-house lady.'

'I remember a certain batch of biscuits.'

'Oh, those biscuits,' she cried. 'Still, from all I heard about the way you devoured them, they couldn't have been so bad. I was *so* low that day, yet somehow I laughed when the nurse told me about those biscuits.'

'I noticed that the twelve nail-holes are still in the library wall where Jeff drove them.'

'Yes.'

It was getting very dark now, a crispness settled in the air; a little gust of wind sent down a last spray of leaves. Roxanne shivered slightly.

'We'd better go in.'

He looked at his watch.

'It's late. I've got to be leaving. I go East tomorrow.'

'Must you?'

They lingered for a moment just below the stoop, watching a moon that seemed full of snow float out of the distance where the lake lay. Summer was gone and now Indian summer. The grass was cold and there was no mist and no dew. After he left she would go in and light the gas and close the shatters, and he would go down the path and on to the village. To these two life had come quickly and gone, leaving not bitterness, but pity; not disillusion, but only pain. There was already enough moonlight when they shook hands for each to see the gathered kindness in the other's eyes.

The Camel's Back

1

The glazed eye of the tired reader resting for a second on the above title will presume it to be merely metaphorical. Stories about the cup and the lip and the bad penny and the new broom rarely have anything to do with cups or lips or pennies or brooms. This story is the exception. It has to do with a material, visible and large-as-life camel's back.

Starting from the neck we shall work towards the tail. I want you to meet Mr Perry Parkhurst, twenty-eight, lawyer, native of Toledo. Perry has nice teeth, a Harvard diploma, parts his hair in the middle. You have met him before – in Cleveland, Portland, St Paul, Indianapolis, Kansas City, and so forth. Baker Brothers, New York, pause on their semi-annual trip through the West to clothe him; Montmorency & Co. dispatch a young man post-haste every three months to see that he has the correct number of little punctures on his shoes. He has a domestic roadster now, will have a French roadster if he lives long enough, and doubtless a Chinese tank if it comes into fashion. He looks like the advertisement of the young man rubbing his sunset-coloured chest with liniment and goes East every other year to his class reunion.

I want you to meet his Love. Her name is Betty Medill, and she would take well in the movies. Her father gives her three hundred a month to dress on, and she has tawny eyes and hair and feather fans of five colours. I shall also introduce her father, Cyrus Medill. Though he is to all appearances flesh and blood, he is, strange to say, commonly known in Toledo as the Aluminum Man. But when he sits in his club window with two or three Iron Men, and the White-Pine Man, and the Brass Man, they look very much as you and I do, only more so, if you know what I mean.

Now during the Christmas holidays of 1919 there took place in Toledo, counting only the people with the italicised *the*, forty-one dinner parties, sixteen dances, six luncheons, male and female, twelve teas, four stag dinners, two weddings, and thirteen bridge parties. It was the cumulative effect of all this that moved Perry Parkhurst on the twenty-ninth day of December to a decision.

This Medill girl would marry him and she wouldn't marry him. She was having such a good time that she hated to take such a definite step. Meanwhile, their secret engagement had got so long that it seemed as if any day it might break off of its own weight. A little man named Warburton, who knew it all, persuaded Perry to superman her – to get a marriage licence and go up to the Medill house and tell her she'd have to marry him at once or call it off for ever. So he presented himself, his heart, his licence, and his ultimatum, and within five minutes they were in the midst of a violent quarrel, a burst of sporadic open fighting such as occurs near the end of all long wars and engagements. It brought about one of those ghastly lapses in which two people who are in love pull up sharp, look at each other coolly and think it's all been a mistake. Afterwards they usually kiss wholesomely and assure the other person it was all their fault. Say it all was my fault! Say it was! I want to hear you say it!

But while reconciliation was trembling in the air, while each was, in a measure, stalling it off, so that they might the more voluptuously and sentimentally enjoy it when it came, they were permanently interrupted by a twenty-minute phone call for Betty from a garrulous aunt. At the end of eighteen minutes Perry Parkhurst, urged on by pride and suspicion and injured dignity, put on his long fur coat, picked up his light brown soft hat and stalked out the door.

'It's all over,' he muttered brokenly as he tried to jam his car into first. 'It's all over – if I have to choke you for an hour, damn you!' The last to the car, which had been standing some time and was quite cold.

He drove downtown – that is, he got into a snow rut that led him downtown. He sat slouched down very low in his seat, much too dispirited to care where he went.

In front of the Clarendon Hotel he was hailed from the sidewalk by a bad man named Baily, who had big teeth and lived at the hotel and had never been in love.

'Perry,' said the bad man softly when the roadster drew up beside him at the curb, 'I've got six quarts of the doggonedest still champagne you ever tasted. A third of it's yours, Perry, if you'll come upstairs and help Martin Macy and me drink it.'

'Baily,' said Perry tensely, 'I'll drink your champagne. I'll drink every drop of it, I don't care if it kills me.'

'Shut up, you nut!' said the bad man gently. 'They don't put wood alcohol in champagne. This is the stuff that proves the world is more than six thousand years old. It's so ancient that the cork is petrified. You have to pull it with a stone drill.'

'Take me upstairs,' said Perry moodily. 'If that cork sees my heart it'll fall out from pure mortification.'

The room upstairs was full of those innocent hotel pictures of little girls eating apples and sitting in swings and talking to dogs. The other decorations were neckties and a pink man reading a pink paper devoted to ladies in pink tights.

'When you have to go into the highways and byways – ' said the pink man, looking reproachfully at Baily and Perry.

'Hello, Martin Macy,' said Perry shortly, 'where's this stone-age champagne?'

'What's the rush? This isn't an operation, understand. This is a party.'

Perry sat down dully and looked disapprovingly at all the neckties.

Baily leisurely opened the door of a wardrobe and brought out six handsome bottles.

'Take off that darn fur coat!' said Martin Macy to Perry. 'Or maybe you'd like to have us open all the windows.'

'Give me champagne,' said Perry.

'Going to the Townsends' circus ball tonight?'

'Am not!'

' 'Vited?'

'Uh–huh.'

'Why not go?'

'Oh, I'm sick of parties,' exclaimed Perry. 'I'm sick of 'em. I've been to so many that I'm sick of 'em.'

'Maybe you're going to the Howard Tates' party?'

'No, I tell you; I'm sick of 'em.'

'Well,' said Macy consolingly, 'the Tates' is just for college kids anyways.'

'I tell you – '

'I thought you'd be going to one of 'em anyways. I see by the papers you haven't missed a one this Christmas.'

'Hm,' grunted Perry morosely.

He would never go to any more parties. Classical phrases played in his mind – that side of his life was closed, closed. Now when a man says 'closed, closed' like that, you can be pretty sure that some woman has double-closed him, so to speak. Perry was also thinking that other classical thought, about how cowardly suicide is. A noble thought that one – warm and inspiring. Think of all the fine men we should lose if suicide were not so cowardly!

An hour later was six o'clock, and Perry had lost all resemblance to the young man in the liniment advertisement. He looked like a rough draft for a riotous cartoon. They were singing – an impromptu song of Baily's improvisation:

> 'One Lump Perry, the parlour snake,
> Famous through the city for the way he drinks his tea;
> Plays with it, toys with it,
> Makes no noise with it,
> Balanced on a napkin on his well-trained knee – '

'Trouble is,' said Perry, who had just banged his hair with Baily's comb and was tying an orange tie round it to get the effect of Julius Caesar, 'that you fellas can't sing worth a damn. Soon's I leave the air and start singing tenor you start singin' tenor too.'

' 'm a natural tenor,' said Macy gravely. 'Voice lacks cultivation, tha's all. Gotta natural voice, m'aunt used say. Naturally good singer.'

'Singers, singers, all good singers,' remarked Baily, who was at the telephone. 'No, not the cabaret; I want night egg. I mean some doggone clerk 'at's got food – food! I want – '

'Julius Caesar,' announced Perry, turning round from the mirror. 'Man of iron will and stern 'termination.'

'Shut up!' yelled Baily. 'Say, iss Mr Baily. Sen' up enormous supper. Use y'own judgement. Right away.'

He connected the receiver and the hook with some difficulty, and then with his lips closed and an expression of solemn intensity in his eyes went to the lower drawer of his dresser and pulled it open.

'Lookit!' he commanded. In his hands he held a truncated garment of pink gingham.

'Pants,' he exclaimed gravely. 'Lookit!'

This was a pink blouse, a red tie, and a Buster Brown collar.

'Lookit!' he repeated. 'Costume for the Townsends' circus ball. I'm li'l' boy carries water for the elephants.'

Perry was impressed in spite of himself.

'I'm going to be Julius Caesar,' he announced after a moment of concentration.

'Thought you weren't going!' said Macy.

'Me? Sure I'm goin'. Never miss a party. Good for the nerves – like celery.'

'Caesar!' scoffed Baily. 'Can't be Caesar! He is not about a circus. Caesar's Shakespeare. Go as a clown.'

Perry shook his head.

'Nope; Caesar,'

'Caesar?'

'Sure. Chariot.'

Light dawned on Baily.

'That's right. Good idea.'

Perry looked round the room searchingly.

'You lend me a bathrobe and this tie,' he said finally. Baily considered.

'No good.'

'Sure, tha's all I need. Caesar was a savage. They can't kick if I come as Caesar, if he was a savage.'

'No,' said Baily, shaking his head slowly. 'Get a costume over at a costumer's. Over at Nolak's.'

'Closed up.'

'Find out.'

After a puzzling five minutes at the phone a small, weary voice managed to convince Perry that it was Mr Nolak speaking, and that they would remain open until eight because of the Townsends' ball. Thus assured, Perry ate a great amount of filet mignon and drank his third of the last bottle of champagne. At eight-fifteen the man in the tall hat who stands in front of the Clarendon found him trying to start his roadster.

'Froze up,' said Perry wisely. 'The cold froze it. The cold air.'

'Froze, eh?'

'Yes. Cold air froze it.'

'Can't start it?'

'Nope. Let it stand here till summer. One those hot ole August days'll thaw it out awright.'

'Goin' let it stand?'

'Sure. Let 'er stand. Take a hot thief to steal it. Gemme taxi.'

The man in the tall hat summoned a taxi.

'Where to, mister?'

'Go to Nolak's – costume fella.'

2

Mrs Nolak was short and ineffectual looking, and on the cessation of the World War had belonged for a while to one of the new nationalities. Owing to unsettled European conditions she had never since been quite sure what she was. The shop in which she and her husband performed their daily stint was dim and ghostly, and peopled with suits of armour and Chinese mandarins, and enormous papier-mâché birds suspended from the ceiling. In a vague background many rows of masks glared eyelessly at the visitor, and there were glass cases full of crowns and sceptres, and jewels and enormous stomachers, and paints, and crape hair, and wigs of all colours.

When Perry ambled into the shop Mrs Nolak was folding up the last troubles of a strenuous day, so she thought, in a drawer full of pink silk stockings.

'Something for you?' she queried pessimistically.

'Want costume of Julius Hur, the charioteer.'

Mrs Nolak was sorry, but every stitch of charioteer had been rented long ago. Was it for the Townsends' circus ball?

It was.

'Sorry,' she said, 'but I don't think there's anything left that's really circus.'

This was an obstacle.

'Hm,' said Perry. An idea struck him suddenly. 'If you've got a piece of canvas I could go's a tent.'

'Sorry, but we haven't anything like that. A hardware store is where you'd have to go to. We have some very nice Confederate soldiers.'

'No. No soldiers.'

'And I have a very handsome king.'

He shook his head.

'Several of the gentlemen,' she continued hopefully, 'are wearing stovepipe hats and swallowtail coats and going as ringmasters – but we're all out of tall hats. I can let you have some crape hair for a moustache.'

'Want somep'n 'stinctive.'

'Something – let's see. Well, we have a lion's head, and a goose, and a camel – '

'Camel?' The idea seized Perry's imagination, gripped it fiercely.

'Yes, but it needs two people.'

'Camel. That's the idea. Lemme see it.'

The camel was produced from his resting place on a top shelf. At first glance he appeared to consist entirely of a very gaunt, cadaverous head and a sizable hump, but on being spread out he was found to possess a dark brown, unwholesome-looking body made of thick, cottony cloth.

'You see it takes two people,' explained Mrs Nolak, holding the camel in frank admiration. 'If you have a friend he could be part of it. You see there's sorta pants for two people. One pair is for the fella in front, and the other pair for the fella in back. The fella in front does the lookin' out through these here eyes, an' the fella in back he's just gotta stoop over an' folla the front fella round.'

'Put it on,' commanded Perry.

Obediently Mrs Nolak put her tabby-cat face inside the camel's head and turned it from side to side ferociously.

Perry was fascinated.

'What noise does a camel make?'

'What?' asked Mrs Nolak as her face emerged, somewhat smudgy. 'Oh, what noise? Why, he sorta brays.'

'Lemme see it in a mirror.'

Before a wide mirror Perry tried on the head and turned from side to side appraisingly. In the dim light the effect was distinctly pleasing. The camel's face was a study in pessimism, decorated with numerous abrasions, and it must be admitted that his coat was in that state of general negligence peculiar to camels – in fact, he needed to be cleaned and pressed – but distinctive he certainly was. He was majestic. He would have attracted attention in any gathering, if only by his melancholy cast of feature and the look of hunger lurking round his shadowy eyes.

'You see you have to have two people,' said Mrs Nolak again.

Perry tentatively gathered up the body and legs and wrapped them about him, tying the hind legs as a girdle round his waist. The effect on the whole was bad. It was even irreverent – like one of those medieval pictures of a monk changed into a beast by the ministrations of Satan. At the very best the ensemble resembled a humpbacked cow sitting on her haunches among blankets.

'Don't look like anything at all,' objected Perry gloomily.

'No,' said Mrs Nolak; 'you see you got to have two people.'

A solution flashed upon Perry.

'You got a date tonight?'

'Oh, I couldn't possibly – '

'Oh, come on,' said Perry encouragingly. 'Sure you can! Here! Be good sport, and climb into these hind legs.'

With difficulty he located them, and extended their yawning depths ingratiatingly. But Mrs Nolak seemed loath. She backed perversely away.

'Oh, no – '

'C'mon! You can be the front if you want to. Or we'll flip a coin.'

'Oh, no – '

'Make it worth your while.'

Mrs Nolak set her lips firmly together.

'Now you just stop!' she said with no coyness implied. 'None of the gentlemen ever acted up this way before. My husband – '

'You got a husband?' demanded Perry. 'Where is he?'

'He's home.'

'Wha's telephone number?'

After considerable parley he obtained the telephone number pertaining to the Nolak penates and got into communication with that small, weary voice he had heard once before that day. But Mr Nolak, though taken off his guard and somewhat confused by Perry's brilliant flow of logic, stuck staunchly to his point. He refused firmly, but with dignity, to help out Mr Parkhurst in the capacity of back part of a camel.

Having rung off, or rather having been rung off on, Perry sat down on a three-legged stool to think it over. He named over to himself those friends on whom he might call, and then his mind paused as Betty Medill's name hazily and sorrowfully occurred to him. He had a sentimental thought. He would ask her. Their love affair was over, but she could not refuse this last request. Surely it was not much to ask – to help him keep up his end of social obligation for one short night. And if she insisted, she could be the front part of the camel and he would go as the back. His magnanimity pleased him. His mind even turned to rosy-coloured dreams of a tender reconciliation inside the camel – there hidden away from all the world . . .

'Now you'd better decide right off.'

The bourgeois voice of Mrs Nolak broke in upon his mellow fancies and roused him to action. He went to the phone and called up the Medill house. Miss Betty was out; had gone out to dinner.

Then, when all seemed lost, the camel's back wandered curiously into the store. He was a dilapidated individual with a cold in his head and a general trend about him of downwardness. His cap was pulled down low on his head, and his chin was pulled down low on his chest, his coat hung down to his shoes, he looked run-down, down at the heels, and – Salvation Army to the contrary – down and out. He said that he was the taxicab-driver that the gentleman had hired at the Clarendon Hotel. He had been instructed to wait outside, but he had waited some time, and a suspicion had grown upon him that the gentleman had gone out the back way with purpose to defraud him – gentlemen sometimes did – so he had come in. He sank down on to the three-legged stool.

'Wanta go to a party?' demanded Perry sternly.

'I gotta work,' answered the taxi-driver lugubriously. 'I gotta keep my job.'

'It's a very good party.'

' 's a very good job.'

'Come on!' urged Perry. 'Be a good fella. See – it's pretty!' He held the camel up and the taxi-driver looked at it cynically.

'Huh!'

Perry searched feverishly among the folds of the cloth. 'See!' he cried enthusiastically, holding up a selection of folds. 'This is your part. You don't even have to talk. All you have to do is to walk – and sit down occasionally. You do all the sitting down. Think of it. I'm on my feet all the time and *you* can sit down some of the time. The only time *I* can sit down is when we're lying down, and you can sit down when – oh, any time. See?'

'What's 'at thing?' demanded the individual dubiously. 'A shroud?'

'Not at all,' said Perry indignantly. 'It's a camel.'

'Huh?'

Then Perry mentioned a sum of money, and the conversation left the land of grunts and assumed a practical tinge. Perry and the taxi-driver tried on the camel in front of the mirror.

'You can't see it,' explained Perry, peering anxiously out through the eyeholes, 'but honestly, ole man, you look sim'ly great! Honestly!'

A grunt from the hump acknowledged this somewhat dubious compliment.

'Honestly, you look great!' repeated Perry enthusiastically. 'Move round a little.'

The hind legs moved forward, giving the effect of a huge cat-camel hunching his back preparatory to a spring.

'No; move sideways.'

The camel's hips went neatly out of joint; a hula dancer would have writhed in envy.

'Good, isn't it?' demanded Perry, turning to Mrs Nolak for approval.

'It looks lovely,' agreed Mrs Nolak.

'We'll take it,' said Perry.

The bundle was stowed under Perry's arm and they left the shop.

'Go to the party!' he commanded as he took his seat in the back.

'What party?'

'Fanzy-dress party.'

'Where'bouts is it?'

This presented a new problem. Perry tried to remember, but the names of all those who had given parties during the holidays danced confusedly before his eyes. He could ask Mrs Nolak, but on looking out the window he saw that the shop was dark. Mrs Nolak had already faded out, a little black smudge far down the snowy street.

'Drive uptown,' directed Perry with fine confidence. 'If you see a party, stop. Otherwise I'll tell you when we get there.'

He fell into a hazy daydream and his thoughts wandered again to Betty – he imagined vaguely that they had had a disagreement because she refused to go to the party as the back part of the camel. He was just slipping off into a chilly doze when he was wakened by the taxi-driver opening the door and shaking him by the arm.

'Here we are, maybe.'

Perry looked out sleepily. A striped awning led from the curb up to a spreading grey stone house, from which issued the low drummy whine of expensive jazz.

He recognised the Howard Tate house.

'Sure,' he said emphatically; ' 'at's it! Tate's party tonight. Sure, everybody's goin'.'

'Say,' said the individual anxiously after another look at the awning, 'you sure these people ain't gonna romp on me for comin' here?'

Perry drew himself up with dignity.

‘ ’f anybody says anything to you, just tell ’em you’re part of my costume.’

The visualisation of himself as a thing rather than a person seemed to reassure the individual.

‘All right,’ he said reluctantly.

Perry stepped out under the shelter of the awning and began unrolling the camel.

‘Let’s go,’ he commanded.

Several minutes later a melancholy, hungry-looking camel, emitting clouds of smoke from his mouth and from the tip of his noble hump, might have been seen crossing the threshold of the Howard Tate residence, passing a startled footman without so much as a snort, and heading directly for the main stairs that led up to the ballroom. The beast walked with a peculiar gait which varied between an uncertain lockstep and a stampede – but can best be described by the word ‘halting’. The camel had a halting gait – and as he walked he alternately elongated and contracted like a gigantic concertina.

3

The Howard Tates are, as everyone who lives in Toledo knows, the most formidable people in town. Mrs Howard Tate was a Chicago Todd before she became a Toledo Tate, and the family generally affect that conscious simplicity which has begun to be the earmark of American aristocracy. The Tates have reached the stage where they talk about pigs and farms and look at you icy-eyed if you are not amused. They have begun to prefer retainers rather than friends as dinner guests, spend a lot of money in a quiet way, and, having lost all sense of competition, are in process of growing quite dull.

The dance this evening was for little Millicent Tate, and though all ages were represented, the dancers were mostly from school and college – the younger married crowd was at the Townsends’ circus ball up at the Tallyho Club. Mrs Tate was standing just inside the ballroom, following Millicent round with her eyes, and beaming whenever she caught her eye. Beside her were two middle-aged sycophants, who were saying what a perfectly exquisite child Millicent was. It was at this moment that Mrs Tate was grasped firmly by the skirt and her youngest daughter, Emily, aged eleven, hurled herself with an 'Oof!' into her mother's arms.

'Why, Emily, what's the trouble?'

'Mamma,' said Emily, wild-eyed but voluble, 'there's something out on the stairs.'

'What?'

'There's a thing out on the stairs, mamma. I think it's a big dog, mamma, but it doesn't look like a dog.'

'What do you mean, Emily?'

The sycophants waved their heads sympathetically.

'Mamma, it looks like a – like a camel.'

Mrs Tate laughed.

'You saw a mean old shadow, dear, that's all.'

'No, I didn't. No, it was some kind of thing, mamma – big. I was going downstairs to see if there were any more people, and this dog or something, he was coming upstairs. Kinda funny, mamma, like he was lame. And then he saw me and gave a sort of growl, and then he slipped at the top of the landing, and I ran.'

Mrs Tate's laugh faded. 'The child must have seen something,' she said.

The sycophants agreed that the child must have seen something – and suddenly all three women took an instinctive step away from the door as the sounds of muffled steps were audible just outside.

And then three startled gasps rang out as a dark brown form rounded the corner, and they saw what was apparently a huge beast looking down at them hungrily.

'Oof!' cried Mrs Tate.

'O–o–oh!' cried the ladies in a chorus.

The camel suddenly humped his back, and the gasps turned to shrieks.

'Oh – look!'

'What is it?'

The dancing stopped, but the dancers hurrying over got quite a different impression of the invader; in fact, the young people immediately suspected that it was a stunt, a hired entertainer come to amuse the party. The boys in long trousers looked at it rather disdainfully, and sauntered over with their hands in their pockets, feeling that their intelligence was being insulted. But the girls uttered little shouts of glee.

'It's a camel!'

'Well, if he isn't the funniest!'

The camel stood there uncertainly, swaying slightly from side to aide, and seeming to take in the room in a careful, appraising glance; then as if he had come to an abrupt decision, he turned and ambled swiftly out the door.

Mr Howard Tate had just come out of the library on the lower floor, and was standing chatting with a young man in the hall. Suddenly they heard the noise of shouting upstairs, and almost immediately a succession of bumping sounds, followed by the precipitous appearance at the foot of the stairway of a large brown beast that seemed to be going somewhere in a great hurry.

'Now what the devil!' said Mr Tate, starting.

The beast picked itself up not without dignity and, affecting an air of extreme nonchalance, as if he had just remembered an important engagement, started at a mixed gait towards the front door. In fact, his front legs began casually to run.

'See here now,' said Mr Tate sternly. 'Here! Grab it, Butterfield! Grab it!'

The young man enveloped the rear of the camel in a pair of compelling arms, and, realising that further locomotion was impossible, the front end submitted to capture and stood resignedly in a state of some agitation. By this time a flood of young people was pouring downstairs, and Mr Tate, suspecting everything from an ingenious burglar to an escaped lunatic, gave crisp directions to the young man: 'Hold him! Lead him in here; we'll soon see.'

The camel consented to be led into the library, and Mr Tate, after locking the door, took a revolver from a table drawer and instructed the young man to take the thing's head off. Then he gasped and returned the revolver to its hiding-place.

'Well, Perry Parkhurst!' he exclaimed in amazement.

'Got the wrong party, Mr Tate,' said Perry sheepishly. 'Hope I didn't scare you.'

'Well – you gave us a thrill, Perry.' Realisation dawned on him. 'You're bound for the Townsends' circus ball.'

'That's the general idea.'

'Let me introduce Mr Butterfield, Mr Parkhurst.' Then turning to Perry: 'Butterfield is staying with us for a few days.'

'I got a little mixed up,' mumbled Perry. 'I'm very sorry.'

'Perfectly all right; most natural mistake in the world. I've got a clown rig and I'm going down there myself after a while.' He turned to Butterfield. 'Better change your mind and come down with us.'

The young man demurred. He was going to bed.

'Have a drink, Perry?' suggested Mr Tate.

'Thanks, I will.'

'And, say,' continued Tate quickly, 'I'd forgotten all about your – friend here.' He indicated the rear part of the camel. 'I didn't mean to seem discourteous. Is it anyone I know? Bring him out.'

'It's not a friend,' explained Perry hurriedly. 'I just rented him.'

'Does he drink?'

'Do you?' demanded Perry, twisting himself tortuously round.

There was a faint sound of assent.

'Sure he does!' said Mr Tate heartily. 'A really efficient camel ought to be able to drink enough so it'd last him three days.'

'Tell you,' said Perry anxiously, 'he isn't exactly dressed up enough to come out. If you give me the bottle I can hand it back to him and he can take his inside.'

From under the cloth was audible the enthusiastic smacking sound inspired by this suggestion. When a butler had appeared with bottles, glasses and siphon, one of the bottles was handed back; thereafter the silent partner could be heard imbibing long potations at frequent intervals.

Thus passed a benign hour. At ten o'clock Mr Tate decided that they'd better be starting. He donned his clown's costume, Perry replaced the camel's head, and side by side they traversed on foot the single block between the Tate house and the Tallyho Club.

The circus ball was in full swing. A great tent fly had been put up inside the ballroom and round the walls had been built rows of booths representing the various attractions of a circus sideshow, but these were now vacated and over the floor swarmed a shouting, laughing medley of youth and colour – clowns, bearded ladies, acrobats, bareback riders, ringmasters, tattooed men and charioteers. The Townsends had determined to assure their party of success, so a great quantity of liquor had been surreptitiously brought over from their house and was now flowing freely. A green ribbon ran along the wall completely round the ballroom, with pointing arrows alongside and signs which instructed the uninitiated to 'Follow the green line!' The green line led down to the bar, where waited pure punch and wicked punch and plain dark-green bottles.

On the wall above the bar was another arrow, red and very wavy, and under it the slogan: 'Now follow this!'

But even amid the luxury of costume and high spirits represented there, the entrance of the camel created something of a stir, and Perry was immediately surrounded by a curious, laughing crowd attempting to penetrate the identity of this beast that stood by the wide doorway eying the dancers with his hungry, melancholy gaze.

And then Perry saw Betty standing in front of a booth, talking to a comic policeman. She was dressed in the costume of an Egyptian snake-charmer: her tawny hair was braided and drawn through brass rings, the effect crowned with a glittering Oriental tiara. Her fair face was stained to a warm olive glow and on her arms and the half moon of her back writhed painted serpents with single eyes of venomous green. Her feet were in sandals and her skirt was slit to the knees, so that when she walked one caught a glimpse of other slim serpents painted just above her bare ankles. Wound about her neck was a glittering cobra. Altogether a charming costume – one that caused the more nervous among the older women to shrink away from her when she passed, and the more troublesome ones to make great talk about 'shouldn't be allowed' and 'perfectly disgraceful'.

But Perry, peering through the uncertain eyes of the camel, saw only her face, radiant, animated, and glowing with excitement, and her arms and shoulders, whose mobile, expressive gestures made her always the outstanding figure in any group. He was fascinated and his fascination exercised a sobering effect on him. With a growing clarity the events of the day came back – rage rose within him, and with a half-formed intention of taking her away from the crowd he started towards her – or rather he elongated slightly, for he had neglected to issue the preparatory command necessary to locomotion.

But at this point fickle Kismet, who for a day had played with him bitterly and sardonically, decided to reward him in full for the amusement he had afforded her. Kismet turned the tawny eyes of the snake-charmer to the camel. Kismet led her to lean towards the man beside her and say, 'Who's that? That camel?'

'Darned if I know.'

But a little man named Warburton, who knew it all, found it necessary to hazard an opinion: 'It came in with Mr Tate. I think part of it's probably Warren Butterfield, the architect from New York, who's visiting the Tates.'

Something stirred in Betty Medill – that age-old interest of the provincial girl in the visiting man.

'Oh,' she said casually after a slight pause.

At the end of the next dance Betty and her partner finished up within a few feet of the camel. With the informal audacity that was the keynote of the evening she reached out and gently rubbed the camel's nose.

'Hello, old camel.'

The camel stirred uneasily.

'You 'fraid of me?' said Betty, lifting her eyebrows in reproof. 'Don't be. You see I'm a snake-charmer, but I'm pretty good at camels too.'

The camel bowed very low and someone made the obvious remark about beauty and the beast.

Mrs Townsend approached the group.

'Well, Mr Butterfield,' she said helpfully, 'I wouldn't have recognised you.'

Perry bowed again and smiled gleefully behind his mask.

'And who is this with you?' she enquired.

'Oh,' said Perry, his voice muffled by the thick cloth and quite unrecognisable, 'he isn't a fellow, Mrs Townsend. He's just part of my costume.'

Mrs Townsend laughed and moved away. Perry turned again to Betty,

'So,' he thought, 'this is how much she cares! On the very day of our final rupture she starts a flirtation with another man – an absolute stranger.'

On an impulse he gave her a soft nudge with his shoulder and waved his head suggestively towards the hall, making it clear that he desired her to leave her partner and accompany him.

'Bye-bye, Rus,' she called to her partner. 'This old camel's got me. Where we going, Prince of Beasts?'

The noble animal made no rejoinder, but stalked gravely along in the direction of a secluded nook on the side stairs.

There she seated herself, and the camel, after some seconds of confusion which included gruff orders and sounds of a heated dispute going on in his interior, placed himself beside her – his hind legs stretching out uncomfortably across two steps.

'Well, old egg,' said Betty cheerfully, 'how do you like our happy party?'

The old egg indicated that he liked it by rolling his head ecstatically and executing a gleeful kick with his hoofs.

'This is the first time that I ever had a tête-à-tête with a man's valet 'round' – she pointed to the hind legs – 'or whatever that is.'

'Oh,' mumbled Perry, 'he's deaf and blind.'

'I should think you'd feel rather handicapped – you can't very well toddle, even if you want to.'

The camel hung his head lugubriously.

'I wish you'd say something,' continued Betty sweetly. 'Say you like me, camel. Say you think I'm beautiful. Say you'd like to belong to a pretty snake-charmer.'

The camel would.

'Will you dance with me, camel?'

The camel would try.

Betty devoted half an hour to the camel. She devoted at least half an hour to all visiting men. It was usually sufficient. When she approached a new man the current débutantes were accustomed to scatter right and left like a close column deploying before a machine-gun. And so to Perry Parkhurst was awarded the unique privilege of seeing his love as others saw her. He was flirted with violently!

4

This paradise of frail foundation was broken into by the sounds of a general ingress to the ballroom; the cotillion was beginning. Betty and the camel joined the crowd, her brown hand resting lightly on his shoulder, defiantly symbolising her complete adoption of him.

When they entered the couples were already seating themselves at tables round the walls, and Mrs Townsend, resplendent as a super bareback rider with rather too rotund calves, was standing in the centre with the ringmaster in charge of arrangements. At a signal to the band everyone rose and began to dance.

'Isn't it just slick!' sighed Betty. 'Do you think you can possibly dance?'

Perry nodded enthusiastically. He felt suddenly exuberant. After all, he was here incognito talking to his love – he could wink patronisingly at the world.

So Perry danced the cotillion. I say danced, but that is stretching the word far beyond the wildest dreams of the jazziest terpsichorean. He suffered his partner to put her hands on his helpless shoulders and pull him here and there over the floor while he hung his huge head docilely over her shoulder and made futile dummy motions with his feet. His hind legs danced in a manner all their own, chiefly by hopping first on one foot and then on the other. Never being sure whether dancing was going on or not, the hind legs played safe by going through a series of steps whenever the music started playing. So the spectacle was frequently presented of the front part of the camel standing at ease and the rear keeping up a constant energetic motion calculated to rouse a sympathetic perspiration in any soft-hearted observer.

He was frequently favoured. He danced first with a tall lady covered with straw who announced jovially that she was a bale of hay and coyly begged him not to eat her.

'I'd like to; you're so sweet,' said the camel gallantly.

Each time the ringmaster shouted his call of 'Men up!' he lumbered ferociously for Betty with the cardboard wienerwurst or the photograph of the bearded lady or whatever the favour chanced to be. Sometimes he reached her first, but usually his rushes were unsuccessful and resulted in intense interior arguments.

'For heaven's sake,' Perry would snarl, fiercely between his clenched teeth, 'get a little pep! I could have gotten her that time if you'd picked your feet up.'

'Well, gimme a little warnin'!'

'I did, darn you.'

'I can't see a doggone thing in here.'

'All you have to do is follow me. It's just like dragging a load of sand round to walk with you.'

'Maybe you wanta try back here.'

'You shut up! If these people found you in this room they'd give you the worst beating you ever had. They'd take your taxi licence away from you!'

Perry surprised himself by the ease with which he made this monstrous threat, but it seemed to have a soporific influence on his companion, for he gave out an 'aw gwan' and subsided into abashed silence.

The ringmaster mounted to the top of the piano and waved his hand for silence.

'Prizes!' he cried. 'Gather round!'

'Yea! Prizes!'

Self-consciously the circle swayed forward. The rather pretty girl who had mustered the nerve to come as a bearded lady trembled with excitement, thinking to be rewarded for an evening's hideousness. The man who had spent the afternoon having tattoo marks painted on him skulked on the edge of the crowd, blushing furiously when anyone told him he was sure to get it.

'Lady and gent performers of this circus,' announced the ringmaster jovially, 'I am sure we will all agree that a good time has been had by all. We will now bestow honour where honour is due by bestowing the prizes. Mrs Townsend has asked me to bestow the prices. Now, fellow performers, the first prize is for that lady who has displayed this evening the most striking, becoming' – at this point the bearded lady sighed resignedly – 'and original costume.' Here the bale of hay pricked up her ears. 'Now I am sure that the decision which has been agreed upon will be unanimous with all here present. The first prize goes to Miss Betty Medill, the charming Egyptian snake-charmer.' There was a burst of applause, chiefly masculine, and Miss Betty Medill, blushing beautifully through her olive paint, was passed up to receive her award. With a tender glance the ringmaster handed down to her a huge bouquet of orchids.

'And now,' he continued, looking round him, 'the other prize is for that man who has the most amusing and original costume. This prize goes without dispute to a guest in our midst, a gentleman who is visiting here but whose stay we all hope will be long and merry – in short, to the noble camel who has entertained us all by his hungry look and his brilliant dancing throughout the evening.'

He ceased and there was a violent clapping, and yeaing, for it was a popular choice. The prize, a large box of cigars, was put aside for the camel, as he was anatomically unable to accept it in person.

'And now,' continued the ringmaster, 'we will wind up the cotillion with the marriage of Mirth to Folly! Form for the grand wedding march, the beautiful snake-charmer and the noble camel in front!'

Betty skipped forward cheerily and wound an olive arm round the camel's neck. Behind them formed the procession of little boys, little girls, country jakes, fat ladies, thin men, sword-swallowers, wild men of Borneo and armless wonders, many of them well in their cups, all of them excited and happy and dazzled by the flow of light and colour round them, and by the familiar faces, strangely unfamiliar under bizarre wigs and barbaric paint. The voluptuous chords of the wedding march done in blasphemous syncopation issued in a delirious blend from the trombones and saxophones – and the march began.

'Aren't you glad, camel?' demanded Betty sweetly as they stepped off. 'Aren't you glad we're going to be married and you're going to belong to the nice snake-charmer ever afterwards?'

The camel's front legs pranced, expressing excessive joy.

'Minister! Minister! Where's the minister?' cried voices out of the revel. 'Who's going to be the clergyman?'

The head of Jumbo, obese negro waiter at the Tally-ho Club for many years, appeared rashly through a half-opened pantry door.

'Oh, Jumbo!'

'Get old Jumbo. He's the fella!'

'Come on, Jumbo. How 'bout marrying us a couple?'

'Yea!'

Jumbo was seized by four comedians, stripped of his apron, and escorted to a raised dais at the head of the ball. There his collar was removed and replaced back side forward with ecclesiastical effect. The parade separated into two lines, leaving an aisle for the bride and groom.

'Lawdy, man,' roared Jumbo, 'Ah got ole Bible 'n' ev'ythin', sho nuff.'

He produced a battered Bible from an interior pocket.

'Yea! Jumbo's got a Bible!'

'Razor, too, I'll bet!'

Together the snake-charmer and the camel ascended the cheering aisle and stopped in front of Jumbo.

'Where's yo' licence, camel?'

A man near by prodded Perry. 'Give him a piece of paper. Anything'll do.'

Perry fumbled confusedly in his pocket, found a folded paper, and pushed it out through the camel's mouth.

Holding it upside down Jumbo pretended to scan it earnestly. 'Dis yeah's a special camel's licence,' he said. 'Get yo' ring ready, camel.'

Inside the camel Perry turned round and addressed his worse half.

'Gimme a ring, for heaven's sake!'

'I ain't got none,' protested a weary voice.

'You have. I saw it.'

'I ain't goin' to take it offen my hand.'

'If you don't I'll kill you.'

There was a gasp and Perry felt a huge affair of rhinestone and brass inserted into his hand.

Again he was nudged from the outside. 'Speak up!'

'I do!' cried Perry quickly.

He heard Betty's responses given in a debonair tone, and even in this burlesque the sound thrilled him.

Then he had pushed the rhinestone through a tear in the camel's coat and was slipping it on her finger, muttering ancient and historic words after Jumbo. He didn't want anyone to know about this ever. His one idea was to slip away without having to disclose his identity, for Mr Tate had so far kept his secret well. A dignified young man, Perry – and this might injure his infant law practice.

'Embrace the bride!'

'Unmask, camel, and kiss her!'

Instinctively his heart beat high as Betty turned to him laughingly and began to strike the cardboard muzzle. He felt his self-control giving way, he longed to surround her with his arms and declare his identity and kiss those lips that smiled only a foot away – when suddenly the laughter and applause round them died off and a curious hush fell over the hall. Perry and Betty looked up in surprise. Jumbo had given vent to a huge, 'Hello!' in such a startled voice that all eyes were bent on him.

'Hello!' he said again. He had turned round the camel's marriage licence, which he had been holding upside down, produced spectacles, and was studying it agonisingly.

'Why,' he exclaimed, and in the pervading silence his words were heard plainly by everyone in the room, 'this yeah's a sho-nuff marriage permit.'

'What?'

'Huh?'

'Say it again, Jumbo!'

'Sure you can read?'

Jumbo waved them to silence and Perry's blood burned to fire in his veins as he realised the break he had made.

'Yassuh!' repeated Jumbo. 'This yeah's a sho-nuff licence, and the pa'ties concerned – one of 'em is dis yeah young lady, Miz Betty Medill, and th' other's Mistah Perry Pa'khurst.'

There was a general gasp, and a low rumble broke out as all eyes fell on the camel. Betty shrank away from him quickly, her tawny eyes giving out sparks of fury.

'Is you Mistah Pa'khurst, you camel?'

Perry made no answer. The crowd pressed up closer and stared at him. He stood frozen rigid with embarrassment, his cardboard face still hungry and sardonic as he regarded the ominous Jumbo.

'Y'all bettah speak up!' said Jumbo slowly, 'this yeah's a mighty serious mattah. Outside mah duties at this club ah happens to be a sho-nuff minister in the Firs' Cullud Baptis' Church. It done look to me as though y'all is gone an' got married.'

5

The scene that followed will go down for ever in the annals of the Tallyho Club. Stout matrons fainted, one-hundred-per-cent Americans swore, wild-eyed débutantes babbled in lightning groups instantly formed and instantly dissolved, and a great buzz of chatter, virulent yet oddly subdued, hummed through the chaotic ballroom. Feverish youths swore they would kill Perry or Jumbo or themselves or someone, and the Baptis' preacheh was besieged by a tempestuous covey of clamorous amateur lawyers, asking questions, making threats, demanding precedents, ordering the bonds annulled, and especially trying to ferret out any hint of prearrangement in what had occurred.

In the corner Mrs Townsend was crying softly on the shoulder of Mr Howard Tate, who was trying vainly to comfort her; they were exchanging 'all my fault' volubly and voluminously. Outside on a snow-covered walk Mr Cyrus Medill, the Aluminum Man, was being paced slowly up and down between two brawny charioteers, giving vent now to a string of unrepeatables, now to wild pleadings that they'd just let him get at Jumbo. He was facetiously attired for the evening as a wild man of Borneo, and the most exacting stage-manager would have acknowledged any improvement in casting the part to be quite impossible.

Meanwhile the two principals held the real centre of the stage. Betty Medill – or was it Betty Parkhurst? – storming furiously, was surrounded by the plainer girls – the prettier ones were too busy talking about her to pay much attention to her – and over on the other side of the hall stood the camel, still intact except for his headpiece, which dangled pathetically on his chest. Perry was earnestly engaged in making protestations of his innocence to a ring of angry, puzzled men. Every few minutes, just as he had apparently proved his case, someone would mention the marriage certificate, and the inquisition would begin again.

A girl named Marion Cloud, considered the second best belle of Toledo, changed the gist of the situation by a remark she made to Betty. 'Well,' she said maliciously, 'it'll all blow over, dear. The courts will annul it without question.'

Betty's angry tears dried miraculously in her eyes, her lips shut tight together, and she looked stonily at Marion. Then she rose and, scattering her sympathisers right and left, walked directly across the room to Perry, who stared at her in terror. Again silence crept down upon the room.

'Will you have the decency to grant me five minutes' convers-ation – or wasn't that included in your plans?'

He nodded, his mouth unable to form words.

Indicating coldly that he was to follow her she walked out into the hall with her chin uptilted and headed for the privacy of one of the little card-rooms.

Perry started after her, but was brought to a jerky halt by the failure of his hind legs to function.

'You stay here!' he commanded savagely.

'I can't,' whined a voice from the hump, 'unless you get out first and let me get out.'

Perry hesitated, but unable any longer to tolerate the eyes of the curious crowd he muttered a command and the camel moved carefully from the room on its four legs.

Betty was waiting for him.

'Well,' she began furiously, 'you see what you've done! You and that crazy licence! I told you you shouldn't have gotten it!'

'My dear girl, I – '

'Don't say "dear girl" to me! Save that for your real wife if you ever get one after this disgraceful performance. And don't try to pretend it wasn't all arranged. You know you gave that coloured waiter money! You know you did! Do you mean to say you didn't try to marry me?'

'No – of course – '

'Yes, you'd better admit it! You tried it, and now what are you going to do? Do you know my father's nearly crazy? It'll serve you right if he tries to kill you. He'll take his gun and put some cold steel in you. Even if this wed – this *thing* can be annulled it'll hang over me all the rest of my life!'

Perry could not resist quoting softly: 'Oh, camel, wouldn't you like to belong to the pretty snake-charmer for all your – '

'Shut-up!' cried Betty.

There was a pause.

'Betty,' said Perry finally, 'there's only one thing to do that will really get us out clear. That's for you to marry me.'

'Marry you!'

'Yes. Really it's the only – '

'You shut up! I wouldn't marry you if – if – '

'I know. If I were the last man on earth. But if you care anything about your reputation – '

'Reputation!' she cried. 'You're a nice one to think about my reputation *now*. Why didn't you think about my reputation before you hired that horrible Jumbo to – to – '

Perry tossed up his hands hopelessly.

'Very well. I'll do anything you want. Lord knows I renounce all claims!'

'But,' said a new voice, 'I don't.'

Perry and Betty started, and she put her hand to her heart.

'For heaven's sake, what was that?'

'It's me,' said the camel's back.

In a minute Perry had whipped off the camel's skin, and a lax, limp object, his clothes hanging on him damply, his hand clenched tightly on an almost empty bottle, stood defiantly before them.

'Oh,' cried Betty, 'you brought that object in here to frighten me! You told me he was deaf – that awful person!'

The camel's back sat down on a chair with a sigh of satisfaction.

'Don't talk 'at way about me, lady. I ain't no person. I'm your husband.'

'Husband!'

The cry was wrung simultaneously from Betty and Perry.

'Why, sure. I'm as much your husband as that gink is. The smoke didn't marry you to the camel's front. He married you to the whole camel. Why, that's my ring you got on your finger!'

With a little yelp she snatched the ring from her finger and flung it passionately on the floor.

'What's all this?' demanded Perry dazedly.

'Jes' that you better fix me an' fix me right. If you don't I'm a-gonna have the same claim you got to bein' married to her!'

'That's bigamy,' said Perry, turning gravely to Betty.

Then came the supreme moment of Perry's evening, the ultimate chance on which he risked his fortunes. He rose and looked first at Betty, where she sat weakly, aghast at this new complication, and then at the individual who swayed from side to side on his chair, uncertainly, menacingly.

'Very well,' said Perry slowly to the individual, 'you can have her. Betty, I'm going to prove to you that as far as I'm concerned our marriage was entirely accidental. I'm going to renounce utterly my rights to have you as my wife, and give you to – to the man whose ring you wear – your lawful husband.'

There was a pause and four horror-stricken eyes were turned on him,

'Goodbye, Betty,' he said brokenly. 'Don't forget me in your new-found happiness. I'm going to leave for the Far West on the morning train. Think of me kindly, Betty.'

With a last glance at them he turned and his head rested on his chest as his hand touched the doorknob.

'Goodbye,' he repeated. He turned the doorknob.

But at this sound the snakes and silk and tawny hair precipitated themselves violently towards him.

'Oh, Perry, don't leave me! Perry, Perry, take me with you!'

Her tears flowed damply on his neck. Calmly he folded his arms about her.

'I don't care,' she cried. 'I love you and if you can wake up a minister at this hour and have it done over again I'll go West with you.'

Over her shoulder the front part of the camel looked at the back part of the camel – and they exchanged a particularly subtle, esoteric sort of wink that only true camels can understand.

Financing Finnegan

1

Finnegan and I have the same literary agent to sell our writings for us – but though I'd often been in Mr Cannon's office just before and just after Finnegan's visits, I had never met him. Likewise we had the same publisher and often when I arrived there Finnegan had just departed. I gathered from a thoughtful sighing way in which they spoke of him –

'Ah – Finnegan – '

'Oh yes, Finnegan was here.'

– that the distinguished author's visit had been not uneventful. Certain remarks implied that he had taken something with him when he went – manuscripts, I supposed, one of those great successful novels of his. He had taken 'it' off for a final revision, a last draft, of which he was rumoured to make ten in order to achieve that facile flow, that ready wit, which distinguished his work. I discovered only gradually that most of Finnegan's visits had to do with money.

'I'm sorry you're leaving,' Mr Cannon would tell me, 'Finnegan will be here tomorrow.' Then after a thoughtful pause, 'I'll probably have to spend some time with him.'

I don't know what note in his voice reminded me of a talk with a nervous bank president when Dillinger was reported in the vicinity. His eyes looked out into the distance and he spoke as to himself: 'Of course he may be bringing a manuscript. He has a novel he's working on, you know. And a play too.'

He spoke as though he were talking about some interesting but remote events of the cinquecento; but his eyes became more hopeful as he added: 'Or maybe a short story.'

'He's very versatile, isn't he?' I said.

'Oh yes,' Mr Cannon perked up. 'He can do anything – anything when he puts his mind to it. There's never been such a talent.'

'I haven't seen much of his work lately.'

'Oh, but he's working hard. Some of the magazines have stories of his that they're holding.'

'Holding for what?'

'Oh, for a more appropriate time – an upswing. They like to think they have something of Finnegan's.'

His was indeed a name with ingots in it. His career had started brilliantly and if it had not kept up to its first exalted level, at least it started brilliantly all over again every few years. He was the perennial man of promise in American letters – what he could actually do with words was astounding, they glowed and coruscated – he wrote sentences, paragraphs, chapters that were masterpieces of fine weaving and spinning. It was only when I met some poor devil of a screenwriter who had been trying to make a logical story out of one of his books that I realised he had his enemies.

'It's all beautiful when you read it,' this man said disgustedly, 'but when you write it down plain it's like a week in the nut-house.'

From Mr Cannon's office I went over to my publishers on Fifth Avenue and there too I learned in no time that Finnegan was expected tomorrow.

Indeed he had thrown such a long shadow before him that the luncheon where I expected to discuss my own work was largely devoted to Finnegan. Again I had the feeling that my host, Mr George Jaggers, was talking not to me but to himself.

'Finnegan's a great writer,' he said.

'Undoubtedly.'

'And he's really quite all right, you know.'

As I hadn't questioned the fact I enquired whether there was any doubt about it.

'Oh no,' he said hurriedly. 'It's just that he's had such a run of hard luck lately – '

I shook my head sympathetically. 'I know. That diving into a half-empty pool was a tough break.'

'Oh, it wasn't half-empty. It was full of water. Full to the brim. You ought to hear Finnegan on the subject – he makes a side-splitting story of it. It seems he was in a run-down condition and just diving from the side of the pool, you know – ' Mr Jaggers pointed his knife and fork at the table, 'and he saw some young girls diving from the fifteen-foot board. He says he thought of his lost youth and went up to do the same and made a beautiful swan dive – but his shoulder broke while he was still in the air.' He looked at me rather anxiously. 'Haven't you heard of cases like that – a ball player throwing his arm out of joint?'

I couldn't think of any orthopaedic parallels at the moment.

'And then,' he continued dreamily, 'Finnegan had to write on the ceiling.'

'On the ceiling?'

'Practically. He didn't give up writing – he has plenty of guts, that fellow, though you may not believe it. He had some sort of arrangement built that was suspended from the ceiling and he lay on his back and wrote in the air.'

I had to grant that it was a courageous arrangement.

'Did it affect his work?' I enquired. 'Did you have to read his stories backward – like Chinese?'

'They were rather confused for a while,' he admitted, 'but he's all right now. I got several letters from him that sounded more like the old Finnegan – full of life and hope and plans for the future – '

The faraway look came into his face and I turned the discussion to affairs closer to my heart. Only when we were back in his office did the subject recur – and I blush as I write this because it includes confessing something I seldom do – reading another man's telegram. It happened because Mr Jaggers was intercepted in the hall and when I went into his office and sat down it was stretched out open before me:

> With fifty I could at least pay typist and get haircut and pencils. Life has become impossible and I exist on dream of good news. Desperately, Finnegan.

I couldn't believe my eyes – fifty dollars, and I happened to know that Finnegan's price for short stories was somewhere around three thousand. George Jaggers found me still staring dazedly at the telegram. After he read it he stared at me with stricken eyes.

'I don't see how I can conscientiously do it,' he said.

I started and glanced around to make sure I was in the prosperous publishing office in New York. Then I understood – I had misread the telegram. Finnegan was asking for fifty thousand as an advance – a demand that would have staggered any publisher no matter who the writer was.

'Only last week,' said Mr Jaggers disconsolately, 'I sent him a hundred dollars. It puts my department in the red every season, so I don't dare tell my partners any more. I take it out of my own pocket – give up a suit and a pair of shoes.'

'You mean Finnegan's broke?'

'Broke!' He looked at me and laughed soundlessly – in fact I didn't exactly like the way that he laughed. My brother had a nervous – but that is afield from this story. After a minute he pulled himself together. 'You won't say anything about this, will you? The truth is Finnegan's been in a slump, he's had blow after blow in the past few years, but now he's snapping out of it and I know we'll get back every cent we've – ' He tried to think of a word but 'given him' slipped out. This time it was he who was eager to change the subject.

Don't let me give the impression that Finnegan's affairs absorbed me during a whole week in New York – it was inevitable, though, that being much in the offices of my agent and my publisher, I happened in on a lot. For instance, two days later, using the telephone in Mr Cannon's office, I was accidentally switched in on a conversation he was having with George Jaggers. It was only partly eavesdropping, you see, because I could only hear one end of the conversation and that isn't as bad as hearing it all.

'But I got the impression he was in good health . . . he did say something about his heart a few months ago but I understood it got well . . . yes, and he talked about some operation he wanted to have – I think he said it was cancer . . . Well, I felt like telling him I had a little operation up my sleeve too, that I'd have had by now if I could afford it . . . No, I didn't say it. He seemed in such good spirits that it would have been a shame to bring him down. He's starting a story today, he read me some of it on the phone . . .

' . . . I did give him twenty-five because he didn't have a cent in his pocket . . . oh, yes – I'm sure he'll be all right now. He sounds as if he means business.'

I understood it all now. The two men had entered into a silent conspiracy to cheer each other up about Finnegan. Their investment in him, in his future, had reached a sum so considerable that Finnegan belonged to them. They could not bear to hear a word against him – even from themselves.

2

I spoke my mind to Mr Cannon. 'If this Finnegan is a four-flusher you can't go on indefinitely giving him money. If he's through he's through and there's nothing to be done about it. It's absurd that you should put off an operation when Finnegan's out somewhere diving into half-empty swimming pools.'

'It was full,' said Mr Cannon patiently – 'full to the brim.'

'Well, full or empty the man sounds like a nuisance to me.'

'Look here,' said Cannon, 'I've got a talk to Hollywood due on the wire. Meanwhile you might glance over that.' He threw a manuscript into my lap. 'Maybe it'll help you understand. He brought it in yesterday.'

It was a short story. I began it in a mood of disgust but before I'd read five minutes I was completely immersed in it, utterly charmed, utterly convinced and wishing to God I could write like that. When Cannon finished his phone call I kept him waiting while I finished it and when I did there were tears in these hard old professional eyes. Any magazine in the country would have run it first in any issue.

But then nobody had ever denied that Finnegan could write.

3

Months passed before I went again to New York, and then, so far as the offices of my agent and my publisher were concerned, I descended upon a quieter, more stable world. There was at last time to talk about my own conscientious if uninspired literary pursuits, to visit Mr Cannon in the country and to kill summer evenings with George Jaggers where the vertical New York starlight falls like lingering lightning into restaurant gardens. Finnegan might have been at the North Pole – and as a matter of fact he was. He had quite a group with him, including three Bryn Mawr anthropologists, and it sounded as if he might collect a lot of material there. They were going to stay several months, and if the thing had somehow the ring of a promising little house party about it, that was probably due to my jealous, cynical disposition.

'We're all just delighted,' said Cannon. 'It's a godsend for him. He was fed up and he needed just this – this – '

'Ice and snow,' I supplied.

'Yes, ice and snow. The last thing he said was characteristic of him. Whatever he writes is going to be pure white – it's going to have a blinding glare about it.'

'I can imagine it will. But tell me – who's financing it? Last time I was here I gathered the man was insolvent.'

'Oh, he was really very decent about that. He owed me some money and I believe he owed George Jaggers a little too – ' He 'believed', the old hypocrite. He knew damn well – 'so before he left he made most of his life insurance over to us. That's in case he doesn't come back – those trips are dangerous of course.'

'I should think so,' I said – 'especially with three anthropologists.'

'So Jaggers and I are absolutely covered in case anything happens – it's as simple as that.'

'Did the life-insurance company finance the trip?'

He fidgeted perceptibly.

'Oh, no. In fact when they learned the reason for the assignments they were a little upset. George Jaggers and I felt that when he had a specific plan like this with a specific book at the end of it, we were justified in backing him a little further.'

'I don't see it,' I said flatly.

'You don't?' The old harassed look came back into his eyes. 'Well, I'll admit we hesitated. In principle I know it's wrong. I used to advance authors small sums from time to time, but lately I've made a rule against it – and kept it. It's only been waived once in the last two years and that was for a woman who was having a bad struggle – Margaret Trahill, do you know her? She was an old girl of Finnegan's, by the way.'

'Remember I don't even know Finnegan.'

'That's right. You must meet him when he comes back – if he does come back. You'd like him – he's utterly charming.'

Again I departed from New York, to imaginative North Poles of my own, while the year rolled through summer and fall. When the first snap of November was in the air, I thought of the Finnegan expedition with a sort of shiver and any envy of the man departed. He was probably earning any loot, literary or anthropological, he might bring back. Then, when I hadn't been back in New York three days, I read in the paper that he and some other members of his party had walked off into a snowstorm when the food supply gave out, and the Arctic had claimed another sacrifice.

I was sorry for him, but practical enough to be glad that Cannon and Jaggers were well protected. Of course, with Finnegan scarcely cold – if such a simile is not too harrowing – they did not talk about it but I gathered that the insurance companies had waived habeas corpus, or whatever it is in their lingo, and it seemed quite sure that they would collect.

His son, a fine looking young fellow, came into George Jaggers's office while I was there and from him I could guess at Finnegan's charm – a shy frankness together with an impression of a very quiet brave battle going on inside of him that he couldn't quite bring himself to talk about – but that showed as heat lightning in his work.

'The boy writes well too,' said George after he had gone. 'He's brought in some remarkable poems. He's not ready to step into his father's shoes, but there's a definite promise.'

'Can I see one of his things?'

'Certainly – here's one he left just as he went out.'

George took a paper from his desk, opened it and cleared his throat. Then he squinted and bent over a little in his chair.

'Dear Mr Jaggers,' he began, 'I didn't like to ask you this in person – ' Jaggers stopped, his eyes reading ahead rapidly.

'How much does he want?' I enquired.

He sighed.

'He gave me the impression that this was some of his work,' he said in a pained voice.

'But it is,' I consoled him. 'Of course he isn't quite ready to step into his father's shoes.'

I was sorry afterwards to have said this, for after all Finnegan had paid his debts, and it was nice to be alive now that better times were back and books were no longer rated as unnecessary luxuries. Many authors I knew who had skimped along during the Depression were now making long-deferred trips or paying off mortgages or turning out the more finished kind of work that can only be done with a certain leisure and security. I had just got a thousand-dollar advance for a venture in Hollywood and was going to fly out with all the verve of the old days when there was chicken feed in every pot. Going in to say goodbye to Cannon and collect the money, it was nice to find he too was profiting – wanted me to go along and see a motor boat he was buying.

But some last-minute stuff came up to delay him and I grew impatient and decided to skip it. Getting no response to a knock on the door of his sanctum, I opened it anyhow.

The inner office seemed in some confusion. Mr Cannon was on several telephones at once and dictating something about an insurance company to a stenographer. One secretary was getting hurriedly into her hat and coat as upon an errand and another was counting bills from her purse.

'It'll be only a minute,' said Cannon, 'it's just a little office riot – you never saw us like this.'

'Is it Finnegan's insurance?' I couldn't help asking. 'Isn't it any good?'

'His insurance – oh, perfectly all right, perfectly. This is just a matter of trying to raise a few hundred in a hurry. The banks are closed and we're all contributing.'

'I've got that money you just gave me,' I said. 'I don't need all of it to get to the coast.' I peeled off a couple of hundred. 'Will this be enough?'

'That'll be fine – it just saves us. Never mind, Miss Carlsen. Mrs Mapes, you needn't go now.'

'I think I'll be running along,' I said.

'Just wait two minutes,' he urged. 'I've only got to take care of this wire. It's really splendid news. Bucks you up.'

It was a cablegram from Oslo, Norway – before I began to read I was full of a premonition.

> Am miraculously safe here but detained by authorities. Please wire passage money for four people and two hundred extra. I am bringing back plenty. Greetings from the dead. Finnegan.

'Yes, that's splendid,' I agreed. 'He'll have a story to tell now.'

'Won't he though,' said Cannon. 'Miss Carlsen, will you wire the parents of those girls – and you'd better inform Mr Jaggers.'

As we walked along the street a few minutes later, I saw that Mr Cannon, as if stunned by the wonder of this news, had fallen into a brown study, and I did not disturb him, for after all I did not know Finnegan and could not wholeheartedly share his joy. His mood of silence continued until we arrived at the door of the motor-boat show. Just under the sign he stopped and stared upward, as if aware for the first time where we were going.

'Oh, my,' he said, stepping back. 'There's no use going in here now. I thought we were going to get a drink.'

We did. Mr Cannon was still a little vague, a little under the spell of the vast surprise – he fumbled so long for the money to pay his round that I insisted it was on me.

I think he was in a daze during that whole time because, though he is a man of the most punctilious accuracy, the two hundred I handed him in his office has never shown to my credit in the statements he has sent me. I imagine, though, that someday I will surely get it because someday Finnegan will click again and I know that people will clamour to read what he writes. Recently I've taken it upon myself to investigate some of the stories about him and I've found that they're mostly as false as the half-empty pool. That pool was full to the brim.

So far there's only been a short story about the polar expedition, a love story. Perhaps it wasn't as big a subject as he expected. But the movies are interested in him – if they can get a good long look at him first – and I have every reason to think that he will come through. He'd better.

Design in Plaster

'How long does the doctor think now?' Mary asked. With his good arm Martin threw back the top of the sheet, disclosing that the plaster armour had been cut away in front in the form of a square, so that his abdomen and the lower part of his diaphragm bulged a little from the aperture. His dislocated arm was still high over his head in an involuntary salute.

'This was a great advance,' he told her. 'But it took the heatwave to make Ottinger put in this window. I can't say much for the view but – have you seen the wire collection?'

'Yes, I've seen it,' his wife answered, trying to look amused.

It was laid out on the bureau like a set of surgeon's tools – wires bent to every length and shape so that the nurse could reach any point inside the plaster cast when perspiration made the itching unbearable.

Martin was ashamed at repeating himself.

'I apologise,' he said. 'After two months you get medical psychology. All this stuff is fascinating to me. In fact – ' he added, and with only faint irony, ' – it is in a way of becoming my life.'

Mary came over and sat beside the bed raising him, cast and all, into her slender arms. He was chief electrical engineer at the studio and his thirty-foot fall wasn't costing a penny in doctor's bills. But that – and the fact that the catastrophe had swung them together after a four months' separation, was its only bright spot.

'I feel so close,' she whispered. 'Even through this plaster.'

'Do you think that's a nice way to talk?'

'Yes.'

'So do I.'

Presently she stood up and rearranged her bright hair in the mirror. He had seen her do it half a thousand times but suddenly there was a quality of remoteness about it that made him sad.

'What are you doing tonight?' he asked.

Mary turned, almost with surprise.

'It seems strange to have you ask me.'

'Why? You almost always tell me. You're my contact with the world of glamour.'

'But you like to keep bargains. That was our arrangement when we began to live apart.'

'You're being very technical.'

'No – but that *was* the arrangement. As a matter of fact I'm not doing anything. Bieman asked me to go to a preview, but he bores me. And that French crowd called up.'

'Which member of it?'

She came closer and looked at him.

'Why, I believe you're jealous,' she said. 'The wife of course. Or *he* did, to be exact, but he was calling for his wife – she'd be there. I've never seen you like this before.'

Martin was wise enough to wink as if it meant nothing and let it die away, but Mary said an unfortunate last word.

'I thought you liked me to go with them.'

'That's it,' Martin tried to go slow, ' – with "them", but now it's "he".'

'They're all leaving Monday,' she said almost impatiently. 'I'll probably never see him again.'

Silence for a minute. Since his accident there were not an unlimited number of things to talk about, except when there was love between them. Or even pity – he was accepting even pity in the past fortnight. Especially their uncertain plans about the future were in need of being preceded by a mood of love.

'I'm going to get up for a minute,' he said suddenly. 'No, don't help me – don't call the nurse. I've got it figured out.'

The cast extended halfway to his knee on one side but with a snake-like motion he managed to get to the side of the bed – then rise with a gigantic heave. He tied on a dressing-gown, still without assistance, and went to the window. Young people were splashing and calling in the outdoor pool of the hotel.

'I'll go along,' said Mary. 'Can I bring you anything tomorrow? Or tonight if you feel lonely?'

'Not tonight. You know I'm always cross at night – and I don't like you making that long drive twice a day. Go along – be happy.'

'Shall I ring for the nurse?'

'I'll ring presently.'

He didn't though – he just stood. He knew that Mary was wearing out, that this resurgence of her love was wearing out. His accident was a very temporary dam of a stream that had begun to overflow months before.

When the pains began at six with their customary regularity the nurse gave him something with codein in it, shook him a cocktail and ordered dinner, one of those dinners it was a struggle to digest since he had been sealed up in his individual bomb-shelter. Then she was off duty four hours and he was alone. Alone with Mary and the Frenchman.

He didn't know the Frenchman except by name but Mary had said once: 'Joris is rather like you – only naturally not formed – rather immature.'

Since she said that, the company of Mary and Joris had grown increasingly unattractive in the long hours between seven and eleven. He had talked with them, driven around with them, gone to pictures and parties with them – sometimes with the half-comforting ghost of Joris's wife along. He had been near as they made love and even that was endurable as long as he could seem to hear and see them. It was when they became hushed and secret that his stomach winced inside the plaster cast. That was when he had pictures of the Frenchman going towards Mary and Mary waiting. Because he was not sure just how Joris felt about her or about the whole situation.

'I told him I loved you,' Mary said – and he believed her, 'I told him that I could never love anyone but you.'

Still he could not be sure how Mary felt as she waited in her apartment for Joris. He could not tell if, when she said good-night at her door, she turned away relieved, or whether she walked around her living-room a little and later, reading her book, dropped it in her lap and looked up at the ceiling. Or whether her phone rang once more for one more good-night.

Martin hadn't worried about any of these things in the first two months of their separation when he had been on his feet and well.

At half-past eight he took up the phone and called her; the line was busy and still busy at a quarter to nine. At nine it was out of order; at nine-fifteen it didn't answer and at a little before nine-thirty it was busy again. Martin got up, slowly drew on his trousers and with the help of a bellboy put on a shirt and coat.

'Don't you want me to come, Mr Harris?' asked the bellboy.

'No thanks. Tell the taxi I'll be right down.'

When the boy had gone he tripped on the slightly raised floor of the bathroom, swung about on one arm and cut his head against the washbowl. It was not so much, but he did a clumsy repair job with the adhesive and, feeling ridiculous at his image in the mirror, sat down and called Mary's number a last time – for no answer. Then he went out, not because he wanted to go to Mary's but because he had to go somewhere towards the flame, and he didn't know any other place to go.

At ten-thirty Mary, in her nightgown, was at the phone.

'Thanks for calling. But, Joris, if you want to know the truth I have a splitting headache. I'm turning in.'

'Mary, listen,' Joris insisted. 'It happens Marianne has a headache too and has turned in. This is the last night I'll have a chance to see you alone. Besides, you told me you'd *never* had a headache.'

Mary laughed.

'That's true – but I *am* tired.'

'I would promise to stay one half-hour – word of honour. I am only just around the corner.'

'No,' she said and a faint touch of annoyance gave firmness to the word. 'Tomorrow I'll have either lunch or dinner if you like, but now I'm going to bed.'

She stopped. She had heard a sound, a weight crunching against the outer door of her apartment. Then three odd, short bell rings.

'There's someone – call me in the morning,' she said. Hurriedly hanging up the phone she got into a dressing-gown.

By the door of her apartment she asked cautiously.

'Who's there?'

No answer – only a heavier sound – a human slipping to the floor.

'Who is it?'

She drew back and away from a frightening moan. There was a little shutter high in the door, like the peephole of a speakeasy, and feeling sure from the sound that whoever it was, wounded or drunk, was on the floor Mary reached up and peeped out. She could see only a hand covered with freshly ripening blood, and shut the trap hurriedly. After a shaken moment, she peered once more.

This time she recognised something – afterwards she could not have said what – a way the arm lay, a corner of the plaster cast – but it was enough to make her open the door quickly and duck down to Martin's side.

'Get doctor,' he whispered. 'Fell on the steps and broke.'

His eyes closed as she ran for the phone.

Doctor and ambulance came at the same time. What Martin had done was simple enough, a little triumph of misfortune. On the first flight of stairs that he had gone up for eight weeks, he had stumbled, tried to save himself with the arm that was no good for anything, then spun down catching and ripping on the stair rail. After that a five-minute drag up to her door.

Mary wanted to exclaim, 'Why? Why?' but there was no one to hear. He came awake as the stretcher was put under him to carry him to the hospital, repair the new breakage with a new cast, start it over again. Seeing Mary he called quickly. 'Don't you come. I don't like anyone around when – when – Promise on your word of honour not to come?'

The orthopaedist said he would phone her in an hour. And five minutes later it was with the confused thought that he was already calling that Mary answered the phone.

'I can't talk, Joris,' she said. 'There was an awful accident – '

'Can I help?'

'It's gone now. It was my husband – '

Suddenly Mary knew she wanted to do anything but wait alone for word from the hospital.

'Come over then,' she said. 'You can take me up there if I'm needed.'

She sat in place by the phone until he came – jumped to her feet with an exclamation at his ring.

'Why? Why?' she sobbed at last. 'I offered to go and see him at his hotel.'

'Not drunk?'

'No, no – he almost never takes a drink. Will you wait right outside my door while I dress and get ready?'

The news came half an hour later that Martin's shoulder was set again, that he was sleeping under the ethylene gas and would sleep till morning. Joris Deglen was very gentle, swinging her feet up on the sofa, putting a pillow at her back and answering her incessant 'Why?' with a different response every time – Martin had been delirious; he was lonely; then at a certain moment telling the truth he had long guessed at: Martin was jealous.

'That was it,' Mary said bitterly. 'We were to be free – only I wasn't free. Only free to sneak about behind his back.'

She was free now though, free as air. And later, when he said he wouldn't go just yet, but would sit in the living-room reading until she quieted down, Mary went into her room with her head clear as morning. After she undressed for the second time that night she stayed for a few minutes before the mirror arranging her hair and keeping her mind free of all thoughts about Martin except that he was sleeping and at the moment felt no pain.

Then she opened her bedroom door and called down the corridor into the living-room: 'Do you want to come and tell me good-night?'

What a Handsome Pair!

1

At four o'clock on a November afternoon in 1902, Teddy Van Beck got out of a hansom cab in front of a brownstone house on Murray Hill. He was a tall, round-shouldered young man with a beaked nose and soft brown eyes in a sensitive face. In his veins quarrelled the blood of colonial governors and celebrated robber barons; in him the synthesis had produced, for that time and place, something different and something new.

His cousin, Helen Van Beck, waited in the drawing-room. Her eyes were red from weeping, but she was young enough for it not to detract from her glossy beauty – a beauty that had reached the point where it seemed to contain in itself the secret of its own growth, as if it would go on increasing for ever.

She was nineteen and, contrary to the evidence, she was extremely happy.

Teddy put his arm around her and kissed her cheek, and found it changing into her ear as she turned her face away. He held her for a moment, his own enthusiasm chilling; then he said: 'You don't seem very glad to see me.'

Helen had a premonition that this was going to be one of the memorable scenes of her life, and with unconscious cruelty she set about extracting from it its full dramatic value. She sat in a corner of the couch, facing an easy-chair.

'Sit there,' she commanded, in what was then admired as a 'regal manner', and then, as Teddy straddled the piano stool: 'No, don't sit there. I can't talk to you if you're going to revolve around.'

'Sit on my lap,' he suggested.

'No.'

Playing a one-handed flourish on the piano, he said, 'I can listen better here.'

Helen gave up hopes of beginning on the sad and quiet note.

'This is a serious matter, Teddy. Don't think I've decided it without a lot of consideration. I've got to ask you – to ask you to release me from our understanding.'

'What?' Teddy's face paled with shock and dismay.

'I'll have to tell you from the beginning. I've realised for a long time that we have nothing in common. You're interested in your music, and I can't even play chopsticks.' Her voice was weary as if with suffering; her small teeth tugged at her lower lip.

'What of it?' he demanded, relieved. 'I'm musician enough for both. You wouldn't have to understand banking to marry a banker, would you?'

'This is different,' Helen answered. 'What would we do together? One important thing is that you don't like riding; you told me you were afraid of horses.'

'Of course I'm afraid of horses,' he said, and added reminiscently: 'They try to bite me.'

'It makes it so – '

'I've never met a horse – socially, that is – who didn't try to bite me. They used to do it when I put the bridle on; then, when I gave up putting the bridle on, they began reaching their heads around trying to get at my calves.'

The eyes of her father, who had given her a Shetland at three, glistened, cold and hard, from her own.

'You don't even like the people I like, let alone the horses,' she said.

'I can stand them. I've stood them all my life.'

'Well, it would be a silly way to start a marriage. I don't see any grounds for mutual – mutual – '

'Riding?'

'Oh, not that.' Helen hesitated, and then said in an unconvinced tone, 'Probably I'm not clever enough for you.'

'Don't talk such stuff!' He demanded some truth: 'Who's the man?'

It took her a moment to collect herself. She had always resented Teddy's tendency to treat women with less ceremony than was the custom of the day. Often he was an unfamiliar, almost frightening young man.

'There is someone,' she admitted. 'It's someone I've always known slightly, but about a month ago, when I went to Southampton, I was – thrown with him.'

'Thrown from a horse?'

'Please, Teddy,' she protested gravely. 'I'd been getting more unhappy about you and me, and whenever I was with him everything seemed all right.' A note of exaltation that she would not conceal came into Helen's voice. She rose and crossed the room, her straight, slim legs outlined by the shadows of her dress. 'We rode and swam and played tennis together – did the things we both liked to do.'

He stared into the vacant space she had created for him. 'Is that all that drew you to this fellow?'

'No, it was more than that. He was thrilling to me like nobody ever has been.' She laughed. 'I think what really started me thinking about it was one day we came in from riding and everybody said aloud what a nice pair we made.'

'Did you kiss him?'

She hesitated. 'Yes, once.'

He got up from the piano stool. 'I feel as if I had a cannon ball in my stomach,' he exclaimed.

The butler announced Mr Stuart Oldhorne.

'Is he the man?' Teddy demanded tensely.

She was suddenly upset and confused. 'He should have come later. Would you rather go without meeting him?'

But Stuart Oldhorne, made confident by his new sense of proprietorship, had followed the butler.

The two men regarded each other with a curious impotence of expression; there can be no communication between men in that position, for their relation is indirect and consists in how much each of them has possessed or will possess of the woman in question, so that their emotions pass through her divided self as through a bad telephone connection.

Stuart Oldhorne sat beside Helen, his polite eyes never leaving Teddy. He had the same glowing physical power as she. He had been a star athlete at Yale and a Rough Rider in Cuba, and was the best young horseman on Long Island. Women loved him not only for his points but for a real sweetness of temper.

'You've lived so much in Europe that I don't often see you,' he said to Teddy. Teddy didn't answer and Stuart Oldhorne turned to Helen: 'I'm early; I didn't realise – '

'You came at the right time,' said Teddy rather harshly. 'I stayed to play you my congratulations.'

To Helen's alarm, he turned and ran his fingers over the keyboard. Then he began.

What he was playing, neither Helen nor Stuart knew, but Teddy always remembered. He put his mind in order with a short résumé of the history of music, beginning with some chords from the *Messiah* and ending with Debussy's *La plus que lent*, which had an evocative quality for him, because he had first heard it the day his brother died. Then, pausing for an instant, he began to play more thoughtfully, and the lovers on the sofa could feel that they were alone – that he had left them and had no more traffic with them – and Helen's discomfort lessened. But the flight, the elusiveness of the music, piqued her, gave her a feeling of annoyance. If Teddy had played the current sentimental song from *Erminie*, and had played it with feeling, she would have understood and been moved, but he was plunging her suddenly into a world of mature emotions, whither her nature neither could nor wished to follow.

She shook herself slightly and said to Stuart: 'Did you buy the horse?'

'Yes, and at a bargain . . . Do you know I love you?'

'I'm glad,' she whispered.

The piano stopped suddenly. Teddy closed it and swung slowly around: 'Did you like my congratulations?'

'Very much,' they said together.

'It was pretty good,' he admitted. 'That last was only based on a little counterpoint. You see, the idea of it was that you make such a handsome pair.'

He laughed unnaturally; Helen followed him out into the hall.

'Goodbye, Teddy,' she said. 'We're going to be good friends, aren't we?'

'Aren't we?' he repeated. He winked without smiling, and with a clicking, despairing sound of his mouth, went out quickly.

For a moment Helen tried vainly to apply a measure to the situation, wondering how she had come off with him, realising reluctantly that she had never for an instant held the situation in her hands. She had a dim realisation that Teddy was larger in scale; then the very largeness frightened her and, with relief and a warm tide of emotion, she hurried into the drawing-room and the shelter of her lover's arms.

Their engagement ran through a halcyon summer. Stuart visited Helen's family at Tuxedo, and Helen visited his family in Wheatley Hills. Before breakfast, their horses' hoofs sedately scattered the dew in sentimental glades, or curtained them with dust as they raced on dirt roads. They bought a tandem bicycle and pedalled all over Long Island – which Mrs Cassius Ruthven, a contemporary Cato, considered 'rather fast' for a couple not yet married. They were seldom at rest, but when they were, they reminded people of His Move on a Gibson pillow.

Helen's taste for sport was advanced for her generation. She rode nearly as well as Stuart and gave him a decent game of tennis. He taught her some polo, and they were golf crazy when it was still considered a comic game. They liked to feel fit and cool together. They thought of themselves as a team, and it was often remarked how well mated they were. A chorus of pleasant envy followed in the wake of their effortless glamour.

They talked.

'It seems a pity you've got to go to the office,' she would say. 'I wish you did something we could do together, like taming lions.'

'I've always thought that at a pinch I could make a living breeding and racing horses,' said Stuart.

'I know you could, you darling.'

In August he bought a Thomas automobile and toured all the way to Chicago with three other men. It was an event of national interest and their pictures were in all the papers. Helen wanted to go, but it wouldn't have been proper, so they compromised by driving down Fifth Avenue on a sunny September morning, one with the fine day and the fashionable crowd, but distinguished by their unity, which made them each as strong as two.

'What do you suppose?' Helen demanded. 'Teddy sent me the oddest present – a cup rack.'

Stuart laughed. 'Obviously, he means that all we'll ever do is win cups.'

'I thought it was rather a slam,' Helen ruminated. 'I saw that he was invited to everything, but he didn't answer a single invitation. Would you mind very much stopping by his apartment now? I haven't seen him for months and I don't like to leave anything unpleasant in the past.'

He wouldn't go in with her. 'I'll sit and answer questions about the auto from passers-by.'

The door was opened by a woman in a cleaning cap, and Helen heard the sound of Teddy's piano from the room beyond. The woman seemed reluctant to admit her.

'He said don't interrupt him, but I suppose if you're his cousin – '

Teddy welcomed her, obviously startled and somewhat upset, but in a minute he was himself again.

'I won't marry you,' he assured her. 'You've had your chance.'

'All right,' she laughed.

'How are you?' He threw a pillow at her. 'You're beautiful! Are you happy with this – this centaur? Does he beat you with his riding crop?' He peered at her closely. 'You look a little duller than when I knew you. I used to whip you up to a nervous excitement that bore a resemblance to intelligence.'

'I'm happy, Teddy. I hope you are.'

'Sure, I'm happy; I'm working. I've got MacDowell on the run and I'm going to have a shebang at Carnegie Hall next September.' His eyes became malicious. 'What did you think of my girl?'

'Your girl?'

'The girl who opened the door for you.'

'Oh, I thought it was a maid.' She flushed and was silent.

He laughed. 'Hey, Betty!' he called. 'You were mistaken for the maid!'

'And that's the fault of my cleaning on Sunday,' answered a voice from the next room.

Teddy lowered his voice. 'Do you like her?' he demanded.

'Teddy!' She teetered on the arm of the sofa, wondering whether she should leave at once.

'What would you think if I married her?' he asked confidentially.

'Teddy!' She was outraged; it had needed but a glance to place the woman as common. 'You're joking. She's older than you . . . You wouldn't be such a fool as to throw away your future that way.'

He didn't answer.

'Is she musical?' Helen demanded. 'Does she help you with your work?'

'She doesn't know a note. Neither did you, but I've got enough music in me for twenty wives.'

Visualising herself as one of them, Helen rose stiffly.

'All I can ask you is to think how your mother would have felt – and those who care for you . . . Goodbye, Teddy.'

He walked out the door with her and down the stairs.

'As a matter of fact, we've been married for two months,' he said casually. 'She was a waitress in a place where I used to eat.'

Helen felt that she should be angry and aloof, but tears of hurt vanity were springing to her eyes.

'And do you love her?'

'I like her; she's a good person and good for me. Love is something else. I loved you, Helen, and that's all dead in me for the present. Maybe it's coming out in my music. Someday I'll probably love other women – or maybe there'll never be anything but you. Goodbye, Helen.'

The declaration touched her. 'I hope you'll be happy, Teddy. Bring your wife to the wedding.'

He bowed noncommittally. When she had gone, he returned thoughtfully to his apartment.

'That was the cousin that I was in love with,' he said.

'And was it?' Betty's face, Irish and placid, brightened with interest. 'She's a pretty thing.'

'She wouldn't have been as good for me as a nice peasant like you.'

'Always thinking of yourself, Teddy Van Beck.'

He laughed. 'Sure I am, but you love me, anyhow?'

'That's a big wur-red.'

'All right. I'll remember that when you come begging around for a kiss. If my grandfather knew I married a bog trotter, he'd turn over in his grave. Now get out and let me finish my work.'

He sat at the piano, a pencil behind his ear. Already his face was resolved, composed, but his eyes grew more intense minute by minute, until there was a glaze in them, behind which they seemed to have joined his ears in counting and hearing. Presently there was no more indication in his face that anything had occurred to disturb the tranquillity of his Sunday morning.

2

Mrs Cassius Ruthven and a friend, veils flung back across their hats, sat in their auto on the edge of the field.

'A young woman playing polo in breeches.' Mrs Ruthven sighed. 'Amy Van Beck's daughter. I thought when Helen organised the Amazons she'd stop at divided skirts. But her husband apparently has no objections, for there he stands, egging her on. Of course, they always have liked the same things.'

'A pair of thoroughbreds, those two,' said the other woman complacently, meaning that she admitted them to be her equals. 'You'd never look at them and think that anything had gone wrong.'

She was referring to Stuart's mistake in the panic of 1907. His father had bequeathed him a precarious situation and Stuart had made an error of judgement. His honour was not questioned and his crowd stood by him loyally, but his usefulness in Wall Street was over and his small fortune was gone.

He stood in a group of men with whom he would presently play, noting things to tell Helen after the game – she wasn't turning with the play soon enough and several times she was unnecessarily ridden off at important moments. Her ponies were sluggish – the penalty for playing with borrowed mounts – but she was, nevertheless, the best player on the field, and in the last minute she made a save that brought applause.

'Good girl! Good girl!'

Stuart had been delegated with the unpleasant duty of chasing the women from the field. They had started an hour late and now a team from New Jersey was waiting to play; he sensed trouble as he cut across to join Helen and walked beside her towards the stables. She was splendid, with her flushed cheeks, her shining, triumphant eyes, her short, excited breath. He temporised for a minute.

'That was good – that last,' he said.

'Thanks. It almost broke my arm. Wasn't I pretty good all through?'

'You were the best out there.'

'I know it.'

He waited while she dismounted and handed the pony to a groom.

'Helen, I believe I've got a job.'

'What is it?'

'Don't jump on the idea till you think it over. Gus Myers wants me to manage his racing stables. Eight thousand a year.'

Helen considered. 'It's a nice salary; and I bet you could make yourself up a nice string from his ponies.'

'The principal thing is that I need the money; I'd have as much as you and things would be easier.'

'You'd have as much as me,' Helen repeated. She almost regretted that he would need no more help from her. 'But with Gus Myers, isn't there a string attached? Wouldn't he expect a boost up?'

'He probably would,' answered Stuart bluntly, 'and if I can help him socially, I will. As a matter of fact, he wants me at a stag dinner tonight.'

'All right, then,' Helen said absently.

Still hesitating to tell her her game was over, Stuart followed her glance towards the field, where a runabout had driven up and parked by the ropes.

'There's your old friend Teddy,' he remarked dryly – 'or rather, your new friend Teddy. He's taking a sudden interest in polo. Perhaps he thinks the horses aren't biting this summer.'

'You're not in a very good humour,' protested Helen. 'You know, if you say the word, I'll never see him again. All I want in the world is for you and I to be together.'

'I know,' he admitted regretfully. 'Selling horses and giving up clubs put a crimp in that. I know the women all fall for Teddy, now he's getting famous, but if he tries to fool around with you I'll break his piano over his head . . . Oh, another thing,' he began, seeing the men already riding on the field. 'About your last chukker – '

As best he could, he put the situation up to her. He was not prepared for the fury that swept over her.

'But it's an outrage! I got up the game and it's been posted on the bulletin board for three days.'

'You started an hour late.'

'And do you know why?' she demanded. 'Because your friend Joe Morgan insisted that Celie ride side-saddle. He tore her habit off her three times, and she only got here by climbing out the kitchen window.'

'I can't do anything about it.'

'Why can't you? Weren't you once a governor of this club? How can women ever expect to be any good if they have to quit every time the men want the field? All the men want is for the women to come up to them in the evening and tell them what a beautiful game they played!'

Still raging and blaming Stuart, she crossed the field to Teddy's car. He got out and greeted her with concentrated intensity: 'I've reached the point where I can neither sleep nor eat from thinking of you. What point is that?'

There was something thrilling about him that she had never been conscious of in the old days; perhaps the stories of his philanderings had made him more romantic to her.

'Well, don't think of me as I am now,' she said. 'My face is getting rougher every day and my muscles lean out of an evening dress like a female impersonator. People are beginning to refer to me as handsome instead of pretty. Besides, I'm in a vile humour. It seems to me women are always just edged out of everything.'

Stuart's game was brutal that afternoon. In the first five minutes, he realised that Teddy's runabout was no longer there, and his long slugs began to tally from all angles. Afterwards, he bumped home across country at a gallop; his mood was not assuaged by a note handed him by the children's nurse:

> *Dear* – Since your friends made it impossible for us to play, I wasn't going to sit there just dripping; so I had Teddy bring me home. And since you'll be out to dinner, I'm going into New York with him to the theatre. I'll either be out on the theatre train or spend the night at mother's.
>
> HELEN

Stuart went upstairs and changed into his dinner coat. He had no defence against the unfamiliar claws of jealousy that began a slow dissection of his insides. Often Helen had gone to plays or dances with other men, but this was different. He felt towards Teddy the faint contempt of the physical man for the artist, but the last six months had bruised his pride. He perceived the possibility that Helen might be seriously interested in someone else.

He was in a bad humour at Gus Myers' dinner – annoyed with his host for talking so freely about their business arrangement. When at last they rose from the table, he decided that it was no go and called Myers aside.

'Look here. I'm afraid this isn't a good idea, after all.'

'Why not?' His host looked at him in alarm. 'Are you going back on me? My dear fellow – '

'I think we'd better call it off.'

'And why, may I ask? Certainly I have the right to ask why.'

Stuart considered. 'All right, I'll tell you. When you made that little speech, you mentioned me as if you had somehow bought me, as if I was a sort of employee in your office. Now, in the sporting world that doesn't go; things are more – more democratic. I grew up with all these men here tonight, and they didn't like it any better than I did.'

'I see,' Mr Myers reflected carefully – 'I see.' Suddenly he clapped Stuart on the back. 'That is exactly the sort of thing I like to be told; it helps me. From now on I won't mention you as if you were in my – as if we had a business arrangement. Is that all right?'

After all, the salary was eight thousand dollars.

'Very well, then,' Stuart agreed. 'But you'll have to excuse me tonight. I'm catching a train to the city.'

'I'll put an automobile at your disposal.'

At ten o'clock he rang the bell of Teddy's apartment on Forty-Eighth Street.

'I'm looking for Mr Van Beck,' he said to the woman who answered the door. 'I know he's gone to the theatre, but I wonder if you can tell me – ' Suddenly he guessed who the woman was. 'I'm Stuart Oldhorne,' he explained. 'I married Mr Van Beck's cousin.'

'Oh, come in,' said Betty pleasantly. 'I know all about who you are.'

She was just this side of forty, stoutish and plain of face, but full of a keen, brisk vitality. In the living-room they sat down.

'You want to see Teddy?'

'He's with my wife and I want to join them after the theatre. I wonder if you know where they went?'

'Oh, so Teddy's with your wife.' There was a faint, pleasant brogue in her voice. 'Well, now, he didn't say exactly where he'd be tonight.'

'Then you don't know?'

'I don't – not for the life of me,' she admitted cheerfully. 'I'm sorry.'

He stood up, and Betty saw the thinly hidden anguish in his face. Suddenly she was really sorry.

'I did hear him say something about the theatre,' she said ruminatively. 'Now sit down and let me think what it was. He goes out so much and a play once a week is enough for me, so that one night mixes up with the others in my head. Didn't your wife say where to meet them?'

'No. I only decided to come in after they'd started. She said she'd catch the theatre train back to Long Island or go to her mother's.'

'That's it,' Betty said triumphantly, striking her hands together like cymbals. 'That's what he said when he called up – that he was putting a lady on the theatre train for Long Island, and would be home himself right afterwards. We've had a child sick and it's driven things from my mind.'

'I'm very sorry I bothered you under those conditions.'

'It's no bother. Sit down. It's only just after ten.'

Feeling easier, Stuart relaxed a little and accepted a cigar.

'No, if I tried to keep up with Teddy, I'd have white hair by now,' Betty said. 'Of course, I go to his concerts, but often I fall asleep – not that he ever knows it. So long as he doesn't take too much to drink and knows where his home is, I don't bother about where he wanders.' As Stuart's face grew serious again, she changed her tone: 'All and all, he's a good husband to me and we have a happy life together, without interfering with each other. How would he do working next to the nursery and groaning at every sound? And how would I do going to Mrs Ruthven's with him, and all of them talking about high society and high art?'

A phrase of Helen's came back to Stuart: 'Always together – I like for us to do everything together.'

'You have children, haven't you, Mr Oldhorne?'

'Yes. My boy's almost big enough to sit a horse.'

'Ah, yes; you're both great for horses.'

'My wife says that as soon as their legs are long enough to reach stirrups, she'll be interested in them again.' This didn't sound right to Stuart and he modified it: 'I mean she always has been interested in them, but she never let them monopolise her or come between us. We've always believed that marriage ought to be founded on companionship, on having the same interests. I mean, you're musical and you help your husband.'

Betty laughed. 'I wish Teddy could hear that. I can't read a note or carry a tune.'

'No?' He was confused. 'I'd somehow got the impression that you were musical.'

'You can't see why else he'd have married me?'

'Not at all. On the contrary.'

After a few minutes, he said good-night, somehow liking her. When he had gone, Betty's expression changed slowly to one of exasperation; she went to the telephone and called her husband's studio: 'There you are, Teddy. Now listen to me carefully. I know your cousin is with you and I want to talk with her . . . Now, don't lie. You put her on the phone. Her husband has been here, and if you don't let me talk to her, it might be a serious matter.'

She could hear an unintelligible colloquy, and then Helen's voice: 'Hello.'

'Good-evening, Mrs Oldhorne. Your husband came here, looking for you and Teddy. I told him I didn't know which play you were at, so you'd better be thinking which one. And I told him Teddy was leaving you at the station in time for the theatre train.'

'Oh, thank you very much. We – '

'Now, you meet your husband or there's trouble for you, or I'm no judge of men. And – wait a minute. Tell Teddy, if he's going to be up late, that Josie's sleeping light, and he's not to touch the piano when he gets home.'

Betty heard Teddy come in at eleven, and she came into the drawing-room smelling of camomile vapour. He greeted her absently; there was a look of suffering in his face and his eyes were bright and far away.

'You call yourself a great musician, Teddy Van Beck,' she said, 'but it seems to me you're much more interested in women.'

'Let me alone, Betty.'

'I do let you alone, but when the husbands start coming here, it's another matter.'

'This was different, Betty. This goes way back into the past.'

'It sounds like the present to me.'

'Don't make any mistake about Helen,' he said. 'She's a good woman.'

'Not through any fault of yours, I know.'

He sank his head wearily in his hands. 'I've tried to forget her. I've avoided her for six years. And then, when I met her a month ago, it all rushed over me. Try and understand, Bet. You're my best friend; you're the only person that ever loved me.'

'When you're good I love you,' she said.

'Don't worry. It's over. She loves her husband; she just came to

New York with me because she's got some spite against him. She follows me a certain distance just like she always has, and then – Anyhow, I'm not going to see her any more. Now go to bed, Bet. I want to play for a while.'

He was on his feet when she stopped him.

'You're not to touch the piano tonight.'

'Oh, I forgot about Josie,' he said remorsefully. 'Well, I'll drink a bottle of beer and then I'll come to bed.'

He came close and put his arm around her.

'Dear Bet, nothing could ever interfere with us.'

'You're a bad boy, Teddy,' she said. 'I wouldn't ever be so bad to you.'

'How do you know, Bet? How do you know what you'd do?'

He smoothed down her plain brown hair, knowing for the thousandth time that she had none of the world's dark magic for him, and that he couldn't live without her for six consecutive hours. 'Dear Bet,' he whispered. 'Dear Bet.'

3

The Oldhornes were visiting. In the last four years, since Stuart had terminated his bondage to Gus Myers, they had become visiting people. The children visited Grandmother Van Beck during the winter and attended school in New York. Stuart and Helen visited friends in Asheville, Aiken and Palm Beach, and in the summer usually occupied a small cottage on someone's Long Island estate. 'My dear, it's just standing there empty. I wouldn't dream of accepting any rent. You'll be doing us a favour by occupying it.'

Usually, they were; they gave out a great deal of themselves in that eternal willingness and enthusiasm which makes a successful guest – it became their profession. Moving through a world that was growing rich with the war in Europe, Stuart had somewhere lost his way. Twice playing brilliant golf in the national amateur, he accepted a job as professional at a club which his father had helped to found. He was restless and unhappy.

This weekend they were visiting a pupil of his. As a consequence of a mixed foursome, the Oldhornes went upstairs to dress for dinner surcharged with the unpleasant accumulation of many unsatisfactory months. In the afternoon, Stuart had played with their hostess and Helen with another man – a situation which Stuart always dreaded, because it forced him into competition with Helen. He had actually tried to miss that putt on the eighteenth – to just miss it. But the ball dropped in the cup. Helen went through the superficial motions of a good loser, but she devoted herself pointedly to her partner for the rest of the afternoon.

Their expressions still counterfeited amusement as they entered their room.

When the door closed, Helen's pleasant expression faded and she walked towards the dressing-table as though her own reflection was the only decent company with which to forgather. Stuart watched her, frowning.

'I know why you're in a rotten humour,' he said; 'though I don't believe you know yourself.'

'I'm not in a rotten humour,' Helen responded in a clipped voice.

'You are; and I know the real reason – the one you don't know. It's because I holed that putt this afternoon.'

She turned slowly, incredulously, from the mirror.

'Oh, so I have a new fault! I've suddenly become, of all things, a poor sport!'

'It's not like you to be a poor sport,' he admitted, 'but otherwise why all this interest in other men, and why do you look at me as if I'm – well, slightly gamey?'

'I'm not aware of it.'

'I am.' He was aware, too, that there was always some man in their life now – some man of power and money who paid court to Helen and gave her the sense of solidity which he failed to provide. He had no cause to be jealous of any particular man, but the pressure of many was irritating. It annoyed him that on so slight a grievance, Helen should remind him by her actions that he no longer filled her entire life.

'If Anne can get any satisfaction out of winning, she's welcome to it,' said Helen suddenly.

'Isn't that rather petty? She isn't in your class; she won't qualify for the third flight in Boston.'

Feeling herself in the wrong, she changed her tone.

'Oh, that isn't it,' she broke out. 'I just keep wishing you and I could play together like we used to. And now you have to play with dubs, and get their wretched shots out of traps. Especially' – she hesitated – 'especially when you're so unnecessarily gallant.'

The faint contempt in her voice, the mock jealousy that covered a growing indifference was apparent to him. There had been a time when, if he danced with another woman, Helen's stricken eyes followed him around the room.

'My gallantry is simply a matter of business,' he answered. 'Lessons have brought in three hundred a month all summer. How could I go to see you play at Boston next week, except that I'm going to coach other women?'

'And you're going to see me win,' announced Helen. 'Do you know that?'

'Naturally, I want nothing more,' Stuart said automatically. But the unnecessary defiance in her voice repelled him, and he suddenly wondered if he really cared whether she won or not.

At the same moment, Helen's mood changed and for a moment she saw the true situation – that she could play in amateur tournaments and Stuart could not, that the new cups in the rack were all hers now, that he had given up the fiercely competitive sportsmanship that had been the breath of life to him in order to provide necessary money.

'Oh, I'm so sorry for you, Stuart!' There were tears in her eyes. 'It seems such a shame that you can't do the things you love, and I can. Perhaps I oughtn't to play this summer.'

'Nonsense,' he said. 'You can't sit home and twirl your thumbs.'

She caught at this: 'You wouldn't want me to. I can't help being good at sports; you taught me nearly all I know. But I wish I could help you.'

'Just try to remember I'm your best friend. Sometimes you act as if we were rivals.'

She hesitated, annoyed by the truth of his words and unwilling to concede an inch; but a wave of memories rushed over her, and she thought how brave he was in his eked-out, pieced-together life; she came and threw her arms around him.

'Darling, darling, things are going to be better. You'll see.'

Helen won the finals in the tournament at Boston the following week. Following around with the crowd, Stuart was very proud of her. He hoped that instead of feeding her egotism, the actual achievement would make things easier between them. He hated the conflict that had grown out of their wanting the same excellences, the same prizes from life.

Afterwards he pursued her progress towards the clubhouse, amused and a little jealous of the pack that fawned around her. He reached the club among the last, and a steward accosted him. 'Professionals are served in the lower grill, please,' the man said.

'That's all right. My name's Oldhorne.'

He started to walk by, but the man barred his way.

'Sorry, sir. I realise that Mrs Oldhorne's playing in the match, but my orders are to direct the professionals to the lower grill, and I understand you are a professional.'

'Why, look here – ' Stuart began, wildly angry, and stopped. A group of people were listening. 'All right; never mind,' he said gruffly, and turned away.

The memory of the experience rankled; it was the determining factor that drove him, some weeks later, to a momentous decision. For a long time he had been playing with the idea of joining the Canadian Air Force, for service in France. He knew that his absence would have little practical bearing on the lives of Helen and the children; happening on some friends who were also full of the restlessness of 1915, the matter was suddenly decided. But he had not counted on the effect upon Helen; her reaction was not so much one of grief or alarm, but as if she had been somehow outwitted.

'But you might have told me!' she wailed. 'You leave me dangling; you simply take yourself away without any warning.'

Once again Helen saw him as the bright and intolerably blinding hero, and her soul winced before him as it had when they first met. He was a warrior; for him, peace was only the interval between wars, and peace was destroying him. Here was the game of games beckoning him – Without throwing over the whole logic of their lives, there was nothing she could say.

'This is my sort of thing,' he said confidently, younger with his excitement. 'A few more years of this life and I'd go to pieces, take to drink. I've somehow lost your respect, and I've got to have that, even if I'm far away.'

She was proud of him again; she talked to everyone of his impending departure. Then, one September afternoon, she came home from the city, full of the old feeling of comradeship and bursting with news, to find him buried in an utter depression.

'Stuart,' she cried, 'I've got the – ' She broke off. 'What's the matter, darling? Is something the matter?'

He looked at her dully. 'They turned me down,' he said.

'What?'

'My left eye.' He laughed bitterly. 'Where that dub cracked me with the brassie. I'm nearly blind in it.'

'Isn't there anything you can do?'

'Nothing.'

'Stuart!' She stared at him aghast. 'Stuart, and I was going to tell you! I was saving it for a surprise. Elsa Prentice has organised a Red Cross unit to serve with the French, and I joined it because I thought it would be wonderful if we both went. We've been measured for uniforms and bought our outfits, and we're sailing the end of next week.'

4

Helen was a blurred figure among other blurred figures on a boat deck, dark against the threat of submarines. When the ship had slid out into the obscure future, Stuart walked eastward along Fifty-Seventh Street. His grief at the severance of many ties was a weight he carried in his body, and he walked slowly, as if adjusting himself to it. To balance this there was a curious sensation of lightness in his mind. For the first time in twelve years he was alone, and the feeling came over him that he was alone for good; knowing Helen and knowing war, he could guess at the experiences she would go through, and he could not form any picture of a renewed life together afterwards. He was discarded; she had proved the stronger at last. It seemed very strange and sad that his marriage should have such an ending.

He came to Carnegie Hall, dark after a concert, and his eye caught the name of Theodore Van Beck, large on the posted bills. As he stared at it, a green door opened in the side of the building and a group of people in evening dress came out. Stuart and Teddy were face to face before they recognised each other.

'Hello, there!' Teddy cried cordially. 'Did Helen sail?'

'Just now.'

'I met her on the street yesterday and she told me. I wanted you both to come to my concert. Well, she's quite a heroine, going off like that . . . Have you met my wife?'

Stuart and Betty smiled at each other.

'We've met.'

'And I didn't know it,' protested Teddy. 'Women need watching when they get towards their dotage . . . Look here, Stuart; we're having a few people up to the apartment. No heavy music or anything. Just supper and a few débutantes to tell me I was divine. It will do you good to come. I imagine you're missing Helen like the devil.'

'I don't think I – '

'Come along. They'll tell you you're divine too.'

Realising that the invitation was inspired by kindliness, Stuart accepted. It was the sort of gathering he had seldom attended, and he was surprised to meet so many people he knew. Teddy played the lion in a manner at once assertive and sceptical. Stuart listened as he enlarged to Mrs Cassius Ruthven on one of his favourite themes: 'People tried to make marriages cooperative and they've ended by becoming competitive. Impossible situation. Smart men will get to fight shy of ornamental women. A man ought to marry somebody who'll be grateful, like Betty here.'

'Now don't talk so much, Theodore Van Beck,' Betty interrupted. 'Since you're such a fine musician, you'd do well to express yourself with music instead of rash words.'

'I don't agree with your husband,' said Mrs Ruthven. 'English girls hunt with their men and play politics with them on absolutely equal terms, and it tends to draw them together.'

'It does not,' insisted Teddy. 'That's why English society is the most disorganised in the world. Betty and I are happy because we haven't any qualities in common at all.'

His exuberance grated on Stuart, and the success that flowed from him swung his mind back to the failure of his own life. He could not know that his life was not destined to be a failure. He could not read the fine story that three years later would be carved proud above his soldier's grave, or know that his restless body, which never spared itself in sport or danger, was destined to give him one last proud gallop at the end.

'They turned me down,' he was saying to Mrs Ruthven. 'I'll have to stick to Squadron A, unless we get drawn in.'

'So Helen's gone.' Mrs Ruthven looked at him, reminiscing. 'I'll never forget your wedding. You were both so handsome, so ideally suited to each other. Everybody spoke of it.'

Stuart remembered; for the moment it seemed that he had little else that it was fun to remember.

'Yes,' he agreed, nodding his head thoughtfully, 'I suppose we were a handsome pair.'